"I really hate people like you," Hadrian said, shaking his head.

"I just got here. I was at sea for a month—*a month*! That's how long I've traveled to get away from this kind of thing." He shook his head in disgust. "And here you are—you too." Hadrian pointed at Pickles as they worked at tying the boy's wrists behind his back. "I didn't ask for your help. I didn't ask for a guide, or a steward, or a houseboy. I was just fine on my own. But no, you had to take my bag and be so good-humored about everything. Worst of all, you didn't run. Maybe you're stupid—I don't know. But I can't help thinking you stuck around to help me."

"I'm sorry I didn't do a better job." Pickles looked up at him with sad eyes.

Hadrian sighed. "Damn it. There you go again." He looked back at the clubmen, already knowing how it would turn out—how it always turned out—but he'd to try anyway. "Look, I'm not a knight. I'm not a squire either, but these swords are mine, and while Pickles thought he was bluffing, I—"

"Oh, just shut up." The one with the torn sleeve took a step and thrust his club to shove Hadrian. On the slippery pier it was easy for Hadrian to put him off balance. He caught the man's arm, twisted the wrist and elbow around, and snapped the bone. The crack sounded like a walnut opening. He gave the screaming clubman a shove, which was followed by a splash as he went into the harbor.

BOOKS BY MICHAEL J. SULLIVAN

THE RIYRIA CHRONICLES

The Crown Tower
The Rose and the Thorn

THE RIYRIA REVELATIONS

Theft of Swords
Rise of Empire
Heir of Novron

THE
CROWN
TOWER

Book One of the
Riyria Chronicles

MICHAEL J. SULLIVAN

www.orbitbooks.net

Orbit
Hachette Book Group
237 Park Avenue, New York, NY 10017
HachetteBookGroup.com

First Edition: August 2013

Orbit is an imprint of Hachette Book Group, Inc. The Orbit name and
logo are trademarks of Little, Brown Book Group Limited.

The Hachette Speakers Bureau provides a wide range of authors for
speaking events. To find out more, go to www.hachettespeakersbureau
.com or call (866) 376-6591.

The publisher is not responsible for websites (or their content) that are
not owned by the publisher.

Library of Congress Cataloging-in-Publication Data
Sullivan, Michael J.
    The crown tower : book one of the Riyria chronicles / Michael J.
Sullivan. — First edition.
        pages cm
    ISBN 978-0-316-24371-1 (trade pbk.) — ISBN978-0-316-24370-4
(ebook)
    I. Title.
    PS3691.U4437C76 2013
    813'.6—dc23
                                        2013004666

10 9 8 7 6 5 4 3 2 1

RRD-C

Printed in the United States of America

*To the readers who believed in me
when no one else would.*

Contents

TRENT

GHENT

ERVANON
Lake Morgan
HERTON

NORTH RIVER

SHERIDAN
UNIVERSITY

LOTHOMAD

ASPER

High
Meadowlands

EAST MARCH

MELENGAR

LONGWOOD

MEDFORD

DRONDIL
FIELDS

Sinara Rose

SLEON
UPLANDS

Lake
WINDERMERE

WEST MARCH

GALILIN

CHADWICK

HIGHLANDS

RILAN VALLEY

ROE

GALEWYR RIVER

FORD

GLOUSTON

AMBER
HEIGHTS

ALB

WARRIC

COLNORA

SHARON
SEA

AQUESTA

BERNUM RIVER

RATIBOR

RHENYDD

KILNAR

VERNES

AUTHOR'S NOTE

Welcome to The Riyria Chronicles.

If you're new to the world of Elan, you might want to read this introduction to help determine where to start, because it might not be here. Even veterans of The Riyria Revelations might want to read this to learn a bit about how this series came into being and what to expect going forward.

The Riyria Chronicles are prequels to my debut series, The Riyria Revelations (originally published by Orbit starting with *Theft of Swords* in November 2011 and concluding with *Heir of Novron* in January 2012). If you prefer your tales in chronological order, start with this book, as I've taken great care to keep the Chronicles spoiler free. Also, no prior knowledge from Revelations is required. I wanted to accommodate readers from both camps (chronological or order of publication). That being said, the Chronicles were actually designed to be read *after* The Riyria Revelations, and veteran readers will be treated to hidden surprises made possible by having the inside scoop on the entire story arc. These won't be significant plot points, just little extra bonuses for *those in the know*. The bottom line is that readers can begin their adventures in Elan starting with either *The Crown Tower* or *Theft of Swords*.

I'd like to take just a moment to talk about the difference

in structure between these two series. For those who don't know, I wrote all six books of The Riyria Revelations before publishing any of them. This was absolutely necessary for that particular series. While I gave each book its own conflict and resolution, there were a number of threads interwoven across the entire series. Mysteries were hinted at, geese needed chasing, and everything was built to support the grand finale where all the secrets were...well...revealed. Because it was a first work, I could afford such luxury; after all, no one was waiting on the next installment.

My approach to The Riyria Chronicles is quite different. I have no idea how many there will be, so I'm designing this as an open-ended series rather than a single tale divided into episodes. The stories are more like stand-alone novels with less integration from one book to another. By doing this I'll be able to stop writing Riyria tales at any time without leaving open questions or unresolved conflicts. There are several reasons for doing this. First and foremost is because I'm incredibly protective of Riyria. I'm very proud of what I've accomplished, and we've all seen series that were once great but ended up going on longer than they should. Second, I have no idea if people will want any more stories with these characters. All told, I've written and published eight novels, and that just might prove to be enough.

So exactly what are The Riyria Chronicles? And why did I opt to write a prequel rather than a sequel? Well, many people already know that Riyria is elvish for *two*; it's also the name adopted by Hadrian Blackwater and Royce Melborn to refer to their thieves-for-hire enterprise. Not surprisingly, then, The Riyria Chronicles will prominently feature the pair. As a carefully designed series, Revelations concludes with the end of an era, and I'm extremely pleased with how the events wrapped up. After working so hard to find the *perfect ending*, I was concerned that any continuation could be seen as "tacked on" and could have the very real possibility of destroying something I consider precious. So the obvious choice was to explore the opposite end.

Chronicles is in essence the origin story of Riyria. In the opening scene of Revelations, Royce and Hadrian were already the best of friends. Having worked together for twelve years, they demonstrate a bond that endears them to many readers. What was most interesting to me, as the author, was to explore how these two very different men influenced each other and how they came to develop the unquestioning trust that exists between them. It occurred to me that upon first meeting, they really wouldn't have liked each other or, more precisely, they would probably have hated each other. The challenge for me was to realistically show how their union came into being, and there is nothing I love more when writing than a good challenge.

Some have suggested that Chronicles was created at the urging of my publisher, who wanted me to return to an established commodity. This is not so. Anyone familiar with me knows that no amount of money could entice me to write something I'm not interested in. So if Orbit wasn't responsible for Chronicles, who was? Well, in large part it was the readers, who insisted that 685,000 words just weren't enough. It is your support that keeps food on my table and a roof over my head. In many ways I feel like an artist of the Renaissance and you are my patrons. But there is another person, and probably the only one, who can actually make me do something. This person plotted to bring Chronicles to life. I was taken in by this mastermind, and how her devious manipulations ensnared me is a tale in itself.

It's the classic story of a husband whose wife falls for another man—a more dashing and charming gent. It sounds tragic, but this tale is a bit different because the love affair is between a real woman and a fictional man. My wife—let's call her Robin (because that's her name)—has developed an infatuation for Hadrian Blackwater. I'm not sure how I feel about enabling my wife's relationship with another man, but at least I know this guy is trustworthy. After finishing the Revelations series, Robin became depressed at having to say goodbye to the world of Elan and especially at having to bid farewell to Hadrian—until she realized I could bring both him and Royce back in the form of prequels. This realization set in motion her diabolical plan to resurrect the pair.

It started when she persuaded me to write a short story so that I would have something for readers during the transition from self- to traditional publishing. Preorder pages for Orbit's editions of Revelations had been posted (but the books were not yet released) and my earlier versions had been removed to make way. For the first time in years, I had nothing "out there," and since my contract allowed me to produce non-book-length works, and because short stories are...well... short, Robin asked me to create an early story starring Royce and Hadrian.

The thing is, I'm not very good at short stories. So I decided to approach the task like a chapter—the first chapter of a novel. I went back in time and wrote a simple little tale about Royce and Hadrian meeting Viscount Albert Winslow. This would have occurred about a year after the duo first met. I published this for free under the title *The Viscount and the Witch* and readers appear to have liked it. Once I had written that story, a seed had been planted, and while I worked on other projects it began to grow. When it became apparent that Revelations had enough momentum, I started what would become *The Rose and the Thorn.*

As I neared that book's end, I realized I had a problem. I couldn't publish a novel about the second year of Royce and Hadrian's relationship. What was I thinking? Going back in time begged the question, How did it all start? What good is a legend without the origin story? The more I thought about it, the more I realized I had to write how Royce and Hadrian first met. When I told my wife, she feigned her support: "Well, whatever you think is best, dear." After leaving the room, I heard the muffled "*Yes!*" and imagined her doing a fist pump, as if she had just scored a winning touchdown. And so *The Crown Tower* was born.

Having accidently written the books spaced a year apart in Elan time, I am now envisioning the possibility of a twelve-book series—one novel for each year prior to the events in Revelations. Will those other stories be written? It's impossible to say until I see how these two books go. But as with all things writerly, I've opened the door and ideas keep walking through. For now, I'm collecting them like pretty shells while I work on other projects.

And so there you have it. A happy accident born from a conniving wife's passion for a fictional man and a legion of readers who wanted to read more. If you are a veteran of The Riyria Revelations, I hope you will enjoy these books as much as you did my others. If you are new to my writing, you might just make some new friends, and if you do, there are six more books just waiting for you to jump into.

Finally, please consider dropping me a line at michael .sullivan.dc@gmail.com after reading to give me your impressions. It is exactly this kind of feedback that got Chronicles written in the first place. So if you do end up wanting more, speaking up is the best way to ensure that.

xvi

CHRONICLE ORDER	PUBLISHED ORDER
The Crown Tower	*Theft of Swords*
The Rose and the Thorn	*Rise of Empire*
Theft of Swords	*Heir of Novron*
Rise of Empire	*The Crown Tower*
Heir of Novron	*The Rose and the Thorn*

CHAPTER 1

PICKLES

Hadrian Blackwater hadn't gone more than five steps off the ship before he was robbed.

The bag—his only bag—was torn from his hand. He never even saw the thief. Hadrian couldn't see much of anything in the lantern-lit chaos surrounding the pier, just a mass of faces, people shoving to get away from the gangway or get nearer to the ship. Used to the rhythms of a pitching deck, he struggled to keep his feet on the stationary dock amidst the jostling scramble. The newly arrived moved hesitantly, causing congestion. Many onshore searched for friends and relatives, yelling, jumping, waving arms—chasing the attention of someone. Others were more professional, holding torches and shouting offers for lodging and jobs. One bald man with a voice like a war trumpet stood on a crate, promising that The Black Cat Tavern offered the strongest ale at the cheapest prices. Twenty feet away, his competition balanced on a wobbly barrel and proclaimed the bald man a liar. He further insisted The Lucky Hat was the only local tavern that didn't substitute dog meat for mutton. Hadrian didn't care. He wanted to get out of the crowd and find the thief who stole his bag. After only a few minutes, he realized that wasn't going to happen. He settled for protecting his purse and considered himself lucky. At least nothing of value was lost—just clothing, but given how cold Avryn was in autumn, that might be a problem.

Hadrian followed the flow of bodies, not that he had much choice. Adrift in the strong current, he bobbed along with his head just above the surface. The dock creaked and moaned under the weight of escaping passengers who hurried away from what had been their cramped home for more than a month. Weeks breathing clean salt air had been replaced by the pungent smells of fish, smoke, and tar. Rising far above the dimly lit docks, the city's lights appeared as brighter points in a starlit world.

Hadrian followed four dark-skinned Calian men hauling crates packed with colorful birds, which squawked and rattled their cages. Behind him walked a poorly dressed man and woman. The man carried *two* bags, one over a shoulder and the other tucked under an arm. Apparently no one was interested in *their* belongings. Hadrian realized he should have worn something else. His eastern attire was not only uselessly thin, but in a land of leather and wool, the bleached white linen thawb and the gold-trimmed cloak screamed *wealth*.

"Here! Over here!" The barely distinguishable voice was one more sound in the maelstrom of shouts, wagon wheels, bells, and whistles. "This way. Yes, you, come. Come!"

Reaching the end of the ramp and clearing most of the congestion, Hadrian spotted an adolescent boy. Dressed in tattered clothes, he waited beneath the fiery glow of a swaying lantern. The wiry youth held Hadrian's bag and beamed an enormous smile. "Yes, yes, you there. Please come. Right over here," he called, waving with his free hand.

"That's my bag!" Hadrian shouted, struggling to reach him and stymied by the remaining crowd blocking the narrow pier.

"Yes! Yes!" The lad grinned wider, his eyes bright with enthusiasm. "You are very lucky I took it from you or someone would have surely stolen it."

"*You* stole it!"

"No. No. Not at all. I have been faithfully protecting your most valued property." The youth straightened his willowy back such that Hadrian thought he might salute. "Someone like you should not be carrying your own bag."

Hadrian squeezed around three women who'd paused to comfort a crying child, only to be halted by an elderly man dragging an incredibly large trunk. The old guy, wraith thin with bright white hair, blocked the narrow isthmus already cluttered by the mountain of bags being recklessly thrown to the pier from the ship.

"What do you mean *someone like me?*" Hadrian shouted over the trunk as the old man struggled in front of him.

"You are a great knight, yes?"

"No, I'm not."

The boy pointed at him. "You must be. Look how big you are and you carry swords—three swords. And that one on your back is huge. Only a knight carries such things."

Hadrian sighed when the old man's trunk became wedged in the gap between the decking and the ramp. He reached down and lifted it free, receiving several vows of gratitude in an unfamiliar language.

"See," the boy said, "only a knight would help a stranger in need like that."

More bags crashed down on the pile beside him. One tumbled off, rolling into the harbor's dark water with a *plunk!* Hadrian pressed forward, both to avoid being hit from above and to retrieve his stolen property. "I'm not a knight. Now give me back my bag."

"I will carry it for you. My name is Pickles, but we must be going. Quickly now." The boy hugged Hadrian's bag and trotted off on dirty bare feet.

"Hey!"

"Quickly, quickly! We should not linger here."

"What's the rush? What are you talking about? And come back here with my bag!"

"You are very lucky to have me. I am an excellent guide. Anything you want, I know where to look. With me you can get the best of everything and all for the least amounts."

Hadrian finally caught up and grabbed his bag. He pulled and got the boy with it, his arms still tightly wrapped around the canvas.

"Ha! See?" The boy grinned. "No one is pulling your bag out of *my* hands!"

"Listen"—Hadrian took a moment to catch his breath—"I don't need a guide. I'm not staying here."

"Where are you going?"

"Up north. Way up north. A place called Sheridan."

"Ah! The university."

This surprised Hadrian. Pickles didn't look like the worldly type. The kid resembled an abandoned dog. The kind that might have once worn a collar but now possessed only fleas, visible ribs, and an overdeveloped sense for survival.

"You are studying to be a scholar? I should have known. My apologies for any insult. You are most smart—so, of course, you will make a great scholar. You should not tip me for making such a mistake. But that is even better. I know just where we must go. There is a barge that travels up the Bernum River. Yes, the barge will be perfect and one leaves tonight. There will not be another for days, and you do not want to stay in an awful city like this. We will be in Sheridan in no time."

"We?" Hadrian smirked.

"You will want me with you, yes? I am not just familiar with Vernes. I am an expert on all of Avryn—I have traveled far. I can help you, a steward who can see to your needs and watch your belongings to keep them safe from thieves while you study. A job I am most good at, yes?"

"I'm not a student, not going to be one either. Just visiting someone, and I don't need a steward."

"Of course you do not need a steward—if you are not going to be a scholar—but as the son of a noble lord just back from the east, you definitely need a houseboy, and I will make a fine houseboy. I will make sure your chamber pot is always emptied, your fire well stoked in winter, and fan you in the summer to keep the flies away."

"Pickles," Hadrian said firmly. "I'm not a lord's son, and I don't need a servant. I—" He stopped after noticing the boy's attention had been drawn away, and his gleeful expression turned fearful. "What's wrong?"

"I told you we needed to hurry. We need to get away from the dock right now!"

Hadrian turned to see men with clubs marching up the pier, their heavy feet causing the dock to bounce.

"Press-gang," Pickles said. "They are always near when ships come in. Newcomers like you can get caught and wake up in the belly of a ship already at sea. Oh no!" Pickles gasped as one spotted them.

After a quick whistle and shoulder tap, four men headed their way. Pickles flinched. The boy's legs flexed, his weight shifting as if to bolt, but he looked at Hadrian, bit his lip, and didn't move.

The clubmen charged but slowed and came to a stop after spotting Hadrian's swords. The four could have been brothers. Each had almost-beards, oily hair, sunbaked skin, and angry faces. The expression must have been popular, as it left permanent creases in their brows.

They studied him for a second, puzzled. Then the foremost

thug, wearing a stained tunic with one torn sleeve, asked, "You a knight?"

"No, I'm not a knight." Hadrian rolled his eyes.

Another laughed and gave the one with the torn sleeve a rough shove. "Daft fool—he's not much older than the boy next to him."

"Don't bleedin' shove me on this slimy dock, ya stupid sod." The man looked back at Hadrian. "He's not that young."

"It's possible," one of the others said. "Kings do stupid things. Heard one knighted his dog once. Sir Spot they called him."

The four laughed. Hadrian was tempted to join in, but he was sobered by the terrified look on Pickles's face.

The one with the torn sleeve took a step closer. "He's got to be at least a squire. Look at all that steel, for Maribor's sake. Where's yer master, boy? He around?"

"I'm not a squire either," Hadrian replied.

"No? What's with all the steel, then?"

"None of your business."

The men laughed. "Oh, you're a tough one, are ya?"

They spread out, taking firmer holds on their sticks. One had a strap of leather run through a hole in the handle and wrapped around his wrist. *Probably figured that was a good idea*, Hadrian thought.

"You better leave us alone," Pickles said, voice wavering. "Do you not know who this is?" He pointed at Hadrian. "He is a famous swordsman—a born killer."

Laughter. "Is that so?" the nearest said, and paused to spit between yellow teeth.

"Oh yes!" Pickles insisted. "He's vicious—an animal—and very touchy, very dangerous."

"A young colt like him, eh?" The man gazed at Hadrian and pushed out his lips in judgment. "Big enough—I'll grant ya that—but it looks to me like he still has his mother's milk dripping down his chin." He focused on Pickles. "And *you're* no vicious killer, are ya, little lad? You're the dirty alley rat I saw yesterday under the alehouse boardwalks trying to catch crumbs. You, my boy, are about to embark on a new career at sea. Best thing for ya really. You'll get food and learn to work—work real hard. It'll make a man out of ya."

Pickles tried to dodge, but the thug grabbed him by the hair.

"Let him go," Hadrian said.

"How did ya put it?" The guy holding Pickles chuckled. "*None of your business?*"

"He's my squire," Hadrian declared.

The men laughed again. "You said you ain't a knight, remember?"

"He works for me—that's good enough."

"No it ain't, 'cause this one works for the maritime industry now." He threw a muscled arm around Pickles's neck and bent the boy over as another moved behind with a length of rope pulled from his belt.

"I said, let him go." Hadrian raised his voice.

"Hey!" the man with the torn sleeve barked. "Don't give us no orders, boy. We ain't taking you, 'cause you're somebody's property, someone who has you hauling three swords, someone who might miss you. That's problems we don't need, see? But don't push it. Push it and we'll break bones. Push us more and we'll drop you in a boat anyway. Push us too far, and you won't even get a boat."

"I really hate people like you," Hadrian said, shaking his head. "I just got here. I was at sea for a month—*a month*! That's how long I've traveled to get away from this kind of thing." He shook his head in disgust. "And here you are— you too." Hadrian pointed at Pickles as they worked at tying the boy's wrists behind his back. "I didn't ask for your help. I didn't ask for a guide, or a steward, or a houseboy. I was just fine on my own. But no, you had to take my bag and be so good-humored about everything. Worst of all, you didn't run. Maybe you're stupid—I don't know. But I can't help thinking you stuck around to help me."

"I'm sorry I didn't do a better job." Pickles looked up at him with sad eyes.

Hadrian sighed. "Damn it. There you go again." He looked back at the clubmen, already knowing how it would turn out—how it always turned out—but he'd to try anyway. "Look, I'm not a knight. I'm not a squire either, but these swords are mine, and while Pickles thought he was bluffing, I—"

"Oh, just shut up." The one with the torn sleeve took a step and thrust his club to shove Hadrian. On the slippery pier it was easy for Hadrian to put him off balance. He caught the man's arm, twisted the wrist and elbow around, and snapped the bone. The crack sounded like a walnut opening. He gave the screaming clubman a shove, which was followed by a splash as he went into the harbor.

Hadrian could have drawn his swords then—almost did out of reflex—but he'd promised himself things would be different. Besides, he stole the man's club before sending him over the side, a solid bit of hickory about an inch in diameter and a little longer than a foot. The grip had been polished smooth from years of use, the other end stained brown from blood that seeped into the wood grain.

The remaining men gave up trying to tie Pickles, but one continued to hold him in a headlock while the other two rushed Hadrian. He read their feet, noting their weight and momentum. Dodging his first attacker's swing, Hadrian tripped the second and struck him in the back of the head as he went down. The sound of club on skull made a hollow thud like slapping a pumpkin, and when the guy hit the deck, he stayed there. The other swung at him again. Hadrian parried with the hickory stick, striking fingers. The man cried out and lost his grip, the club left dangling from the leather strap around his wrist. Hadrian grabbed the weapon, twisted it tight, bent the man's arm back, and pulled hard. The bone didn't break, but the shoulder popped. The man's quivering legs signaled the fight had left him, and Hadrian sent him over the side to join his friend.

By the time Hadrian turned to face the last of the four, Pickles was standing alone and rubbing his neck. His would-be captor sprinted into the distance.

"Is he going to come back with friends, you think?" Hadrian asked.

Pickles didn't say anything. He just stared at Hadrian, his mouth open.

"No sense lingering to find out, I suppose," Hadrian answered himself. "So where's this barge you were talking about?"

꒰

Away from the seaside pier, the city of Vernes was still choked and stifling. Narrow brick roads formed a maze overshadowed by balconies that nearly touched. Lanterns and moonlight were equally scarce, and down some lonely pathways there was no light at all. Hadrian was thankful to have Pickles. Recovered from his fright, the "alley rat" acted more like a hunting dog. He trotted through the city's corridors, leaping puddles that stank of waste and ducking wash lines and scaffolding with practiced ease.

"That's the living quarters for most of the shipwrights, and over there is the dormitory for the dockworkers." Pickles pointed to a grim building near the wharf with three stories, one door, and few windows. "Most of the men around this ward

live there or at the sister building on the south end. So much
here is shipping. Now, up there, high on that hill—see it? That
is the citadel."

Hadrian lifted his head and made out the dark silhouette of
a fortress illuminated by torches.

"Not really a castle, more like a counting house for traders
and merchants. Walls have to be high and thick for all the gold
it is they stuff up there. This is where all the money from the
sea goes. Everything else runs downhill—but gold flows up."

Pickles sidestepped a toppled bucket and spooked a pair
of cat-sized rats that ran for deeper shadows. Halfway past a
doorway Hadrian realized a pile of discarded rags was actually an ancient-looking man seated on a stoop. With a frazzled
gray beard and a face thick with folds, he never moved, not
even to blink. Hadrian only noticed him after his smoking
pipe's bowl glowed bright orange.

"It is a filthy city," Pickles called back to him. "I am
pleased we are leaving. Too many foreigners here—too many
easterners—many probably arrived with you. Strange folk, the
Calians. Their women practice witchcraft and tell fortunes,
but I say it is best not to know too much about one's future.
We will not have to worry about such things in the north. In
Warric, they burn witches in the winter to keep warm. At least
that is what I have heard." Pickles stopped abruptly and spun.
"What is your name?"

"Finally decided to ask, eh?" Hadrian chuckled.

"I will need to know if I am going to book you passage."

"I can take care of that myself. Assuming, of course, you
are actually taking me to a barge and not just to some dark
corner where you'll clunk me on the head and do a more thor-
ough job of robbing me."

Pickles looked hurt. "I would do no such thing. Do you
think me such a fool? First, I have seen what you do to people

who try to *clunk you on the head*. Second, we have already passed a dozen perfectly dark corners." Pickles beamed his big smile, which Hadrian took to be one part mischief, one part pride, and two parts just-plain-happy-to-be-alive joy. He couldn't argue with that. He also couldn't remember the last time he felt the way Pickles looked.

The press-gang leader was right. Pickles could only be four or five years younger than Hadrian. *Five*, he thought. *He's five years younger than I am. He's me before I left. Did I smile like that back then?* He wondered how long Pickles had been on his own and if he'd still have that smile in five years.

"Hadrian, Hadrian Blackwater." He extended his hand.

The boy nodded. "A good name. Very good. Better than Pickles—but then what is not?"

"Did your mother name you that?"

"Oh, most certainly. Rumor has it I was both conceived and born on the same crate of pickles. How can one deny such a legend? Even if it isn't true, I think it should be."

Crawling out of the labyrinth, they emerged onto a wider avenue. They had gained height, and Hadrian could see the pier and the masts of the ship he arrived on below. A good-sized crowd was still gathered—people looking for a place to stay or searching for belongings. Hadrian remembered the bag that had rolled into the harbor. How many others would find themselves stranded in a new city with little to nothing?

The bark of a dog caused Hadrian to turn. Looking down the narrow street, he thought he caught movement but couldn't be sure. The twisted length of the alley had but one lantern. Moonlight illuminated the rest, casting patches of blue-gray. A square here, a rectangle there, not nearly enough to see by and barely enough to judge distance. Had it been another rat? Seemed bigger. He waited, staring. Nothing moved.

When he looked back, Pickles had crossed most of the

plaza to the far side where, to Hadrian's delight, there was another dock. This one sat on the mouth of the great Bernum River, which in the night appeared as a wide expanse of darkness. He cast one last look backward toward the narrow streets. Still nothing moved. *Ghosts.* That's all—his past stalking him.

Hadrian reeked of death. It wasn't the sort of stench others could smell or that water could wash, but it lingered on him like sweat-saturated pores after a long night of drinking. Only this odor didn't come from alcohol; it came from blood. Not from drinking it—although Hadrian knew some who had. His stink came from wallowing in it. But all that was over now, or so he told himself with the certainty of the recently sober. That had been a different Hadrian, a younger version who he'd left on the other side of the world and who he was still running from.

Realizing Pickles still had his bag, Hadrian ran to close the distance. Before he caught up, Pickles was in trouble again.

"It is his!" Pickles cried, pointing at Hadrian. "I was helping him reach the barge before it left."

The boy was surrounded by six soldiers. Most wore chain and held square shields. The one in the middle, with a fancy plume on his helmet, wore layered plate on his shoulders and chest as well as a studded leather skirt. He was the one Pickles was speaking to while two others restrained the boy. They all looked over as Hadrian approached.

"This your bag?" the officer asked.

"It is, and he's telling the truth." Hadrian pointed. "He is escorting me to that barge over there."

"In a hurry to leave our fair city, are you?" The officer's tone was suspicious, and his eyes scanned Hadrian as he talked.

"No offense to Vernes, but yes. I have business up north."

The officer moved a step closer. "What's your name?"

"Hadrian Blackwater."

"Where you from?"

"Hintindar originally."

"Originally?" The skepticism in his voice rose along with his eyebrows.

Hadrian nodded. "I've been in Calis for several years. Just returned from Dagastan on that ship down there."

The officer glanced at the dock, then at Hadrian's knee-length thawb, loose cotton pants, and keffiyeh headdress. He leaned in, sniffed, and grimaced. "You've definitely been on a ship, and that outfit is certainly Calian." He sighed, then turned to Pickles. "But this one hasn't been on any ship. He says he's going with you. Is that right?"

Hadrian glanced at Pickles and saw the hope in the boy's eyes. "Yeah. I've hired him to be my...ah...my...servant."

"Whose idea was that? His or yours?"

"His, but he's been very helpful. I wouldn't have found this barge without him."

"You just got off one ship," the officer said. "Seems odd you're so eager to get on another."

"Well, actually I'm not, but Pickles says the barge is about to leave and there won't be another for days. Is that true?"

"Yes," the officer said, "and awfully convenient too."

"Can I ask what the problem is? Is there a law against hiring a guide and paying for him to travel with you?"

"No, but we've had some nasty business here in town—real nasty business. So naturally we're interested in anyone eager to leave, at least anyone who's been around during the last few days." He looked squarely at Pickles.

"I haven't done anything," Pickles said.

"So you say, but even if you haven't, maybe you know

something about it. Either way you might feel the need to disappear, and latching on to someone above suspicion would be a good way to get clear of trouble, wouldn't it?"

"But I don't know anything about the killings."

The officer turned to Hadrian. "You're free to go your way, and you'd best be quick. They've already called for boarders."

"What about Pickles?"

He shook his head. "I can't let him go with you. Unlikely he's guilty of murder, but he might know who is. Street orphans see a lot that they don't like to talk about if they think they can avoid it."

"But I'm telling you, I don't know *anything*. I haven't even been on the hill."

"Then you've nothing to worry about."

"But—" Pickles looked as if he might cry. "He was going to take me out of here. We were going to go north. We were going to go to a university."

"Hoy! Hoy! Last call for passengers! Barge to Colnora! Last call!" a voice bellowed.

"Listen"—Hadrian opened his purse—"you did me a service, and that's worth payment. Now, after you finish with their questions, if you still want to work for me, you can use this money to meet me in Sheridan. Catch the next barge or buckboard north, whatever. I'll be there for a month maybe, a couple of weeks at least." Hadrian pressed a coin into the boy's hand. "If you come, ask for Professor Arcadius. He's the one I'm meeting with, and he should be able to tell you how to find me. Okay?"

Pickles nodded and looked a bit better. Glancing down at the coin, his eyes widened, and the old giant smile of his returned. "Yes, sir! I will be there straightaway. You can most certainly count on me. Now you must run before the barge leaves."

Hadrian gave him a nod, picked up his bag, and jogged to the dock where a man waited at the gangway of a long flat boat.

CHAPTER 2

GWEN

Gwen knew she would be too late the moment the screams began on the second floor. The ceiling shook, casting dirt into the drinks of those huddled at the bar. Overhead, the pounding sounded like he was taking a club to Avon's head.

No, not a club. He's hammering her head against the floor.

"Avon!" Gwen yelled, charging the stairs.

Unwilling to slow for the turn, she slammed her shoulder into the wall at the top of the flight, knocking loose a little mirror that fell and shattered. Gwen sprinted down the hall. The screams sounded inhuman, like something from a slaughterhouse—the futile cries of the doomed.

Stane is killing her.

Gwen clawed at the latch and pushed, but the inside bolt had been thrown. The door refused to budge. She threw herself against it, but the wood ignored her slight weight. Inside, the pounding softened, turning mushy. No longer a muffled thump, it had become a wet smack. The screams faded to whispered moans.

Gwen wrenched open the door across the hall where Mae had been entertaining a redheaded man from East March. Mae screamed in fear. Whatever business they had been engaged in had stopped with Avon's shrieks. Gwen kicked at the loose post of the bed's footboard. The carpenter had constructed the frame from solid stumps of maple, but he'd done a lousy job fitting the pieces together. Two more kicks and the leg toppled, collapsing the mattress to the floor along with Mae and the redhead from East March.

Running like a jousting knight, Gwen drove the post into Avon's door. The impact threw the ram from her hands but left a sizable dent in its surface and splintered the frame. Scrambling, she grabbed it once more just as Raynor Grue appeared at the top of the stairs.

"Damn it, ya stupid bitch! Stop!"

With every ounce of her strength, Gwen rammed the door again, aiming for the same spot and hitting it, more or less. The frame shattered, and the door burst open. The momentum carried her through, and she landed on the floor in a pool of blood.

"Great Maribor's beard!" Grue cursed, standing in the doorway.

Stane was on top of Avon, his hands still around her neck. "She wouldn't stop screaming."

Avon's eyes were open but not seeing, her blond hair stained crimson.

"Get outta here!" Grue said, grabbing Gwen and dragging her into the corridor. "Go downstairs! Ya owe me for a new bloody door and a bed."

"Is she dead?" Stane asked, still straddling her with his naked legs, his skin slick with sweat, his chest splattered with blood.

Grue nudged Avon's head with his boot. "Yeah, ya killed her."

"You bastard!" Gwen launched herself at Stane.

Grue caught her and shoved her backward, causing Gwen to stumble and fall. "Shut up!" he yelled.

"I'm sorry, Grue," Stane offered.

Grue grimaced and shook his head, surveying the blood spreading across the wooden floor. Gwen could tell from the way he stood and the downward curl of his mouth that he wasn't seeing Avon as a beautiful young girl gone before her time but merely as a mess to be cleaned up.

Grue sighed. "I don't want no apology, Stane. You're gonna have to pay for this. Avon was popular."

"How much?"

Grue thought a moment the way he always did, chewing on a toothpick and sucking on his teeth. "Eighty-five silver tenents."

"Silver? Eighty-five? She only cost six coppers!"

"Ya done killed her, ya stupid son of a bitch! I'm out everything she would have made in the future. I should charge ya gold!"

"I ain't got that much."

"You'll have to get it."

Stane nodded. "I'll get it."

"Tonight."

Stane hesitated, then agreed. "Okay, tonight."

"Gwen, get a bucket and clean this up. You, too, Mae. Red, you're done for the night. Go on and get outta here, and send Willard up on your way out. I'll need help getting her body down the stairs."

"You can't let him get away with this," Gwen said through clenched teeth as she got to her feet. The tears hadn't started yet, and she wondered why. Maybe she was still too angry. The smashing of the door had gotten her blood up, and she hadn't calmed down yet.

"He's paying for the damages, just like you will."

"In that case, I'm not done damaging." Gwen picked up the bedpost and charged at Stane's head. She might have made it, but Grue caught her arm. He spun her, striking her cheek hard with the flat of his hand. She fell backward again. The bedpost hit what was left of the doorframe and rolled harmlessly down the hall.

"Get your ass downstairs! Mae, get in here with that bucket, and where's Willard? *Willard!*"

Gwen sat, dazed. If he had used his fist, she would've been down awhile, maybe spitting teeth. But Grue knew how to handle his girls, and he avoided marking them if he could. With the heat still on her cheek and the jaw-rattling pain reaching around her face, Gwen got up and ran downstairs. Everyone in the bar got out of her way as she barreled through the front door of The Hideous Head Tavern and Alehouse, heading straight for the sheriff's office.

The night was cold with the blow of an autumn wind, but she barely noticed as she ran through the cracked-mud streets of Medford. No one was out—all the decent folk were asleep.

She didn't knock, just shoved the door open.

Ethan was asleep in a chair, his head nestled in his arms on the table. Gwen kicked the table's leg, and he popped up like a flushed quail.

"What the—" He sounded angry.

Good.

She wanted him furious. She wanted him seething.

"Stane just murdered Avon at The Hideous Head," she yelled, making Ethan flinch. "The bastard hammered her head against the floor until he split her skull. I told Grue he'd do it. I told him not to let Stane back in, but he didn't listen. Now get over there!"

"All right, all right." Ethan grabbed his sword belt off the chair and buckled it as he followed her out.

"He blackened Jollin's eye just three days back," she told him as they walked down Wayward Street. Ethan wasn't moving fast enough to suit her. Not that time was essential. Avon wouldn't be getting any better, and Stane wouldn't be getting any smarter. Still, she wanted to see justice done, done right and done fast. Stane didn't deserve to live any longer than Avon, and every breath he took was a crime in Gwen's eyes. "And he broke Abby's arm a little more than a month ago. Grue was a fool to force Avon to go with him. She knew, and she was scared, but that's how Stane likes us. Fear excites him, and the more excited he gets, the more damage he does. And Avon—Maribor love her—she was absolutely terrified. Grue should have known better."

The door to the tavern was still open, casting a long slant of light across the porch and into the rutted road. Maybe she had broken that one too; she hoped so. The drunks had left, likely chased out. Grue and Willard were bringing Avon down, wrapped in the blanket from the bed. One end was dripping a dark line down the steps.

"What ya doing here, Ethan?" The cords of Grue's neck stood out from the strain. He wasn't yelling, just angry, which meant he was back to normal.

"What do you mean? Your girl came and got me."

"I didn't send her."

"Well, she woke me out of a dead sleep, so here I am. What's going on?"

"Nothing," Grue said.

"Don't look like nothing. Is that Avon in the blanket?"

"What's it to you?"

"It's my job to make sure justice is done. Stane upstairs?"

"Yep."

"Well, get him down here."

Grue frowned, hesitated, then set his end of the burden down. "Go get him, Willard."

As angry as Gwen was at Stane and Grue, she couldn't

help feeling she was also to blame. More than anyone, she had known what would happen. She should have done something—gotten Avon out of there—only she couldn't even get herself out. But maybe she could have done something, anything. She didn't. Now Avon was dead.

Gwen stared at the little puddle forming around the end of the blanket and wondered how she was still standing. Guilt tore at her insides, pulling her apart. *How is it possible to remain upright after being gutted?*

Stane came downstairs buttoning his pants, finger streaks of blood smeared across his sun-bleached shirt. There was more on his face where he'd wiped his nose.

"You kill this girl?" Ethan asked.

Stane didn't speak. He just nodded and sniffled.

"That's a serious crime. You understand that, right?"

"Yes, sir."

Gwen spotted Grue glaring at her. She'd pay later, but it was worth a beating to see Stane suffer the same punishment as Avon. It wouldn't be the same, of course. Ethan wouldn't bash his head against the floor over and over. They would just hang him. It would be public, though. He'd suffer humiliation before he died. At least that would be something.

Ethan brushed the hair from his face, letting his hand rub the back of his neck. He chewed his lower lip while staring at the blanket-wrapped body. Finally, he took a breath and addressed Stane. "You're gonna need to make restitution."

"What's that?" Stane asked nervously.

"You need to compensate Grue for damages. Pay him for his loss."

"We done settled that already," Grue said. "He's gonna pay me eighty-five."

"Silver...right?" Ethan asked, nodding. "Seems fair. Any other damages?"

"A busted door, mirror, and bed, but that was her doing." Grue pointed at Gwen. "She's gonna pay for them."

"She bust up the place trying to get that one out?" Ethan gestured at the blanket.

"I suppose so."

"Seems to me she wouldn't have done all that if he wasn't beating on Avon, so Stane is gonna take care of those too. Understand?"

"Yes, sir."

The sheriff nodded. "Okay, then."

Ethan took a step back, and Gwen saw him start to turn. "That's all? That's not right. He needs to pay."

"He is. Eighty-five and—"

"A woman is dead! He killed her and needs to die."

"A whore," Grue corrected.

Gwen glared.

"A *whore* is dead, and that's not the same thing. No one is gonna execute a working man for getting a little carried away."

"She's *dead*!"

"And *I'm* the injured party. If I say the settlement is fair, then that's the end of it. This never was any of your concern. Now shut up."

"You can't do this," Gwen said to Ethan.

"She got any family?" he asked.

Gwen shook her head. "If any of us had family, do you think we'd be here?"

"Then that makes him responsible for her. He's satisfied, so this affair is done." He turned back to Grue. "Make sure you get the body out of the city walls before noon, or the constable will have my ass, and I'll be after yours to replace it. Understand?"

Grue nodded and Ethan left.

The two men hoisted the bundle again and headed for the

front door. As they passed Gwen, Grue said, "Guess who's getting a beating when I get back?"

Grue and Willard headed out, leaving Gwen staring across at Mae and Jollin. Between them stood Stane.

He gave her a smile and a wink. "I'm gonna enjoy having you." Lowering his voice, he added, "As soon as I get me another eighty-five saved up." He took a step toward her.

"He won't ever let you in here again."

"Grue?" He laughed. "Avon ain't the first. There was another girl in Roe. If I can pay, they'll wrap you in a bow." He looked at Mae and then Jollin. "Don't worry. I won't forget you two neither."

He gave another little laugh that turned Gwen's stomach. Stane walked to the door, but instead of leaving, he stuck his head out and looked both ways before closing it. When he turned around, he was grinning and his eyes were fixed on Gwen.

"Run!" Jollin shouted.

As Gwen ran for the back door, she heard him curse. He fell hard, probably slipping in the puddle of Avon's blood. It sounded like a chair or a table fell over, too, but by then Gwen was running in the dark, her skirt hiked. She sprinted up the alley past the tanner's shop to the "bridges," a couple of narrow wooden planks crossing the river of sewage that ran behind the buildings. She was too scared, going too fast. Her feet skipped off slick, unsteady boards, and she fell forward into the muck. Gwen's arms sank to the elbows, but she saved her face.

She expected him to be on her, bloody hands closing around her throat and forcing her into the foul soup, which smelled of urine and dung. She spun, but he wasn't there. No one was. Gwen was alone.

Pulling her arms out, she wiped them on any clean parts

of her dress she could find. She found few, and in her frustration the tears finally came. Sitting next to the filthy trench, she sobbed so hard her stomach hurt, and each gasp of air was thick with sewage.

"I don't know what to do!" she cried out loud. "Tell me what to do!" She scooped a fistful of manure and mud and flung it as hard as she could. Tilting her head back, she screamed at the sky. "Do you hear me? I'm not strong enough. I'm like my mother and I'll break." She sucked in a shuddering breath. "And if I don't break first, he'll kill me. Me, Jollin, Mae, and all the rest. I can't...I can't wait anymore. Do you hear me? I can't. It's been five years! I just can't wait for him any longer."

She shivered, panting for air and listening for a reply, but all she heard was the wind.

CHAPTER 3

THE BERNUM RIVER BARGE

Hadrian crouched on the deck of the river barge as two large workhorses drew the boat up the Bernum River. Lifting his head, he peered through the morning mist, trying to catch a glimpse of something familiar. He could see farmland nestled in the hills beyond the bank and the faint outlines of small towns. Everything seemed strange. This was an alien land, filled with odd people, customs, and accents. He felt uncomfortable and out of place, never certain just how to act or what to say. Everyone, he imagined, saw him for the outsider he was, although at that moment he guessed he was less than a half day's walk from home.

The plump man came out of the boat's cabin, slapping his chest and taking deep breaths. "Crisp morning, eh?" he said, looking at the sky.

He might have been speaking to the god Maribor, but Hadrian replied just the same. "Chilly. I'm not used to the cold." He had selected this spot to be sheltered from the wind. He wore everything he owned, including two pairs of pajama-loose pants, his traveling and dress thawb, a wide-wrap belt, his cloak, and a head wrap. Even so, he was still cold. He planned to buy wool when they reached Colnora, something heavy that weighed like armor. He felt naked without the extra pounds.

"You're just up from Dagastan, right? Warm there, I imagine."
Hadrian tightened his thawb. "Linen weather when I left."

"I'm envious." The man drew his robe tight. He glanced around the barge with a disappointed scowl, as if expecting some miraculous transformation to have occurred overnight. He shrugged and mimicked Hadrian by settling down out of the wind until they faced each other. "I'm Sebastian of Iber." The man extended a hand.

"Hadrian," he said, shaking the man's hand. "You're with the other two?" Hadrian had seen them the night before, Sebastian and two companions, all dressed similarly in finely crafted robes. For all his rushing, the barge ended up being delayed as dockworkers strained to hoist numerous trunks on board. The three had shouted orders and reprimanded the workers for each bump or jostle.

The man nodded. "Samuel and Eugene. We're in the same business."

"Merchants?"

Sebastian smiled. "Something like that." His sight drifted to the swords slung at Hadrian's sides. "And you? Soldier?"

He grinned back. "Something like that."

Sebastian chuckled. "Well said. But seriously, there's no reason for arms. The rest of us don't wear steel, so I don't see why you're bothering...Oh, right...I see!"

Hadrian studied the man. In his experience there were two types: the kind you could trust and the *other kind*. Over the past five years, Hadrian had come to rely on men who wore metal, had scars, and whistled through gaps of missing teeth. Sebastian wore thick robes—plush and pricey—and sported golden rings on each hand. Hadrian had seen his type as well. Whatever Sebastian had been about to say, he guessed he wouldn't like it. "You see...*what?*"

Sebastian lowered his voice. "You've heard about the murders. The town guards were everywhere and asking questions even as we set out."

"You're talking about the murders in Vernes?"

"Yes, exactly. Three over the same number of nights."

"And you suspect me?" Hadrian asked.

Sebastian chuckled. "Absolutely not! You were one of those just off the *Eastern Star* out of Calis. Your clothes betray you. It would make more sense to suspect myself. At least I had the opportunity. You weren't even in town."

"So you're saying I should suspect you?"

"Not at all. My associates can vouch for my whereabouts, and the steersman will tell you we had our passage booked weeks in advance. Besides, do I look like an assassin?"

Hadrian had never seen an assassin, but Sebastian didn't seem a likely candidate. Round and soft with pudgy fingers and an infectious smile, he would be more the sort to order his killings by way of an unsigned letter.

"I'll tell you who does, though." Sebastian's eyes strayed toward the front of the boat where a cloaked figure stood near the prow. He had his back to them, and rather than seek the warmth of sunlight, he stood in the shadow of the stacked crates. "*He* looks like an assassin."

"You suspect him because he wears a hood?"

"No, it's his eyes. Have you seen them? Cold, I tell you. Dead eyes. The kind used to seeing and handing out death."

Hadrian smirked. "You can tell that from a man's eyes, can you?"

"Absolutely. A man accustomed to killing has the look of a wolf—empty of soul and hungry for blood." Sebastian leaned forward but kept his sight on the man at the bow. "Just as learning certain truths robs us of innocence, taking lives robs a man of his soul. Each killing steals a bit of humanity until a murderer is nothing more than an animal. A hunger replaces the spirit. A want for what was lost, but as with innocence, the soul can never be replaced. Joy, love, and peace flee such a vessel and in their stead blooms a desire for blood and death."

Sebastian spoke with a serious tone, as a man who knew such things. His self-confidence and easy manner exuded a worldliness that suggested wisdom born from experience. But if what Sebastian had said was true, Hadrian doubted the plump merchant from Vernes would choose to sit so close once he'd seen Hadrian's eyes.

"I'll tell you something else. He came aboard at the last minute without a single bag or trunk."

"And how do you know that?"

"I was on the deck when he booked his passage. Why was he so late? Who jumps on a boat bound so far north on a whim? And why no baggage? People don't just set off on long excursions like they do for an afternoon pleasure cruise, do they? Maybe he evaded the guards' searches and saw the barge as a means of escape."

"I arrived late as well."

"But you carried a bag at least."

"There you are, Sebastian!" His two associates stepped out of the cabin.

Samuel was the older one. Tall and thin, he appeared to have been stretched out like dough. His robe hung loose, the sleeves so long they completely covered his hands, revealing only the tips of his fingers. The other was Eugene. He was much younger, more Hadrian's age, and his body hadn't yet decided if it wanted to be more like Samuel's or round and plump like Sebastian's. He, too, wore a fine robe, a dark burgundy held at the shoulder by a handsome gold clasp.

Both wore a look of exhaustion, as if they had been at hard labor all night rather than just risen from bed. Samuel caught sight of the hooded traveler at the bow and nudged Eugene. "Doesn't he sleep?"

"A tormented conscience will do that," Eugene replied.

"A man like that has no conscience," Sebastian declared, if a declaration could be made via a whisper.

Overhead, an unbalanced chevron of geese crossed the blue sky, honking. Everyone looked up to watch their passing, then adjusted cloaks and robes as if the geese had alerted them that winter was coming. Eugene and Samuel joined Sebastian, all three huddling for warmth.

Sebastian nodded his way. "This is Hadrian…er, Hadrian…" He snapped his fingers and looked for help.

"Blackwater." He extended his hand and shook with each.

"And where do you hail from, Hadrian?" Eugene asked.

"Nowhere really."

"A man with no home?" Samuel's voice was nasal and a bit suspicious. Hadrian imagined him the type of man to count money handed him by a priest.

"What do you mean?" Eugene asked. "He came off the boat from Calis. We talked about it just last night."

"Don't be a fool, Eugene," Sebastian said. "Do you think Calians have sandy hair and blue eyes? Calians are swarthy brutes and clever beyond measure. Never trust one, any of you."

"What were you doing in Calis, then?" Eugene's tone was inquisitorial and spiteful, as if Hadrian had been the one to declare him foolish.

"Working."

"Making his fortune, I suspect," Sebastian said, motioning toward Hadrian. "The man wears a heavy purse. You should be half as successful, Eugene."

"All Calian copper dins, I'll wager." Eugene sustained his bitter tone. "If not, he'd have a fine wool robe like us."

"He wears a fine steel sword, two of them in fact. So you might consider your words more carefully," Sebastian said.

"Three," Samuel added. "He keeps another in his cabin. A big one."

"There you have it, Eugene. The man spends all his coin on steel, but by all means go right on insulting him. I'm certain Samuel and I can manage just fine without you."

Eugene folded his arms across his chest and watched the passing hills.

"What is your trade?" Samuel asked, his eyes focusing on Hadrian's purse.

"I used to be a soldier."

"A soldier? I've never heard of a rich soldier. In whose army?"

All of them, Hadrian almost said but resisted the urge. While funny at first, the reality depressed him an instant later, and he had no desire to explain a past that he had crossed an ocean to leave behind. "I moved around a lot." A simple sidestep, an effortless maneuver. In combat this tactic decided nothing, although if done enough, it could sometimes tire or frustrate an opponent into resignation. Samuel looked like the stubborn type, but at that moment the cabin door opened again. This time the woman emerged.

Her name was Vivian, and the merchants had lavished all their attentions on her the night before. Her emergence cast the same spell, and the three jumped to their feet the moment she stepped on deck. Unlike the others, Vivian did not bundle herself in woolen robes or cloaks. She wore only a simple gray gown, the sort a young wife of a successful journeyman might choose. It hardly mattered what she wore. Hadrian thought she could make a gunnysack look stunning. Vivian was beautiful, which was saying a great deal, as Hadrian was fresh out of Calis, where the native women, particularly the Tenkins, were perhaps the most beautiful in the world. Vivian was nothing like them, and he guessed that was part of her allure. Fair-haired, pale, and delicate, she seemed like a porcelain figurine amidst the men. She was the first western woman Hadrian had consorted with in two years.

Samuel helped Vivian settle discreetly between himself and Sebastian, leaving Eugene to take a seat next to Hadrian. "Did you sleep well?" Eugene asked, leaning in closer to her than necessary.

"Not at all. I had nightmares, dreadful nightmares brought on by last night's events."

"Nightmares?" Sebastian scowled. "There is no need to concern yourself, dear lady. Vernes and those heinous crimes are far behind us. Besides, everyone knows the rogue was known to kill only men."

"That's precious little comfort, sir, and *that* man"—she indicated the solitary figure at the front of the boat—"frightens me."

"Never fear, dear lady. Only a fool would try something nefarious on so small a boat," Samuel said. "There is no privacy to commit a crime and no retreat in its wake."

"Its *wake*—how witty of you, Samuel," Vivian said, but the merchant did not seem to understand his own wordplay.

"And look here." Sebastian pointed toward Hadrian. "We have a young soldier on board. He is fresh from the wilds of Dagastan. You will keep her safe from any would-be brute, won't you?"

"Of course," Hadrian replied, and meant it, although he hoped not to be tested. He started regretting wearing the swords. In Calis, they were as commonplace as his linen thawb or keffiyeh, and in truth a man would be thought strange without at least one displayed at his side. He'd forgotten they were a rarity in Avryn, but to start leaving them in his cabin now would be awkward. After five years his swords had become as much a part of him as his fingers, and their absence would be as distracting as a lost tooth. While he was certain Sebastian's earlier conclusions had been based more on stories than first-hand experience, Hadrian knew the merchant was right about one thing—killing carried a price.

"There, you see." Sebastian clapped his hands as if he had just performed a magic trick. "You're safe."

Vivian offered a weak smile, but her eyes glanced once more toward the bow and the man in the hood.

"Perhaps one of us should talk to him?" Eugene suggested. "If we find out his story, there might be nothing to fear."

"Our young apprentice has a point," Sebastian said with enough surprise in his voice to draw a scowl from the younger man. "It's upsetting to have a tiger about and not know if it's hungry. Go speak to him, Eugene."

"No thank you. I had the idea."

"Well I certainly can't," Sebastian said. "I'm far too talkative. It's a trait that has often led to problems. We don't want to provoke the man unnecessarily. What about you, Samuel?"

"Are you insane? You don't send a lamb to question a tiger. The soldier should go. He has nothing to be afraid of. Even a murderer would think twice before challenging a man with two swords."

They all looked at Hadrian.

"What do you want to know?"

"His name," Sebastian suggested. "Where he's from. What he does—"

"If he's the murderer—" Vivian burst in.

"I'm not so sure you'll want to lead with that," Samuel said.

"But isn't that what we all want to know?"

"Yes, but who would admit to such a thing? Better to get enough information to build a picture and then infer the truth from that."

"But if you ask straight out, that will serve as a warning that we're wise to him and on our guard. Any plans he might have will be spoiled and abandoned."

"How about I just see how things go," Hadrian said, rising.

The team of horses moved along the towpath, hauling the barge smoothly up the river. Still, Hadrian carefully checked his footing as he climbed the short steps of the foredeck and skirted around boxes covered in tarpaulins and lashed with fishing nets. From his new vantage point he could see the expanse of the Bernum. The wind caught him full face, bringing the smell of pine with its cold chill. *Wool*, he promised himself again. *A thick shirt and heavy cloak.*

"Excuse me," Hadrian said, and the man turned partway but not far enough to reveal features, not even a nose. After Sebastian's comments Hadrian was curious about the man's eyes. "My name is Hadrian Blackwater."

"Congratulations." The reply was as cold as the wind that carried it.

"Uh...what's yours?"

The man turned away. "Leave me alone."

"Just being friendly. We're all cooped up on this barge for a couple of days. Might as well get to know each other."

Nothing. Like talking to a wall.

Walls usually surrounded fortresses. To get in you could lay siege, dig under, or slip an agent inside. Maybe Vivian had the right idea. There was always the suicidal frontal assault. "Just thought you should know that there might be a killer on board."

The head turned to face him again. This time it came farther around and Hadrian caught a glimpse of one eye. It did not glow, nor did Hadrian see an elongated pupil, but Sebastian might have a point. Hadrian saw menace there, a piercing glare he'd seen many times before, usually followed by the clash of steel.

"I'm certain there is more than one," the hooded man said. "Now go away."

This gate was tightly sealed. Hadrian gave up and returned to the others.

"Well?" Vivian was the first to speak.

Hadrian shrugged. "Doesn't like to talk much."

"What about his eyes? He has eyes like a wolf, doesn't he?" Sebastian asked.

"Well, he's not a friendly sort—that much is certain. As to his eyes...I wouldn't exactly call that conclusive proof."

"He *is* the killer. I knew it!" Sebastian gloated.

"At least we know," Samuel agreed while struggling to roll his sleeves up in a way they would stay. "Now we can take steps to protect ourselves."

"We don't know anything," Hadrian said. "Just because he's solitary doesn't mean he's a killer."

"I agree with Samuel," Vivian said. "We need to act. What steps can we take?" She was pressed close to Sebastian as if he were a campfire, her arms crossed over her breasts and hands tucked under for warmth.

"Well, it wouldn't hurt to avoid being alone with him," Hadrian said. "And the locks on the cabin door are well made. I suggest you secure them whenever you're in your room."

"Why don't we just shutter the entire cabin area?" Eugene asked.

"I think he might object to being locked out, especially when he paid for a berth like the rest of us," Hadrian explained.

"The rest of us are not murderers," Eugene said.

"As far as we know, neither is he."

"We could tie him up," Sebastian suggested.

"Are you serious?" Hadrian asked.

"That's a good idea!" Samuel agreed. "We could all have at him. He's not big. We could pin him down, tie his hands and feet, and then lock him in the hold until the trip is over. Once we reach Colnora, we can turn him over to the city guard. They can take him back downriver and hand him over to the authorities in Vernes. We might even get a reward for his capture."

"You can't do that," Hadrian said. "We don't know if he's done anything wrong."

"You saw his eyes. Do you honestly think that man is innocent? Even if he didn't kill those men in Vernes, he's done something...something bad."

Hadrian had listened to Sebastian's kind before and always hated himself afterward. People believe what they want when no one offers the truth.

"And how would you feel if we did that to you?" Hadrian asked Sebastian.

"Don't be ridiculous. I'm not like him. I'm a decent man."

"Are you? How do I know?"

"Because I'm telling you so."

"And what if he said the same thing?"

"Did he?"

"I didn't ask."

Sebastian wore a smug look as he addressed his reply more to the others than to Hadrian. "You didn't have to. You can tell just by looking at him. He has blood on his hands. The man is evil, I tell you."

Hadrian looked from one face to another and saw the inexplicable conviction. Their actions made no sense, until he factored in fear. Fear made all the difference between rational and insane and could even masquerade one for the other. Once a herd starts stampeding, only a fool stands in the way.

Wishing Pickles had made the boat with him, Hadrian pushed to his feet.

"Where are you going?" Vivian asked.

"I can't agree. So leave me out." He took a step, then

paused. "Oh, and if you try to tie him, shove him overboard, or anything like that, you can expect I'll help him—not you."

Silence followed. Shocked faces stared up as the boat creaked. Hadrian walked toward the stern, hoping to break their line of sight behind the cabin structure.

"He's young and naïve," he heard Sebastian say.

Hadrian was young. He couldn't deny that, but he measured the time spent in Calis in dog years. He had learned many things and had been too anxious to seek those lessons, too eager to refuse his father's tongs and hammer.

He climbed to the stern and leaned against the gunwale, looking east. The grass was still green in most of the low areas, but leaves on the high slopes were turning. Somewhere in the distance, beyond his sight, stood a tiny manorial village that he had not seen in five years. Hadrian imagined that everything there would have remained the same. Change came slowly to places like Hintindar, where generations lived and died in isolated repetition. Some were bound to the land and unable to leave, others—like his father—were unwilling. The people from his hometown occupied a handful of shacks running along a narrow road between a stone bridge and His Lordship's manor—a road that began nowhere and ended in the same place. Hadrian had left at fifteen, and this was as close as he'd come to returning... and as close as he ever planned to.

Picturing the village, he realized he was wrong about the lack of change. There would be something new—a grave marker on the hill between the two southern fields. Most likely it would be just a stick or maybe an engraved board. The name would be burned in but no date. The villagers didn't understand calendars.

"Gonna be a nice day, it is," the steersman said. One hand rested on the tiller and his feet were up.

Hadrian nodded and realized he no longer shivered. The mist

was thinning as the day brightened. Sunlight cut shafts through the trees, dappling the water behind them. The Bernum was a deep, wide river, especially where it neared the sea. The waterway looked tranquil, lazily meandering through the spread fingers of the low hills. But this was an illusion that concealed a fierce undercurrent in which men, women, and livestock had been lost. In spring the lowlands flooded, which explained the lack of farms close to the banks. Occasionally they passed the foundation of a house or barn; the Bernum never permitted crowding, not for long. Hadrian's father had spoken of the river as if it were a living thing, like an evil woman who lured men to cool themselves in her waters. She would let them swim to the center, then drag them down. He also said that if the river were ever dammed—which he insisted was impossible—thousands of skeletons would be uncovered. The river never gave up her dead.

Hadrian hadn't believed the stories. Even as a kid, he hadn't been the type to accept what couldn't be seen. His father had told him a great many such things.

"You're a quiet one, aren't you?" the steersman said with an inviting tone, earthy as well-turned soil. He possessed the engraved face of a life spent on water, his hands a pair of driftwood. "Didn't see much of you last night. Sorta like that other one—the fella up on the bow. Name's Farlan, by the way."

"I'm Hadrian."

"I know. I try to know all the passengers. Well, their names anyway. Don't want to be too nosy. Some boatmen are. Comes with the territory. Riding the river up and down, all you ever see are the banks. It's nice to have people to talk to, even if it's only for the length of the trip. It's good to meet you, sir. Hope your stay is a fine one. Not like I'm a captain of a ship or nothing, but I like my passengers to be happy with the service."

Hadrian motioned toward the front of the ship. "And what is his name?"

"Oh, *him*. He didn't offer, and I didn't press. He's the kind you best leave to himself and hope he does the same in return. Don't want to be irritating a man like that."

"And what kind of man is he?"

"A bit obvious, isn't it, sir?"

"You think he's the killer?"

"Well, I don't know either way, but I can't say I'm not concerned."

"If you were suspicious, why didn't you report him to the city guard?"

"I should have—would have if I wasn't so stressed about setting out. All those crates had put us behind schedule, and I don't like keeping the postilions and their teams waiting. Patrol came by earlier and searched the ship, but he wasn't a passenger then. He came aboard just as we were shoving off. I was rushing to get under way and just wasn't paying attention. After we were on the river, I realized how stupid I had been. I should have just let the postilion wait and made an excuse, like I forgot to get enough oil for the lamps or something. But I didn't, so now I'll have to wait until we reach Colnora."

"What then?"

"I'll tell the sheriff about the murders and my suspicions about that one. Sheriff Malet's a good man…smart. He'll conduct an investigation and get to the truth of the matter. If I were you, I wouldn't count on getting on your way straight off. I'm sure he'll want to talk to everyone."

"Well, I'm not in any hurry. I just hope he'll have better luck with that guy than I did." Hadrian glanced once more toward the bow and the solitary man standing there.

꒰꒱

They gathered for lunch on the deck, and just as Farlan had predicted, the mist and chill were burned away by a hot afternoon sun. The barge docked at a posthouse, where Farlan secured it by looping a rope around the bollard, and the postilion unhitched his team. A new boy brought over a fresh pair of horses and started attaching their harnesses.

Farlan set out the midday meal. Nothing warm was brought up, but the cold chicken, day-old bread, and fresh apples made for a better meal than the salted pork and sea biscuits Hadrian had become used to on the *Eastern Star*. The barge wasn't soft travel, but it was efficient, operating both day and night. The passengers were little more than extra freight filling open space. The trip cost a copper a mile, which may be expensive to a man used to using his feet but was nothing to someone accustomed to a carriage. Pickles had made a good choice; the ride was gentler than the bounce and jiggle of a coach.

"So what is it you do, Sebastian?" Hadrian asked before sitting down with his wooden plate. He wasn't actually interested, but he wanted to steer the conversation away from any plans for the hooded traveler.

"Are you familiar with Vernes, Hadrian?"

"Me? No. I pretty much came straight from the ship to the barge. Why? Are you famous?"

"In a way. I run the most prestigious jewelry shop in all of Vernes."

Vivian had resumed the same place from earlier in the day but now balanced a plate on her lap. Her portions were small, the kind of meal a mother might serve to a child. She nodded in agreement. "Sebastian's is the oldest jewelry store in the city."

"Are all of you jewelry merchants?" Hadrian asked.

"Samuel is my cousin and Eugene is the son of my sister. They learned the business from me, and I loaned Samuel the money to start his own place." Sebastian gave a wicked smile. "Customers who are angry with my prices or poor service or who just don't like the cut of my clothing will stomp out of my shop declaring I've just lost an important sale. Out of spite they will walk down the street and pay more for a similar item at Samuel's shop. They think they're enacting their revenge, but as I am part owner in both, they still pay me after all."

"And Eugene?" Hadrian asked.

"That's why we're traveling to Colnora, to get him a shop," Samuel said.

Sebastian added, "It's time the boy went out on his own."

"I'm not a boy," Eugene said.

"Until you've paid back the loan, you're whatever I say you are."

Eugene scowled, but when he opened his mouth, it was merely to fill it with chicken.

"And you, dear lady?" Hadrian turned to Vivian, who was biting most delicately into a slice of apple. "What puts you here with us?"

The woman's smile vanished, her gaze fixated on her plate of food.

"Did I say something wrong?"

She shook her head but did not speak. Sebastian placed a hand on her shoulder and patted gently.

"Excuse me, please." She stood and moved to the bow of the barge, left empty because the hooded man was stretching his legs on the towpath.

"I didn't mean anything," Hadrian told the rest, feeling terrible.

Sebastian said in a supportive tone, "It's not your fault. I suspect that lady has been through something terrible."

"What do you mean?"

"Few women travel unescorted. And did you see how little food she took? She is clearly distressed."

"Maybe she just doesn't eat much, and she could be on her way to meet, you know, someone."

"Perhaps, but I think it's likely she's terrified, and the rumors, of course, have us all on edge."

Vivian had abandoned her plate and sat on one of the crates staring at the river. Raising a hand, she wiped away tears.

Hadrian sighed. He had always been a bit awkward around women and often found himself saying the wrong things. He wanted to go to her and lend comfort, but he was sure to just make matters worse. Hadrian didn't think he could feel lonelier than he already did, but then again, he hadn't been correct about a lot of things lately.

৵

After the meal they set off again. Farlan went below to sleep as the relief steersman took his shift. Hadrian failed to catch his name. He was younger and, despite his beard and brooding eyebrows, appeared baby-faced in contrast to Farlan. Taking his post without saying a word, he lacked the older steersman's friendliness.

Vivian vanished into her cabin as soon as they set out. Perhaps she worried the hooded man would resume his station at the bow. But the front of the riverboat remained vacant.

Hadrian spent the day watching the landscape slip by and sharpening his short sword. Maintaining his weapons was as much a habit for him as biting nails might be for someone else. Doing so helped him think, relax, and work out troubles. And he had a need for all three.

Vivian reappeared shortly after sunset. She didn't settle in with the merchants this time. Finding the bow empty, she returned there and sat near the swaying light of the lantern as the stars came out. The loss of the sun invited back the autumn chill, and after seeing her shiver, Hadrian walked to the bow.

"Here," he said, pulling off his cloak and draping it over her shoulders. "It's not much, but it ought to help a little."

"Thank you."

"I should have given it to you earlier. I'm an idiot. I'd like to apologize."

Vivian looked up, surprised. "For not lending me your cloak?"

"For upsetting you earlier."

She appeared puzzled, then realization dawned. "Has that been bothering you all this time?" She touched his hand. "Sit, won't you?"

"Are you sure? I haven't been particularly courteous."

"Were I to guess, I would think you a gentleman—a knight in disguise."

Hadrian chuckled. "Everyone wants me to be a knight."

"Pardon?"

"Nothing. I'm not a knight. I'm just not experienced speaking in refined company."

"Is that how you see me?"

"Compared to the folks I'm used to? Yes."

Vivian looked down for a moment. "I'm not cultured or sophisticated. I was born poor. Any change in status came through marriage, but now..."

She let the statement hang for a moment while she stared at the deck.

"What is it?" Hadrian asked.

"The reason I'm here...the reason I'm alone...is that my husband is dead. He was killed two days ago, one of those murdered in Vernes. I was afraid for my life and I...and I... fled. Now I think I made a terrible mistake."

"Why would anyone want to kill you or your husband?"

"Daniel was a wealthy man, and a rich man has many enemies. Our home was ransacked. Even the tapestries were pulled down. I was so terrified that I ran with nothing but the clothes on my back. I didn't even take a cloak. I traded my wedding ring for fare, but I fear I brought my troubles with me. I don't think the killer found whatever he was looking for, and he has followed me on board to obtain it."

"What do you think he's after?"

"I don't know. It doesn't matter. I don't have it, but he won't believe me—won't even ask. He'll just kill me like he did my husband, then ransack my cabin."

She made a slight motion with her head, and Hadrian noticed Vivian was looking over his shoulder. He turned and saw that the hooded man was also back on deck, standing at the rail near the stern. Hadrian prided himself on never judging a person by appearance, but he couldn't deny the malevolence wrapping that man. His silence and the dark hood, which he hadn't lowered since they had set out, were disconcerting. He was unsociable and hostile.

If Hadrian believed in such things, he might suspect him to be an evil spirit, a phantom, or a dark warlock of some sort. This, he was certain, was how such stories started. After the passengers disembarked in Colnora, they would tell their tales of the mysterious, faceless man, and the story would grow with each recitation. Before long, people would gather around hearths to hear about how Death himself haunted the Bernum River, wrapped in a dark hooded cloak.

"I don't know what I will do when we reach Colnora."

"Do you have relatives there? Do you know anyone who can help?"

She shook her head and Hadrian thought he saw her lip tremble. "This isn't your problem, is it? I'm sure I'll get by somehow."

"Listen, Farlan is going to alert the sheriff in Colnora when we arrive and there will be an investigation. If the hooded man is guilty, he'll be tried and convicted. Then you can go back home to Vernes. The thieves couldn't have taken everything.

Your house is still there and you can rent rooms out or something like that."

She looked back toward the hooded man and lowered her voice. "What if I never reach Colnora? What if he kills me right here on this barge?"

"I won't let that happen."

"I wish I could believe that, but you won't be able to stop him. He could slip into my cabin, and in the morning I would be dead and no one would care."

"Here's what you should do. Lock your door, and block it with whatever you can find. He won't be able to reach you without making a racket, and I'll come right away."

She wiped her eyes. "I'll do that, thank you. I just hope it will be enough."

CHAPTER 4

THE HIDEOUS HEAD

After the beating, even the weight of the empty buckets hurt Gwen's back and shoulders as they swung from the yoke. Grue had been hard on her for involving Ethan. He'd left no marks, though; damaged goods were sold at reduced rates.

Reaching Wayward Street's common well, she dropped the pails and sat on the edge, looking back the way she had come. It was still early, the sun just peeking between the bent roof of the tavern and the lopsided one of the building across the street. Avon had told her it was once an inn, but that was long ago. She could almost picture it. No one stayed there now, except for the rats and the dogs that ate them. The state of the inn was indicative of the whole Lower Quarter, Wayward Street especially—a dead end in every sense.

For as long as Gwen could remember, her mother had spoken about Medford and how they would one day make it their home. Gwen imagined it must be a beautiful place, full of fine carriages and stone houses. She had dreamed they would live in one of those beautiful homes with a fountain outside for water and market sellers who would sing and chant like those in Calis. Even as she sat on the stone lip of the well, Gwen marveled at how different her reality turned out to be.

Did my mother have any real idea about where we were headed?

Her mother had been dedicated to a single purpose—reaching Medford. She had spoken of the city for years. Looking back, Gwen now saw things that a child missed. They had traveled alone. A woman with a child in tow would never set out to cross a continent on her own, without a good reason, even if they were headed for a paradise. Besides, Tenkin women *never* traveled unescorted.

Strange as well was the name Illia had picked for her only daughter: Gwendolyn. Her mother was born to the Owanda tribe, and custom dictated Gwen should have been named after an ancestor, but surely no one in their bloodline had ever been called Gwendolyn. A pretty name, but it wasn't Tenkin. Gwendolyn was a name given to pale, blond-haired girls with blue eyes. Gwen hadn't even seen blond hair until they had reached Vernes, and even there it was rare. Not until years later, when Gwen finally reached the north, did she meet other girls with similar names. Still, even this concession had not been enough to find her acceptance in the foreign lands. All the light-skinned travelers and shopkeepers eyed her with contempt.

In Calis, people were equally suspicious of pale visitors. Most Calians thought the foreigners were ill, but that didn't prevent Tenkins from doing business with them. The same could not be said in the north. Even in Vernes, Gwen and her mother were shunned.

They might have died of starvation if not for her mother's gift. Vernes was rich with Calian immigrants. They had settlements in the hills outside the city, a large camp with colorful tents just like in Dagastan or Ardor, and the camp leaders understood the values of a seer. Illia was able to find work reading the palms of fellow Calians delighted to have such a fine fortune-teller among them.

The talent was always passed from mother to daughter, and Illia had taught Gwen everything she knew.

"You can't read your own future," Illia had told her, "any more than you can see your own face, but just as you can sometimes see your reflection in a darkened glass or calm pool, you can find your way in the stories of others."

She had taught Gwen to read, to *see*, using customers' hands. "What do you see?" she had asked while holding out a man's weathered palm.

"A boat, a big ship with sails," Gwen had answered.

"What color?"

"Blue."

"That is likely the past."

Gwen had looked at the man whose hand she held, and he nodded. "I arrived by ship yesterday."

"Recent events are the easiest. They're the strongest," Illia had told them.

At first all she could see was the recent past, and her mother completed her readings so that the customers wouldn't become annoyed. This was how all the lessons had gone, and Gwen wondered why her mother had never offered her own hands for practice. Initially, Gwen thought it was because they were too closely related for it to work, but as Gwen's skill increased, Illia took to wearing gloves.

Eventually they joined with a caravan headed north, but they had to leave it when Illia became sick. Gwen had brought her mother into a city where it had taken days to find a doctor who would see her, but nothing helped. Knowing her mother would die, Gwen finally asked all her pent-up questions. *Why did we leave Calis? Why did you give me a northern name?* And most importantly, *Why does it mean so much to you for us to go to this mythical place called Medford?*

Stubbornly her mother had refused to answer, except to say

that God had told her to go. When Gwen asked which god, her mother had replied, "The one who walks as a man."

Gwen had used nearly all their money paying for the cramped room where Illia ultimately died. For days Gwen had done little more than wipe her mother's head with a damp rag while Illia lingered without opening her eyes or speaking a word. Then one morning she had stirred. "Promise me... promise you'll go to Medford as we've always planned. Promise me you won't stop until you reach it and that you'll make a life there. You must do what I failed to do. You must be there for *him*."

Gwen didn't know who her mother was referring to and she never learned any more about *him* from her, but she had agreed just the same. She would have sworn to marry a goblin and live on a cloud if her mother had asked her to.

Illia died two days later in that little room in an unfamiliar town far from both Calis and Medford. Gwen had been just fourteen.

Allowing her mother the luxury of dying in a bed had left Gwen destitute. She didn't have enough money for food, much less for a burial. She couldn't stomach turning her mother's body over to the city guard, who had always been so cruel. Alone in the tiny room, Gwen did the only thing she could; she sat and wept. She almost hadn't heard the knocking over her own tears.

The man at the door had been tall and thin and carried a leather satchel over one shoulder.

"Excuse me, but I am here to see Illia," he had said politely.

"My mother has died." Gwen wiped her face. It hadn't occurred to her at the time to wonder how the man knew where to find them.

He had nodded without surprise. "I'm sorry." Lifting his eyes to the bed where Illia lay wrapped in her favorite shawl, he added, "Your mother used to read my palm, and the last time I had no money to pay her. I've come to settle my debt." He had placed six coins in Gwen's hand, making her gasp when she noticed the color.

Gwen shook her head. "This is too much. Mother charged three copper dins. This is...this is..." She couldn't bring herself to say what she had thought. Holding the metal coins was like cupping summer or sunshine. She recalled thinking, *Such power should not be in such dirty hands.*

"It was a *very* good fortune she told."

The encounter had been so strange. This man hadn't even been Calian, and as far as Gwen knew, Illia hadn't told the fortunes of westerners.

Gwen had seen the smile on the man's face—a nice face, a friendly face.

Over the years she had relived that moment a hundred times, asking herself how it happened. Part of it was his eyes, so inviting they drew her in. Another part was her desperation. Gwen was alone and frightened. She was looking for answers, not only about who he was but also who she was as well. What should she do now that the driving force in her life was gone? She had so many questions that when she looked, she took the questions with her.

Illia had taught Gwen all about reading fortunes from the lines of a palm, but her mother had never mentioned anything about what happened when a Tenkin seer peered deep into a person's eyes. The way her mother explained it, the lines on a person's hand were the stories of an individual's life written by the soul. They could be read as easily as a book, but Gwen discovered the eyes were windows. There was no reading possible; no such control existed. Looking through eyes was like jumping off a cliff into a lake with no idea what the water would be like or how deep it went, and as she learned that day...it was possible to drown.

She would have too—if he hadn't turned away. Looking into his eyes was to see eternity. Gwen had been spared madness only because he'd been quick, but she had caught a glimpse, and a glimpse was more than enough. All the strength had left her legs and she collapsed before him, sobbing.

A gentle hand had touched her head, and she heard him say, "You'll be all right. Use one coin to see that your mother is taken care of. Be generous—she deserves the best. Use a second to pay for your expenses to reach Medford, and be frugal. Save the remaining four. Hide them away. You mustn't spend them, no matter how bad things get. Wait until it's absolutely necessary."

"Why?" She didn't know whether she had said the word or if her memory had merely filled that hole. She couldn't imagine having the power of speech, not after looking in his eyes—after seeing what she had seen.

"A desperate man will come to you in Medford. He will come at night, dressed in his own blood and begging for help. You must be there. You must save him."

The man had walked to her mother's side where he stood and lingered for a moment. When he turned, Gwen had seen tears on his cheeks. "Take care of her. She was a good woman."

That had been a lifetime ago and so very far away. The four hidden coins were holy relics to her now. She kept them beneath the knotted board in the little room at the end of the corridor, the same one with the loose bedpost. She had cherished them for five years, told no one of their existence, and prayed to them often.

"Stupid, useless, bloody piece of crap!" The sound of Dixon the carter startled her. He kicked the wheel of his wagon, whose axle was still broken, propped outside Bennington's Warehouse like a wounded animal. Dixon didn't look much better. While the man was still big as an ox, his cheeks were growing hollow. Wayward Street was the end of the road for many people. He paused when he saw her notice him and tipped his hat.

The gesture made her smile, and she nodded in return.

The sun had cleared the crooked roofs, painting the street in gold. Clouds were moving in, and clouds in autumn meant a cold rain. She looked at Dixon sympathetically. At least she had a roof and food, such that it was. Gwen considered her life could be worse—and then it was. Marching down the street was Stane with a bundle of wood under one arm and a hammer in the other.

⁂

"Lumber," Gwen said to Grue after Stane carried his burden up the stairs of The Hideous Head. "Where did he get lumber?"

"Don't know and don't care. He's fixing the doorframe. 'Bout time too. Probably doin' a lousy job. He's a fisherman or a dockworker or some such thing, not a woodie."

Gwen found it odd that Grue didn't know Stane was the net hauler for the *Lady Banshee*. Maybe he did know but was playing stupid to distance himself. Grue was like that—not the type of man to stand beside you when the weather changed. Of course, it was possible he really didn't know. After all, Grue only served the bastard drinks. He didn't sleep with him or have to listen to his chatter afterward.

Grue was wiping slop from the surface of the pine-plank bar. She wondered why he bothered. No one cared. The men who came each night would hunker down along the sewer out back so long as Grue continued to serve the drinks. Still carrying the filthy rag, Grue crossed to the base of the steps and yelled, "That door better open and close without sticking!"

The only reply was the sound of hammer on wood.

"So he's been paid?"

"Seems that way." Grue returned to the bar and rocked the kegs to determine how full they were. "Everyone working the docks gets their due on the new moon, and last night was pretty dark."

"How much? How much did he get paid?"

"How the hell should I know?"

"More than eighty-five?"

Grue paused, turned to her, and shook the bar towel in her face. "He paid that already."

"I know. And now he has more."

"So? That's good for us. He's got the coin to fix the door *and* pay for drinks."

"And women?"

"What are ya getting at, ya stupid tart?"

"You can't sell me to him, Grue. You just can't."

"The man paid his debt." Grue walked over to the slate and tapped it, his wet fingers leaving black dots among the list of names and the amount each owed. Stane's entry was gone, leaving a blank space. "His slate is clean."

"If he has the money, he'll kill me. He knows he can get away with it now. He even knows the cost—how much you charge for the pleasure."

Grue huffed. "That's not true. What happened was an unfortunate accident. You make it sound like Stane is a monster and kills girls for fun."

"He does!"

Grue frowned. "No, he doesn't. He's bought you several times, and you're still alive. Why, he's had every girl in here a dozen times. Stane's always been a good customer. You just have to understand, men like him—fellas who spend day after day dealing with stinking fish and taking orders from boat handlers and dock foremen—they need a break. They need to feel like men, so they like to roughhouse a bit. Grabbing a girl by the hair, giving her a little shake, it gives him the sense he can control something—*anything*. And that's what he's here for. That's what they all come for, to see what it's like to be in charge of their own lives."

She folded her arms and shifted her weight.

"It was an accident, Gwen. Besides, do you really think I'd put up with him—with anyone—killing my girls? That sort of thing's not very good for business. Not only do I have to find a decent replacement, but also people don't like the disturbance. I lose customers, and then there's the need to scrub the bloody floor. Trust me, if I thought Avon's death was anything more than an unfortunate accident, Stane wouldn't be allowed in here."

"But he *has* done it before. He told me there was another girl in Roe."

Grue rolled his eyes. "And why would he tell you that? Next thing you'll be accusing him of spreading the plague and drowning puppies. By Mar, Gwen! I know you're still upset, but Stane's not a killer. And I had a long talk with him. There won't be any more trouble—understand?"

Gwen certainly did not but didn't see the point in saying so.

"I told him that if he rented a horse and then broke the thing's leg—"

"A horse? You compared us to a horse?"

Grue smirked. "It's what he understands."

Gwen was pretty sure it was what Grue understood too.

"Stane agreed to behave," Grue said.

"He'll kill me, Raynor." She hoped that by using his first name her plea would sound more personal, as if she were talking to an old friend instead of the man who had forced her into prostitution. "He wants me dead because I ran to the sheriff."

"Well, I guess ya shoulda thought about that before, don't ya think?"

She didn't answer. How could she answer that? If she were a man, she'd give him the beating of his life, but if she were a man, she wouldn't need to.

Seeing her face, he softened slightly. "Look, I'm just saying ya bring things on yourself. Besides, if Stane really did want to kill you, he wouldn't have to come here to see it done. But it doesn't matter anyway. He's getting Jollin."

"He asked? And you agreed? You're actually going to sell another girl to him?"

"Ale, gambling, and women is how I make my living. That's all there is to it."

"Don't you do it! Goddammit, Grue, you can't. You just can't!"

"I already told ya, he didn't ask for you."

"I don't care. He'll kill her. Don't you see that?"

"He's got nothing against Jollin."

"He had nothing against Avon either. He just liked seeing her scared."

"Getting real tired of your mouth, Gwen. Drop it." Grue shoved her roughly out of his way and returned to checking the kegs, giving the Ole Roundhouse Nut Brown a stronger rocking than necessary.

"You don't own us."

"Oh no?"

"Ethan won't let you keep us here against our will. The sheriffs have to report to the high constable, who reports to the king, and King Amrath cares about—"

"What in Novron's name do ya know about King Amrath and his thinking? Or the sheriff's for that matter? You're just an ignorant whore, Gwen, and that's why I don't have to keep ya at all. I told you that. You can leave any time you want." He grabbed a fistful of her hair and dragged her to the door, shoving her out to the porch. "There...go. Go on, get!" He stared at her. "Where ya gonna go? What ya gonna do? Winter is coming and nights are already getting chilly. Where ya gonna sleep? How ya gonna eat?"

"I can do the same thing I've been doing."

"Like ya did last time? Like Hilda? Go ahead, try again. I told ya I wouldn't stand in your way. I just won't take ya back this time. But you go on. You might last longer than she did. She survived a couple weeks. Maybe you can do better. I actually think ya will. You're smarter. I bet you'll last a whole month. Well...maybe not. She wasn't a foreigner."

Hilda and Avon had been at the Head before Gwen arrived. Neither one ever admitted how long they'd been there. Hilda had been bent on getting out. She'd saved her meager tips, and after a beating one night, she'd run away. Rumors said she tried to find legitimate work but couldn't. She resorted to applying at another alehouse, but they all knew she was Grue's girl and refused. With no other choice, she sold herself on the street, taking men into the alley behind the tannery. She survived all of two weeks. Ethan found her. She'd been robbed and strangled. They never bothered to look for the killer. It could have been anyone.

Grue stepped back, clearing the doorway. "Ya want to live? Ya stay here, and to stay here, ya do as I say." He rubbed his feebly thin beard, which was no more than tufts of hair that refused to grow together or to a length longer than three inches. "Listen," he began in a softer tone, "I was trying not to scare ya, but even I know putting you and Stane together ain't a good idea. So he's getting Jollin."

Gwen's eyes widened. "He *did* ask for me!"

"Yeah, but he's not getting ya. Not tonight. Not until I can tell he's gotten over this whole thing."

"But it's not something he'll get over—it's the way he *is*, Grue. And even if it wasn't, he'd do it out of spite, out of revenge. He'll kill Jollin because he knows it will hurt me. And if that's the best he can do, then he'll settle for that."

Grue ran a hand down his face and shook his fist at her. "Gwen, I'm tired of arguing with ya. It's not for you to say. He's getting Jollin, right after he finishes the door. I've already made up my mind."

"I'm warning you, Grue—"

He slapped her hard, enough to make her stagger but not fall. Still, the crack echoed between The Hideous Head and the inn across the street. "First ya threaten to leave, then ya threaten *me*? That Calian blood of yours is gonna be the death of you. I shoulda never taken you in. You're more trouble than you're worth. I knew men would find you exotic, a novelty. But if I had known how much trouble you'd cause…"

He took her by the shoulders, his long dirty fingers squeezing like bird's claws. "Now I'm gonna tell ya what you're gonna do, and you're gonna do it. Understand?" He gave her a rough shake. "I want *you* to go wake Jollin up and get a room ready for them. Make up the little one, best not to have Stane in the one with the bloody spot. No sense giving him any ideas."

He pulled her back into the tavern and pushed her toward the stairs. She staggered into a table and chair. "And I don't want to hear another word." He raised a pointed finger. "Not…a…single…word."

Thud, thud, thud. Stane's hammer pounded.

When Gwen entered the girls' room, they were all sleeping as close as puppies on the two mattresses lying on the floor. Work at the Head rarely started before sundown, so they napped during the day. Aside from Gwen, Jollin was the oldest. Rose was the youngest—fourteen, maybe, but Gwen never got a straight answer out of the girl, so she really didn't know. Mae was the smallest, like a delicate bird, and Gwen always cringed when she saw the girl go upstairs with some of the big brutes who had to keep ducking even after entering the tavern. Etta, who had never been much of a looker, was now worse thanks to a smashed-in nose and two missing front teeth, the remains of a beating that had left her unconscious for a day and a half. She did most of the serving and cleaning chores around the Head. Christy and Abby could have been sisters, they looked so much alike, but Christy came from Cold Hollow and Abby was a native of Wayward Street. All of them had been born in Medford or one of the nearby villages or farms. None had traveled more than a couple of miles their whole lives—except Gwen—who had come from another world.

Thud, thud, thud. "Almost done, Grue," Stane shouted.

Gwen had crossed a continent, traversing two nations and five kingdoms. She'd seen mountains, jungles, and great rivers. She'd stood in the capital of the east and the largest city in the west, but in all her travels, nothing had ever compared to the sight she'd seen in that tiny room where her dead mother had passed—what she had seen in the eyes of the man who had placed six gold coins in her hand.

Wait until it's absolutely necessary.

"Get up! Get up, all of you." She shook each of them. "Gather your things and hurry!"

They rose slowly, stretching—cats now instead of puppies.

"What's going on?" Jollin asked, wiping her face and squinting at the light outside the windows.

"We need to leave."

"Leave? What do you mean?" Jollin asked.

"We can't stay here anymore."

Jollin rolled her eyes. "Not again. Gwen, if you want to try and leave again, go."

"I can't go alone. None of us can make it on our own, but together we just might survive."

"Survive where? Survive how?"

"I have some money," Gwen said.

"We all have *some* money," Christy said. "But it won't be enough."

"No, I have *real* money."

"How much?" Abby asked.

Gwen took a breath. "I have four gold coins."

"Bull!" Abby challenged.

"Four gold?" Mae muttered. "That's not possible. You could never save up that much, not if you slept with every man in Medford."

"I didn't make it. It was given to me. I just didn't know how best to spend it...until now."

Jollin was nodding. "I knew you had stashed some money away, but I never thought it was that much. Still, that isn't enough."

"Then we'll just have to make more," Gwen said.

"So what are you planning?" Abby asked.

Gwen wasn't—that was the problem. She hadn't a clue. All she knew for certain was that she wasn't going to end up like Avon, and to have any chance at survival, she couldn't manage on her own. Maybe together they would stand a better chance. She went to the window, looking out at the muddy streets of the Lower Quarter. "I've got it all worked out—just trust me."

"No one will hire us," Jollin told her. "A home wealthy enough to afford a girl would never employ one who has no letter of reference, even to scrub floors and empty chamber pots. And the guilds don't take girls as apprentices."

"She's right," Etta said. "No one's gonna hire me. Who'd want to look at my face each day? I don't like looking at it myself."

"You know all this, Gwen. You tried and failed, remember? And have you forgotten about Hilda?"

"Hilda tried it alone. So did I," Gwen said. "That's what we did wrong. If we all go together—"

"Then we can keep each other company as we starve?"

"Maybe if we went somewhere else," Mae said. "A place where no one knows us."

Jollin shook her head. "They're gonna want to know. Folks don't hire people unless they know their past. We'd be strangers and no one is gonna hire a stranger over someone they've known for years."

"I watched my mother starve," Rose said. "I won't do that."

"No, leaving is just too risky," Jollin concluded. "Even if we had enough means for food, we'd have no place to sleep but the street. How long before we were robbed and strangled too? Gwen, if we had any alternatives, do you think any of us would be here?"

Gwen turned from the window. "But I have gold."

"That's great, Gwen. Buy yourself a nice dress or something." Jollin crawled back into the bed and reached for the covers.

"But you don't understand—"

"I do understand. It's you who keeps thinking there is somewhere better than this. Yeah, Grue can be a bastard, but there are plenty of things worse than him. Trust me. I know. As much as we hate it here, the truth is that if we leave, it's almost certain we'll die. You know this better than any of us."

Gwen nodded. "You're right." She slapped her arms against her sides and nodded again. "You're absolutely right."

"What do you know? She can be reasoned with."

Jollin pulled the covers over her head and used a pillow to deafen the sound of the hammering.

"Is that pounding keeping you awake?" Gwen asked. "Jollin, do you know what that is? That's Stane fixing the door I busted."

"So?" She lowered the covers to peer at her.

"So he's got money, and Grue plans on letting him have you."

All the color drained from Jollin's face. She slowly sat up. "Me?"

"He'll beat her to death," Etta said with a lisp that made the word *death* sound like *deaf,* and coming from that busted mouth it was more than just words.

"Yeah, he will, and she won't be the last—unless we leave...now."

"But you almost died when you tried, and Hilda—"

"Both Hilda and I made the same mistake...We tried to make it on our own. Plus Hilda only had a few coppers, so she was stranded on the street, and when I ran, I didn't have my coins...They were hidden up here. With them we can get our own place—a safe place. So what if no one will hire us. Who cares! Grue makes good money from us, and Hilda had the right idea about keeping it all. We can start our own place. Individually none of us can survive—that's what I didn't understand—but together we have a chance. Certainly a better chance than hoping that Stane will lose his job or become a human being."

Gwen looked around and could see them weighing the possibilities.

"Look, I'm going to get the money. Those who want to come with me, have your stuff packed, because if we are going to do this, it's got to be now."

Gwen rushed out of the room, as much to avoid any questions as to leave before Stane finished. Truth was, the idea had only just come to her, and she was a long way from fitting all the pieces into place.

Thud, thud, thud. Stane was on his knees hammering the pale new plank against the frame. He smiled at her. "I'm almost done here. Gonna have a little fun after I—"

Gwen stepped into the little room across from him and

slammed the door behind her. She waited with her back against it, making sure he didn't follow. She heard the scrape of a planer and guessed she was safe...for now. The little bedchamber didn't have a bolt like the other room, which had always been a problem. She'd never checked the money in the daylight, and she wasn't *just checking* this time.

She crossed the room, dragged the table out of the way, and pried up the board, praying. That she had managed to keep them hidden for so long, right under Grue's nose, had been a miracle. The men knew to pay Raynor directly, but some of the better ones tipped. It was never more than a copper or two, and Grue let them keep what was given. But he had no idea of the fortune she kept under the bedroom floor. Had he known, he would've killed her for them himself.

The board popped up, and the bag was there. She'd sewn it from the sleeve that Gideon Hawk had torn off her dress the night he'd had eight drinks instead of the usual four. At last count she had had forty-five copper dins in addition to the four gold tenents. A weighty sum and more than just her life's savings—it was a sacred treasure. She stuffed the pouch between her breasts and went back out.

Stane was swinging the door open and closed, checking the clearance as she walked past. "Tell Jollin to brush her hair but leave it down."

When Gwen entered the bedroom, the girls were all up and waiting—every one of them.

"Gwen," Etta said, "I don't know what in the kingdom you were thinking when you told us to pack our stuff—you know we ain't got no stuff."

"Dear blessed Maribor, Gwen," Jollin whispered. "I hope you know what you're doing."

"Just follow me."

They were all barefoot. Grue never saw the point in shoes,

but seven women descending the wooden steps were about as quiet as a runaway wagon.

"What's going on?" he said, coming out of the little store-room near the kitchen, just as Gwen pulled open the door.

She stopped short, pushing the rest of them out to the porch, where they stood confused. The cats had turned into ducklings and Gwen their reluctant mother, standing between them and a vicious dog. "I warned you. Now we're leaving."

"God, you're a stupid whore! I just got done telling ya—there's no place for you to go. This is the only place any of ya have. But go on. You all go ahead and leave. Go wander around town awhile. When you get tired—when it's dark and cold and you're hungry—you'll realize just how good you had it and will come right back. But know this: When you do, you'll stop this nonsense and do as I say. Oh, and I'll be getting the belt out again for causing so much trouble."

Gwen stepped outside and closed the door.

Her hands were shaking and the tremor traveled the length of her body until she thought she might collapse right there on the porch.

"Where *are* we going, Gwen?" Abby asked.

"You don't know, do you?" Jollin said.

"You wouldn't do that to us, would you?" Mae asked. "Get Raynor mad like that and not have someplace to go?"

Rose touched Gwen on the arm, those big doe eyes focused on her. "Please tell us. Where are we going?"

Gwen stood shivering, her back to the door. The sun was finally high enough to erase the shadows cast by The Hideous Head, and across from Wayward Street stood the dilapidated inn.

"There." Gwen pointed.

"You're crazy," Jollin said.

"Maybe." Gwen nodded. "But it's better than being dead."

Chapter 5

Murder on the Bernum

Thought something might have happened to you," Sebastian said the next morning as Hadrian stepped onto the deck. "Eugene tried your room, but your door was locked and you didn't answer."

Hadrian glanced up at the sky. The sun was nearly overhead.

They were all up and gathered in the middle of the boat again, except the fellow in the hood, who remained aloof and at that moment was nowhere to be seen. Vivian sat in the center of them, wearing Hadrian's cloak and a pleasant smile.

"I stayed up late. Must have slept in." He sounded guilty, like a kid accused of laziness.

"Well, I barely got a wink myself," Sebastian said.

"I don't think any of us slept much," Samuel added.

Hadrian reached into a bucket hanging from the rail and caught enough water to wipe his face. He stretched and yawned. Waking up late always left him feeling tired and sluggish. He had spent most of the night with the door to his room open and an eye on the tiny corridor leading to the other cabins. He watched the lamp sway for hours but never saw anyone. Finally, as the sun came up, he had locked his door and crawled into bed, feeling foolish.

Hadrian sat down next to Eugene. The youngest merchant

had his hands fanned out and stared at them admiringly. His nails were ragged and dirty, so Hadrian guessed he was looking at his rings. With three on each hand, he had almost as many as Sebastian. Hadrian didn't wear rings. He never saw the point. A wealthy warlord gave him one once, but Hadrian hadn't liked the way it interfered with his grip, and he left it as a tip for a barmaid. He imagined that, being jewelers, the men with him had different opinions.

Across from Hadrian, Vivian sat wrapped in his cloak. With her knees pulled up to her chest, she vanished within its folds. Hadrian had never liked the thin garment, what the Calians called a bisht. He had bought it from a zealous bazaar hawker in Dagastan just before boarding the ship to Avryn. Never good at bartering, Hadrian had spent more than was necessary. He'd done a lot of that while in the east, and the cloak was a physical reminder of his time in Calis. Still, it looked good on her.

The barge continued upriver, stopping only to change horses and drivers and bring on a relief steersman so Farlan could sleep. The world around the Bernum had changed dramatically overnight. The river was narrower, more turbulent, and the banks had risen. Canyon walls cast the river in shadow, and the towpath transformed from a country lane into a narrow track that skirted cliffs where pines struggled to find purchase in thin soil, leaving roots exposed.

This was the landscape of the north he remembered—mountains and ravines, snow and ice. So much had happened in the two years since he'd left. Beyond the cliffs were the lands of Warric, the kingdom just to the north of his childhood home. Old Clovis Ethelred had been the king. A cruel ruler, but then Hadrian had yet to meet another sort. Ethelred had built a fine army. Hadrian felt he possessed a particularly expert opinion on that subject, as he had both fought against and been a member of its ranks. That was how he knew the cliffs and canyons of the area; that was how he remembered them, as a young soldier driven through the crags and up the mountains, holding the high ground against the enemy who months before had been his friends.

He chanced another glance at Vivian. When she returned his gaze, he quickly looked away, staring at the banks of the river, realizing too late that his sudden shift would be taken as an admission of guilt.

"Do you know where you'll be staying while in Colnora, Mr. Blackwater?" she asked.

"I have no plans at present," Hadrian admitted.

"But you're a soldier." Eugene's tone was dismissive and superior enough to irritate.

"And you're a merchant," Hadrian said, although he was thinking of another word instead of *merchant.*

Eugene smirked. "I meant you'll be staying at some barracks, won't you?"

"Actually...I'm retired."

"Retired?" Sebastian chuckled. "You don't look old enough to have done much more than enlist."

"And yet..." Hadrian smiled at them, spreading his hands out.

"What are your plans, then?" Samuel said.

Hadrian was beginning to see why the hooded man kept his distance. "Just traveling."

"To where?"

"North."

"That's a very big place. Anywhere in—"

The boat bucked, glancing off a boulder. The tow cable went slack, then snapped taut again. Hadrian looked back and noticed the lack of a steersman. "Where's Farlan?"

Sebastian tilted his head to peer around the others. "I don't know."

They all got up, and Hadrian led the way to the rear of the boat, where they found no sign of the ship's guide. Sebastian gestured to the rope looped around the tiller's handle. "He does that when he needs a break, but he's never gone long. Perhaps he's preparing breakfast. It's getting late."

Looking back, Hadrian saw the river, which had been relatively flat and straight for miles, was now becoming rife with boulders and starting to zigzag with the emergence of the high cliffs.

He glanced toward the cabins. "After a bump like that, don't you think he'd come up?"

They all looked expectantly toward the door, but when it opened, it was the hooded man peering out. Still with hood up, he looked around, then without a word went back below.

"Someone isn't concerned," Sebastian observed.

"Has anyone seen Farlan today?" Hadrian asked.

The three merchants and Vivian exchanged glances.

"Now that you mention it...no. No, I haven't. Anyone else?" Sebastian asked.

They all shook their heads.

"The relief steersman got off after supper last night, didn't he?" Hadrian asked.

"I believe so," Sebastian replied. "When they traded out the horses."

"Is it possible that Farlan got off, too, and we didn't notice?" Hadrian asked.

"Maybe it was some kind of mistake," Eugene said. "A scheduling error or something like that? Maybe the driver started hauling before Farlan got back on?"

"I think Farlan would have told him to stop."

Sebastian said, "Flag the postilion."

Samuel whistled and Eugene waved until the driver halted the horses. Hadrian loosed the tiller and brought the barge over to the bank, where it was inclined to go anyway, being swept to shore by the current. The merchants conducted a search but failed to find the missing steersman. They all disembarked, even the hooded man, who observed from a distance.

"Relief steersmen come and go, but Farlan don't never leave the boat. He cast off after I got my gals here hitched and ready," the postilion told them. His name was Andrew, an older fellow with short-cropped hair who seemed out of his depth when speaking to customers and kept patting the rumps of the horses self-consciously. "Never seen old Farlan step on land except to help load supplies or cargo."

"Then where is he?" Sebastian asked.

"Coulda fallen in the river," the postilion said. "Some have. Not Farlan, but I heard of others that did."

"Shouldn't we wait?" Hadrian asked. "Could he have swum to shore and is running to catch up to us?"

Andrew shook his head. "If he went in, he's likely drowned. This river is evil through and through, but especially round here. The current is strong and sweeps you along. If you fall in near the center, it won't let you get near the banks, plus there's an undertow that will drag down even the strongest swimmer. You get rolled and churned like a deer in a gator's locked jaws. Bodies don't never pop up. The river swallows them whole."

"But what if he did make it?" Hadrian asked.

Andrew shrugged. "He'd be fine, as long as he wasn't bashed up too bad. He'd likely walk back to the last post station or just sit and wait for the next boat coming up."

"Why downriver? Why not up?"

"There ain't no more stations ahead. We're entering the canyons. Next stop is Colnora. I suppose he might head to the city, but walking downhill is easier than up."

"So there aren't any more steersmen to replace him?"

Andrew shook his head again. "Or team changes. From here on it's just me, Bessie, and Gertrude."

"Then what are we going to do?" Samuel asked.

"You'll have to stay here while I go down to the last post. Even if Farlan isn't there, I'll need to grab another steersman to finish the trip."

"How long will that take?" Sebastian asked.

"Most of the day I 'spect, and that's if someone's available. Might not be, then it could be three days if we have to wait for another barge."

"That's unacceptable," Samuel declared.

"Absolutely unacceptable," Sebastian agreed. "We can handle the steering."

Andrew rubbed the horses in a circular pattern, looking like he wished he were somewhere else. "Well, I suppose that might be okay, but Colnora is still a day away and this last part is—"

"Then I say we do that," Sebastian declared loud enough for his voice to bounce off the cliff and echo back.

"Who's going to handle the rudder?" Eugene asked.

"We'll take turns. You can start us off, Eugene. I'm sure it's not hard." He looked to Andrew.

"Just keep her near the middle and avoid the rocks. That's all there is to it. These ladies here do all the hard work." He patted the rump of one of the horses.

⌇

They set out once more, this time with Eugene at the tiller. He looked unsure of himself, and while Hadrian was no hand with a boat, he sat with the apprentice merchant for a while until he appeared more comfortable skirting the rocks. Hadrian couldn't tell if Eugene was grateful or irritated with his presence, and eventually took his leave.

"He was murdered," Samuel told Hadrian when he returned

to the center of the barge where the two jewelers and Vivian were gathered. The hooded man had returned to the bow, probably wary of Eugene's steering and not wanting to be caught below. Samuel nodded in his direction. "That one slit his throat and dropped him in the river."

"We don't know that," Hadrian said. By the looks on their faces, he was the only one who believed it.

"Do you really think an experienced steersman fell overboard on a route he's probably traveled a hundred times?" Sebastian asked.

"No, but I'm also not willing to jump to the worst possible conclusion."

"Open your eyes, you foolish boy," Samuel said in a loud voice. "A man is dead! And there is no denying who is responsible."

Hadrian cringed. "You want to say that just a little louder? I don't think Andrew and Bessie heard. Look, you insist that Farlan has been killed, but you are forgetting one very important thing."

"Which is?" Samuel inquired.

"Why?" Hadrian let the word hang in the air. "Can you tell me why he would want Farlan dead? Because I can't think of a single good reason beyond just being crazy, and he hasn't seemed crazy so far."

That seemed to knock the wind out of the merchants' sails. They exchanged glances and seemed genuinely perplexed. While they pondered, Vivian's small wavering voice spoke up: "I think I do."

All three men looked her way.

"He was there last night, wasn't he?" she asked, looking toward the bow. "When the two of us were talking? He wasn't far away when you told me about Farlan getting the sheriff to investigate the murders in Vernes."

"Is that so?" Sebastian asked.

Hadrian nodded.

"He had to make Farlan disappear," Samuel said as his sight shifted to the bow as well. "No Farlan, no investigation, problem solved."

"Well, there you have it," Sebastian declared. "Now it makes perfect sense, but..."

"But what? Hadrian asked.

"Now we *must* take steps," Sebastian said.

"What do you mean?" Hadrian asked.

"We know, don't we? We all know it now."

"Know what?"

"That not only is he the murderer of Vernes, but of Farlan as well. What's more—he knows that we know. If he was willing to kill Farlan, he won't stop. His only choice is to kill *all* of us."

"You can't be serious," Hadrian said. "There are five of us, six counting Andrew. I think the odds are well in our favor."

"He'll just catch us off guard while we sleep or when alone at the tiller. Like a predator winnowing a herd, he'll pick us off one by one."

"That settles it, then," Samuel whispered this time. "We have to kill him first. It's us or him. He's no bigger than Eugene—smaller even—and I don't see any weapons. We could do it right now. The three of us. Hadrian, lend us your swords and get that big one from your cabin. We'll all have at him and then roll the bastard into the water, just like he did to Farlan."

Sebastian was nodding with stern resolution, a judge presiding over a hearing.

Hadrian had spilled enough blood for three lifetimes. However, it was possible, probable even, that they were right. Even more condemning was Mr. Hood himself. Why was he so distant? He must be able to hear their conversations. Why not deny the charges if he was innocent? His behavior invited suspicion and his attitude was worrisome, but that wasn't proof.

"No," Hadrian replied. "I won't kill a man on speculation. Something happened to Farlan, something unexplained, but we don't even know if he's dead. Even if it was murder, who's to say it was him? So the man keeps to himself, big deal. So you don't like the look of his eyes. What does that prove? Why couldn't it have been Eugene, or one of you two, or even me for that matter?"

The two merchants shook their heads in dismay, their mouths agape.

"There's just too much we don't know," Hadrian continued. "I think we should do exactly what Farlan had been planning. We get through the rest of today and tonight, and when we arrive in Colnora, Andrew can fetch the sheriff. If it makes you feel any better, I'll ensure that nobody leaves until he arrives and gets to the bottom of all this."

"You can't be serious," Sebastian said.

"Farlan might be safe and sound, drinking hot soup back at the last outpost. How will you feel when he turns up in Colnora and you know you killed an innocent man?"

"Do you really expect us to do nothing except wait to be slaughtered?"

"I expect you to let the law decide what's to be done." Hadrian stood up, taking advantage of his superior height to make his point. "And if you attempt to lay a hand on him, I'll see that you lose it."

"You would defend a killer!"

"No, but I'll protect what could be an innocent man from a mindless mob. You've had it out for him since he came on board."

"And what about Miss Vivian? Didn't you promise her just yesterday that you would protect her?"

"I did and I will." He looked directly at her. "I'll keep you safe. I promise you that."

"And what about us?" Samuel asked.

"I suggest you stay together. You said it yourself, about being vulnerable when alone. Don't give him any opportunities, and I'm sure you'll be fine."

"That won't change anything. Can't you see the danger we are all in? You're blind and a fool!" Samuel said.

Hadrian laid a hand casually on the pommel of his short sword and Samuel stiffened. "I'll add deaf to that list, but only this once," Hadrian said softly.

He walked away, annoyed by the smallness of the boat and feeling Samuel's glare on his back. Sebastian's mood was harder to gauge. Hadrian thought it a fair bet that both merchants were displeased with him; whether that constituted a change in their opinion was difficult to tell.

From the high rail of the gunwale, Hadrian realized he could climb onto the top of the cabin area—a modestly sloped roof made from pitch-covered boards. In the direct sun the pitch was soft, but not tacky. He sat alone on what he realized was the highest point on the barge. From here, he had a clear view of the entire deck. At the stern, Eugene sat with his feet up, much the way Farlan had, and Hadrian hoped the old steersman had made it to shore. From the little interaction between them, he had liked the man. Below, Sebastian and Samuel continued to speak, but now in hushed whispers, huddled close together in their matching robes, Vivian at their sides. On the bow, the hooded man appeared oblivious as he stared out at the river.

⟡

Hadrian was back at his new favorite spot on top of the cabins, staring at the stars. With nothing to lean back against, it wasn't as comfortable as sitting on deck, but the difficulty of reaching it—requiring a significant effort to climb—guaranteed privacy. None of the jewelers were going to scale the railing in their fancy, flowing robes, nor was Vivian. That left only the hooded man, and Hadrian doubted he would make an appearance.

The day had passed uneventfully. Without Farlan, they managed as best they could. Sebastian, Samuel, and Vivian had set out the midday meal as well as supper. Hadrian had served his time at the tiller after Eugene. Samuel took the duty next and Sebastian would take the last leg. Although whose turn it actually was would make little difference. All three merchants were gathered at the back of the boat, and Hadrian guessed none of them would sleep at all that night. They would keep each other awake, and safe, trading off as needed. The hooded man continued his vigil at the front of the boat, and Vivian had locked herself in her cabin for the duration.

The river continued to narrow and the canyon walls rose ever higher. Hadrian knew the navigable portion of the Bernum River ended at Amber Falls, just south of Colnora. He didn't have a clue how he knew this, any more than he knew not to stick his hand in a fire or stand on a hill in a lightning storm. Someone must have told him, but he couldn't remember who or when. A lot of his knowledge had been gained that way, and he guessed a good deal of it was wrong.

As a boy living in a small village, he had heard many stories delivered by visitors—tinkers mostly. They had been the only ones to enter the Hintindar Valley on a regular basis, and Hadrian suspected that little had changed since he had left. Usually it would be Packer the Red, who could be spotted a mile out by the sound of his rattling wagon and the sight of his flaming hair. When the sun was setting, it looked as if Packer's head was literally on fire. The tinker sold and traded with practiced skill, but his stories had always been free, which granted him a welcomed place in everyone's home.

Packer said he had traveled to the far reaches of the known world, from the deep forests near the Nidwalden—which he claimed marked the boundary with the ancient elven kingdom—to the immeasurably high towers of Drumindor, an ancient dwarven fortress that could spew molten stone hundreds of feet through the air. Everyone delighted in his tales, which usually featured Packer on lonely roads in the middle of the night. Most often he spun fantastical stories about encounters with ghosts, goblins, or faeries who attempted to lure him to an untimely death.

When Hadrian was young, one of his favorite tales was about Packer finding himself surrounded by a bunch of goblins. He had described them as little green men with pointed ears, bulbous eyes, and horns. Fastidious little folk who Packer declared wore formal coats and tall hats. They were dapper in the moonlight and spoke with Calian accents. The goblins had wanted to take Packer to their city to wed their queen, but the tinker outsmarted them. He convinced the goblins that a copper pot had magical properties and when worn on the head showed visions of the future. Packer's grand tale had kept everyone in the village huddled at the hearth, riveted and squealing at every turn, Hadrian included. He had clearly imagined the goblins Packer described and believed every word. That was long before Hadrian had left Hintindar, before he had gone to Calis and seen a real goblin. By that time, Hadrian had already begun to doubt Packer's worldliness, but he knew just how ridiculous the tinker's stories had been the moment he entered the jungles and saw his first Ba Ran Ghazel. Packer had never seen a real goblin. If he had, he never would have lived to tell the tale.

Much of Hadrian's education had been gained kneeling

around various hearths in the winter or beneath shady trees in summer, told by people who never traveled more than a few miles from home. No one in Hintindar knew anything about what lay beyond the valley, except Lord Baldwin and his father.

Danbury Blackwater hadn't been from Hintindar. His father had come to the village only a few years before his son's birth, but he never spoke of the days of his youth. Presumably because there was nothing to tell. Danbury was a simple man, more concerned with creating a plowshare than adventuring. Hadrian resented his small-minded attitude, and it was just one of the reasons he had left home, anxious to find out more about the world.

Packer may have lied about his goblins, ghosts, faeries, and elves, but his geography was impeccable. The river would indeed end at Amber Falls near Apeladorn's largest city—Colnora. Beyond that, the river would fracture into a handful of fast-flowing, rough cascades that came from the highlands where Hadrian had spent most of his soldiering years. In all that time, though, Hadrian had never set foot in the city.

He yawned, regretting the hours of lost sleep. His legs were stiff, and just as he stood up to stretch, the hooded man headed toward the cabin door. Hadrian moved quickly and climbed down. He entered the cabin area only to find Mr. Hood simply going to his room.

Hadrian headed for his own door, but his footsteps must have unnerved Vivian, who called out in a wavering voice, "Who is it? Who's there?"

"Don't worry, Miss Vivian. It's just me, Hadrian."

"Oh, thank Maribor. Can you please wait just a minute?"

Hadrian heard dragging noises, and after some fumbling with the lock, the door opened.

She waved him in, opening the door wider. "I need to give you back your cloak and want to ask you something."

All the ship's cabins were the same, except perhaps the one the merchants rented, which Hadrian expected was a double where Eugene probably was forced to sleep on the floor. Vivian's room was identical to his with one narrow bed and a trunk beside it that doubled as a table. A lantern hung from the ceiling, and Hadrian bumped it with his head just as he always did in his own room.

After entering, he was surprised that Vivian motioned for him to close the door. She worked at the ties of the cloak, her hands shaking. "Thank you for this," she said when she finally got it free.

He took it from her and she rubbed her arms.

"You can keep it, if you're still cold. I don't mind."

She shook her head. "No, that won't be necessary. At least I hope not."

Hadrian wasn't sure what she meant.

Vivian licked her lips, then said in a whisper, "I know this will sound unusual, but then again this night can hardly be considered a common situation." She hesitated, the cabin's lantern casting a halo of light around her thin frame. "I don't mind telling you, Mr. Blackwater, that I am very frightened. I fear that if I close my eyes tonight, I shall never open them again."

"I said I'd protect you. I may seem young, but you can trust me. I'll be right next door. If anything—"

"That's precisely the problem. What if he blocks your door and you can't get out? Or what if you fall asleep and don't hear him breaking in? How long does it take to slit a throat?"

Her hand went to her neck, then lowered slowly, brushing past her breast. She took a breath, closed her eyes, and said, "I would feel much safer if you spent the night *in* my room."

Hadrian raised his eyebrows.

"I can't begin to tell you how I would appreciate it. These

last few days have been the worst of my life. I've lost everything. My whole life and I'm certain that man is planning to kill me." She shivered, drawing closer. "Please, it would mean so much. I'll make certain you stay *very* warm tonight." She took his hand in hers.

Hadrian narrowed his eyes. He was young, not stupid. "All right. I'll...I'll sit here next to the door—put my back against it, so even if I fall asleep, there's no way anyone can get in without my knowing. How's that?" It wasn't a serious question. He just wanted to see her reaction.

She didn't keep him waiting.

No stunned surprise, no frustration at his ignorance or her need to spell things out, no clumsy debate. She merely faced him and began to untie the delicate ribbons of her gown. The lantern caused her shadow to sway in a slow rhythm, side to side, keeping time to the musical creaking of the wooden vessel. Loosing her bodice, she continued to tug at the satin, working free the strained material that pulled away and revealed pale skin. Hadrian finally understood why she was always so cold—all she wore was the dress.

Vivian had stopped shivering. Any chill that the cabin originally held had burned away. Her nimble fingers no longer trembled, and her eyes never left his. "I want to thank you for spending the night with me," she said in a breathy whisper. "I know it's a terrible hardship. I only hope I can make your sacrifice worthwhile."

"I don't want to ruin the moment, but didn't your husband just die? Murdered you said."

"What's your point?" Her hands were back at work, this time on his sword belt.

"I'm guessing you weren't the faithful type."

"The man is dead. I'm alive, and I'd like to stay that way." She arched her back, rose on her toes, and closed her eyes.

"Then I'd get your hands off my belt."

Her eyes opened. "What?"

"You want to tell me what's really going on?"

"I don't understand."

"Neither do I—that's the problem. Your husband wasn't killed, was he?"

"No, but that doesn't mean I don't need a protector."

"From what?"

That's when the screams began.

ॐ

Hadrian reached the deck with sword in hand, but found no one.

The cries had stopped long before he opened Vivian's door. He had told her to lock it behind him, then raced to the deck. He listened for the scuffle of a fight, but the cries had ended decisively. There should have been the sound of boots on decking, the killer running away, but all Hadrian heard was the lap of water.

He waited.

Silence.

No, not silence—the river still spoke. For days the voice of the river breaking against the bow had been a constant frothy rush. Now the tone was different. The lapping against the hull was a lower pitch, quieter. It didn't feel right. And that wasn't the only change. The barge was no longer moving.

He scanned the open planking.

Nothing moved.

Hadrian walked slowly to the stern and found Samuel not far from the tiller. He was facedown in a spreading pool of blood.

Where are Sebastian and Eugene?

Hadrian had seen plenty of death. He'd killed more men

than he wanted to remember but had convinced himself that each one was necessary. This was a lie—one he never actually believed, no matter how much he wanted it to be true. Still, all his fights had been on battlefields or in arenas. This was different—unprovoked butchery.

The night, which had been so tranquil, wore a new expression. Quaint swinging lanterns offered poor light and the moon showed less than half a face, giving life to a thousand silhouettes. Hadrian wasn't afraid for himself; what had happened was over. As far as he could tell, the deck was secure, leaving only the hold and the cabins. Taking a lantern, he crept to the bow where he found the other two merchants. Both dead. Throats cut. Lying in their own blood.

A few feet from their bodies was the trapdoor leading to the hold, the padlock gone, hatch open. Hadrian peered in. Crates, sacks, bags, and boxes were tightly packed. No one waited in the shadows. Again he listened, again silence. His short sword ready, Hadrian moved through the narrow pathways that ran half the length of the barge. He found the huge trunks belonging to the merchants. They, too, were unlocked. Inside were more robes, silver plates, silverware, gold goblets, necklaces, candelabras, bowls, and crystal stemware. He also found a small chest and a strongbox. Both were open, two padlocks lying nearby. Inside, he found nothing.

Leaving everything as he found it, Hadrian climbed back onto the deck.

Everything was still quiet...and dead.

At that moment, Hadrian remembered Andrew and the fact that the barge wasn't moving. In the dim moonlight, all he saw was the outline of the horse team illuminated by Andrew's lantern.

Hadrian returned to the cabins.

He found the hallway as he had left it, Vivian's door intact. He knew she would be terrified, and this time for good reason. At least he could report they were safe. The hooded man was gone.

"Unlock the door, Miss Vivian," he said, knocking. "It's—"

The door creaked inward. The shock of its movement halted his breathing and set his heart pounding. Pushing it revealed the little cabin still illuminated by the lantern. The door stopped short with a dull gut-wrenching thump. All he saw beyond its edge was a hand—her hand, fingers slightly curled. Vivian lay on her stomach in a lake of blood that spilled out across the floor, soaking into the dry wood.

What if I never reach Colnora? What if he kills me right here on this barge?

Hadrian felt sick. He shook his head as he backed out, knocking it against the lantern and setting the shadows dancing around the walls.

He had promised to protect her. He had assured her she was safe.

Walking backward out of the cabin, he noticed the crimson stains he was tracking on the corridor floor.

What is it with me and death? Hundreds of miles and I'm still leaving bloody footprints.

Hadrian returned to his cabin and gathered his belongings. His one bag, comprising the accumulated wealth of his life. Hoisting it made him think of Pickles. That officer on the dock might just have saved the boy's life. Hadrian's great sword still hung on the wall peg. He slipped the baldric over his shoulder, centered the spadone on his back, and climbed to the deck.

Without the pull of the horses or proper steering, the barge had already closed the distance to the towpath like the pendulum of a clock. Hadrian made an easy jump from the barge and landed on solid ground. Reaching the horses, his fears were confirmed. Andrew was gone. There was no body, but the pool of blood and the trail leading to the river told the story.

Standing on the towpath, Hadrian was at the base of the exposed stone cliff that blocked out most of the sky. Andrew's lantern displayed his shadow against the stone wall as if he were a giant. Other than the blood and the missing postilion, the scene was as quiet as the boat. The lead line of the horses had been fastened to a tree, and Bessie and Gertrude waited for a signal to start again.

Hadrian tied off the bow line to another tree, then unfastened the horses from their harnesses. Given the strong current, he wedged the bar of the tackle between two boulders just to make sure the boat remained secure. Then he returned to the horses. He tied Bessie—or was it Gertrude?—to the same tree as the boat's line and leapt on the other's back. "No sense leaving you here," Hadrian told the animal, and gave it a light kick. The horse wasn't trained for riding and refused to do more than plod. The animal's pace was aggravatingly slow but better than walking.

Hadrian couldn't help wondering if he might stumble upon the hooded man in some inn or tavern. He imagined him drinking with his feet up and boasting about how he'd just slaughtered a boat full of people on the Bernum. Picturing the scene made Hadrian feel better.

He was tired of killing, but for the hooded man he could make an exception.

CHAPTER 6

THE RUINS OF WAYWARD

For two years Gwen had looked out of the windows of The Hideous Head Tavern at the dilapidated building, but until that day she had never gone into it. Many others had. When their strength ran out and the cold of winter came, the desperate always sought shelter in its ruins. Many died there. Every year Ethan dragged at least one frozen corpse from its fallen timbers. The Lower Quarter was the bottom of the city's sink and the dead end of Wayward Street was the drain. As Gwen stood in the ramshackle remains of the old inn, she wondered how long she had before the drain's whirlpool sucked them all down.

Two walls were solid; one tilted inward, warped into a wave, and the last was mostly missing. Part of the second floor had collapsed, as had a good portion of the roof. Through the gaping holes she could see clouds drifting past. At least three small trees, one four feet tall with a trunk as thick as her thumb, grew up through the floor.

"This isn't too bad," Rose said.

Gwen looked around but couldn't see her. Since crossing the street, the girls had wandered the ruins like ghosts. "Where are you?"

"I don't know...the parlor?"

The parlor? Gwen almost laughed. Not just because of the

absurdity of the statement, but because of the way Rose had said it, her voice as carefree as a cloudless sky. Gwen spotted Jollin circling the shattered staircase, her arms folded tight, head bowed as she shuffled through the debris. Their eyes met, and the two shared a smile that conveyed the same thought. *Only Rose would see a parlor in this dump.*

They all moved toward the sound of Rose's voice and found the only room with four walls. Shattered remains of old furniture were scattered on the floor as well as a thick layer of dust, dirt, and animal droppings. A family of swallows nested in a pile of twigs set on the rafters and the floor beneath it was thick with white and gray splatter. What caught everyone's attention, however, was the fireplace. Unlike the timber and plaster walls, the fieldstone chimney ignored the ravages of time and looked nearly perfect, even elegant.

"Look!" Rose said, spinning around with a pair of iron tongs in her hand. "I found this under that stuff in the corner. We can have a fire."

Up until that point, Gwen was all but certain she had made the biggest mistake of her life, which just happened to be the same as her last biggest error—leaving Grue.

On her first day after finally achieving her mother's dream of reaching Medford, Gwen thought she was both blessed and outright lucky. Not only had she finally made it, but she had also landed a job that very afternoon—as a barmaid at The Hideous Head. Grue provided her room and board. The room was shared, of course, so she hid her coins in the floorboards in the little room across the hall—one of the rooms with just a single bed. She should have realized that Grue wasn't extending kindness. No one had been kind to her in the north. She was different, and the farther she traveled the more looks she got—all of them loathsome. When she'd discovered that *barmaid* meant "whore," she had tried to leave.

Grue beat her.

After that, he kept a close eye on Gwen, never letting her near an open door. Weeks later Grue became careless. She was alone at the bar, the door left open. She ran. Her coins were still under the floorboards, but she was free. At least she had thought so.

Gwen wandered the city looking for work, for handouts, for help. She found indifference, and in some cases hatred. They called her things she only understood as insults—names for lowborn Calians. After more than a week—she never really knew how long—of surviving only on bits of food she found in piles of trash, she discovered she couldn't walk straight or see clearly, and she even had trouble just standing up. Like Hilda, she went to other brothels and received the same refusal. This was how she knew the rumors about Hilda weren't rumors at all. That's when Gwen became terrified. That's when she realized she was going to die.

Wait until it's absolutely necessary.

She couldn't think of a more dire circumstance. She had to use the coins…only she didn't have them. Hunger drove her back. She had to chance it. There was no hope of sneaking in, and she expected Grue to beat her again. Maybe this time he'd kill her, but she had no choice. She would die anyway.

To Gwen's surprise, Grue didn't kill her. He didn't even beat her. He just stared and shook his head sadly. He sent Gwen to bed and ordered food brought up—soup at first, and then some bread. She told herself she'd get the coins when she was better. She ate and slept, and slept and ate. Days went by. The other girls visited, hugged her, kissed her, and cried about how happy they were she was all right. It had been the first time since her mother's death that she'd felt a kind touch. She cried too.

Eventually Grue came. "I didn't have to take you back.

You know that, right?" he had said, standing above her, arms folded. "You're young and stupid, but maybe now you see what's really out there. No one's going to help you. No one gives a damn about you. Whatever terrible things you think about me or have heard, let me tell you this—most are true. I'm a bad man, but I don't lie. Fancy people, people with good reputations, they lie. I don't give a rat's ass what anyone thinks of me. I haven't cared for a long time. So believe me when I tell you, I wouldn't cry a tear if you died, and I didn't lose a minute's sleep when you ran. But the truth is I can make more money with you than without you, so that makes me the only person in the world who cares what happens to your sorry ass.

"I'm not going to lock you up like before. I'm not going to watch you either. You want to leave, go ahead. You can crawl away and die like all the rest." He turned and reached for the door latch. "Starting tomorrow, you go back to work."

That night Gwen didn't sleep. She could have taken the coins and run. But a week on the streets had proved that all doors, except the Hideous Head's, were closed to her in Medford. If she wanted to survive, she'd have to go back south. Four coins were more than enough to reach Vernes or even Calis. And while northerners would charge her with witchcraft for reading fortunes, she could make a small living among her own kind the way her mother had.

All she needed to do was forget about her mother's dying wish.

Should have been a simple thing. What value were the demands of a dead woman in the face of slavery? Maybe if her mother had known... but that was the problem. To anyone else, prophesies were flimsy things, silly things, childish fantasies. Gwen and her mother knew better. Illia had abandoned everything. She'd given up her family, her home, her very life to get her daughter to Medford—and Gwen knew why.

Her mother *had* known. She'd read Gwen's palm and understood the price her daughter would pay. Illia had sent her just the same—made her promise. If she couldn't trust her mother, who could she trust?

Besides, Gwen had seen *him* herself. She'd looked into that man's eyes, understood who he was, and seen the truth. No matter what, Gwen had to stay in Medford, to survive any way possible. Nothing else mattered, not her comfort, not her safety, dignity, or even her life. Those coins were meant for something more than just food.

Wait until it's absolutely necessary.

This must have been what he had meant. But autumn was no time to declare independence. She should have started planning sooner, done some research, and lined up a place to go—a real place, not this pile of wood. Stane might have murdered Jollin if they hadn't left, but Gwen could end up killing them all.

Then Rose spoke, and the sound of her voice was music.

"Isn't it beautiful?" she asked, pointing at the fireplace with the tongs, wielding them like a sword. Her tone was almost giddy. "This is going to be great."

Gwen looked at Rose's cheery face and started to cry. She crossed the room, threw her arms around the smaller girl, and hugged her. "Thank you," she whispered.

Pulling back, she was met with Rose's puzzled expression. "They're just tongs."

"They're a start. And yes, we can have a fire, so we won't freeze."

"What are we going to eat?" Abby asked, staring down at the pile of bird droppings with a grimace.

"I'll go buy some food," Gwen replied.

"Grue won't sell us any," Jollin said. "And if he says so, no one in the Lower Quarter will either."

Gwen nodded. "We'll do our shopping in the Merchant Quarter." She looked around. "We'll get blankets and some tools too."

"Tools?"

"We'll need to fix this place up."

"What kind of tools?" Etta asked, though with her missing teeth it sounded more like, *what kind of thules*, and she looked worried, as if Gwen planned to have them rebuild the foundation that afternoon.

"A broom would be nice, don't you think? We don't want to sleep in this dirt."

"But we can't just stay here," Jollin said. Her hands had moved to her hips and the smile they had shared was already a distant memory.

Gwen hadn't determined anything yet. She hadn't thought any further ahead than that they could camp there for at least one night, but the moment Jollin said it—maybe it was the *way* she said it—Gwen made a decision.

"Why not?"

"They won't let us."

"Who are *they*?" Gwen asked.

"The city. This isn't ours."

"Whose is it?"

"I don't know—but I know they won't let us just live here."

"I don't intend to *just live here*." Gwen was angry. She was tired of having all doors closed to her. Maybe Jollin was right, but she wasn't about to give up, not now that it seemed like she was finally able to make her own way. What came out of her mouth next was more spite than sense. "Grue made a fortune off us. We'll do the same thing on our own, right here, and we won't have to walk around in rags." She looked at her dirt-caked feet. "And we are going to get shoes, damn it!"

Jollin rolled her eyes.

"No one is using this place," Gwen protested, as if Jollin had just laid out a careful argument. "No one has in years. Why would anyone care?"

"That doesn't matter. There are rules about businesses."

"What are they?"

Jollin shrugged. "I'm a stupid whore. How should I know!"

"Well I'm sick of rules!" Gwen shouted. "Do you want to go back? Then go! I'm sure Stane is still waiting. He wasn't there for me, you know. Have you forgotten about that? Grue promised you to him. I could have sat downstairs and listened to the rhythm of your head bashing against the bedroom floor. You want to be another stain that Grue needs to hide from the customers? Is that what you want? Is it? Is it?"

Jollin didn't respond.

"I'm the one risking four gold coins! And Grue promised to keep Stane away from me. But not you—oh no—not any of you. He was going to feed each of you to him. Why not? Look at the profit he made from Avon's death. You're just whores, just dirt, and there's plenty more out there. I'm trying to make this work...I'm trying to save everyone, and all I've heard is complaining!"

Gwen saw it then, a small quiver of Jollin's lower lip. She was breathing through her nose, her chest rising and falling at twice the normal speed, and there was a growing glassiness to her eyes. She wasn't fighting because she was angry; she was panicking. She was terrified for the same reasons that Gwen had hoped to rely on her—Jollin was the most sensible.

Gwen softened. "It's okay," she said, taking Jollin's hand and rubbing it in both of hers. "It's all going to be fine. You just have to trust me."

"But you don't know how to start a business. You don't even know if we can—if it's allowed."

"I'm actually a bit tired of *what's allowed*," Gwen growled.

"What's allowed is for men to beat and kill us, to keep us as slaves and make money off our humiliation. I'm tired of being kept barefoot and in rags—that's what's been allowed. I'm sick of it. Sick to death... if that's what it comes to. They taught us the one thing we can make money at, so that's what we'll do— at least for now. And we'll do it in Medford because we know this place. We already have paying customers and only one enemy. But you're right. We don't know everything we need to yet, so we'll find out. When we go to the Merchant Quarter, I'll ask. They all have businesses—they can tell us."

"It'll cost money. A *lot* of money, Gwen. I have no idea how much."

Gwen considered the gold coins nested between her breasts. She had always thought they amounted to a fortune and each held the magical power to grant any wish, but would they be enough?

"Why don't we go find out?"

⸎

The city of Medford was divided into four parts, five if you counted the castle in the middle, but that was like including the bone in a cut of meat. No one had much use for the castle or the king. The Gentry Quarter encompassed the city's main northern gate. The Merchant Quarter was where the gentry went to shop and entertain themselves, the Artisan Quarter did the work of the city, and the Lower Quarter was the sewer.

Gwen had never spent much time outside the Lower Quarter. Here the lanes were wider and bustled with carts, horses, and people carrying baskets on their heads or shoulders. She heard the shouts of men, the squeal of pigs, and the nonstop hammering of commerce. Everyone had places to be and rushed to get there. They paid little attention to the group of women dressed in rags and lacking shoes, who moved slower than the current, unsure where to go. On the occasions when others did notice them, Gwen caught stares, scowls, and smirks.

The lady behind the woolen goods counter, however, didn't give Gwen a dirty look. She didn't look at all.

"I'd like to buy seven blankets," Gwen declared.

The woman ignored her.

"Those over there would be good." Gwen pointed at what she hoped were the cheapest in the shop.

Again the woman refused to acknowledge her existence or even look up.

"I have money," she said, her voice dwindling, already knowing it wouldn't matter.

Gwen lowered her head in defeat and walked away.

"Give me the purse," Jollin said. Taking it, she strode to the counter.

"May I help you?" the woman asked with a practiced smile.

"How much are those blankets?"

"One for seven dins, two for a ses."

"I'll give you three ses for seven."

"For three ses you get six."

"Three ses, three din," Jollin said. "Has a nice ring, doesn't it?"

"Three ses and six din sounds better."

"Three and five."

The woman nodded and fetched the blankets as Jollin pulled out a golden coin. Surprise painted the shopkeeper's face. As the change was counted out, Jollin handed the purse back to Gwen and the blankets to another of the girls.

"*She* has that kind of money?" The shopkeeper indicated Gwen.

"Yes, and more. A shame you were so rude. My lady will be filling carts with her purchases today, but no more from here. Perhaps this will teach you not to be so judgmental. My lady is very generous to those who understand that true beauty is found inside, and cruel to those with little, tiny, shriveled, warped hearts and sick, twisted minds so small and—"

"Jollin!" Gwen snapped.

"Ah, you see, my lady is anxious to leave your establishment and find somewhere she is more welcome."

"But I'm—" the shopkeeper started.

"—a bitch?" Jollin offered a sweet smile. "I couldn't agree more."

With that, Jollin left the shop.

Gwen and the other girls followed, all of them laughing and patting Jollin on the back. Afterward, Jollin and Abby were sent for food while Mae and Rose set off to get a broom. The rest waited with Gwen, standing in the shade of the pottery shop's awning watching everyone. Mae and Rose returned first and were so proud of their purchase that they took turns sweeping the street. Gwen wondered if it was the first thing they'd ever bought. Jollin and Abby came back with cheese and bread.

"Is that all?" Gwen asked.

"I don't know if we can afford anything else," Jollin said.

"How expensive *is* food? We should have—"

"It's not that. I talked to the baker and he says you need to purchase a royal writ."

"What? For food?"

"No—to open a business. Called it a certificate of permit or something like that. You can't open one without it or they'll arrest you."

"How do you get one?"

"You have to go to the city assessor's office in Gentry Square. They're expensive."

"How much?"

"He didn't know. The baker said it would be different based on the type of business. I think we might be in trouble."

"Well let's not declare failure before we even start. Let's go back to the inn," Gwen said. She added with disgust, "Unless there's a law against seven girls eating bread and cheese in an abandoned rat farm?"

‍‌⁂

By the time they trekked to the Merchant Quarter, bought supplies, and returned to Wayward Street, the sun had set and the cold crept in. As awful as the dilapidated building looked in daylight, the dark brought a whole new level of dread. Unlike the Merchant Quarter, where business owners lit up their storefronts, the Lower Quarter was dark. On Wayward, only the firelight spilled out of The Hideous Head's windows to illuminate the street in stretched rectangles. Gwen wanted to kick herself for not adding a lantern to their shopping list, but it would be the first thing during tomorrow's trip.

Gwen could hear the clink of glasses and Dizzy the Piper playing at the tavern. The muffled sound of his whistle served as a musical reminder of their freedom, or was it banishment? In the dark such a thing was hard to determine. On the street, even in the ruins of the building, the gusting wind was louder as it creaked shutters and tortured dead leaves. The interior of the parlor was visible only by angles of moonlight that revealed the many holes and gaps through which the wind found reeds of its own to whistle with, the wind's tune far more doleful than Dizzy's.

Abby and Etta set to making the fire. The two crouched like conspirators in the dark before the stone hearth. Gwen wondered why Grue kept them on at all, especially Etta, who hadn't made a copper in almost a year. Both had spent a good deal of time in the Head's kitchen, Abby because she was big-boned and stocky and Etta because her looks never matched the person inside. Even Gwen had questioned the wisdom of bringing Etta. She couldn't afford to tie their survival to so much dead weight. But excluding her could breed resentment and cause too much trouble in the long run. She'd just have to find some way for them to contribute.

In order to survive, she needed to be tougher, stronger. She looked back toward the lights of the tavern.

After the incident with the man with the gold coins, Gwen discovered he wasn't the only one whose eyes she could see through. It took a bit of concentration, of focus, but she'd done it with others. Bits and pieces of lives were revealed— few ever pleasant—and the process was disturbing. She'd often had nightmares afterward. But in the two years she'd been at the Head, Gwen had never looked in Grue's eyes. Not because she was afraid of the evils he had done, but because she might understand why he'd done them.

They had plenty of scrap wood, dry leaves, and twigs, and Gwen saw a flame for a while. It didn't last, but they were all soon choking on smoke and for the first time Gwen was happy the parlor had so many holes.

"What's wrong?" Mae asked from somewhere in the dark.

"Chimney's blocked," Etta said, her voice muted as if she'd climbed up inside. "All kinds of nests and leaves I think. There's no draft."

"Well, don't try it again, or we'll all have to sleep in the street," Jollin said, then coughed to prove the point.

With no fire they ate in the dark.

Gwen had hoped for a cheery fire and a hot meal. The two might have been enough to transform the inn, at least for a while, into something familiar, something good. Instead, they clustered in the corner of the parlor away from most of the holes, huddling for warmth as they ate in silence, listening to the singing of a ghostly wind.

Jollin turned and asked her softly, "Do you think we can afford it?"

Gwen could hear it in her voice—she wanted to be reassured.

"We still have a lot of money." Gwen tore off a small piece of the bread loaf they passed around.

"But we'll need that to fix this place. How we going to do that?" Abby asked, her voice coming out of the darkness.

"Let's just wait to see how much this permit thing costs." Gwen felt cheese pass into her hands.

The smoke had cleared, but the smell lingered. The wind blew harder, and Gwen wondered if it heralded a storm. The air was cold and damp—rain maybe. Through the holes in the ceiling, she looked up at the sky. That was all they needed. They shuffled closer, each pulling their thin wool coverings tight.

"What was this place?" Mae asked. She was entirely wrapped in her blanket, with part of it over her head like a hood. She sat next to Rose and the two tiny girls looked like sisters, except Mae had blond hair and Rose brown.

"Used to be an inn," Jollin explained.

"What happened to it?"

Jollin shrugged, a shaft of moonlight making her shoulders appear and disappear.

"The way I heard it—" Abby began.

"You didn't hear anything," Jollin said.

"But I—"

"I said you didn't hear anything."

"Why?" Mae asked. "What didn't she hear?"

Rose, who was nodding off to sleep between Mae and Etta, blinked and looked up.

"It's just a rumor," Jollin said.

"What is?" This time it was Rose who asked.

Jollin looked at Gwen apologetically. "Some people say the owner murdered his wife," Jollin told them. "And then her ghost came back for revenge."

Gwen watched as they all looked around at the moonlight-pierced darkness that left so many patches of impenetrable mystery. Upstairs they could hear a slapping that Gwen knew was a shutter but that sounded disturbingly like Avon's head. There was also a faint scratching somewhere, maybe a mouse, maybe a squirrel, maybe a dead woman's fingernails.

"Good for her!" Rose said so loudly it left each of them staring. "Maybe Avon will do the same to Grue and Stane."

Jollin looked to Gwen and smiled.

Gwen smiled back. "Maybe she will."

Chapter 7

Colnora

A light rain began to fall by the time Hadrian reached the city. From the dock where the towpath ended, a wider and much steeper road climbed the canyon wall. Hadrian dismounted before the climb. The poor animal had hauled a barge all day and didn't need his extra burden. By the time they reached the top, both were puffing. Their breath formed clouds more from the wet than the temperature, which didn't seem so cold given the exertion of the climb.

At the top, the streets turned to cobblestone that was tricky to walk on. Still, it was better than the dirt, which the rain would have turned into a muddy mess. Hadrian figured it must be close to dawn. The city had pole lamps, but none were lit. Few people were on the streets, and those who were moved slow, yawning and sneering at the sky. Colnora fit its reputation for size with a maze of streets and hundreds of buildings comprised of homes and shops of every sort imaginable. One store just sold ladies' hats. How a place could survive selling just hats baffled him, much less one catering only to ladies. Another sold slippers for men—not boots, not shoes, just slippers. Hadrian had never worn slippers in his life. The sign above the big window instructed LEAVE THE MUD ON THE STREET! Hadrian wondered if the store owner had ever seen the street, as the one in front of his shop lacked even a hint of dirt. He felt like a ghost in a graveyard or a thief in a mansion—all the buildings and thoroughfares dark and silent except for the patter and ping of the morning rain.

Hadrian was exhausted. Any reserves he once had were stolen by the climb. He considered looking for an inn or even a dry porch. Anyplace he could get out of the wet and close his eyes for a few hours. Only he knew he wouldn't be able to sleep. Vivian haunted him. So did the others, but he kept seeing her lying in that cabin, facedown in that dark pool. Her hand bent, her head turned away—that at least was a mercy.

He wandered up the street with his giant horse clopping beside him. Everything since the river had been uphill, as if they had built the city on a mountaintop. The higher he went the nicer the buildings became, and he remembered Pickles's comment: *Everything else runs downhill, but gold flows up*. Homes here were made from crafted stone, three and four stories tall with numerous glass windows, gates of bronze-paneled reliefs, and even little towers as if every house was a tiny castle. He wasn't sure what neighborhood he was in, but he didn't feel comfortable. Hadrian had never seen such luxury. There were sidewalks and gutters with storm drains that kept the street clear. *Street*. Hadrian chuckled. *Street* was too small a word for the thoroughfares near the top. These were boulevards made of luxurious brick and three times the width of any normal avenue with rows of trees, gardens, and fountains lining islands in the center. Most surprising of all was the total lack of horse manure, and Hadrian wondered if they polished the bricks at night.

He wandered, making turns at random, looking to the signboards for clues. He reached a short wall and, peering over, realized how far he'd come. Far below was the river, a small line at the base of a canyon, and what looked like the roof of a boathouse appearing the size of a copper din held at arm's length.

Certain he'd find nothing at the top, Hadrian descended by a different route. At last he spotted a signboard with a crown and sword. The building it was attached to looked like an errant castle turret made from large blocks of stone complete with a crenellated parapet two stories up. Hadrian tied his horse to the post and climbed up the porch steps. He beat on the door at its base. After the fourth clubbing, he debated drawing his big sword—the butt of it made a decent sledge—but the door opened. Behind it stood a beefy man with a day-old beard and an unfriendly look on a freshly bruised face. "What?"

"You the city watch?" Hadrian asked.

"Sheriff Malet," he croaked, his eyes only half open.

"There's been a murder—several in fact—down on the river."

Malet looked up at the weather with a sneer. "Bugger me."

He waved Hadrian into a small room with a stove, table, rumpled bed, and enough swords, shields, and other tools of war to outfit a small army.

"Mind your feet and keep your puddle at the door." Malet was alone and holding a candle that illuminated his face from below, casting shadows that along with his puffed and bloodied face made him look as grotesque as a stone gargoyle. He set the candle on the table and stared at Hadrian.

"What's your name?"

"Hadrian Blackwater."

"Where's Blackwater?"

"It's not a place."

Malet, who was wearing only a nightshirt, grabbed a pair of trousers off the floor. Sitting on the corner of a dark wood desk, he stuffed his legs in. "What kind of profession is it, then?"

"It's just a surname. Doesn't mean anything."

Malet glared at him with weary eyes. "What good is it if it don't tell me something about you?"

"Why don't you just call me Hadrian."

"I'll do that." He stood up and buckled his trousers. "Where *are* you from, Hadrian?"

"Hintindar originally—a little village south of here in Rhenydd."

"Originally? What's that supposed to mean? You got yourself born someplace else recently?"

"I just meant I haven't been there in many years."

"Many years? You don't look old enough to have lived many years." His eyes shifted to his swords. "That's a lot of hardware you're carrying, Hadrian. You a weaponsmith maybe?"

"Father was a blacksmith."

"But you're not?"

"Listen, I just came here to report the killings—you want to hear about those?"

Malet sucked on his teeth. "You know where the killer is right now?"

"No."

"Bodies likely to get up and walk away soon?"

"No."

"Then what's your rush?"

"I'm a bit tired."

Malet's bushy eyebrows rose. "Really? I'm so sorry for you. Turns out I'm a little worn out myself. I spent all day stopping a bloody riot from breaking out over on the west side because some dumb bastard spit the wrong way. Two of my men are laid up with knife wounds as parting gifts. And just a few hours ago I got my nose mashed dragging two drunks out of The Gray Mouse Tavern who were busting up the place because they thought it would be funny. I only just collapsed into bed when some other bastard couldn't wait until morning before hammering on my door. I know I wasn't asleep long because I still have the same damn headache I went to bed with. Now, I didn't bang on *your* door, did I, Hadrian? So don't complain to me about being tired." He turned to a small stove. "Care for coffee?"

"Don't you want to go see the bodies?"

Malet sighed and raised a hand to the bridge of his nose. "Are they in the street outside?"

"No, down on the river, about three miles I guess."

"Then no, I don't want to go see the bodies."

"Why not?"

The sheriff glanced over his shoulder with a mix of disbelief and annoyance. "It's dark and it's raining, and I'm not trekking down that ruddy mud slide until the sun comes up. In my experience the dead are a very patient lot. I don't think they'll mind waiting a few hours, do you? Now, you want coffee or not?"

"Yes."

"Good." He began stuffing the stove with split wood stacked beside it. "Go ahead and tell me your story."

Hadrian took a seat at the little table and explained the events of the last several days while Sheriff Malet made his coffee and continued to dress. By the time he was done with both, the previously black window revealed the soaked street in a growing hazy light.

"And this barge is about three miles down the river along the towpath?" the sheriff asked, sitting opposite him at the little table by the window, his hands hugging the metal cup under his nose.

"Yeah, I secured it well enough before coming here." The coffee was bitter and far weaker than Hadrian was used to. In Calis, coffee was common in every house, but it was a rare, and he imagined expensive, luxury in Avryn.

"And you never met any of these people before?"

"No, sir."

"You've never been to Colnora before now?"

"No, sir."

"And you insist that a guy in a dark cloak with a hood killed everyone on the boat as well as three others in Vernes, then just vanished."

"Yes."

"So tell me, Hadrian. How did *you* survive?"

"I suppose because I was the only one who was armed. I also didn't sleep, which is why I'd like to get this taken care of sooner rather than later."

"Uh-huh. And how did this fella manage to murder everyone on a tiny barge without you ever seeing him kill anyone? You didn't, right? He butchered all those people, including the woman you were with—this Vivian—and then got away, and you never even saw him swim to shore?"

"I don't know how he did it."

"Uh-huh." He took a loud sip from his cup. "So you're not a blacksmith...What are you, Hadrian?"

"Nothing at the moment."

"Looking for work, then?"

"I will be. Right now I'm on my way to Sheridan."

"The university? Why?"

"A friend of the family sent me word that my father had passed and asked me to visit."

"Thought you were from Hintindar."

"I am."

"But your father died in Sheridan?"

"No, he died in Hintindar—I'm guessing. But the friend lives in Sheridan. He has some things to give me."

"And the swords?"

"I was a soldier."

"Deserter?"

"Why are you interrogating me?"

"Because you come here with a story of being the only survivor of a slaughter, and that makes you the obvious suspect."

"If I had killed them, why would I come to you? Why wouldn't I just disappear?"

"Maybe that's just the point. Maybe you think by pinning these deaths on Duster I'd never suspect you."

"Who's Duster?"

The sheriff smirked and took another sip.

"Am I supposed to know? Because I don't."

Malet stared at him a moment with a puzzled look. Then with a rise of his brows, he set his coffee back down, making a little clink. "A year ago last summer, this town was terrorized by a series of exceptionally gruesome murders perpetrated by someone called *Duster*, or *the Duster*. The magistrate, lawyers, merchants, some of my men, and a number of disreputable malcontents were butchered and hung up like decorations. Every morning there were new ornaments, gruesome bits of artwork. No one was safe. Even members of the Black Diamond were butchered. The killing spree went on all summer. The streets went empty, 'cause folks were too scared to go out. Commerce was crippled, and I had every bloody merchant calling me every name you can imagine."

"And this was all because of one guy?"

"That's the rumor."

"You never caught him?"

"Nope. The killings just stopped one day. And every day since then the people of this city have given thanks to Novron and Maribor. So you can see why I'm not too pleased to hear your story."

"What makes you think it's the same guy?"

The sheriff shrugged. "Few people ever saw the killer, but the ones who did reported he wore a black cloak with a hood."

Malet glanced out the window, drained his cup, and fetched his coat off a wall peg. "Let's go see what you left on the river."

✌

Rain poured as they rode the slick towpath where rivulets etched the mud. Hadrian now understood Malet's concern about hazarding the trip in the dark. The canyon gave birth to dozens of various-sized waterfalls that saturated the trail. Most of the bigger ones they managed to walk around; some even had wooden awnings built for the purpose that he hadn't noticed on the way up in the dark. Others they carefully trudged through, and on one occasion they dismounted and led their horses across on foot. Hadrian couldn't get any wetter, but soaked as he was and still dressed in his useless linen, the gusts that blew through the ravine drove him to shiver.

Hadrian led the way on the single-lane towpath and slowly came to a stop.

"Something wrong?" the sheriff asked.

"Yeah, this is the place. It was right here."

"The boat?"

"Yes."

Malet circled his horse, a tired spotted bay with a ratty black mane. "I thought you tied it."

"I did. Right here." Hadrian slid to the ground, his feet slapping the muck.

Peering downriver, he found no sign of the barge.

"Well...I guess the rising current might have loosened the rope." He found the tree he had tied the barge to and saw a slight mark, yet nothing so certain as a rope burn.

Malet pursed his lips and nodded. "I suppose that's possible."

Hadrian searched the path for the wedged tow bar, but it, too, was gone. More disturbing was the lack of discarded tack, the horse collars, and the other half of the team. Nothing remained. He trotted farther down the path until he reached a slight bend that gave him a clear view of the open river—still no barge.

"Why don't we head back up and talk to Bennett at the shipping dock," Malet said as Hadrian returned. "I'd like to hear what he makes of his missing boat."

Hadrian nodded.

Nestled in the crux of the canyon walls, just past the river dock, stood a wooden building. It possessed all the charm of a mining shack but sported the elongated frame of a boat-house. A sign mounted on the roof read COLNORA-VERNES SHIPPING & BARGE SERVICE.

"Closed! Go way!" they heard when Malet banged on the door.

"Open up, Billy," Malet said. "Need to talk to you about your boat that was due in today."

The door drew back a crack and a small bald man peered out. "Whose—whatsa?"

"The barge you're expecting this morning, it's not coming. According to this fella, everyone's been murdered."

The old man squinted at him. "What are you talking about? What barge?"

"What do you mean, *what barge*?"

"Ain't no barge expected in today. Next barge is in three days."

"That so?" Malet asked.

"Honest," Bennett replied, rubbing his sleeves.

"You got a barge pilot named Farlan working for you?" the sheriff asked. "He a steersman a yours?"

Bennett shook his head. "Never heard of him."

"Heard of him working for anyone, maybe even a free-boater?"

Again Bennett shook his head.

"How about your postilion? You have one named Andrew?"

"Never heard of him neither."

Malet turned back to Hadrian. The sheriff didn't look pleased.

"What about this horse?" Hadrian asked, slapping what he had concluded must have been Gertrude.

"What about it?"

"This horse was one of the pair used to drag the barge."

"This your horse?" the sheriff asked Bennett.

The bald man stuck his head out the door, caught some runoff from the roof, then pulled it back in. He wiped off the rain with his sleeve, then said with a grimace, "Never saw that horse before in my life."

"Well, what about the jewelers?" Hadrian turned to Malet with a bit more emotion than he had planned. This whole affair was making him out to look crazy. What was worse, he was starting to question his own sanity. "Have you heard of any new shops that are opening soon?"

Malet peered at him, rain running off his nose. "No, I haven't. What about you, Bennett?"

"Can't say that I have."

"All right, Billy, sorry to get you up. You can go back to bed."

Without even a parting word, the door closed.

The sheriff's look turned harsher. "You said you were heading to Sheridan, right?"

Hadrian nodded.

"Maybe you should get going before I start reflecting on how you woke me up before dawn and dragged me out into this piss. If I wasn't so tired, and you didn't look as miserable as I feel, I'd lock you up for being a nuisance."

Hadrian watched the sheriff ride back up the hill, grumbling as he went. He tried making sense of it all, but there was none to be found.

CHAPTER 8

MEDFORD HOUSE

The driving rain soaked Gwen and Rose as they stood in line on the street outside the office of the city assessor. Even in a downpour the Gentry Quarter looked beautiful. The water drained away, running along stone curbs until it vanished altogether through grated sewers. No mud here; the roads were all brick, the houses tall and lovely.

"Is it going to look like that?" Rose asked Gwen. The younger girl looked like an otter with her hair slicked back. She was pointing at the big house across the street. A handsome powder blue building stood behind a small neat fence, its facade dominated by a gable housing a huge decorative window. A square tower rose on one side and extended a full story above the house's highest point, making it look castle-like. A covered porch wrapped the front and sides with white painted balustrades, which gave the place a frilly, feminine quality.

"If we make the old inn look like that," Gwen said, "the constable will have us burned as witches."

"We can do it. I just know we can."

Gwen offered a little smile. "Well, we'll see. We're not dead yet."

This was the best encouragement she could offer that morning. The rain didn't help. After shivering all night, they were rewarded with a chilling downpour at dawn. The girls' faces were pale, lips bluish, teeth chattering. Gwen got them up and working. Mae swept the floor with their new broom, but she might as well have been trying to clean a dirt field. Even in the rain, a few people trotting by to make deliveries to the Head paused to stare. Crazy as the work was, it kept the girls warm and prevented Gwen from screaming.

She left Jollin in charge and took Rose with her to Gentry Square. Without the magical permit, she was afraid Ethan would chase them out, so she planned to be the first in line that morning. The rain would actually help in one regard. Ethan wouldn't be eager to make his rounds in the storm. Gwen didn't know what would be required to get a certificate; she just prayed it wouldn't cost too much.

"Next!" A man with a long coat beat on the wooden porch with his staff.

Gwen grabbed Rose's hand and pulled her inside.

Instantly the world went quiet. The pour of rain reduced to a distant hum, the sounds of traffic were locked outside, and no one inside said a word. An old man in a doublet with a starched collar sat at a large table. Behind him, four much younger men scurried, shuffling stacks of parchments and leaf-books.

There was no chair on their side of the desk.

"Still raining I see," the old man said.

"Yes, sir," Gwen replied with an abrupt curtsy, the sort her mother had taught. She hadn't performed it in years and felt awkward.

"What can I do for you?"

His question caught her off guard. She had expected to be rebuffed, insulted, or ignored the way the woolen merchant had treated her. Gwen had brought Rose along for that very reason, figuring no one could say no to Rose's big round eyes, but he wasn't even looking at Rose.

"Ah...there's an unused building on Wayward Street in the Lower Quarter across from The Hideous Head Tavern and Alehouse. I—"

"Hold on." The old man leaned back and looked over his shoulder. "LQ—quad fourteen," he shouted, and one of the younger men trotted to a shelf and began flipping through parchments.

"I—" Gwen began again, but the assessor held up a hand.

"Wait until I see what we're talking about. It's a big city, and I can't be expected to know every corner, much less one as small as quad fourteen in the LQ. Not a lot of activity down that way."

Gwen nodded. Water ran down her forehead and into her eyes. She blinked rather than wipe her face, not certain if doing so would be considered proper. In the silence that followed, she was amazed how loud the sound of dripping clothes could be.

"You're not from around here, are you?" the assessor asked.

"I was born in Calis."

"I can see that. What's your name?"

"Gwen DeLancy."

"Uh-huh. And who's this with you? Not your sister." He offered a wry smile.

"No. This is Rose."

"Where are you from?"

Rose smiled sweetly, playing her part perfectly, because she wasn't acting. "Near Cold Hollow, between the King's Road and—"

"I know where it is."

"We're..."—Gwen hesitated—"business partners."

"Really? Don't see too many young girls running businesses."

"We're unusual that way."

"You are indeed."

The clerk laid a pile of parchments on the desk before the assessor, who carefully flipped through them. "You're talking about lot four-sixty-eight, The Wayward Traveler Inn."

"It's not an inn anymore—just a pile of warped boards."

The assessor nodded. "That would explain why no taxes have been paid on the lot in . . . eight years, seven months, and six days. What do you want with it?"

"I would like to buy it."

"Buy it?"

"Yes."

"You can't *buy* it."

Gwen's shoulders drooped with the finality of the words. "But no one is using it."

"That doesn't matter. All the land in the kingdom of Melengar is owned by His Majesty. He doesn't part with any of it—ever. So unless you have an army that can move in and hold"—he looked again at the parchment—"lot four-sixty-eight against Melengar's military might, then the king will be keeping it."

"But wait—what about The Hideous Head across the street? Raynor Grue owns that."

The old man shook his head and sighed. "I just told you, the king owns everything in his kingdom. Raynor Grue doesn't own"—once more he looked at the parchments—"lot four-sixty-seven. He merely has the privilege granted by His Majesty to operate a tavern and alehouse at that location."

"*Privilege*? You mean a permit?"

"Certificate of Royal Permit."

"Then I would like one of those."

"What kind of business do you intend to operate?"

"A brothel."

The assessor tilted his head down and peered first at Gwen, then at Rose. "I see."

"Is that a problem?"

"Do you have any family near Cold Hollow?" he asked Rose.

"Yes," Rose replied. "My mother—I buried her there last year."

"And your father?"

"If I had one of those, I'd probably still have a mother."

The man nodded with a solemn expression.

"And you?"

"My parents are dead as well. That's why we need to start a business."

The old man pursed his lips and shook his head. "It will cost you two gold tenents for the certificate, plus eighteen copper din for the filing fee. Do you have that much?"

"Ah...yes. Yes, we do." *Only two!*

The man appeared surprised and showed her a slight smile. He took a parchment and, dipping his quill, began to write. "You will hereafter be assessed taxes relative to the income you accrue. If you fail to accrue any income within the first six months after the issuing of your permit, or if you fail to pay the required taxes within one month after the last assessed period, to be conducted henceforth on a biannual basis, you will be evicted with no reimbursements of investment." He spoke rapidly, reciting with a bored tone. "Do you have the two tenents and eighteen din with you now?"

"Oh—yes." Gwen pulled the purse out from between her breasts.

"The certificate will stand valid for one year. After that, you will need to obtain a new one."

"We can start living there right away—today, right?"

"You can do whatever you want so long as it is legal, doesn't threaten the security of the city or kingdom, provides taxable income, and the king approves."

"The king will visit?" Gwen asked, shocked.

The assessor looked up and chuckled. "No. His Majesty will not be paying a visit. But someone from the Lower Quarter's merchants' guild will."

"And if he approves of what we're doing, we get to keep it?" Gwen held out the coins.

"You get to *use* it," he corrected. "Be aware that any improvements made on the site will become property of the king and that your certificate can be revoked at any time by a royal writ."

Gwen snatched back the money. "What does that mean?"

"If the king wants to, he can kick you out."

Gwen looked worried.

The old man leaned forward. "Be successful, but not *too* successful."

She nodded as if she understood and let go of the coins, feeling both relieved and terrified. She'd just secured a home for all of them; she'd also just handed over most of their money in return for a broken-down hovel.

⟡

"It's ours," Gwen told them all when she and Rose returned.

The rain still poured, but Gwen didn't mind as much. The building was theirs, every ugly rotting beam. The day had warmed, but the rain continued, which Gwen saw as a benefit. Just like with Ethan, the downpour would keep people indoors. Until she was able to get the place sealed up, she felt they were as exposed as mice in a field. While the rain was a nuisance, it had the added benefit of grounding the hawks, allowing her time to dig a burrow. Puppies, cats, ducks, and now mice, why she always thought of them in terms of small animals she had no idea except that such things were cute but also often a burden.

"A man will be by in a few days, and if he approves, this will all be ours."

"All this?" Jollin said in a sour tone.

While Rose and Gwen were gone, the remaining girls had only managed to clear away a small bit of refuse and block a few holes with flimsy boards. More of the wind had been shut out, and rain stopped pouring into the parlor, but beyond that the place was still a disaster of fallen timbers and open walls.

"It will look better," Rose assured them. "We just need to fix it up."

"Going to be cold and wet tonight," Mae said. "And all the sweeping in the world won't help that."

Gwen nodded. "Need to get that chimney clear and the fireplace cleaned out before dark. We'll burn scrap wood to help clear the clutter. I have money left over, enough to buy some lumber, but we'll need to reuse as much as we can."

"But we don't know anything about carpentry," Etta said. "We're never going to be able to fix this."

"And me and Abby tried to move some of them bigger beams." Christy pointed at what must have been a brace beam that had fallen across the stairs. "We couldn't budge them."

"We're going to need help." Gwen began nodding slowly as she surveyed the wreckage once more.

"No one's gonna help us," Jollin said. "No one cares about a bunch of runaway whores so dumb that the farthest they got away was across the stupid street."

Once again Gwen was thankful for the rain, which poured loud enough to mask the silence that followed. They had reached the moment of real decision. The day before had been fear driven. No one had time to think clearly. Left to themselves all day, forced to work hard after a lifetime of making a living on their backs and facing another night sleeping in the cold and wet, they had the opportunity to reflect.

Gwen hadn't done anything to instill confidence or offer hope beyond picking a spot to sleep and providing a bit of food and some thin blankets. Right across the street the Head loomed, whispering of warmth. Gwen had ideas, but what good were ideas compared to dry beds?

"We'll need someone strong," Rose said. "Someone who will work cheap."

Maribor love her, Gwen thought, and then she said, "Or for free."

"Like that will happen." Jollin sat down on the wooden step of a stair that went nowhere except up into a fist of splintered wood. "Why don't we all just kneel and pray for our troubles to end. That has just as much chance of success."

"We'll see," Gwen said. "You get everyone digging out that chimney and moving all that junk away from the fireplace, and I'll see what I can do."

"Gwen plans to make this into a palace," Rose told them all.

At first it sounded like a joke, the cruel sort, only the tone was wrong. "We saw this house in Gentry Square and we're going to make this place like that. And what a place! It had a tower and everything."

Gwen smiled at her sadly. That house was likely the home of a baron or sea captain. It had probably cost chests of gold bars and maybe even favors from the nobility. All they had left was a single gold coin and the combined life savings of each, which amounted to a handful of dins and ses. A lovely dream, but impossible. Rose suffered from the faith of innocence.

"Medford House," Rose said.

"What?" Jollin asked.

"We'll call it Medford House. Can we, Gwen? It will be the finest in the city."

No one laughed. They should have. Jollin of all people should have guffawed until she was blue, but she didn't.

"Medford House it is," Gwen agreed. "But we've got to get this place cleaned up. We'll need to open for business as soon as we can."

"How long do you think we have?" Mae asked.

"I don't know." Gwen stared out at the gushing rain that made the puddles in the street look like they were boiling. "Everyone help Jollin. I'll be back in a few minutes."

Gwen left the skeletal shelter of the ruined inn and stepped back out into the deluge.

Unlike the Gentry Quarter, Wayward Street lacked fancy gutters and always became a brown pond on days like this. If the rain came down long enough, the water would reach the level of the bridge's trench and the streets would be swimming in the stench of horse apples and drunkards' piss.

Being completely soaked, Gwen made no pretense to cover her head or look for high ground. She walked through the pools, splashing as she went. As desperate and precarious as their situation was, she felt good. This was the first time she had walked down Wayward without feeling the suck of the drain. She was under no constraints except those she set for herself. She could go where she wished and stay as long as she liked. With an unexpected grin, Gwen aimed for the biggest puddle and stomped her way through it.

She passed the common well and walked over to the broken cart. Dixon sat next to it, elbows on knees, chin on hands, the water streaming off his face as if he were a fountain's statue.

Gwen sat down beside him, planting herself in a pool of muddy water. She waited a minute while staring at the cart before them, then said, "Nice day for a cart-watching."

Dixon rotated his head to look at her, and a waterfall ran off the brim of his hat. "I thought so."

"Listen, I know you're a busy man, but you see that old

building?" She pointed. "Me and the rest of the girls who used to work at The Hideous Head are going to fix it up."

"Oh yeah? Been watching—wondering what you all were up to. Thinking of doing something with it?"

"Going to start a brothel."

"Good for you."

"Yeah, well, we're gonna be having a nice evening meal in a little while. Might even be hot if we can get the fireplace to suck smoke." She shrugged. "Won't be much, you understand, but if we can get a fire going—there's that, you know?"

"Sounds nice."

"We'd like you to join us."

"Me?" he asked, surprised.

"Don't get your hopes up. Even the bread is pretty soggy."

"Oddly enough, that's exactly the way I like my bread."

"Then you'll come?"

He hung his head, draining the gathered water from his hat. "I ain't got no money, Gwen. At this point, if I had a coin, I'd flip it to see if I'd buy food or drink—with a bottle of hard liquor appearing the most sensible. Food would just extend my misery."

"Don't need your money. We're not open for business yet. I'm just asking you to a meal, nothing else." Gwen wiped the rain-slicked hair from her face. "Well, that's not entirely true. I'd like to offer you a job."

"What kind of job?"

"Hard labor." She saw no reason to lie. "We have a few coins left for supplies, and if we can just straighten that place up a little—make a couple of rooms livable, get some beds— we should be able to make some money." Gwen thought a moment and laughed. "Rose wants to make it into a palace. All fancy and pretty like the places on the Gentry Square. She wants to call it Medford House, expects it to be the best brothel in the city."

"We are talking about the old inn, right? The one you just pointed to—the one that's keeling over like it's drunk and trying to lean on the tavern next to it?"

"That's the one."

"You know you're gonna need a certificate, and they cost—"

"Already got it."

He blinked. "You do?"

"Yes, sir, I do." She clapped a hand to her chest where her copy of the document was hidden and stuck to her skin. "Signed just an hour ago over at the office of the city assessor." Gwen nodded and allowed herself a smile. "It may be nothing right now, and it'll probably never be as grand as Rose wants, but it's something."

"What do you want me for?"

"Have you ever seen Mae?"

"Little one, right?"

"Size of a songbird. Ever see a songbird lift a rough hewed oak beam over its shoulder?"

"Can't say I have."

"And you won't." She touched his arm. "You need an ox for that sort of work."

"You want me to help you build a house?"

"I want you to help me build *the House*."

He smiled at her. "The fact that I haven't managed to fix this cart in a week doesn't dissuade you none?"

"If you see a carpenter willing to work for soggy bread, please point him out. Otherwise, at the moment, I'm willing to settle for a strong back."

"I got that."

"Can I tell the ladies you'll be visiting?"

Dixon looked back at the cart as if it were a dead body. "If you got some rope, I could clear that chimney for you."

"I could get some rope."

"Don't buy it. Borrow some from Henry the Fisher at the south docks. He ain't using it today. Tell him it's for me. He'll be…" He looked at her and chuckled. "How about I go get it."

"Whatever you think is best."

"Best not to send a woman who looks like you across town to a surly fisherman's bar." He stared at her a moment and shook his head.

"What?"

"You're a beautiful woman, Gwen."

"Thank you, Dixon."

"What I meant is that no one should ever mistake you for a man."

"I don't think anyone ever has."

"You keep acting this way and they might. For a second there I did."

"That's not good news for a woman in my profession."

"How do you think it makes me feel? Just got a new job and discovered I'm blind all in the same day."

"Just so long as you're not deaf and dumb."

"No promises. You get me as I am."

"I'll take it."

✧

Gwen went with Dixon to find Henry the Fisher. Henry worked off his boat, running nets and traps along the Galewyr, then hauling back his catch to sell to the fisheries at the Riverside docks. That was also where he moored his boat during inclement weather because it was just a stone's throw from The Three Sheets Alehouse. The tavern would have been a competitor to The Hideous Head if they were in the same quarter, or the same league. Three Sheets was a category better despite catering to the raucous sailors and fishermen of the docks. The walls, ceiling, and even floors were whitewashed and likely mopped out regularly, as Gwen could smell the lye as she entered.

"The owner is a retired ship captain," Dixon mentioned as they stepped into a room decorated with ship's wheels, rigging, and nets. "You might want to wait outside."

"Are you trying to protect me from the depravity of tavern life?"

Dixon smiled. "No, but walking in with you would be like heading up to the bar with drinks already in hand. The Sheets has its own women."

Gwen waited at the doorway, watching the crowd. The Head never had such business, rainy day or not. All the faces were unfamiliar, not that she remembered everyone with whom she had done business. Outside of a few regulars, most were vague memories. Strangers in the night who she thought she might know better by feel. Few Hideous Head customers came from the docks—too far a walk when thirsty, too far for the return trip when drunk. She knew a few boatmen, though, not that they spent the night chatting about careers, but the smell of fish was a powerful hint. They also all dressed alike. Fishermen and dockworkers had the same woolly uniforms and calloused hands that felt like sandpaper.

If she was going to make Medford House a success, she would need to pull in clients from outside the Lower Quarter, from places like this. Gwen had a good idea how much Grue charged, although he tried to keep that hidden. No sense in admitting the small fortune he was making off their labors. He also didn't charge the same rate for all the girls. If the girls knew there was a difference, it might cause trouble. She actually thought that was smart. Grue was many things, but stupid wasn't among them—neither was *successful businessman*. He got by, maybe better than got by, but being the only tavern on

Wayward, he should have been much better off. Where all his money went she had no idea. All she knew was none of it went back into the Head. Grue figured that the men drinking at his rail didn't care if the floor was dirt or marble. He was right, but he never considered how cleaning the place up might bring in a new crowd—a patronage that *did* care about such things because they had enough money to afford better places.

She turned and studied the street. The riverside docks were reputed to be the sorriest places in the city, but Gwen didn't think it looked any worse than Wayward Street. While the fish stink was arguably stronger than the bridges' stench, the general appearance of the locals convinced Gwen the docks had nothing on the Lower Quarter for penury. She should be able to do just as well as Three Sheets.

A man walked by with a rack of fresh-cut boards. A girl passed with a bolt of cloth. A bricklayer set his empty hod near the door before going in. This was the Artisan Quarter. Everything Gwen could ever want was right here—the workers to build her house and the clientele to pay for it. She just needed to get the cart rolling downhill.

Dixon came out alone.

"Not there?"

"He's there. Where else would he be? But he sees no reason to step out in the rain just to give me a length of rope. We can grab it off his lady."

"He's married?"

"His boat."

She followed him around the wooden pier. The Three Sheets was just two buildings away from the river; only the fishery shed and the fleet office separated them. She imagined men docking and delivering their catch to the first, picking up their pay at the second, and spending it all at the third.

Gwen rarely had a chance to see the big river and she still

couldn't. Riverboats with single and double masts blocked much of the view; the rain hid the rest. Tied to bollards and cleats, boats bobbed in the swells. Most were covered in taut stretched tarps while a few others were upended on the dock; their buoys, nets, and oars tucked underneath. Each had names painted across the bows: *Lady Luck*, *Sister Syn*, *Bobbing Beulah*.

"Why are all boats named after women?" she asked.

Dixon shrugged. "I named my cart Dolly after the horse that used to pull it. I was used to shouting at her to get moving. Just kept doing it after the old girl died."

Dixon found Henry's boat, the *Loralee*, and searched under the tarp. As he did, Gwen stared off at the shipyard that lay upriver. She could see a big scaffold like a gallows with an arm that extended out over the boat slips, from which dangled a huge block and tackle. Even in the rain she could hear the beating of hammers.

"Do you know where there are carpentry shops?" she asked when Dixon returned with the rope looped over his body like a sash.

"Artisan Row would be a good place to look."

Gwen smiled. She should have known.

They were coming back up the boardwalk when Gwen saw her first familiar face. Stane glared at her with the expression of a dog finding an intruder in its yard.

"Looking for me?" he asked, taking no notice of Dixon.

"No," she said, and kept walking.

Stane grabbed her wrist. "You came all this way—you should at least say hello."

"Let me go." She pulled.

His fingers tightened. "It was very rude the way you walked out. Did you come to apologize?"

"I don't think she likes the way you're holding on to her," Dixon said.

"Bugger off," Stane said, his eyes never leaving Gwen.

"I don't think you understand," Dixon went on. "My horse died a year ago."

Stane looked up at him for the first time, puzzled. "So what?"

"So because I don't have a horse no more, I've spent the last year pushing and pulling a heavy cart around the streets of this city."

"And I care, why?"

"Because you ain't nearly as heavy, and I might accidentally break something when I throw you in the river." Dixon took hold of the arm that was holding Gwen, and Stane winced as he let go.

Dixon shoved him hard against the wall of the fishery shed.

"I have a lot of friends who work around here," Stane said. "I wouldn't come back."

"And if I were you, I'd stay out of the Lower Quarter, because I don't like men who hurt women, and I don't need a lot of friends."

Dixon stayed between Stane and Gwen until they were back to the street.

"Thank you," Gwen said. "But you should be careful. He was the one who killed Avon."

Dixon stopped. His face reddened and he turned back.

"Don't," she said, putting a hand on his arm.

"Is that why you all left?"

"He was coming back for the rest of us, and Grue had no problem with that."

"I would."

Gwen smiled and took his hand. "Congratulations, you're the first." She started forward again, but Dixon hesitated, still looking back.

"Leave him. He's not a threat anymore."

"He bothers you again, and he won't be anything anymore."

They trudged on through the rain, back to Artisan Row. Each quarter had better and worse areas, and the block that backed up against the entrance to the Lower Quarter was the artisan's version of Wayward Street. The Row they called it, a line of narrow two-story shops so tiny that much of the work was done on the street. Usually this jammed traffic, forcing people to maneuver around cutting tables, looms, and racks, but the rain was keeping everyone inside, where little appeared to be getting done.

The signboard on one of the buildings read WILLIAMS BROTHERS BUILDERS. Beneath the words were a hammer and saw.

"How's this?" she asked Dixon.

"One's as good as any other, I guess."

She nodded and paused under a porch eave to twist the water out of her hair and skirt before entering. She drew looks. The rain had kept the men from working and a dozen stood, sat, or paced the interior, which was a bed of sawdust and woodworking tools. She marched to the counter, straightened up to make certain to look the man behind it in the eye, and said, "I want to hire you to build a house at the end of Wayward Street in the Lower Quarter."

No one answered.

"Lady here is speaking to you," Dixon said, his voice a low growl.

"Ain't no lady here, friend," a man who'd been seated on a stool said. He was blond, thin, wore a leather apron, and had a stick of graphite tucked behind his right ear.

"Ain't no friend here neither," Dixon replied.

Gwen pulled the little bag from between her breasts, fished out the last gold coin, and held it up. "How much will this buy me?"

The man on the stool got up and took the coin from her,

scratching it with his thumbnail. An eyebrow rose as did the tone and volume of his voice. "Depends on the price of lumber. What were you looking for?"

"I want a house, like the one across the street from the office of the assessor in Gentry Square, to be built on the foundation of a mess presently at the end of Wayward Street. I want two stories and lots of bedrooms plus a spacious parlor, a drawing room, and...and a small office—yes, a main floor office as well. Oh, and I want a porch that wraps around the front and sides with fancy spindles holding up the handrail."

The builder stared at her as dumbfounded as if she had been drinking paint.

"It'll take a lot more than this."

"I suspected as much. But I'll settle for one room for now."

"A room?"

"Build me one room inside that ruin—just four walls and a door. Oh, and fix the roof so it doesn't leak. You can reuse whatever you salvage from what's there. Can you do that in return for this coin?"

The man looked at the coin, thought a moment, and then nodded.

"Good. Do that first and we'll be able to start earning more. As coins come in, I'll have you do some more. Deal?"

"You're that Calian whore. The one who works at the Head?"

"I was."

"Was what? A Calian or a whore?"

Dixon took a step forward, but Gwen stopped him with a touch of her hand.

"Both. I'm from Medford now, and I'm a business owner."

The man narrowed his eyes. "What business?"

"Medford House, the best damn brothel in the city."

"Never heard of it."

"Strange—you're the one building the place."

CHAPTER 9

THE PROFESSOR

Hadrian stayed five days in Colnora while the rain poured, sleeping most of the time. The rest he spent wandering the streets, visiting taverns and inns, looking for that familiar hooded head. He never found him but saw Vivian's face everywhere. Just about everything from his journey since leaving Vernes had been erased. If not for the horse, he might have concluded it had all been a bad dream. When the rain finally relented, he was glad to get on his way. He needed to put distance between himself and the strangeness, to add miles to separate him from still more ghosts.

He had a new mount, thanks to trading the heavy tow horse for a pretty rouncey named Dancer, who sported two rear white socks and a white diamond on her forehead. He had new clothes too—wool and leather, sturdy and warm. In no time at all the rain made them feel like old friends. For two days he had traveled, hood up and head down, but never lost the haunted sensation.

With the city far behind, he entered farmlands of brightly painted barns that faded to gray the farther north he went. Soon the barns disappeared, as did the fields, and he found himself on the third morning in a thick wood. The tunnel of oak, thrashed by another storm, cast a leafy bed of red and gold over the road. Big leaves, bright and beautiful against the black mud. Something about the wet always brought out the best colors. Trunks and branches became ink-black, but the otherwise dull leaves were yellow as gold and red as blood.

Hadrian drew his horse to a stop and waited. He was alone, but it didn't feel that way.

The air was still. He could hear the patter of water dripping from the trees, the deep breath of the rouncey, and the jangle of the bridle as she shook her head. She didn't like stopping. Dancer felt uneasy too.

This was how bad things always started in stories told at campfires or around small tavern tables. The young man rode deep into a forest. He was alone in the gray stillness, and all he could hear was the sound of dripping water, the hush of leaves, and then... A hundred things could follow. The man would see a light in the trees and follow it to his doom, or he would hear the pursuit of some creature stalking him.

"You think I'm crazy, don't you?" Hadrian asked Dancer. "Ask Sheriff Malet in Colnora and he'll agree with you."

He gave a gentle nudge and the rouncey started forward again. The moment she did, Hadrian caught sight of movement. Not a falling leaf—something big, something dark, moving somewhere behind the bright colors. He turned and stared. Only trees.

"Did you see that?" he whispered.

Dancer continued to plod forward.

Hadrian kept his eyes fixed on the spot but saw nothing. Soon he was carried too far down the road to matter, but he continued to cast nervous glances over his shoulder. In the stories the stalker would be half-man half-wolf, a troll, or a ghost. And if it were one of Packer's tales, it would have been a goblin wearing a waistcoat and a tall hat. While his imagination could conjure many possibilities, at least he knew it wasn't a goblin.

Perhaps a highwayman? A lone rider like himself, with new clothes and tack, would prove a tempting target. He continued to travel, keeping an eye to the wood and an ear to the breeze, but nothing ever revealed itself.

What little geographical information Hadrian retained from his nights before the hearth with Packer ended mostly with Colnora, as did his personal travels as a soldier. He was still in Warric, still in the kingdom of Ethelred, though near the north end. Sheridan was north of Warric—he knew that much. Somewhere along the road, but exactly how far he didn't have a clear idea, and he wasn't certain if there would be a sign or indication of the school along the way. He had passed several trails, which he ignored, guessing a university would be along the path most heavily traveled. The only thing north of Sheridan that Packer had ever mentioned was a land called Trent. The old tinker had described that place as a mountainous realm settled by violent people. Hadrian didn't think he'd overshot, but he'd done stupider things.

By midmorning he entered a small village of simple thatch-roofed homes, zigzagging fences, and stone-cleared fields. No inhabitants were visible in the drizzle. He considered tapping on the door of a house that had smoke rising from the chimney when he spotted a man wheeling a manure cart.

"What village is this?"

The cart driver looked up slowly, as if his head weighed more than most. Hadrian recognized the body language. He'd encountered it often, usually in the company of a well-armed troop. Fear. The reaction was no less irrational than a deer's flight, and Hadrian was certain that if this man and his cart could bolt with the speed of a whitetail, he would have already been gone. Hadrian had been in the employ of many armies, and none had questioned the right to seize such a village. The commander would take the best home for his headquarters. He'd give the others to his lieutenants, driving the previous owners out into the elements, keeping even their blankets. Pretty daughters were allowed to stay. Should the father object, he might receive only a beating—if the commander was in a good mood. But commanders of war-faring men were rarely in good moods. Hadrian could not recall if he'd ever stayed in this particular village. They all appeared alike, just as all the battlefields blurred meaninglessly together in his mind. Fear was a taught lesson, though, and Hadrian guessed this man had seen or felt the pain of men on horseback before.

Hadrian dismounted and softened his tone. "Pardon me, sir, I didn't mean to startle you. I am merely passing through and hoped you could lend me directions."

The man stole a peek at his face.

Hadrian smiled.

The man smiled in return. "Windham."

"Is that the name of the village, or yours?"

The man looked embarrassed. "Ah, the village, sir. My name is Pratt, sir."

"Nice to meet you, Pratt. And what river is that?"

"The Galewyr, sir."

"And that would make this what kingdom?"

"We're standing in the province of Chadwick, in the kingdom of Warric."

"Still in Avryn, then?"

The man looked surprised. "Of course, sir. But that far bank begins the kingdom of Melengar."

"Still in Avryn?"

"Yes, sir."

The man set the cart back on its haunches and wiped his face with the crux of his sleeve. "Are you headed to Trent, then?"

"No, to Sheridan. I've just been traveling for several days and thought I might have overshot."

"To Sheridan? Oh no, sir. You have half a day's ride before you."

Hadrian looked up at the leaking gray sky. "Wonderful. Anything you can tell me of the road ahead?"

"I don't cross the river, sir."

"Are there hostilities between the banks?"

"Oh no, Ethelred and Amrath have been peaceful neighbors for years. There hasn't been a guard on the Gateway Bridge as long as I've lived here, and I've lived here all my life. I've just never had an occasion to cross. Bib the Potter, he's been over. He sells his clays in the city of Medford. Goes twice a year, he does. That's the royal seat of Melengar. It's just up that way." He pointed across the river and slightly to the left of the bridge. All Hadrian could see was vague gray shapes curtained off by the rain. "On a clear night in winter when the leaves are gone, you can see the lights of Essendon Castle, and on Wintertide morning you can hear the bells of Mares Cathedral. Bib, he brings back salt and colored cloths, and once he even came back with a wife. A pretty girl, but"—he lowered his voice—"she's lazy as a milkweed. He can't get her to fix a meal, which is just as well since she also can't cook any better than a woodchuck. Bib's place is a wreck now."

"So to get to Sheridan, do you know how I would go?"

"Certainly. I ain't never been, but plenty of folk going both ways through here. I talk to a few. Not many as nice as you, but I've talked to some. Seems the road splits just past the river. No sign or nothing Bib says, but the left heads to Medford—that's the King's Road. You want to stay right all the way up through East March, past the High Meadowlands. Bib's never been that way—he only goes to Medford—but others say the school is near the Meadowlands, off to the east a bit."

"Well thank you...Pratt, is it?"

"Yes, sir. Where you coming from, sir?"

"Colnora."

"I heard of that. Big city they say. Not sure why people would want to live so close to one another. Unnatural really. And it's people like that who come up here to escape Maribor's wrath when he lets them know it. That's what happened when that plague came through here six years ago. Plenty good folk died, and it was them that brought it. If it weren't for Merton of Fallon Mire, we'd all be dead, I suspect. How are things down there now?"

"Strange, Pratt. Wet and strange."

‍ﾟ

By evening, the sun managed to cut holes in the clouds, and slanted shafts of light streamed into Sheridan Valley as Hadrian approached. That Maribor-chosen look gave Hadrian hope his luck might have changed, but he wasn't holding his breath.

Hadrian had been on a miserable streak ever since receiving the letter. How it found him in the wilds of the east was a miracle—or a curse. He was still working that one out. He had been deep in Calis in the city of Mandalin—the big arena with the white towers—which always had the best crowds. He performed three fights that night but remembered only the last one. Maybe he would have felt the same way afterward even if he hadn't read the letter. He wanted to think so to restore some of his self-respect, help ease his guilt. The notion that it took his father's death for him to quit suggested a connection and made him culpable. The idea was irrational, but sometimes those were the best kind. He wasn't responsible, but he wasn't innocent.

Pratt's directions proved accurate, and the moment Hadrian spotted the bell tower to the east, he figured he had found his goal. He couldn't remember a more pleasant valley. University buildings circled the shaded common like the stone monoliths in the jungles of the Gur Em. The tribal shrines had the same mystical quality, both sacred and inscrutable. These were just a lot larger. At the center stood a huge statue of a man holding a book in one hand and a sword in the other. Hadrian had no idea who he might be, perhaps the school's founder. Maybe it wasn't a statue at all but the giant who had constructed the mammoth buildings, somehow turned to stone. At least that would explain the stone halls. Hadrian hadn't seen any exposed rock for miles, and it would take ten heavy horses and a greased sled just to move one of the blocks, much less stack them four stories high. If it wasn't a giant, he couldn't think of any other way to account for the place.

As he ambled into the circle, he spotted dozens of young men all dressed in gowns. They moved along walkways, careful not to get the hems of their robes wet in the lingering puddles. A number paused to look his way, making Hadrian uncomfortable, as he had no idea where to go. He had expected the university to be a single building, likely no more than one room, where he could just knock and ask for the professor. What he found was a good-sized town.

Reaching a bench, he dismounted and tied Dancer to the arm.

"Are you intending to be a student here?" one of the older boys asked, looking him over.

Hadrian got the impression from the wrinkled nose that the student didn't approve. The boy had a haughty tone for someone so young, small, and weaponless. "I'm here to see a man by the name of Arcadius."

"*Professor* Arcadius is in Glen Hall."

"Which one of these..." He looked up at the columned buildings that appeared even taller with his feet on the grass.

"The big one," the boy said.

Hadrian almost chuckled, wondering which ones the boy thought were small.

The student pointed to the hall with the bell tower.

"Ah...thanks."

"You didn't answer me. Do you expect to attend this school?"

"Naw—already graduated."

The young man looked stunned. "From Sheridan?"

Hadrian shook his head and grinned. "Different school. Easier to get into but literally murder to pass. Hey, watch my horse, will you? But be careful—she bites."

He left the boy and three others standing bewildered by the bench, watching him cross to the big doors of Glen Hall.

Inside, the architecture continued to amaze him. Hadrian had spent most of his years since leaving Hintindar living in military camps. His scenery had been limited to tents and campfires, forests and fields. He'd seen a few castles, usually while storming the walls, but remembered little. A hundred men swinging sharpened steel and firing arrows made it hard to observe the subtle nuances of chiseled stone and carved woodwork. The closest thing to what he saw here would have been the arenas—the ones he fought in near the end after he'd left the jungle. Grand amphitheaters with ascending tiers filled with stomping feet and clapping hands. They had some of the scale but none of the quality. Glen Hall made him feel he should remove his boots.

The ceiling was three stories above the entrance, where a chandelier holding two dozen candles burned pointlessly, given that tall windows cast radiant spears across the marble. Voices echoed down from a grand stair that was wide enough for five men to walk arm in arm. He moved across the polished foyer, his boots clacking, and peered around corners. The only face he saw was that of an old man captured in a painting as tall as himself. He paused, wondering how a person went about making a portrait of that size.

The bell in the tower began to ring and the pensive mood shattered, replaced by scuffling feet and excited voices. A herd of young men rumbled down the stairs. Gowns of various shades poured through the front doors or peeled off to the side corridors. Hadrian pressed himself against a wall as if caught in a canyon during a stampede.

"No, that's not right. Professor Arcadius said Morning Star was the stone that glowed," one boy said. He was either tall for his age or one of the oldest.

"It was magnesia," replied the one walking with him, holding a book to his chest. He was shorter and thin as a willow; Hadrian almost mistook him for a girl.

"I don't think so."

"Care to wager?" The boy with the book took hold of the other's arm, causing the flow of traffic to break around them. "You take my chores for a month?"

"I'm the son of a baron. I can't scrub floors."

"Sure you can. I'll teach you. Even the son of a baron can learn how to scrub floors."

The baron's son smirked.

"All right, Angdon, how about we trade meals for a month?"

"Are you insane?"

"It's not poison."

"It would be to me. I don't know how you eat that slop."

"You're scared because you know I'm right."

The baron's son pushed the other to the floor and stood grinning. "I'm not afraid of anything. You'd best remember that." He turned sharply, intent on making a dramatic exit. He would have succeeded except that Hadrian was standing in his way and Angdon, the baron's son, walked straight into him. "Watch where you're going, clod!"

"No, sorry, the name's Hadrian." He stuck out his open hand and accompanied it with a smile.

Angdon glared. "I don't care who you are. Go away."

"Love to. Could you show me how to get to Professor Arcadius's office?"

"I'm not your personal escort."

Hadrian could see the anger in the boy's eyes. The kid was mad, but Hadrian was older and taller. Angdon had also noticed the swords and was smarter than the boy near the bench, since he decided not to press the matter.

"It was Morning Star," Angdon called over his shoulder while walking away.

"Magnesia," the other boy muttered.

"Friend of yours?" Hadrian offered his hand, pulling the fallen student to his feet.

"Angdon is noble," the boy explained.

"You're not?"

The boy looked surprised. "Are you joking? I'm a merchant's son. Silks, satins, and velvets, which"—he slapped at the material of his gown with a miserable look—"are now filthy."

"Hadrian." He held out his hand again.

"Bartholomew." The boy shook, giving up on his gown. "I can show you where the professor's room is if you like."

"Awful nice of you."

"No problem, this way."

Bartholomew trotted up the stairs, taking them two at a time. When they reached the second floor, he turned down a corridor, then another, and stopped before a door at the end of a hall. He beat on the wood with the bottom of his fist. "Visitor for you, Professor."

After a short delay the door pulled back to reveal the face of an elderly man with a white beard and spectacles. What Hadrian knew of Arcadius was limited to boyhood memories of a stranger who visited his father on a few occasions. He would appear unexpectedly, stay with them for a few days, and then leave, often without saying goodbye. He performed magic tricks to amuse the children of the village, making flowers appear and lighting candles with a wave of his hand, and once he claimed to have made it rain, although it had already been quite cloudy that day. Hadrian had always liked the old man, who was soft-spoken and friendlier than his own father. When Hadrian was six years old—shortly after his mother died—Arcadius visited for the last time. He and Danbury had talked late into the night. He never came back after that, and his father never spoke about the old man.

Hadrian stepped forward. "Hello, I'm—"

Arcadius raised his hand, stopping him, then stroked his beard while his tongue explored the ridge of his teeth. "The thing about the old is that we never change so much as the young. We slip in degrees, adding rings like trees—a new wrinkle here, a shade less color there, but the young transform like caterpillars into butterflies. They become whole new people as if overnight." He nodded as a smile grew. "Hadrian Blackwater, how you have grown." He turned to the boy. "Thank you, Bartholomew. Oh, and it was Morning Star—but the white kind, not the red."

The boy paused, stunned. "But..."

"Out you go." The old man shooed him. "Close the door on your way in, Hadrian, won't you, please."

Hadrian took a step and then paused. Chaos hardly described the interior of the office before him, which appeared as if mayhem incarnate had been locked behind a door. The room was a warehouse of oddities, but mostly it was filled with books. Hadrian had never seen so many in one place. Shelves ran to the ceiling and each was filled, so more books were piled in stacks like pillars that teetered and swayed. Many had fallen, scattering the volumes across the floor like the remains of some ancient ruin. Among them stood barrels, bottles, and jars of all sizes. Rocks and stones, feathers, and dried plants were stuck in every visible crevice. An old wasp nest hung in the corner above a cage housing a family of opossums. There were other cages as well, housing birds, rodents, and reptiles. The room was alive with squawks, chirps, and chatters.

Hadrian failed to see the route Arcadius had used and was left to his own judgment on how best to cross the sea of debris. Stepping carefully, he joined the old man, who sat on a tall stool at a small wooden desk.

Arcadius took off his glasses and began wiping the lenses with a cloth that might have been a sock. "So you received my letter, then?"

"I'm not sure how. I was in Mandalin, in Calis."

"Ah...the ancient capital of the Eastern Empire. How is it? Still standing, I assume."

"Some of it."

"To answer your question, I sent Tribian DeVole to find you and deliver my missive. The man is nearly as tenacious as a sentinel and having been born there is well acquainted with the east."

"I still don't see how he could find me, or how you even knew I was in Calis."

"Magic."

"Magic?"

"Didn't your father ever tell you I was a wizard?"

"My father never discussed you."

Arcadius opened his mouth, then stopped and nodded. "Yes, I can see that." He breathed on the other lens and began rubbing it with the cloth.

"If you can do magic, why not fix your eyes?"

"I am." Arcadius slipped on the spectacles. "There—all better."

"That's not really magic."

"Isn't it? If I shot an arrow and killed Phineas, the frog in that cage behind you, would that be magic?"

"No."

"But if I snapped my fingers and poor Phineas dropped dead, it would be, right?"

"I suppose."

"What's the difference?"

"People can't normally kill frogs by snapping fingers."

"Close. The correct answer is, it's magic because you don't know *how* I killed the frog. If you knew I'd poisoned pathetic little Phineas moments before you entered, would it still be magic?"

"No."

"Now let me ask you this... how does wearing these glasses make it possible for me to see more clearly?"

"I don't know."

"Magic!" The old man smiled brightly, looking over his glasses. "You see, as I get older I have more trouble seeing. The world hasn't changed—my eyes have. Noting the way glass alters perception through focus, I'm able to create these bits of glass that assist my eyes by magnifying my vision. That's what magic is, you see. Observations, coupled with logic, knowledge, and reasoning, provide a wizard such as myself with an understanding of nature. This allows me to harness its power." The professor looked up as if hearing something. "Relax, Phineas. I didn't really poison you."

Hadrian turned and indeed there was a frog in a cage behind him. When Hadrian turned back, Arcadius was busy adjusting the position of his stool.

"In your case," he went on, "it was a simple matter of putting one's ear to the ground and listening for news of a great warrior. I know the kind of training your father provided you. He also informed me of your intentions after you left Hintindar. Together those bits of knowledge all but guaranteed you would be famous by now. Determining your location was easy."

Hadrian nodded, feeling foolish for having asked. "I want to thank you for notifying me and for taking a hand in administering my father's affairs in my absence. I'm glad he had someone he could count on, especially since you seemed to have stopped coming around."

"Your father and I were old friends. I met him long before you were born—just about the time he settled in Hintindar. I visited him often in those days, but the years and our ages got in the way. It's hard to travel long distances when walking across the hall is a challenge. That happens...time slips by unseen."

"How did you hear of his death?"

"I visited him last year and we reminisced about old times. He was very sickly, and I knew his time was short, so I asked to be notified of any change in his condition."

"Did you go back to Hintindar, then?"

"No, and I don't suppose I ever shall."

"But you said you had artifacts of my father's to give me."

"*An* artifact to be precise. The last time I visited Danbury he gave me instructions that I should give it to you."

Judging by the state of the room, Hadrian wondered at the odds of finding this heirloom, assuming it was smaller than a dog. Looking up, he noticed an owl roosting on the second-story balcony rail, the random collection of boxes and chests, and the near-complete human skeleton that dangled from a Vasarian battle spear driven into the wall.

Arcadius smiled and pulled a chain with an amulet from

around his neck. Hadrian knew the medallion. His father had worn it every day of his life, even when sleeping or bathing. The amulet was such an integral part of him that seeing it there was like looking at a finger severed from his hand. Whatever fantasies Hadrian might have held that his father still lived were snuffed out, and for an instant he saw the bloodied tiger again, taking its last breath, eyes still open and staring back with the single question: *Why?*

"Would you like to sit down?" Arcadius asked, his tone gentle. "I think there's another chair in here. Should be five, in fact. I suppose you could just use my stool. I sit too much anyway."

Hadrian wiped his eyes. "I'm fine."

Arcadius offered the sock, but Hadrian shook his head.

"Did he speak of me?"

Arcadius, who had gotten to his feet, returned to his seat. He removed the necklace and placed it on a pile of clutter in front of Hadrian. "He told me of your leaving. Something about an argument between you two, but he didn't elaborate, and I didn't press."

"I called him a coward. It was the worst thing I could think of, and the last thing I said to him."

"I wouldn't be too concerned. He's been called worse."

"Not by his son. Not by the one person he had left in the world." Hadrian let his head hang over the desk, over the medallion. The circle of silver was just a bit larger than a coin and was comprised of a ring of twisted knots. "Where did he get this? Did my mother give it to him?"

"No, I suspect this medallion is an heirloom that has been handed down through generations. It is very precious. Your father asked me to tell you what his father had told him. That you should wear it always, never sell it, and give it to your son should you have one. This was the first part of what became his dying wish."

Hadrian picked up the chain, letting the medallion swing from his fingers. "And the second?"

"We'll get to that, but that's enough for now. You've had a long trip and your clothes look wet. I suspect you'd like a chance to dry them, perhaps take a bath, have a tasty meal and a good night's sleep in a warm bed. Sadly, I can only offer you three of the four...Tonight is meat pies."

"Thank you. I am a bit..." His voice cracked and he could only shrug.

"I understand." Arcadius looked across the room and shouted, "Bartholomew!"

The door to the office creaked open. "Sir?"

"Be a good lad and see that Hadrian gets a meal and a bed. I believe Vincent Quinn is away, so there should be a vacancy in the north wing dormitories."

"Ah...certainly, but...ah...how did you know I was still here?"

"Magic." The old wizard winked at Hadrian.

⟡

"Pickles!" Hadrian grinned upon seeing the boy.

Bartholomew led Hadrian up a flight of steps to the dormitory, a long room lined with a row of neatly made beds. All were empty except one. Hearing his name, the Vernes street urchin popped up and offered Hadrian his familiar smile.

"I have made it, good sir. Rushed as fast as I could, fearful I would miss you, but here I am and arriving in this wonderful place two days ahead of you."

"I had some problems and spent some time in Colnora. You were lucky to have missed that barge."

Hadrian found the boy's hand and squeezed tight. They were nearly strangers, but also foreigners with a common history. Even if they had shared only a few minutes walking through a rat-infested city, at that moment, Pickles was Hadrian's oldest and dearest friend.

"I must apologize again, good sir, for being arrested just as you needed me most."

"You don't need to apologize for that, and you can call me Hadrian."

Pickles looked shocked. "I am your humble servant. I cannot call you by name."

"Well, *sir* makes me uncomfortable—and people might think I'm impersonating a knight."

Pickles wrinkled his forehead in contemplation. Then the smile returned. "Master Hadrian, then."

Not what he wanted, but he could settle for that.

"This is an amazing place, Master Hadrian. Never have I seen anything like it. So clean. It does not smell at all of fish or horse droppings."

Horses. *Dancer.* He'd forgotten all about her.

"I've got to find a place for my horse."

"I know a place," Pickles said proudly. "I saw the stable. I can take care of all your livery problems. Besides, I need to go down to drop off this book."

Hadrian noticed a surprisingly large tome on the bed. "You can read?"

Pickles shook his head. "Oh no, of course not, but this book has many pictures. The professor said I could look through it to pass the time while I waited for you to arrive as long as I returned it to the library in the east building where he had borrowed it from. I will drop it off and then see to your horse. Where is it that you left this animal?"

"I'll show you."

"You do not need to. I am your happy servant. You can stay here and be most lazy."

Hadrian looked at the stark room that reminded him of too many barracks. "That's okay, I've been most lazy enough."

❧

The sun, having disappeared behind the hills, left only an afterglow in the sky. Across the common a boy with a ladder was busy lighting lamps. Walking beside Hadrian, Pickles struggled with the book, which was as cumbersome as a prize pumpkin. The boy grunted as he shifted the weight from arm to arm.

"Can I help with that?" Hadrian asked.

"Oh no!" Pickles burst out as he sped up, walking faster and faster to prove he had everything under control, or maybe just to reach his destination before his arms gave out.

Next to Glen Hall was a smaller building. Hadrian finally noticed that there were indeed different sizes, although still imposing. This one was filled with cubicles, desks, large tables, and chairs in disarray. The library was not very large, but the walls were devoted entirely to shelves on which were books. Far fewer books than Hadrian would have expected. Many of the shelves had dead space, and he guessed the books that belonged there were on loan to students. Pickles let his book slap down on the central table where it landed with an echoing thud.

"There!" he said with a dramatic expulsion of air and collapsed over the table, as if suffering from a mortal blow. "I am not cut out for being a scholar." He slowly rose, breathing hard. "I do not see how you do it. I understand swords are heavy."

"Bad swords are."

"There are good and bad swords?"

"Just like people."

"Really?" Pickles appeared unconvinced.

"Bad swords are just uselessly heavy, whereas well-made ones are quite light and well balanced."

"I still doubt I could lift one."

Hadrian drew his short sword and held out the pommel to him.

Pickles eyed the weapon skeptically. "This does not look like a good sword. Pardon me for saying so, Master Hadrian, but it looks very tired."

"Looks are often deceiving."

Pickles's big smile grew even larger.

The boy reached out and wrapped both hands around the grip, grimacing with anticipation. Then Hadrian let go, and the blade swept up so sharply that Pickles nearly fell backward.

"It is light. Not so light as a feather, but much more than expected."

"Two and a half pounds."

Pickles let go with his left hand to hold it up with only his right. "It does not feel even *that* heavy."

"Because of the balance I mentioned."

"Does it not *need* to be heavy?"

"It doesn't take much to penetrate skin. Faster is better."

Pickles dipped his wrist and swung the blade through the air. "I almost feel heroic with this in my hand."

"And *almost* is as close as anyone ever feels with one of those."

Pickles held the sword out at arm's length and peered one-eyed down the length of the blade. "So was this made by an illustrious weapons master?"

"I made it."

"You, Master Hadrian? Truly?"

"My father was a smith. I grew up beside a forge."

"Oh." Pickles looked embarrassed. "My most humble apologies, Master Hadrian. I am so very sorry about saying it is looking tired."

"It's tired," Hadrian said. "And ugly—an ugly tool for an ugly purpose."

"That one is not." He pointed to the spadone on Hadrian's back.

"I didn't make that one."

Hadrian took his weapon back and dropped the blade into its scabbard, where it landed with a clap.

They returned to the common, and he removed the straps that held his gear to Dancer while Pickles untied her lead. When Hadrian hoisted his pack to one shoulder and looked up, he saw the last thing he expected. On the third floor of Glen Hall, in the last window on the left, a man peered out—a man in a dark hood. It took a moment for Hadrian to realize what he was seeing, and the man stepped back, receding into the darkness and dissolving like a ghost.

"Did you see that?" Hadrian asked.

"See what?"

Hadrian pointed. "Up in that window just now—a man in a hood."

"No, Master Hadrian, I am not seeing anyone. Which window exactly?"

Hadrian pointed. "That one."

Pickles stared a moment, then shook his head. "Are you sure you saw someone? Why would anybody wear a hood inside? It is very warm in there."

"I don't know," Hadrian muttered, still staring. "You're sure you didn't see it?"

"No, sir—I mean master."

Hadrian felt foolish. It couldn't be *him*. If anything, it had to be a student.

"Should I be running up to see if there is a person in a hood up there?"

"No, let's get Dancer put away," Hadrian said, but took one more look at the window before giving up.

⌘

After settling Dancer, they climbed the steps and entered the big doors of Glen Hall once again. The interior appeared so different from the first time, less bright, less inviting. The chandelier and the wall lanterns were not quite up to the task of illuminating the huge entryway and dark stretches of corridors now that the sun was down. It felt like a cave, deep and black.

"The professor said you were welcome in the dining hall," Pickles explained as Hadrian dropped off his pack and swords on his borrowed bed.

"What about you?"

"Me? I will stay here and guard your many precious things from many prying eyes and many empty fingers."

"It's a school, Pickles. Theft isn't allowed."

"It is not allowed in Vernes either, but you would be surprised how many things disappear each day."

"This is different. You think a kid is going to walk off with my spadone? Where would he hide it?"

Pickles pondered this, looking at the huge blade lying on the bed, then said, "Still, it is my task to watch your many wonderful possessions so they will not be stolen."

"I insist you come."

"But I—"

Hadrian folded his arms sternly. "What is more important? My things or my person? It's inappropriate to walk around a school with weapons, but what will I do if I'm attacked?"

This brought a curious look from Pickles. "I am thinking

bad things would happen to anyone who would attack you, Master Hadrian."

Hadrian frowned. "I still need you to watch my back. A simple warning could save my life."

"Oh yes. This is true." Pickles's head was bouncing up and down in a motion that was far too enthusiastic to be a mere nod. "You are far too trusting. I will come and do the watching and the warning."

As Hadrian started to walk out, Pickles grabbed Hadrian's belongings and stuffed them under the mattress. Then he grinned up at him. "There, now no empty hands will be touching Master Hadrian's many wonderful things."

"Lead on, Pickles."

They entered a large hall with long tables where boys crowded together, eating. A few banners hung from the ceiling, but aside from those everything was made from wood, stone, or pewter. The chatter from what looked to be a hundred students created a roaring din.

Pickles had a dreamy look. "Wonderful place. You just walk in and they give you food." He grabbed a pair of pies from the kitchen table where they were being shoveled out on large wooden pallets; then together they squeezed into seats near the end of a long table. The two stood out, as they were the only ones not in gowns.

As hungry as he was, Hadrian only stared at the pie. He started thinking about the window and the hooded man again.

It couldn't be him. Why would he be here?

Hadrian was a witness to the murders. He could identify him—the only one left who could.

A witness to what? There is no boat, no jewelers, no Vivian.

It had been just a moment. Perhaps he didn't see anyone at all. He might have been tricked by the light or lack thereof. Pickles had been right there, and he hadn't seen a thing.

He couldn't find me here anyway, could he? Did I mention Sheridan on the barge?

He wasn't sure. He might have. There had been a lot of talk, the merchants and Vivian always asking questions. It was possible. But how did he get into the school? Not that anyone had stopped or questioned Hadrian. The boys on the common didn't count. Neither would have likely spoken to the hooded man, and had they, Hadrian was certain he would have been even less deterred than Hadrian had.

"Who are you? You're not students."

Hadrian recognized the face. Angdon, the baron's son, who'd run into him in the foyer.

"Guests," Hadrian replied. "And we already met. I'm Hadrian, remember? Bumped into me just an hour or two ago."

"Oh yes—the ignorant oaf who doesn't know how to get out of the way."

"You got all that just from walking into me, did you?"

"You didn't move, and you didn't know where you were going, so yes. And who's this creature with you?"

Hadrian didn't like the baron's son very much. "This fine young man across from us is Pickles."

"Pickles? What kind of name is that?" one of the other boys said.

Hadrian saw Pickles diminish.

"Memorable, wouldn't you say?" Hadrian responded brightly.

"It's ridiculous—but clearly fitting," Angdon said. "And whose guest are you that you've come to steal *our* food?"

"Professor Arcadius. Oh, and you were right about the Morning Star—the white not the red," Hadrian offered.

"Do you think that makes you clever? Do you think I will praise you now for siding with me?"

"Just thought you'd like to know."

"I already know. I don't need an ignorant peasant boy to confirm my education. I also don't need your filthy presence at my table. Take your stolen pie and your Pickle and eat outside where you belong. You miserable—"

All Hadrian saw was Pickles's pie slam into Angdon's face. The plate fell away, taking the lower crust with it. The rest hung on the boy's cheeks for a second. The incident would have been hilarious if the pie hadn't been piping hot. Angdon screamed, clawing the pie from his face.

Across from Angdon, Pickles's face was also red. He was up on his feet, his hands clenched into fists, and Hadrian wondered if the boy was about to leap the table after the wailing baron's son.

Scooping up his own pie, Hadrian grabbed Pickles and headed out of the dining hall while the other boys searched for towels and water to aid their friend.

"You shouldn't have done that," Hadrian said, rushing Pickles from the room.

"You are so right. I should have beaten him with the leg of a stool."

"That's not what I meant. You were supposed to be doing the watching and the warning, remember? Not the hitting and the punching."

They slowed down when they reached the stairs. "Forget it. We'll share this pie in the dormitory. I wasn't hungry anyway."

"You should have let me fight him."

"You'd get in trouble for doing that. He's the son of a baron—a noble."

"He did not seem very noble."

"Besides, Angdon is bigger than you are."

Pickles nodded. "But I am tougher than he is."

"He has a lot of friends."

"Maybe," Pickles said. Stopping on the steps, he added, "But I have one worth more than all of his combined."

Hadrian couldn't help but smile. "Yes, you do. And apparently so do I."

CHAPTER 10

THE HOODED MAN

Hadrian spent the night in the vacated bed of Vincent Quinn, who was decidedly shorter than Hadrian, or perhaps he also settled for dangling his feet off the end. The beds were all filled now with a kennel of boys that reminded Hadrian of any number of barracks he'd slept in. Hives of men, living austere lives with no more property than what they could carry—the war hounds of a duke or king. Not a bad life, but without purpose. That's what ruined it for him. A soldier was meant to be a wheel on a wagon, to roll when ordered. Hadrian always found himself more interested in the choice of direction and annoyed by the sense he was a sword being used to chop wood.

Pickles was in his own borrowed bed, somewhere at the far end. None of the boys spoke to either of them, but they received plenty of stares. Whispers passed between the aisles, and Hadrian caught the words *meat pie* more than once. The mattress was hard—not as nice as the room in Colnora but better than the cold ground. He undressed, stretched out, closed his eyes, and fell asleep.

꒰꒱

It might have been a nightmare that woke him. Hadrian had more than his share, but they dissolved upon waking, leaving little more than a residue of unease. He opened his eyes. It was still dark, with just a hint of gray. He closed them again but that was no use. Instead, he lay there, staring up at the dark ceiling beams, listening to the snoring of a student named Benny and thinking about the hood he'd seen in the window. Maybe that had been the nightmare.

Have you seen his eyes? Cold, I tell you. Dead eyes.

Going back to sleep was a battle he couldn't win. He decided to retreat from the field. Hadrian put his bare feet to the floor. Cold. He expected to find the morning warmer than those he'd experienced on the road. This was the first time in two days that he had woken up dry, but he'd also woken up naked. Casting aside the blanket, Hadrian shivered. The heat of a dozen boys should have warmed the dorm like horses in a stable, and maybe it did, but this was a big room. He grabbed up his clothes, a bit stiff but dry. Pulling them on, the little bed creaked under his movements.

Hadrian had no sense of time, except that he could see. The utter black of the room had retreated to vague shapes, and the windows, invisible before, were now a source of gray light. Nothing but a soothing chorus of deep breaths and the occasional rustled blanket broke the stillness. The nightmare—whatever it had been—left him with an unease that caused Hadrian to reach for his weapons. He buckled his belt, taking great care with his swords to keep metal from striking metal. When he took a step, a board cried with his weight. One student looked up with squinting eyes before turning over and burrowing back under his covers.

Outside the dorm, Glen Hall was filled with silent corridors of dimly lit wood and stone. Hadrian paused when he reached the main stair and glanced up the steps. He was on the second floor. The window he had seen the hood through had been on the third.

Are you up there?

It took a special kind of madness to believe that a killer had stalked him all the way to the university and even greater levels of lunacy to think he was still there. Yet Hadrian had been wrong on the barge and it had cost the lives of six people.

He climbed the steps, slowing down as he reached the north corridor. The lamps were out and he felt his way along the wall until he came to the end of the hallway. Lifting the latch, Hadrian opened the last door on the common's side. It swung inward with only a modest creak. Already the early dawn had grown to a bright gray and revealed the interior of the small room. The size of a large closet, the space was used for storage and filled with crates, buckets, even a stack of cut lumber.

Looking to the far side, Hadrian saw the window with the half-moon top he remembered from the previous day. This was it. Third floor—end of the row.

Hadrian walked over and looked out. Below lay the common. Now empty, even tranquil with the dawn, he imagined himself and Pickles standing near the bench where Dancer had been tied.

A storage room.

Students wouldn't come in there.

He has wolf eyes, doesn't he?

⌘

Hadrian wandered the corridors that morning like a ghost. Glen Hall was larger and more confusing than he expected. He thought of waking Pickles—he probably knew the way better—but decided against it. They would be moving on soon and it was best he got as much sleep as he could.

Eventually Hadrian landed on the main floor and spotted the giant painting. He was near the main entrance and from there he knew the way to the meal hall. He could also hear sounds of plates and banging pots. Other early risers with books in hand waited with him in line for something hot before finding seats at the many vacant tables. Unlike the day before, what conversations there were came in the form of whispers.

"How did you sleep?" Cutting through the quiet with total disregard, came Arcadius's voice.

The professor sat near the fire where most everyone had gravitated, as the stone still held the night's chill. On the table before him rested a cup and a small empty plate. The professor looked much as he had the day before with his white hair cascading in all directions like water hitting rocks. He continued to wear his glasses perched on the end of his nose, though he still did not look through them, and remained dressed in his deep blue robe, littered at that moment with crumbs.

"I don't know, I just sort of put my head down and closed my eyes."

The old man smiled. "You should be a student here. It usually takes months to break the habit of making unwarranted assumptions. Try the hot cider. It's soft but if you get it with cinnamon it adds a little zest to your morning."

Hadrian grabbed one and Arcadius indicated he should sit beside him. Hadrian settled in, feeling the growing warmth of the morning logs against his side. The steam from his mug billowed into his face and he warmed his hands against the cup. The professor reclined in a lush leather chair, one of only four in the room, indicating either he was one of the first to arrive or professorships had privileges.

"When I think about it, that's my biggest problem," Arcadius said, rubbing the sides of his own mug.

"What's that?"

"Getting students to unlearn what they think they know. To erase bad habits." The old man took a dainty sip even though his drink no longer steamed. "You see, everyone is born with questions." Arcadius held up his mug. "Empty cups all too eager to be filled with anything that comes by, even if it's nonsense. For example, what color is this table?"

"Brown."

"How do you know that?"

"I can see it."

"But can you describe a color without using a reference? How would you, for example, explain the color blue to a person blind from birth?"

Hadrian considered saying it was cool, or tranquil, or like the sky or water, but none really defined *blue*. Arcadius's robe was blue and it was none of those things.

"You can't," the professor said at length. "We only know colors by relationships. Your father likely pointed to hundreds of objects whose only common feature was the color, and eventually you understood that the commonality of color equaled the word he used. A lot of things are that way, abstract ideas that have no object to define them. Right and wrong, for example. Problems tend to occur when people are eager to fill their cups and accept ideas by those who might be, metaphorically, color blind. Once an idea is learned, once it settles in, it becomes comfortable and hard to discard, like an old hat. And trust me, I have many old hats. Some I haven't worn in years, but I still keep them. Emotion gets in the way of practicality. By virtue of time spent, even ideas become old friends, and if you can't bear to lose an old hat that you never wear, imagine how much harder it is to abandon ideas you grew up with. The longer the relationship, the harder it is. This is why I try to get them young, before their minds petrify with the nonsense they learn out there in the color-blind world. I'm not always successful." He stared at an older boy seated across from them and winked, causing the boy to scowl and turn away.

"I take it you found your friend Pickles?"

"Yes. We had dinner together."

"I heard about that. Something about a thrown meat pie. Where did you meet this rash young man? Surely not in Calis."

"In Vernes. On the way here. He's not entirely civilized."

"So I've heard. But tell me, what have you done with yourself since leaving home?"

"You must know some of it or guessed in order to have found me."

"Your father said you became a soldier."

"I told him I was leaving to join the army of King Urith."

"And did you?"

He nodded over his cup, smelling the cinnamon.

"But you didn't stay?"

"There was some trouble."

"Veteran soldiers are rarely forgiving of being bested in combat, especially when the humiliation comes at the hand of a fifteen-year-old boy."

Hadrian peered at the old man through the steam. "Took a while to learn that. I guess I thought they'd be impressed, clap me on the back, and cheer. Didn't turn out that way."

"So you moved on?"

"I did better in the army of Warric under King Ethelred. I wasn't so quick to show off and I lied about my age. Made captain, but Ethelred got in an argument with Urith and I found myself lining up against men I had fought beside for almost a year. I resigned, hoping to join the ranks of a king farther away. I just kept moving until eventually I was in Calis."

"The perfect place for a man to disappear."

"I thought so, too, and it was—in a way." Hadrian looked over his shoulder at the doorway as more students staggered in, their gowns disheveled. "Part of me certainly disappeared."

Arcadius used his finger to stir his drink. "How do you mean?"

"The jungles have a way of changing you...or...I don't know, maybe they just bring out what was already part of you. There's no boundaries, no rules, no social structure to get entangled in—no anchor. You see yourself raw, and I didn't like what I had become. Something snapped when I got your letter."

Hadrian looked down at his swords. He'd strapped them on that morning with no more thought than when he pulled on his boots—less so, the boots were new.

"Have you drawn them since leaving Calis?"

"Not to fight with."

Arcadius nodded behind his own cup. His eyes looked strangely bright and alert for such an old face, polished diamonds in an ancient setting.

"I can't help thinking how many men would be alive today if I had listened to my father and stayed in Hintindar."

"They might have died anyway, hazards of the profession."

Hadrian nodded. "Maybe, but at least their blood wouldn't have been on my swords."

Arcadius smiled. "Strange attitude for a career soldier."

"You can thank my father for that. Him and his stupid chicken."

"How's that?"

"Danbury gave me a newborn chick for my tenth birthday and told me it was my responsibility to keep the bird alive, to keep it safe. I diligently watched after the bird. Named it Gretchen and hand-fed the thing. I even slept with it nestled in my arms. A year later, my father declared his son would have roast chicken for his birthday. We didn't have any other chickens. I pleaded and swore that if he killed Gretchen, I wouldn't eat a bite. Only my father had no intention of killing Gretchen. He handed me the axe. 'Learn the value of a life before you take it,' he told me.

"I refused. We went without food that day and the next. I

was determined to outlast my father, but the old man was a rock. For all my pride, my sense of compassion, my loyalty, it only took two days. I cried through the meal but ate every bite—nothing went to waste. I refused to speak to my father for a month, and I never forgave him. I hated my old man off and on, for one thing or another, until the day I left. It took five years of combat to realize the value of that meal, the reason I never took pleasure in killing or turned a blind eye to pain."

"All that from just one chicken?"

"No. The chicken was just the start. There were other lessons." Hadrian glanced at the other boys seated nearby pretending not to listen. "You should be happy to have the professor here as a teacher. There are worse masters."

"He was teaching you the value of life," Arcadius said.

"While at the same time training me on the most efficient ways to take it? What kind of man teaches his son to fly but instills a fear of heights? I wanted to *do* something with my life. Use the skills he pounded into me. What good is it being great with a sword if all you are going to do is make plowshares? I saw the others—rich knights who were praised by great lords for their skill—and I knew I could beat all of them. They had everything: horses, fancy women, estates, armor. I had nothing. I thought if I could just show them..." Hadrian drained the last of his cider and looked back at the line for breakfast, which had grown longer.

"So tell me, Hadrian, what do you plan to do now that you're back? I assume you aren't going to be joining the military ranks of any local potentate."

"My soldiering days are over."

"How will you live, then?"

"I haven't thought about it. I have coin to last me a little while. After that, I don't know...I guess I'm sort of avoiding the issue, really. Drifting sounds good at the moment. I don't know why...Maybe I'm hoping something will just turn up—that something will find me."

"Really?"

Hadrian shrugged.

The professor leaned forward, started to say something, then hesitated and sat back again. "Must have been a long trip from Calis to here. I trust your travels were pleasant at least."

"Actually no—and it's good you brought it up. Have you seen anyone around the school recently who isn't a student? Someone wearing a dark cloak who keeps the hood up?"

"Why do you ask?"

"Six people were murdered on the barge I took up from Vernes to Colnora. Five in one night, throats slit. A guy in a hood slipped away before I could find him. I'm thinking he might have followed me here."

Arcadius glanced at the other boys around them. "Why don't we go back to my office. This fire is getting a bit too hot now."

"Did I say—"

Arcadius held up a hand. "We'll talk more in my office where I only need to be concerned with Sisarus the Squirrel spreading rumors."

Arcadius was slow on the stairs, holding up the hem of his robes and revealing a pair of matching blue slippers.

Leave the mud on the street!

They reached the professor's door, where Arcadius stopped and turned to Hadrian. "Do you remember yesterday when I spoke about your father's dying wish?"

Before Hadrian could reply, the professor swung open the door. Inside, across the room, sat the hooded man.

❧

He sat alone in a corner below the wasp nest and near the reptile cage. Wrapped as always in his black cloak, hood raised so his face was hidden. Still, Hadrian was sure it was him. He looked smaller sitting down, a black puddle or errant shadow, but the garment was unmistakable.

The professor walked in, oblivious to the intruder.

"Professor!" Hadrian rushed past him, drawing both swords. Just having them in his hands made him feel better than he had in days. As much as he disliked what they had accomplished together, they were still the best friends he had.

The hooded man did not move, not even a flinch.

Hadrian positioned himself between Arcadius and the killer. "Professor, you need to get out."

To his surprise, Arcadius was busy closing and locking the door behind them.

"It's him," Hadrian declared in a low tone, pointing with a sword. "The murderer from the barge."

"Yes, yes. That's Royce," Arcadius said. "And you can put the swords down."

"You know him?"

"Of course, I sent him to escort you here. I told him to look for a man wearing three swords. Not too many of those, and even fewer arriving from Calis. He was supposed to show you the way here." The professor glared at the hooded man and added in a louder, reproachful tone, "I had expected him to actually *greet you* and introduce himself like any *civilized* person would. I was hoping you would get acquainted during the trip here."

"I got him here alive—that was hard enough," Royce said.

"You killed those people!" Hadrian shouted now. There was no way he was sheathing his swords, not with the hooded man in the room.

"Yes." The reply was as casual as if Hadrian had asked about the weather. "Well, that's overstating—I didn't kill *all* of them."

"Meaning I'm still alive?" Hadrian said. "Is that why you've come here? To finish the job? I think you'll find that's a mistake." Hadrian raised his blades and advanced.

"Hadrian! Stop!"

The hooded man did move then, faster than any man Hadrian had ever seen. He scaled the shelving and hoisted himself to the second-story balcony, out of reach. Overhead the owl screeched, and a flustered pigeon batted its wings inside a cage. Hadrian halted more out of surprise at the man's athleticism than from the professor's words. He wasn't sure what he had seen. The man had become a blur of motion.

"Royce isn't trying to kill you," Arcadius said.

"He just said so!"

"No, he didn't. He—"

"If I wanted you dead, you wouldn't be annoying me with your stupidity right now." Royce's voice came from above.

"Royce, please!" The professor had his hands up, waving, his voice exasperated.

"Why did you do it?" Hadrian asked. "Why did you kill everyone?"

"To save your life."

Hadrian wasn't sure he'd heard right. "What?"

"I *had* hoped this meeting would begin on a better footing," the professor said, moving to position himself in front of Hadrian. "But I suppose that was wishful thinking, wasn't it?"

"Telling me in advance might have helped. Maybe a polite 'Oh, by the way, we'll be having morning tea with a murderer'! This man killed three merchants, a woman, a postilion named Andrew, and Farlan the boatman. All of whom—"

"Not the boatman." The voice—as that was all it really was to Hadrian, a disembodied sound emanating from the darkened depths of the cloak—had a distinct edge. "The woman killed the boatman."

"The woman? Vivian? Are you insane?"

The very idea made him take a step toward the wrought-iron stairs.

"And why would she do that?" Hadrian shouted to the upper story.

"She told you herself. Farlan was going to have the sheriff investigate."

"Yeah, investigate *you*!"

"But *I* didn't kill anyone. Well, not anyone in Vernes... well, not recently."

"And Vivian did?"

"Yes."

"Do you really expect me to believe that?"

"Believe what you want. They knew an investigation would match all the loot in their crates to missing items from the homes of those murdered in Vernes."

"Wait... *their* crates? What are you talking about? Are you also accusing the gem merchants of being involved?"

"By Mar, you are slow." Royce made a noise that might have been laughter. "First Farlan opened his trap about reporting to Malet, and then after they killed him for it, you went and declared your intentions to do the same stupid thing. You painted a target on your back and left it for me to erase."

"And you couldn't come up with any better solution than killing everyone?" Arcadius asked, disgusted. "You know how I feel about that."

"And you know how little I care about how you feel," Royce replied. "You wanted him here alive—he's here. Be happy. And if it makes you feel better, I didn't start it. They came after me. The fat one and the younger one tried to jump me as I was coming out of the forward hold. I guess they didn't like the idea of me discovering their secret."

"Or maybe Sebastian and Eugene just thought you were the

killer," Hadrian said. "And attacked you out of fear. You don't know. You don't have any evidence to accuse them any more than they had to accuse you."

"I watched the woman kill the boatman," Royce said. "She thought everyone was below. She sat next to him, all warm and friendly. Said she was cold—lonely. The boatman was happy for the company. She reached around his head with a knife, and he was still smiling when she slit his throat. She couldn't get his body in the water—too heavy—so she fetched Samuel and Sebastian for that.

"The way I figure it, she'd done the same to the men in Vernes—got all friendly with them, then cut their throats. The other three did the heavy lifting. Not a bad system."

There was a pause as Hadrian tried to process this.

You want to tell me what's really going on?

I don't understand, Vivian said.

Neither do I—that's the problem. Your husband wasn't killed, was he?

He'd known something wasn't right. A woman who'd just lost her husband wouldn't be inviting him to her room. And how odd had it been that everyone was so insistent that the hooded man was responsible for everything, despite any real evidence.

After a moment, he sheathed his swords.

"Does that mean he plans to play nice? Can I come down?"

"Yes, yes, I'm sure it's quite safe now," Arcadius replied. "Isn't it, Hadrian?"

He nodded.

Royce descended effortlessly. He still kept his distance and his hood raised, but it was farther back and now Hadrian could see more of his face. His skin was as pale as his nose had suggested, his features were sharp, with distinct planes, eyes cold, calculating.

Hadrian was running the sequence of events through his head. "The barge—how did you make a whole barge disappear?"

"I didn't. I sent it, and everything else, downriver with the current. All of five minutes' work. Then I had a talk with the owner of the barge at his office. Convinced him to tell Malet he didn't have a barge coming in that day. I'm certain the boat's been found by now. Word might have even gotten back to Malet, who's likely kicking himself for not having listened to you."

"Wait a minute, you killed Andrew. Are you going to say he was in on this too?"

Royce shook his hood. "No, but you don't kill four people and leave a witness behind. That's just unprofessional."

"You left *me* alive."

"I was *protecting* you."

"You really shouldn't kill innocent people, Royce." The professor scowled at him.

"And you really shouldn't expect me to listen to you."

"And the barge owner?" Hadrian asked. "Did you kill him later to cover your tracks?"

"I didn't leave any tracks."

Arcadius spoke up. "I guess I'm at least partially to blame. I should have known better. Royce isn't terribly..." He sighed. "Well, social, I guess you could say. But now that we have that matter cleared up, can we discuss the original topic of this morning's meeting?"

"Which is?" Hadrian asked.

The old man took his glasses off and wiped them once more with the same sock that he appeared to leave on his desk for that very reason. Either the tension had steamed the lenses or cleaning them served the same purpose as biting nails, or in Hadrian's case, heavy drinking. "Your father asked me to look out for you upon your return. He anticipated your present state and knew you might need some guidance."

"Do I really need to be here for this?" Royce asked.

"Actually you do, because this involves you as well." The professor turned back to Hadrian. "As I was saying, I promised I would help you find a purpose."

"And what does your great wisdom suggest?"

"There's no need to take that tone." The old man tilted his head, peering at Hadrian as if he were still looking over his glasses.

"Sorry, but he makes me nervous." Hadrian jerked his head at Royce.

"He makes everyone nervous. You'll get used to it."

"I don't plan on needing to."

"Well that's just the thing. I brought you both here because I want you to become partners."

Both heads turned.

"You're not serious?" Royce said.

Hadrian started to laugh. "Forget it."

"I'm afraid I am, and I won't. Both of you are at an impasse, both have unique skills and yet suffer from the question of *What now?* As a teacher of young minds, I can tell that neither of you are ready for the world by yourself. Together, however, there might be hope for you both. To put it in simple terms, I think you will be a good influence on each other. Besides, I have a task that needs doing, and the only chance of success is to have you two work together. My hope is that once you see the benefits of each other's skills, you'll see the value in forming a longer-term business venture."

Royce moved forward out of the recesses, and Hadrian marveled at how easily he traversed the treacherous landscape. He glared menacingly at Arcadius and accentuated his words with a point of his finger. "Look, old man...I don't need him for the job. I don't want a partner, and if I *were* looking for one, what I'd require is someone with stealth, finesse, and some level of intelligence."

"I'm sure Hadrian possesses all of those qualities and others that you haven't listed. As far as skills he doesn't have, you'll just have to teach him."

"I don't need him."

"I say you do."

"You're a fool."

"It's my payment, Royce."

Royce drew back his hood, revealing black hair. He was younger than Hadrian had thought, maybe five or ten years older than himself. "You promised it would be just one job. I won't be saddled with him for life."

"And I'll keep that promise."

"You're certain?"

"Yes."

"And that's it? Afterward I'm through with both of you?"

"If that's what you wish." Arcadius had his glasses back on and sat with his hands folded at his desk like a man who'd just laid out his cards and was happy with his bet. "Although I would hope you'd still visit from time to time."

"What if he dies? I can't be responsible for his stupidity."

"I don't expect you to. But I will hold you to an honest attempt—a fair treatment. You can't set him up to fail."

Royce looked over at Hadrian and smiled. "Agreed."

"I don't know what you two think you're talking about," Hadrian said. "I just came up here to get whatever my father had left. That business is done, so I'll be leaving."

"And go where?" the professor asked. "Do you have a plan? An idea? Even a hint of what to do with the rest of your life? You wanted to know the other thing your father asked of me— your father's dying wish."

"Not if you're going to say it's partnering up with…" Hadrian hooked his thumb at Royce.

"Actually, yes."

"And you expect me to believe you?"

"Why not? You believed everything Vivian and her boys said." Royce resumed his earlier seat beneath the wasp nest, this time putting his feet up on a crate marked DANGEROUS: DO NOT OPEN UNTIL SPRING.

"You're not helping, Royce." Arcadius leaned forward and this time peered at Hadrian over his glasses. Why he wore the things when he never looked through them was baffling. "It's the truth. You don't honestly think your father trained you the way he did so that you could be a Hintindar blacksmith, do you?"

"That's what he said."

"That's what he told a young boy with dreams of grandeur. The rest of the tale he was saving for later, only that boy ran away never knowing the truth."

"And what is the truth?"

"You can only discover that by teaming with Royce."

"Or you could just tell me."

"If it was that easy, your father would have told you himself. This—like any real truth—must be discovered on your own. Honestly, I have no idea what your father might have told you. I do know he felt you were too optimistic, too naïve, and Royce is…well…not. At our last meeting, I spoke to him of Royce. It was Danbury's idea—his last wish—that if I ever found his wayward son, I should introduce the two of you. I think he felt Royce could provide you with that last piece of the puzzle, the one thing he failed to give you. Consider it one last chicken test if you will, one whose lesson you might not see the virtue of just yet." The professor stroked his beard around the edges of his mouth. "I suspect you have regrets at how you left home.

Guilt perhaps. This is your chance to ease that feeling. This is the door your father left open for you. Besides, you don't need to marry Royce—just accept this single assignment."

"What assignment?" Hadrian asked.

"I need for you to fetch me a book. It's a journal written by a former professor here at the university."

"He means he wants us to steal a book." Royce had picked up what looked to be a six-inch incisor from a bear and was rolling it between his hands.

"More like borrow without permission," Arcadius explained.

"Can't you just ask, especially since you only want to borrow it?" Hadrian said.

"I'm afraid that won't be possible. First, it would be heretical to read *this* book, and second, the owner doesn't lend his things. In fact, the owner has lived his entire life sealed off from the entire world."

"Who are we talking about here?"

"The head of the Nyphron Church, his supreme holiness, the Patriarch Nilnev."

Hadrian laughed. "The Patriarch? *The* Patriarch?"

The old man didn't look amused. "At last count there was still just the one."

Hadrian continued to chuckle, shaking his head as he walked in a small circle, stepping carefully to avoid islands of books. "Honestly, did you really have to go that far?"

"How do you mean?"

"Couldn't you have demanded we steal the moon away from the stars? Why not request I help abduct the daughter of the Lord God Maribor?"

"Maribor doesn't have a daughter," Arcadius replied without a hint of humor.

"Well, *that* explains it, then."

Royce smiled. "I'm starting to like him."

"And *I* don't trust *you*," Hadrian said.

Royce nodded approvingly. "That's the smartest thing I've heard you say yet. You might be right, old man. I think I've already been a good influence on him."

"This isn't a joke, Hadrian," Arcadius said, his tone leveling deeper than he had yet heard it. "Royce has been planning this job for months. He's confident it can be done."

"It can be, but by me alone. I hadn't been counting on anyone else, and certainly not him," Royce corrected.

"It has to be with Hadrian or not at all."

"Well that cinches it, then. Not at all."

"Fine. But then your debt to me remains unpaid. If you want to be rid of that obligation, this is my price. Complete it *with* my rules and conditions. That's the deal."

"What book are we talking about?" Hadrian asked.

"The journal of Edmund Hall."

Somehow Hadrian expected he would have recognized the title. He should have known better. While his father had taught him to read, Hadrian didn't know many books and certainly wouldn't know a rare or important one from any other.

"What kind of book is it?"

"It's the rarest kind. Not only is there only the one but also, as far as I can determine, just one person has ever read its contents."

"Let me guess, the Patriarch?"

The old man nodded. "Legend claims that Edmund Hall found the ancient city of Percepliquis. After returning, he was immediately arrested. He, and his book, were sealed away in Ervanon and never seen again. As that was more than a hundred years ago, I think we must give up hope for Mr. Hall, but his book should still be there with the rest of the ancient treasures of Glenmorgan."

"Why do you want it?"

"That is my affair."

Hadrian thought to press the issue, but expected that would be fruitless. "And why do you need me? I don't know the first thing about thieving."

"Excellent point," Royce said. "Exactly why do you want him to tag along?"

Arcadius turned his attention to the man with the hood. "Hadrian is an accomplished fighter, and I think your plan is vulnerable as long as you are relying so heavily on stealth. If anything goes wrong, you'll be thanking me for forcing him to go with you."

Royce eyed Hadrian with a skeptical expression. "He'll never manage the climb."

"Climb?" Hadrian asked.

"The treasure room is at the top of the Crown Tower," Arcadius explained.

Even Hadrian had heard of that. Even farmers in Hintindar knew of the Crown Tower. Supposedly it was the leftover corner of some ancient but legendary castle.

"I'm in good shape. A few stairs aren't going to kill me."

"The tower is heavily guarded in every way, except against a person climbing up the outside," Royce replied, his eyes fixed on the long fang he continued to twirl.

"Isn't that because... well, I've heard it's sort of tall."

"The tallest surviving structure built by man," Arcadius said.

"Should I bring a lunch?"

"Considering we'll begin after dusk and climb all night, I'd suggest a late dinner," Royce replied.

"I was joking."

"I wasn't. But I only ask one thing."

"What's that?"

"When you fall to your death, do so quietly."

"It will only take a day or two," the professor assured him. "Ride up, fetch the book, and then you're free to live your life knowing you've done everything your father asked. What do you say?"

"I'll think about it."

～

The rains of the last few days had given way to a perfect autumn sky. Clear blue, the likes of which were unable to survive the haze of summer and the kind Hadrian hadn't seen in almost two years. In the jungles he rarely saw the sky or a horizon. When he did, it was masked in steam. This was the kind of day he would have spent working beside his father at the anvil, then sparring; finally, he would sneak away to the oak on the hill and daydream. He would peer into that endless blue and imagine himself as a noble knight returning from battle, victorious, of course, and Lord Baldwin of the manor would welcome him to his table. While modest, he would be coaxed into recounting his deeds of valor: how he slew the beast, saved the kingdom, and won the heart of the fair princess. He could see it all so clear, like a reflection on a still pond that was lost the moment he reached for it. The dream took a mortal blow the day of his first battle, the day he killed the bearded man. The first of many, but he still saw his face, still met him in nightmares. All the chickens in the world couldn't prepare him for that. His idyllic vision of kingdom saving and knightly valor wasn't so pretty after that. The sky stopped being blue, and he found a new color, a bright color, that splattered everything its ugly hue.

Now Hadrian was back under that blue autumn sky. The father who had forbidden him from striving for his dream was dead, but the professor was right—he had no idea what to do anymore. Once, he thought he knew. It had been as clear as the sky and as simple as a boy's dream.

Not a dream...a promise.

It did feel that way. But how important was it to keep a promise to a child, especially when that child had died years ago in a faraway land?

Hadrian wandered to the stable, looking for Pickles. He hadn't been in the dorm when Hadrian returned, nor was he in the dining hall. The only place left to look was the stable. Entering, he found Dancer neatly brushed, watered, and fed. Even her shoes and legs were cleaned of the mud from the day before, but still no sign of Pickles.

"I thought I might find you out here," Arcadius said with a hand up to block the glare of the sun until he entered the barn.

"Don't you ever teach?"

"Always." He grinned. "And I've just completed my lecture on advanced alchemy, thank you. Now I hoped to discover how *you* were doing."

"Translated that means if I will accept my father's last will and testament?"

"Something like that."

"Who is this Royce..."

"Melborn."

"Yes, Royce Melborn." Hadrian recalled Sheriff Malet and wondered what he could tell about a man from his name, and he didn't like where that took him.

Arcadius smiled. "He's like the pup of a renowned hunting dog who's been beaten badly by every master he's had. He's a gem worthy of a little work, but he'll test you—he'll test you a lot. Royce doesn't make friends easily and he doesn't make it easy to be his friend. Don't get angry. That's what he's looking for. That's what he expects. He'll try to drive you away, but you'll fool him. Listen to him. Trust him. That's what he won't expect. It won't be easy. You'll have to be very patient.

But if you are, you'll make a friend for life—the kind that will walk unarmed into the jaws of a dragon if you asked him to." Arcadius could tell Hadrian wasn't buying it and lowered his tone. "For all your tribulations, you, my lad, have lived a privileged existence in comparison. For one, Royce has never known his parents. He doesn't have so much as a vague image, a familiar tune, or tone of a voice. He was abandoned as an infant in a filthy city. He doesn't even know how he survived, or at least he refuses to say. He doesn't trust me at all, and yet he trusts me more than anyone. That should tell you a great deal. All I've really coaxed out of him—he would say stolen— is that he was raised by wolves."

"Wolves?"

"Ask him about it sometime."

"He doesn't seem like the chatty type—and certainly not with me." Hadrian picked up a brush from the rail and began going over Dancer's coat. She might not need it, but he guessed she liked it just the same.

"I suppose you're right, and all his stories are depressing anyway, but those are the sorts of tales you tell when at the age of seven you have to smother your friends in their sleep so you can survive. Royce took his first life around that age. He doesn't actually know how old he is, you understand. A lot of the things we take for granted are alien to him."

"How did you two meet?"

"I bought him."

Hadrian paused his brushing. "Okay . . . not what I thought you'd say."

"What did you think?"

Hadrian threw up his hands. He honestly didn't know. "Just not that."

"It must be my sweet disposition that misled you into thinking I was above slavery."

"He's your *slave?*" Dancer turned her head and nudged him with her nose. Hadrian was still holding the brush but had forgotten what he had been doing with it.

Arcadius laughed. "Of course not. I *am* above slavery—hideous practice—and Royce would have killed me if I had tried. He really can't abide people controlling him, which interestingly makes me both his worst enemy and his best friend. A very delicate and dangerous line to walk. Like befriending a tiger."

Hadrian stared. "Did you say befriending a *tiger?*"

"Yes. Why?"

"You're just not the first person to compare him to a tiger."

"Is that significant?"

"I don't know."

Arcadius looked at him curiously, but Hadrian wasn't going to explain. He refused to think about it. He merely found it odd that two people had used the word *tiger*—two people who'd likely never seen one, but Hadrian had.

Dancer shifted weight and began whipping her tail at a fly. Hadrian remembered the brush and went back to the horse's coat. "So why *aren't* you dead? Or more specifically, why hasn't he killed you?"

Arcadius lifted an empty bucket from a hook on the wall, set it on its end, and slowly eased himself onto it. "Standing too long hurts my back, and I was on my feet through most of the lecture. I hope you don't mind. Age is a terrible thing—perhaps that's why Royce leaves me to it, or perhaps there's a sliver of humanity left in him. You see, he was imprisoned in Manzant, a salt mine. A truly ghastly place where the salt is rumored to leech the soul out of a man before taking his life. I paid handsomely for his release, on the condition he come with me. He took my advice and let me teach him."

"Was that wise letting him out? My thought is men don't find themselves in prison by accident."

"It certainly was no accident, but oddly enough he'd been sent there for a crime he didn't commit."

"I doubt there are any crimes that man hasn't committed."

"You are probably right. I should have been more precise. He didn't commit the particular crime for which he was imprisoned." The old man winced as he struggled to shift into a comfortable, or at least less painful, position. The professor wanted to be in that stable about as much as Hadrian enjoyed riding in the rain.

"Why are you out here telling me all this? Are you trying to make me feel sorry for the guy? He doesn't exactly invite pity."

"I'm trying to help you understand him. To show you that he's a product of the life he has lived and the people he has met."

"Why?"

"Because I'm hoping you might change that. All the people he has known have hurt, betrayed, or abandoned him."

"I can see why."

"I think you'll find he has hidden qualities—just as we all do. He would be a good influence on you too."

"I'm not sure how. I already know how to kill. You think he might show me how to lose the remorse?"

"No, but you left home before your father could finish raising you. Since then you've lived in military camps or worse. That's an isolated existence, a perverted microcosm, a false semblance of reality. The real world doesn't live by rules, and what Danbury and your barracks life instilled in you is a pale reflection of what you'll face. You haven't really embraced the world. You haven't seen how the mechanism works or been bitten by the beast. Just as Royce is too cynical, you're too trusting."

"I'm not too trusting."

"You were almost murdered on that barge. At the very least, you already owe Royce your life. What he saw, what you missed, is proof that you could learn from him. Royce is a survivor. You've never seen the beast, and he's lived his whole life in its stomach, yet managed not to be digested.

"And given that Royce deals in a very dangerous profession, he could benefit from the training your father gave you. He could use someone watching his back. For all his skills, he doesn't have eyes on both sides of his head." The professor clapped his hands on his thighs. "Just earlier you mentioned how the idea of soldiering was repugnant. You are tired of killing, but fighting is your talent, so what can you do? Here is your opportunity. I'm sure Royce will provide you with direction and many opportunities to use your talents."

Hadrian stopped and this time put the brush down. Until that moment he had assumed the old man was only making guesses. Damn fine guesses, but then the professor wasn't stupid. He had already used enough words he didn't know, like *microcosm* and *semblance,* to prove that. Yet he was hinting at something now that suggested he knew more than he let on. Had his man, this Tribian DeVole, returned first? Perhaps he sent reports back. *You're not going to believe what this kid has been doing out here! Yeah, I can find him. Be hard not to.* Maybe that's why he mentioned the tiger. It shouldn't bother him—it didn't bother him. Arcadius wasn't his father. He was just some old acquaintance who he met a couple of times so long ago he could barely remember.

The guilt returned like a weight on his chest. The news of his father's death had been a shock, a blow to be sure, but he couldn't deny a degree of relief—he wouldn't have to face him and explain where he'd been and what he had done. Danbury's death had opened the door for Hadrian's return. That his newly won freedom was wrought from the blood of his father made it feel like a punishment. As with all punishments, once endured it's best to forget and move on. Hadrian had thought he could leave his past in Calis, but Arcadius must have a piece of it, a secret kernel he wasn't revealing.

"Speaking of trust," Hadrian said. "I don't buy this story of my father's last wish being to pair up with this guy to steal a book. You never spoke with him about Royce and me, did you?"

"Actually I did," Arcadius said. "I told him the day he gave me the amulet. I had only recently found Royce and we discussed him at length—the problems I was having with him." The old man pushed slowly to his feet, wincing as he did. "But no, you're right—I never discussed a plan where his son was sent to steal a book. Danbury was too much like you to have agreed to theft. So this task I have set before you is of my own making, but your father did feel very much as I do that you could learn much from working with Royce and he from you. If it makes it easier, consider doing this for me as reimbursement for settling your father's affairs."

"You're asking for payment?"

"If it will get you to go with Royce—yes. This mission is very important to me."

Hadrian wasn't convinced of anything except that this mission was indeed important to the professor. If that was true, he ought to be able to get something worthwhile out of him.

"What about Pickles?"

"Excuse me?"

"If I do this, I want him to stay here and get an education—a chance at a real life. I imagine you could arrange such a thing."

Arcadius licked his lips and stroked his beard in thought, then began to nod. "I could speak to the headmaster. I think I can arrange something."

"And it would be for just this one job, right?"

Arcadius hesitated, then smiled. "Absolutely."

CHAPTER 11

TRAINING

The claw slipped again. It came off the edge of the stone and Hadrian felt his stomach rise as he fell. He dropped less than two stories and landed in a thick pile of straw, but it still hurt. With the wind knocked from him, he lay staring up at the sky and the wall.

Royce's shadow crossed his face. "That was pathetic."

"You're enjoying this a little too much for me to think you're honestly trying to help."

"Trust me. I want you to improve. I want you to fall from much higher up."

Hadrian reached out a hand, but Royce turned his back and walked away. "Try again."

"You know, I'm bigger than you are."

"I'm not surprised nature chose to curse you."

While glaring at Royce, Hadrian rolled to his feet and dusted the straw off.

Hadrian had learned to read body movements as a second language. It was an important part of combat and a form of foresight. Seeing where the weight rested, how the shoulders turned, and the direction of the eyes allowed him to read a person's next move and determine their level of threat. Even when not in combat, the way a man carried himself revealed his confidence and the degree of balance he possessed. How he placed his feet when walking communicated athletic ability and training. Hadrian's father had taught him that no one could completely hide who they were, and most never tried. Everyone was a stack of accumulated experience, and seeing how that pile wobbled when it moved could reveal secrets.

After watching Royce during the past few days, Hadrian had revised his opinion of the man. On the boat, he had remained wrapped in the folds of a long cloak, and he almost never moved, leaving Hadrian ignorant. All he could base his assessment on was the man's size, which while not unusually small, was not imposing in the slightest. He also was careful not to display a weapon, which Hadrian also would have used as a window into his opponent's abilities and weaknesses. These concealments he soon determined were not by chance. The man was a locked box and worked hard to remain sealed. He was not the sort to give away anything.

He was also amazing.

During their practices, Royce tossed aside the cloak, and at first Hadrian couldn't believe what he was seeing. While the language of other men's bodies talked in prose, Royce's spoke poetry. He didn't move like anyone Hadrian had ever seen. The closest comparison he settled on was the simple elegance and acrobatics of a squirrel. He could go from absolute stillness to blinding movement. His sense of balance and timing was such that Hadrian watched in awe and found himself wanting to applaud. Using the hand-claws, he could scale the full height of Glen Hall's outer wall in less time than it would take Hadrian to run up the stairs. Such ability caused Hadrian to realize the man was far more dangerous than his wolfish eyes ever let on.

The more he saw, the more he missed his weapons.

Hadrian's swords, like Royce's cloak, were up in the little

room on the attic level that Arcadius had arranged the two to share, along with Pickles, who spent most of his time guarding the gear and looking through picture books. Royce had protested, but the professor stood his ground. Hadrian had hoped Royce would win the battle, as sharing a room with him felt like sleeping beneath the blade of a guillotine. Pickles never commented about Royce but always kept a wary eye.

The arrangement wasn't as bad as Hadrian had expected. Royce never entered the room until late. He would slip inside and sleep in his clothes. He never spoke and refused to even look at either of them. In the morning he would vanish without so much as a clearing of his throat or a yawning stretch. He didn't seem human.

Hadrian made another attempt to climb the north wall and slipped after rising only a few feet off the ground. On the next try he managed to get as high as the third-floor window before a gust of wind distracted him. The hand-claw got caught in the ivy, and his foot slipped off its perch. He bruised his cheek and thought he might have broken his foot on that fall.

"You're hopeless," Royce said as Hadrian writhed on the straw, grabbing his leg. "The Crown Tower is sixty stories tall, and you can't manage three. This will never work."

Royce pulled the claws off him and was gone before he could get up.

By the time Hadrian reached Arcadius's office, Royce was already there and shouting. "I just told you he can't even get to the third-story window. It's been three days and he's not improving. We're losing the season, and I don't want to be scaling that thing with ice on it."

"Ah, Hadrian, come in." The professor waved. The old man had a sack under one arm and was working his way around the room feeding his animals. "Hurt your foot?"

"Landed badly."

"Next time try breaking the fall with your neck," Royce said with no sense of humor. "That would be less painful for both of us."

"Royce," Arcadius said, pausing over the chattering raccoon's cage to peer out the window. "If Hadrian *had* broken his leg and you needed to get him up the Crown Tower, how would you do that?"

"I wouldn't. I'd leave him—unless he was moaning or crying. Then I'd cut his throat and see about dragging him to—"

"Yes, yes, but if you *had* to get him up. How would you do it?"

Royce scowled a moment longer; then Hadrian watched as his expression changed. With as much ease as blowing out a candle's flame, the frustration vanished and his eyes focused. He turned to the exterior wall of the office and let his fingers run over the stone. "I'd bring rope and some sort of harness. Then I'd nail thin spikes into the seams of the stone—something I could hook the rope to that he might pull himself up with."

"Why don't you try that, then?"

The frustration returned and he whirled. "It takes too long. I can get up in about an hour, two at the most, but if I have to build a rope hoist, we're talking four, five, maybe six hours."

"Lucky you," Arcadius said with a smile. "Winter is coming—the nights are getting longer. You'll have plenty of time."

"Hanging on the side of a wall takes energy. I'll be exhausted."

"Bring your own harness—that way you can rest while he climbs."

"This is ridiculous." Royce's voice was rising. "If you really want that stupid book, just let me go get it. I'll be up and down."

"That's not the deal."

"Why isn't it the deal?" Royce snapped. "Why do I have to bring him? And if I do, why can't he just stay with the horses? He'd serve an actual purpose then. Is this why you got me out of Manzant, to toy with me? Am I one of your many caged animals? Is it fun to tie my feet together and see if I can run? Are you keeping notes?"

Royce's voice was more than a snarl this time, and Hadrian didn't like how his muscles flexed. The dog was more than growling; his teeth were bared and his fur up.

Arcadius set the bag down and faced Royce without fear. "You'll take him up the tower and get the book. That's the deal."

Royce took an aggressive step forward.

The professor didn't flinch. Hadrian wasn't certain the old man was even breathing.

Stand perfectly still, his father had told Hadrian once when they had come upon a bear and her cubs. *Just let them pass. She's as scared of you as you are of her. Fear makes anyone do stupid things. Take a step forward and she'll figure she's got nothing to lose. Take a step away, and she'll think she has the upper hand and will press the advantage. The only way to win is to stand still and make her move first.*

Arcadius was playing the same game and doing it well. Royce broke eye contact and walked out.

"We're done until I make you a harness," he said. "Something capable of lifting your dead weight."

Royce flew by and slammed the door as he left, managing to blow out a nearby candle. The room was silent for a second and both continued to look at the door.

"He's right." Hadrian limped in and sat on the edge of the professor's desk. "I'm only going to be a burden. You should let him do it alone."

Arcadius took a deep breath and sighed. The old man looked

weary. His head hung low, and his shoulders drooped. He reached out and supported himself on the edge of his little desk as he walked around it and sat slowly on the simple stool. He sighed again and stroked his beard. "Tell me, Hadrian, how did you learn to swing a sword?"

"How's that?"

"When your father first started teaching you, did he give you that big spadone and the two of you go at it?"

"He started teaching me when I was four years old. I couldn't lift any sword, much less that one."

"So how did you manage it? How did you gain the strength to wield that giant metal blade?"

Hadrian remembered the wooden trainers he had used, but those were light as air. "The hammer," he said, thinking out loud. "He had me pounding on the anvil as soon as I was tall enough to reach it. You swing a hammer long enough, your arms and shoulders build muscle."

"Exactly. You don't get stronger from lying around, or even from simply lifting your arms above your head. You need weight. You need resistance. You need challenge. And how did Danbury shape metal?"

"Metal?"

"Yes, how did he start?"

"Heated the metal, then beat it into a shape."

"And what if he was making a sword—a good sword? One that had to be both sharp and strong? How did he do that?"

"You have to start with good metal, just the right mix of carbon and iron. Then you fold it."

"Fold it? Why?"

"It evenly disperses the carbon and iron in layers, making them work together by providing both strength and flexibility as well as the hardness needed to keep a sharp edge."

"How hot does the forge need to be to do that?"

"Very. And you have to leave the metal buried in the coal for a long time, until it is just the perfect color of gold."

"You've made swords, haven't you?"

"I made the ones I carry."

"Do you think making a fine sword is a pleasant process?"

"Pleasant?" Hadrian thought about it. "Not really. It's a lot of work and can be a torment. It takes a lot of time, and you're never sure if it will work until you drop it in the water and see the tempering. Only then can you know how well the iron and carbon bonded."

"Ever consider how the sword feels about it?"

Hadrian look puzzled. "The sword? No."

Arcadius returned to feeding his animals. "That's why it's easier to be a blacksmith."

⚶

Even after two days, Royce was still working on the harnesses, which was fine with Hadrian, who was in no rush. Whatever he was working on could define the line between life and death, so Hadrian liked to think that Royce was taking some time with it. However, this left Hadrian nothing to do. His ankle needed time to heal, but with the days so beautiful, he loathed to remain indoors.

He was on the common, staring up at the statue. In his time at the school he had learned the stone giant was actually a sculpture of Glenmorgan the First. Apparently he had come close to reuniting the four nations of man after the old empire fell into civil war. A big deal, he was told. Glenmorgan set his capital up north in Ervanon and built a massive palace there. He also built the university. It intrigued Hadrian that a world conqueror would also create a place of learning. Hadrian was trying to get a good look at his face because he thought he might have liked this man.

"Can you read?" Pickles asked.

"Yes," Hadrian replied, his sight still focused on the statue. "My father taught me. Why do you…" Hadrian turned his attention to Pickles and saw the boy's face was puffed and bruised. One eye had swollen closed and his upper lip inflated up to his nose.

Hadrian sat up. "Angdon?"

"You were right about his friends." Pickles settled himself on the grass, moving slowly, cringing as he did. Once he settled himself against the base of the statue, he took a few calming breaths.

"Did the others hold you?"

Pickles shook his head. "They most certainly would have, but they had no need. He is a better fighter than I am."

"I can see that."

"All of them are."

"Nobles being trained for combat start at a young age." Hadrian stretched his ankle, testing it. No pain—nothing sharp, just a dull ache and a little stiffness. "So why did you want to know if I could read?"

"I thought perhaps you could teach me. I have never seen so many books."

"Right now I think you'd have a hard time seeing anything. Are you all right?"

"I am fine."

"Of course you are. Instead of teaching you to read, maybe I ought to teach you to fight better."

"That is why I want you to teach me to read." Pickles struggled to bring up his famous smile, but winced. "I have already determined how it is that I shall be beating that son of a baron—Angdon."

"Really?"

Pickles leaned over slightly as if he were imparting a secret. "By being a most successful merchant, I will make piles of gold, travel in a fine carriage, wear the finest of silks, and live in a most luxurious palace. By obtaining the life he wants and achieving it by my own labor and my own very smart thinking, I will win. He will still have the title of noble, but I will have the life of a noble. If I could read, I could learn to be like those most powerful men in the citadel back in Vernes."

"You've been speaking to Professor Arcadius, haven't you?"

"A little."

"No one talks to Arcadius *a little*."

"Will you? I will trade whatever payment you had planned to give me."

"I see. Well, I've got good news and bad news. The bad news is that if you really want to become successful, to do all you just said, you're going to need to know a whole lot more than just how to read. The good news is, you're in the middle of a renowned university."

"But they will not teach one such as me. This school is for nobles' and merchants' sons, and I'm...well...I'm not anything."

"Professor Arcadius is an important man here, and he wants me to do something for him. In fact, I'm going to be leaving soon and you'll be staying here."

"But I—"

"No buts. You'll stay here and the professor will see that you get a first-rate education, or I won't do his job."

"Such a thing is of great value, yes? Why would you do that for me—me who is not even your real servant?"

"Because I don't want to do the job, but I can see I'm going to anyway. So I might as well get something for it—or at least one of us should. And maybe one day when you have your piles of gold, you'll hire me to guard it for you, yes?"

"Absolutely!" Despite the pain, Pickles's face beamed again. "What is it the professor wishes you to do?"

Hadrian looked back at Glen Hall and the blue sky above it. "Honestly, Pickles...I'm not sure."

༜

Later that same day Hadrian went in search of Royce.

His foot was feeling better. He noticed only a minor twinge when he put his full weight on it, which left him limping slightly. He'd survived dozens of battles without a scratch, but one afternoon with Royce had left him a cripple.

He searched the school and the grounds with no results and was heading for Arcadius's office when he was stopped by a student.

"You're Hadrian, right?"

Hadrian hadn't seen the kid before, or at least he didn't think so. The school had a lot of students and most looked the same to him. "Yes."

"Ah...your friend, the young one who speaks funny, he—"

"Pickles?"

"Yeah...I guess."

"What about him?"

Hadrian had taken his battered friend to see the professor, who in turn had taken him to the school physician. Hadrian expected Pickles would remain there for the day but perhaps not. He had only suffered a beating. Nothing was broken.

"He sent me to get you. He's out in the stable."

"In the stable?"

"Said it was important. He wants you to come quick."

Hadrian was moving down the stairs before the boy finished speaking. He forgot the pain in his foot and pushed out of the school doors into the courtyard. Even though it was still early evening, the valley, surrounded by high hills, was cast in shadow. Built on the west side of the common, which received the least light, the stable was already cast in deep shadow, the interior dark.

"Pickles?" Hadrian called out as he poked his head inside. "Are you okay?"

There was no answer, and Hadrian walked the length of the aisle to where Dancer stood. He greeted the horse, clapping her rump. She responded with a stomp of one hoof and a tail swish.

Dancer turned her head, and he imagined she smiled. Hadrian always felt that it was a mistake of the gods not to grant animals the ability to smile and laugh. Every living thing should have that pleasure, and yet when he thought about it, the idea of his horse laughing at him might not be such a great idea.

The light entering the stable from the courtyard flickered. Turning, Hadrian noted silhouettes in the doorway. "Pickles?"

It wasn't Pickles. He counted five before they began pulling the doors closed. A lantern flared and Hadrian saw Angdon. He wasn't wearing his robe. Instead, he was dressed in wool britches and a light shirt—what nobles might call work clothes. It was obvious why Pickles had lost the fight. Angdon was smaller than Hadrian, but not by a lot, and he had a heft to his shoulders and arms, the sort Hadrian usually only saw on field hands or his father.

"Sorry, Pickles won't be coming. Let's see now, your name is Hadrian, you said." Angdon slapped an axe handle against his palm. The other boys had sticks as well—not a gown among them. "You appear to be missing your swords, *Hadrian*."

"They aren't missing. I left them in my room." Hadrian thought the boy might be smart enough to understand the threat he implied, but Angdon missed it.

"You'll regret that decision."

"Why's that?"

The boys moved forward, clapping their sticks. They fanned out, staring him down, banging the barrels and stalls with threatening grins. This was the fun part for them—intimidation. Bullies lived for this, and it wasn't much different on the field of combat; the methods were just more dramatic and multiplied by thousands.

Hadrian recalled how each battle began with two sides facing off. Lines of men stretching as far as he could see, five or ten deep with a grassy gap of less than a hundred yards between them. They would stare at one another, then beat on their shields with swords and axes. Finally, they'd howl like wolves. No one ordered this; no commander instructed they act like animals—that came naturally to men pumping themselves up to kill. Both sides did their best to frighten the other. That's where the real battle took place. On any field that Hadrian had fought on, a balanced scale was set—until the two groups saw each other. The more numerous group added weight to their side of the scale. No one likes to be outnumbered. Cavalry was scary, and seeing horses might tip the scale back. The shouting was an effort to tilt the scales because the winner wasn't the side that fought best. No battle ever came down to the last man standing. The winner was always the group that drilled their side of the scale and sent the others running first. Hadrian had seen winning sides flee because they thought they were losing.

Establishing superiority early on, nailing fear and hopelessness into the other side, made any conflict easier. Hadrian understood this even more than Angdon, but like howling, such things came naturally to men looking to cause harm. This was the crucial moment of any fight, and Hadrian's role, as one against many, was to cower and quake, and if possible cry and beg.

"You're friends with Pickles." Angdon said it as an accusation. "The two of you like embarrassing me. Think it's funny to belittle your betters. Only I don't. None of us do."

"I saw what you did to Pickles. Seemed a bit harsh for throwing a pie."

"We taught Pickles a lesson. This is a school after all. Most of what they teach here is useless—just words. Words don't mean anything outside this valley. But I teach something important, a real-world education. Lessons that can help a person their whole life, and I'm going to teach you one right now, *Hadrian*. I'm going to demonstrate why you should respect your betters."

"Appreciate the thought, but I'm not a student."

"It's a free lesson." Angdon circled Hadrian and with both hands took a solid grip on the axe handle.

Hadrian spread his feet slightly. He bent his knees and balanced his weight. He watched Angdon's body and the direction of his eyes. He would swing right to left, aiming for Hadrian's side rather than his head. The boy intended a beating, not a killing. Behind him, the rustle of straw indicated the others were closing in.

Angdon twisted and raised the axe handle. Muscles stood out on his neck as he started his swing, only the handle failed to move. A shadow appeared to envelop the young man from behind.

"Mufftt..." Angdon uttered softly as his back arched and his eyes widened.

He collapsed, dropping to his knees, where he hovered for a moment and then crumbled to his side. Blood stained Angdon's work shirt, spreading out and soaking through the linen.

The shadow behind him remained standing. A faceless black cloak and hood. The grim reaper took a single step forward and the others bolted, clawing at the doors. Bursting outside, they ran, dropping the lantern in the grass where it went out, spewing a slender thread of smoke.

"What did you do that for?" Hadrian shouted, and moved to the boy's side.

Royce stepped back into the dark recesses, gathered up an armful of leather straps, and walked out.

⊰⊱

"We've talked about this before, Royce," Arcadius yelled at him. "You aren't to hurt the students."

"You said don't *kill*," Royce replied. "If you don't want misunderstandings, then be specific. The little baron boy will live. Trust me, I *know* where to stick a knife."

They were back in the professor's office. Hadrian had carried Angdon to the school infirmary, then marched up to see Arcadius, who had summoned Royce. The thief's hood was down, and he carried his armload of straps and buckles, which he set on one of the crates. He continued to sew with a thick hooked needle as if he were a lady at a quilting bee.

"There will be an investigation," the professor said. "The headmaster will demand it."

"Not a problem as long as he doesn't bother me," Royce said.

"I'm afraid he just may insist on arresting you."

"Bad luck for him."

"I won't have you turning this university into another Colnora."

"Shouldn't have brought me here, then."

Arcadius slumped in frustration. He walked around his desk and sat down looking weary. The professor was easily the oldest person Hadrian had ever known, and at that moment he looked as if he had gained a decade.

"Why did you do it?" Arcadius asked.

"He was trying to help me," Hadrian said.

Royce looked up from his crafting to smile at Arcadius. "He flatters himself. The little brats were planning to pound him with axe handles. Knowing how fragile he is, and how you'd make me wait until he recovered, and because winter is coming, I stepped in."

"I didn't need your help," Hadrian said.

Royce smirked. "Of course you didn't. You were on top of things as always. That's why you made five enemies in four days. Why you were suckered in by such an obvious ploy. Why you let them follow you in and block your exit, and why you failed to carry any weapon at all. But no, you didn't need my help, just like you didn't on the boat. You're a crafty one you are, lulling us all into a false sense of superiority by acting the perfect fool."

"I figured it out by the way." Royce turned to Arcadius. "Why you want me to take him. Why you insist I get him to the top. You've made a bet. You've wagered against me I suspect. You got me out of Manzant to have a grand contest, a game for the pleasure of... whom? That's the part I can't figure out. Some other instructor? Some wealthy duke perhaps? *Or someone I know personally?*" Royce spoke this last bit with a clear tone of threat and glared at the professor with a look that caused Arcadius to take a step back. "I warn you, I've been challenged before. That's how it all started, you know? Hoyte tried to kill me the same way. In case you haven't heard, Hoyte is dead. I did him slow and left him displayed. So if you're looking for entertainment, I can guarantee you'll get it."

"This isn't a game," Arcadius assured him. "And none of this matters anymore. Angdon has been stabbed. Restitution will be sought, which means you two must leave."

Royce turned to Hadrian. "Get your things and saddle that horse. I'll meet you in the stable."

"I don't agree with what you did," Hadrian told him. "But thanks just the same."

Royce shook his head. "You realize I'm just taking you to die."

"I hope to disappoint you."

"You won't."

CHAPTER 12

RAYNOR GRUE

Grue sat at the rickety table near the only window in The Hideous Head clear enough to see out of. Someone had splashed a drink and wiped the glass, taking a circle of grit with it. Maybe they licked it off—he wouldn't put it past some of the drunks who filled the Head each night. They wouldn't be spending their evenings at that end of town if they had the sense Muriel gave a dog. Through the hand-sized circle of near-clarity, Grue stared across the street.

Once upon a time, the place had been known as The Wayward Traveler, a handsome establishment he had been told. The road was named after it, and the joint did a fine business for years, passing between various owners before failing. Some said it had been a gruesome murder that kept business away. Others claimed that the wife of the proprietor had run off with another man, leaving the owner too devastated to carry on. All Grue knew for certain was that the Wayward's roof had collapsed during the winter he turned twelve. No one had touched it since then, except to steal clapboards for their hearth fires. Over the years, the Wayward had developed the perfect shade of despair gray, which, along with the other shops and homes, gave the Lower Quarter its atmosphere. Yet in no time at all the whores had made a bright eyesore of it.

The hammering had started a week ago. Intermittent drumming that came and went. A wall had gone up and then another. They had a bed in there too. He had seen the mattress carried in, just one as far as he knew. Occasionally someone walked by with a stack of planks and a satchel. Always faces Grue didn't recognize, woodies from Artisan Row. Had to be. No one in the Lower Quarter would help them, not without his say-so.

After the rain, Grue had heard the hammering every day and didn't like it. All that noise across the street and all that silence where he sat irritated him. He had never realized before, but he'd grown used to the pitter-patter of little bare feet and the musical rhythms of bed frames. Grue never cared for the quiet—never trusted it. Silence was the result of someone getting strangled.

The fresh-cut wood being nailed up, lacking the gray patina of time, looked naked—a pale ass grinning across the road at him. The woodies had started on the second floor that morning, and Grue had stabbed his eggs as they hoisted the lumber. He wasn't the only one. Groups of fools had gathered to watch. Four over at the livery, two who stood in the muck of the street, and three on his own porch, as if it were a tournament viewing stand instead of the entrance to an alehouse. He had cut them some slack since it had been in the morning. Being a business owner, he never wanted to be accused of contributing to the delinquency of the Quarter. Grue himself never drank *before the mist was off the fields.* He was certain a priest of Novron had once told him doing otherwise was an affront to the gods, although it might just as easily have been the lyric to a song only partially remembered. Whatever the source, Grue took it to heart and refused to trust men who didn't do likewise. Not that he would refuse to sell drinks to anyone. As Grue saw it, if Maribor didn't prevent the sun from shining on the shoulders of the daft and the dubious, then who was he to deny them spirits? But he could never trust such vile sorts, and he respected the moral fortitude of those who lingered on his doorstep, but come midday they had better buy drinks or they could stand in the mud with the rest of the laggards.

"Putting glass in the windows." The sound of Willard's voice was like rocks rubbing together. It wasn't so much Willard's fault; he was born with gravel in his throat. The real problem was with Grue, who had drunk too much the night before. Third night in a row he had fallen asleep at that table. He glanced at the pane with the clean hole. Maybe he had been the one who splashed the drink on the glass. He seemed to recall an argument he'd had with the window the night before. Something about it being dirty.

He had expected the whores to be back by then.

He figured they'd wander around for a day or two, getting footsore and hungry. Then, as the sun set and the winds blew cold, the lot of them would knock on his door with bowed heads, sullen faces, and every one of them shivering on his porch. He had planned to make them spend a cold night on the stoop. Lessons had to be learned. A horse you broke once, and as long as you rode it regular, the training stuck, but harlots needed constant education. He especially wanted to break them of their habit of following *her*.

He watched Gwen from his filthy window. She was out on that broken cart pointing and shouting like some sea captain. He didn't like it. With all this freedom, Gwen's head was going to swell too big to fit through his door. She always had been too full of herself. The first day he laid eyes on her he knew he was looking at a headache. Even while she'd dressed in that patched and frayed skirt, there had been no doubt she was stunning. Dark-skinned, dark-eyed, and that long black hair like some she-demon from the south whose eyes spoke of wickedness—the sort men enjoyed. He offered her a job, and she had accepted. But then she tried to pretend she didn't understand and acted as if all that was required was to just serve drinks. It took three rounds with the belt to set her straight.

"Them's nice windows," Willard said.

"Are all them kegs full?" The sound of Grue's own voice hurt his head.

"Just about."

"I don't want no *just about*!" Willard was a big boy, with hands the size of barrel tops, but he was lazy as a fieldstone. Grue had found him asleep at the bar one night. The boy didn't have any place to go. He'd been working as a road mender, drinking his pay and passing out at the tavern where his coworkers nudged him awake in the mornings. As it turned out, Willard had been drinking on credit, so Grue demanded he work his debt off. Two years later, Willard was still working on that debt.

Grue looked back across the street. Willard was right—they *were* nice windows, thin glass and big. Must have cost a bag of silver.

How'd she do it?

Had to be skimming, doing extras without him knowing and pocketing the coin. He wasn't sure how that was possible. He kept close watch, and her customers knew better than to sidestep him. Everyone who entered the Head understood how things worked.

Raynor Grue ruled Wayward Street.

No great accomplishment, but he took pride in it just the same. Most of the buildings were just storage sheds filled with the junk of those who lived and worked in better places. Wayward—sometimes called the *Last Street in Medford*—divided the have-nothings from the are-nothings. Ironically the only other successful business on the street was that of Kenyon the Clean. He made soap, the stench of which had forced him to the Last Street in Medford, where his smell was no worse than the rest. The other inhabitants were part-time workers and full-time drinkers, like Mason Grumon and the intermittent blacksmith shop that he opened whenever he was sober.

Being the man with the choke hold on the neighborhood's lifeblood made Raynor Grue the King of Wayward, the tyrant of the taps. Not only did he rule the only alehouse on the street, ale that he and Willard brewed in the cellar, but he also offered gambling and, until a week ago, women.

Somehow Gwen had put money aside and a lot of it. She would have needed at least a gold tenent or two to afford the paper on that building. Of course, it wasn't hers yet, and Grue, like any monarch, was stingy about losing even a corner of his kingdom. He wasn't an evil dictator, merely pragmatic, and as he watched her through the window, he decided to prove that.

"Make sure those kegs are set by the time I return, and don't forget to get the wedges under them. I'm tired of pulling barrels that still have a gallon left. Wrenched my back last night on one."

"Where you going?" Willard asked with a sudden interest that reminded Grue of a dog chasing him to the door.

"Nowhere. Get back to work."

Outside, the sun was hotter than expected. The rain had suggested an early winter, but the gods were erratic. Grue wasn't an ardent follower of the Nyphron Church, but that didn't mean he wasn't religious. On the contrary, he considered himself more pious than everyone else because he believed in ten times as many gods. He prayed to the god of ale daily and was perhaps the only one who knew him to be of a very different mind from his brother, the god of beer, and their wicked sister the goddess of wine. Recently he had the notion that the god of gambling, who he called Walter, was the very same deity that controlled the weather and was fickle to an extreme. Walter was in a warm sunny mood today, which just proved how out of step Grue and Walter often were.

Grue plodded through the mostly dried ruts of the thoroughfare, coming up on Gwen who was still on the cart, her back turned. The dress she wore looked clean, and he was wondering how she managed that when Gwen turned and started at the sight of him.

"Grue!" she gasped like she had never expected to see him ten feet from the front of his own home and business.

"Did you think I died?"

"Ah...no, of course not." She settled back until her butt pressed against the far rail of the cart. She bought the place directly across from him, but now she couldn't get far enough away.

"Whatcha building, girl?"

"A...brothel." She said the word quietly, as if ashamed, like a child caught holding his father's lucky silver piece in front of Braxton's Gambling House and Spirits Emporium.

"Where'd you get all the money?"

"Making it as we go."

"I see." He nodded and walked halfway around her, pausing to look at the construction as if he were noticing it all for the first time. "Looks like it might be a real nice place."

"Thank you." The words sounded like they had to claw their way out of her throat.

"How come you never asked me if you could do this?"

"Didn't think I had to."

"No? Figured you could just build a whorehouse across the street from my establishment but didn't think I would care, huh?"

"Thought maybe you might like it." She was lying; he could

hear it in the weak and hopeful tone she used. The same he had once used in front of Braxton's just before his father removed his front tooth with a ceramic mug. "A nicer place will draw more customers, and we'll make sure they're thirsty. Your business will double."

Staring up at her on that cart irritated him. He resented the very idea of having to look up at her, but more than that, Walter had put the blazing sun right behind her head, making him squint and hurting his eyes, which had grown accustomed to dark rooms with dirty windows. "You got big ideas. I can see that. But you're still a whore—*my whore*—and this is my street. Nothing happens here without my say-so. And I didn't say so. Now you and the others have had a nice vacation, a chance to see the world and breathe the air. Honestly, I think you were right to walk out. That unfortunate business with Avon...well, that was a stink that needed airing. Everyone benefited from a break, but now this foolishness is going to stop. I'm a patient man, but you girls are costing me money. You're spending good coin on this foolishness and I won't have it. Now, I want you to send these woodies back to their own quarter and herd the girls to the Head. I'm feeling tired today, so if you're quick about it, I'll likely forget the whole thing— might even let you keep whatever you made bouncing on that new bed. Keep me waiting, and I'll introduce you to the new belt I bought."

"We're never coming back, Grue." This she said louder and the tone was new. It didn't even sound like her voice.

"Don't test me, Gwen. I like you. I really do, but I can't afford to have one of my whores acting all high and mighty. You'll do as you're told, or even Etta will be feeling sorry for you. Now, get down off that bleeding cart."

Gwen stood firm, which just made him mad. He was trying to be nice—forgiving her for running out and being stupid. She ought to be grateful, but she was defying him right in the middle of the street—in front of the blasted woodies. She had her chance and Grue had had enough of being humiliated. Being nice never worked; it just dug a deeper hole to climb out of. He didn't actually own a new belt, but after he was done with Gwen, he'd likely need one.

Grue set one foot on the cart and was in the process of climbing up when a rough hand grabbed him around the throat and threw him backward. He landed on the dirt, banging his hungover head against a wheel rut.

"That's my cart, Raynor. Touch it again and I'll break your bloody neck."

Walter was in his eyes again, but Grue could just make out Dixon the Carter standing over him.

"And that goes for the cargo as well."

Grue crawled to his feet and dusted himself off, feeling the wet from where his back had hit a puddle. "That was a mistake, carter."

Dixon took a step closer, and Grue took a step back.

"I just want ya to know that I offered to settle this proper. I was willing to let it all be forgotten, and it was you who turned me down," Grue said to Gwen. "I just want you to remember that."

All the construction had stopped and the woodies were staring. The rest of the whores were out too.

"I want all of you to remember that...when the time comes."

ॐ

Nine hours later Grue was still feeling the sting of his fall and finding more places where the mud stubbornly stuck to his skin. He was back in his tavern, the bear returned to his cave to lick his wounds and sharpen his teeth. He'd been there all day and much of the night, sitting, waiting, and thinking.

He sat at the table near the bar, trying not to look at the front door, thinking it must be like watched pots. It hurt to move. Grue wasn't a young man and falls were chancy things. Nothing was broken, though perhaps his reputation had been bruised.

The story would have run like urine down a drainpipe. *Grue has lost control of Wayward. Women push him around. His own whores shove him in the mud and laugh.* He didn't recall anyone laughing; no one had so much as smiled. If anything, Gwen had looked terrified when he hit the street, but that didn't matter. They likely laughed afterward, and even if they didn't, the stories would say they did, which made it so. He could have rallied his troops. Willard knew a couple of dockworkers he called Gritty and Brock—big fellas with big fists. The three of them would make a mess of Dixon. And if he was really serious, he'd call Stane—that man was crazy and would do anything for a bottle, a girl, and a blind eye. Dixon would pay, that was a promise he had already made to himself, but that was a present he could wait on.

Grue had other plans.

The candle on the table flickered and he noticed the tin candle plate—the only one left. He had it set out special.

Remembering not to glance at the door, he turned toward the bar and focused on the painting there. He had been look-ing at it a lot that day; it helped to calm him. The whole of The Hideous Head had been built from the scavenged wood and cannibalized parts of other nearby buildings. In that sense the Head was a genuine product of the Lower Quarter—a child of all that had come before—the bastard son of a dozen parents, disowned by all. The front door, which he refused to look at for fear it would never open, originally came from the Way-ward and was still the best door on the street. The windows—the two larger ones that faced the front—came from a failed tailor shop. The smaller window, legend held, was ripped from the hull of a ship that ran aground off the Riverside docks. In these artifacts the tavern was a storehouse that preserved the history of the Lower Quarter.

That's how Raynor Grue liked to see it. He had a tendency to *decide* what the facts were—made life easier that way. He could be a miserable old rotter who lived in squalor, preying on people's vices, or he could be a reputable businessman living in a treasure house of artifacts and providing amusement to hardworking men. Both were true in their own way. Grue preferred the latter. Partly because he really believed he provided a needed service and partly because he knew this was as good as his life would get.

The Hideous Head predated Grue by more years than he knew, and much of it was a mystery like the picture of the lake above the bar. Painted on a panel of wood, it had darkened with the years so that now it appeared as a night scene. He had sat for hours staring at that painting, wondering how it got there, who painted it, but most often how he wished he could be there under that dark sky next to that lake. At times, usually after a minimum of six drinks, he could hear the lapping of the water and the honk of the geese that were so subtly suggested with two dabs of paint. The picture was only one of hundreds of the Head's many curiosities, and over the years he added his own embellishments to mystify the next owner. The tin candle plate on the table was one of those. He'd bought ten from a visiting tinker on a night he was too drunk to be talking business. Nine had vanished over the years—stolen. The one in front of him was the last. He dug it out of hiding to help dress the place up.

He heard the drum of hooves and the snort of a horse and knew his invited guest had finally arrived. Of the fifteen or so regulars who kept Grue in business and the twenty-odd walk-ins, none rode horses.

"Willard," he called across to the bar. "Bring that bottle I have inside the coin box and two glasses—the ones off the top shelf."

The front door to The Hideous Head opened, letting in a burst of brisk autumn air that flickered the candle on the tin. Reginald Lampwick entered, sweeping his cloak in an effort to not get it caught in the door. He had on his wide-brim, tied tight under his chin, and a set of gloves that he tugged off one finger at a time as he scanned the tables. Spotting Grue, he strode over, his big boots thumping.

"Sir." Grue stood up and dipped his head respectfully.

"Raynor," Reginald said, never offering his hand. Grue didn't expect him to.

Willard arrived with the bottle and glasses.

"I can't stay," Reginald said.

"It's a cold night," Grue told him. "Made colder by the ride from Gentry Quarter. It's the least I can do."

Grue went ahead and filled the glasses. He would drink both if Reginald walked out. He would need to. No amount of staring at a painting would help him if Reginald didn't at least listen. Reginald looked at the glass but made no move to touch it.

"You have no idea what I'm about to say," Grue told him. "But that doesn't matter, does it? You don't like me, and just coming here has you raw. You probably cursed me a dozen times already."

"You underestimate yourself, limiting the number to twelve."

Grue smiled. At least he had read the man correctly. "And over the course of your long journey you've decided whatever I say will be a waste of time."

"The odds are in favor of such."

"You can cause me a lot of trouble, sir. I don't want to rankle you any more than I already have. Please, drink." He indicated the bottle. "It's the best I have. Got it off a trader up from Colnora twelve years ago. Had a fancy label with a picture of a naked woman on it that peeled off a few years back. It's good and suitably expensive even for your tastes, I should think. If you drink and you like it, then your trip won't be a total loss no matter what I say."

Reginald picked up the heavy glass with a dainty pinch of two fingers. He sniffed first and then sipped. He remained stone-faced, which irritated Grue. The liquor was good—his guest could have given him that much.

Reginald said nothing, but he removed his hat and cloak and sat down. "So what's so important that you insisted I visit your miserable excuse for a business?"

Grue tapped the window with the lip of his glass. "Your boss granted a certificate for the place across the street."

Reginald looked, then nodded. "A woman named Gwen DeLancy applied for operation rights a week ago. A brothel, I believe."

"A whorehouse to be run by a whore. Does that seem right to you? A *foreign* one at that."

Reginald shrugged. "It's unusual but not unheard of. I take it you're not pleased with the prospect."

"You're damn right I'm not. Those tarts over there used to work for me." Grue swallowed his drink, letting the whiskey burn a path down his throat, and then refilled the glasses. "I make profit from three things: ale, gambling, and women. Across the street is a third of my profit—more even, as the gambling hasn't paid well lately." This was a lie, but he wasn't about to admit financial success to Reginald. Grue never cared for the Lower Quarter's merchants' guild and how they helped the city assessors determine taxes. Traitors, all of them. Being the ward's inspector, Reginald was the worst of the turncoats and the less he knew the better.

"Get to the point."

"You haven't submitted a report on the site yet?"

"No. I have a list and those already paying revenue super-
sede those just applying."

Good news. Grue took a sip, this time letting the liquor linger a bit. "That's fine with me. In fact, I'd like you to pad that
list, push this little operation down a few more names."

"Why?"

"You must have seen it. The whores are putting up a bloody
palace over there. Two stories, new wood, windows—I've even
heard rumor they plan on painting it. The longer you wait, the
more work will be done."

Reginald took a deep swig that pursed his lips again and
squinted his eyes. When he spoke, his voice was strained.
"What does this have to do with you?"

Grue held up his glass so that the candlelight showed
through the murky liquid, revealing the copper color. "I want
you to wait until the place is nearly done, then disapprove the
application. The next day I will apply for the same application
and you'll approve that one."

"And why in the name of Novron would I do that?"

"Because I will give you *half* of everything I make... *before
taxes*."

For Grue, the next few heartbeats determined everything. He
studied every line on the inspector's face. Nothing. Reginald
would make a great gambler but Grue was better. Even nothing was something. He hadn't said no.

He could have thrown up his hands or turned over the table
in outrage. The inspector didn't move at all, not even a twitch
of his eyebrows. He was either thinking it over or waiting to
hear more—probably both—and that gave Grue his chance.

"Would you believe me if I told you that I've lied about how
much I've made off those girls?" Admitting this was equal

to showing discards. If Reggie didn't go for the deal, Grue wouldn't be pulling any income from prostitution any longer, so it didn't matter. If he went for the deal, they would be partners and he knew a tax inspector would be keen to watch the sales of a business's interest he was part owner in. Best to admit it now and take advantage of the possible benefits of honesty and enticement. "I made more off them than from ale. Just look over there. You know how they're paying for all that? They have one bed. One! And that single mattress is financing walls, windows, and doors. Getting a wider business from the Merchant Quarter is what they're doing. All those woodies and trade folk who got money to throw around. Now, I don't know if they're taking it in trade or not, but that's the kind of profit you can expect. And like I said, that's just one bed. Once that place is finished, if they do a nice job, it will pull business from all over the city. We add a few more girls, a few more beds, and this sort of liquor we're drinking now we'll be using to rinse our mouths with later."

It was slight, but Grue saw the corners of Reggie's lips rise a hair.

"You're an honest man and I *know* you've never considered this sort of an arrangement with anyone else you assess." Grue wasn't certain this was a lie, but he also wasn't certain the sun would rise in the morning. "But you work hard riding all over the county, and for what? Not enough I'm sure. And what will you do when you get too old to make the rounds? Be nice to know you've got an income—your own little industry pumping money into your purse, wouldn't it?"

Reginald no longer sipped or swigged; he downed the remainder of his drink in a single swallow and tapped the glass for more.

"No one needs to know," Grue continued, pulling the cork again. "You don't want this getting out, and neither do I. I have a reputation to maintain down here. People need to believe that I control things—on Wayward Street at least. Those whores are challenging me, and it would be best if it appeared I took them down on my own. So all you need to do is take your time getting to them—just a few more days I suspect will do fine—then break the bad news. I'll have my application ready. You just check it off, push it through, and I'll do the rest."

The inspector looked around the room with the nonchalance of a bear in a parlor.

"What do you say?"

Reginald met his stare and held up his glass, smiling. Grue clinked it with his own.

CHAPTER 13

IBERTON

Hadrian followed behind Royce. There was enough room to ride alongside, as the road north was as wide as three oxcarts, but he hung back. Traveling next to him would feel too friendly, and Hadrian had no such feelings. It was possible that Royce had saved his life on the barge, but for all the wrong reasons. And while he had helped him in the stables, again he had not acted out of friendship or loyalty. Hadrian was nothing but a stone in a stream he needed to cross, useful only so long as his foot was on him.

The two rode for hours. The sun had set and the moon had taken its place, but Royce hadn't said a word since they left Arcadius's office, hadn't even looked at him. Hadrian could have fallen asleep, or off a cliff, and Royce would have neither known nor cared.

They traveled through a bleak world, barren of trees. A windswept highland inhabited mostly by rocks and tall grasses, which grew in patches and all leaned the same way, bowing in submission to the prevailing wind. In the distance, he could see rocky mountains, jagged, dark, and grim. This was Ghent—at least that's what Royce and Arcadius called it. Neither had felt it necessary for him to know the details of their mission. Arcadius appeared to care only that Hadrian go along, not that he be an informed member of the team. This was fine. Hadrian didn't want to be there at all. Stealing was wrong. He believed that but was unable to muster much indignation, given he'd done far worse over his few short years. He was trying to be better, but so far all he'd managed to do was run away. Hadrian had fled his home, deserted one army for the next, abandoned Avryn for Calis, and finally with no place left to run, he'd returned home. Hadrian had even run away from Vernes when he might have stayed to help Pickles, and he left Colnora rather than attempt to solve the riddle of the barge. Now he was to be a thief, which didn't sit well with him. But he was stealing only a dusty journal, not the food from a family's mouth. And if it could change Pickles's life from one of desperate poverty to one of almost limitless hope, then it might be the most virtuous thing he'd ever done.

Hadrian tried not to think too much. He didn't ask questions, which he imagined was the real reason why he knew so little, but it was impossible to spend three days in Sheridan and not learn something. First, he discovered that wool was the number one industry in the area and that there were far more sheep than people. Second, he discovered Ghent, or more precisely the city of Ervanon, was once the capital of three of the four nations of men, having been the home of a short-lived empire. Hadrian found neither of these facts particularly interesting or important. The third item, however, surprised him. Ghent, while being the northernmost region of the country of Avryn, was not a kingdom or principality. Ghent was an ecclesiastical dominion, ruled by the Nyphron Church, and Ervanon was the center of the church and home of the Patriarch. This last bit Hadrian remembered having heard before. His father never spoke of the church, and Hintindar had no priest, but everyone knew of the Patriarch just as everyone knew of the gods Novron and Maribor. This meant he would be thieving from the church.

If he hadn't already angered the gods, this ought to cinch the deal.

So far Hadrian wasn't terribly impressed with Ghent. The hillsides had the expressions of old war veterans, scarred and withered. The fields were empty, picked clean, trampled of life. The road had once been paved in stone. Hadrian saw them in patches, now mostly buried in dirt. The whole place seemed used up, sucked dry. Something that may have once been great remained a dust-covered memory.

They came to a bend in the road where it turned more west than north, and there at the turn was a squat fir tree that for the last quarter mile Hadrian had suspected might be a bear.

Coincidentally, at the same time as they passed the tree, Hadrian finally reached the conclusion that Arcadius was senile. The man was old to be sure. Older than anyone he'd ever met. Older even than his father, who at the time of his departure was the oldest man in Hintindar—though everyone said he carried his age well. The professor didn't carry his age well at all, and old folks sometimes went batty. One didn't even need to be that old. Hadrian knew a warlord in the Gur Em who spoke of himself as if he were another person in the room. Sometimes he got in arguments to the point of refusing to speak to himself anymore and insisted others relay messages "to that idiot." And the warlord was nowhere near Arcadius's age. The best that could be said for Arcadius was that he carried his insanity well. So well in fact that it took Hadrian all the way to the bear tree to conclude the professor was crazy.

He had to be. There was just no sense in asking him to pair up with Royce.

If Hadrian had an opposite in the world, it rode on the dark gray horse ahead of him, and this thought entertained Hadrian for several hours. Even the way he rode was different. Royce held the reins close while Hadrian gave Dancer plenty of slack.

Royce crouched and leaned forward; Hadrian slouched back, rolling with the animal's gait. Hadrian often stared at the road below or even at the saddle as he passed the time, tying and untying knots in the saddle straps. Royce was always turning and peering everywhere—except back, of course.

Why would Arcadius insist that he go? Why say this was his father's dying wish? It couldn't be for the book they were after. As Royce had declared a dozen times, he would stand a better chance alone. As much as Hadrian wanted to prove him wrong, he had to agree. He was a soldier, not a thief. If they wanted to besiege this tower, at least then he could contribute, but as it was, Hadrian saw no purpose in his tagging along. He was dead weight being dragged by a person who resented his presence, and that always made for a fun outing.

Royce veered off the road, guiding his horse around the scrub and rocks, climbing and then descending a hill that left them out of sight of the highway. Hadrian followed and found him dismounted next to a rash of bushes, tying his animal. Hadrian remained mounted, watching as Royce saw to his horse's needs; then, finding a suitable place, he unrolled his blanket and lay down.

"I take it we're camping here, then?"

Royce said nothing, still refusing to acknowledge his existence.

"You could have said, 'We're going to bed down here for the rest of the night.' No, wait, you're right, too much. How about 'sleeping here'? Two words. Even you could manage that, right? I mean, I know you can talk. You had plenty to say back in Arcadius's office. Couldn't keep the words from coming out then, but no, utterly impossible to indicate in any way that we'll be stopping here for the night."

Hadrian dismounted and began unloading Dancer. "How long were we on the road?" He paused to look up at the moon.

"What? Five, six hours? Not a damn word. *Getting chilly out, don't you think, Hadrian? Moon looks like a fingernail, ain't that right, Hadrian? That tree looks like a goddamn bear, don't it, Hadrian?* Nothing. By the way, in case you hadn't noticed, I was attacked by a goshawk and a pig-riding dwarf that shot eggs at me with a sling. I was knocked from my horse and wrestled with the dwarf, the hawk, *and* the pig for what had to be half an hour. The dwarf kept smashing eggs in my face, and that ruddy pig pinned me down, licking them off. I only got away because the dwarf ran out of eggs. Then the hawk turned into a moth that became distracted by the light of the moon."

Royce shifted to his side, hood up.

"Yeah, well...thank Maribor and Novron I didn't need your help *that* time."

"Didn't care for my help too much in the stable," Royce said.

"It speaks!" Picking a spot on the other side of the horses, Hadrian laid out his ground cover and draped his blanket over the top. "And I *did* thank you for that."

"And I was touched by your heartfelt gratitude."

"You didn't need to stab him. And you didn't need to kill all those people on the barge. You could have just told me who you were, who they were, and what they were planning."

"You have your ways. I have mine. I haven't been impressed by your methods. Mine work."

"Well, then by all means stick with yours. Maybe you'll get lucky and find yourself back in prison. I hear there's a whole bunch of like-minded people in there."

"Say hello to the worms for me, then," Royce said.

"Worms?"

"Graves are where people who think like you end up."

"No, they don't. Only the lucky ones. You need someone to

bury you for that. You know anyone who'd go to that trouble for you?"

"If I'm dead, why would I care? If I'm not, it'd better be a very deep hole."

"You have any friends?"

"One."

"Arcadius?"

"No."

"Where is this friend?"

"No idea."

"When was the last time you saw him?"

"When he framed me for murder and sent me to prison."

"I don't think you understand the meaning of the word *friend*."

"And I think you live in a fairy-tale world where words have consistent meanings. Can you read and write?"

"My father taught me."

"Good for you. Ever notice how the word *friend* is only one letter away from *fiend*? Maybe it's a coincidence, maybe not."

"You're an optimistic fellow, I'll give you that." Hadrian threw a second blanket over himself and turned to his side, setting his back to Royce.

"Did you save any?" Royce asked.

"Any what?"

"Of those eggs. If you did, we could cook them for breakfast in the morning."

Hadrian lay silent for a moment confused; then it hit him and he almost laughed.

॰ॐ॰

For a second day Royce and Hadrian traveled in silence. It didn't bother Hadrian anymore. The crack about the eggs had sapped some of the tension—maybe Royce was human after all. Hadrian wasn't the chatty type to begin with. He just felt they had been in the middle of a conversation when they escaped Sheridan and the following silence festered like a sliver in his skin. The sliver was still there, but it was one of those deep ones that would need to work itself out. He'd been through worse, and this was only going to last a couple days. That had been the promise at least.

For the last several miles Hadrian had seen what he thought was a figment of his imagination like the bear tree, only this was much farther away and much larger. A single vertical line like a massive pole stuck into the horizon. With each passing hour, the pole got bigger. By the time they stopped for a midday meal, the pole had become a tower, and it was still miles away.

"That's it, isn't it?" Hadrian asked.

Royce was on his knees searching through a canvas bag. He looked up and Hadrian nodded toward the horizon. "The tower? Yeah. Still about a day away."

Hadrian stood staring. Everything at that distance had a bluish cast, a muted washed-out color that began to blend with the sky. The tower stood at the apex of a massive hill that dominated the plain.

A perfect place for armies.

Hadrian could imagine rows of foot soldiers lined up in the open fields. Cavalry wheeling in wide arcs. Legions upon legions could maneuver without effort, and likely did. That tower was a ruin—all that remained of a bigger structure. It must have been mammoth. He could almost see it, this massive fortress on the rise overlooking the vast expanse. The final battle of a war had scarred this land, and it centered on the rise and the castle that once crowned it.

Hadrian sat on a patch of grass, putting his back against a rock, and opened his own food sack. He had lots of apples rolling around the bottom, cheap and plentiful around this time of year. They didn't have them in Calis and he'd bought a half dozen. He bit into one and fished out a chunk of cheese to go with it.

"What was that you slept on last night?" Royce asked.

Hadrian thought of saying "the ground," then realized what he was getting at. "Canvas I coated in pitch. In the Gur Em everything is wet. You lay out a blanket and it will soak through. The pitch keeps the water out. This isn't a jungle but I remember dew getting my bedding soaked just the same."

Royce was nodding. "Interesting. Hadn't thought of that. Good idea. Teach you that in the military?"

"No." Hadrian shrugged. "Just got tired of sleeping soaked, and I was on a dock one day watching a sailor paint the top of his hat with pitch. Said he was waterproofing it. That gave me the idea."

"Clever," Royce said. There was a note of surprise as he peered at Hadrian through squinting eyes.

"I can make you one if you like. Just need to get another piece of canvas and find some pitch."

"That's okay. I'll manage."

"Not a lot of trouble and it can be tricky to get right. Too little pitch and the water still gets in. Too much and it will crack when you roll it. Water gets in the cracks and—"

"I'll be fine."

"No, really, I can show you—"

"I don't need your help," Royce growled. He reached back and pulled up his hood, which had been down most of the day.

There was no further conversation. They ate, mounted, and moved on.

Clouds rolled through, large gray things. A curtain of rain swept the horizon to the west but never came at them. Looking behind him, Hadrian realized what Dancer had known for some time—they had been slowly climbing for miles. Visibility was impressive. He couldn't ever recall seeing so far. Whole forests looked like bushes, and the mountains that had appeared so grim and imposing the day before were tiny things. The tower continued to grow. Less blue, less hazy, the once-featureless column was made of blocks. Battlements ringed the top and were made of a different material, something bright like chalk—marble maybe. The whole thing had likely been dressed in the white stone—the whole castle perhaps—but the pretty material would have been scavenged. Hadrian had seen such things in Old Calis. Great fortresses gutted, the once-noble edifices used for field walls to corral sheep. The higher stone would have been too difficult to get. As pretty as the white slabs were, they weren't worth dying for. The effect was dramatic—a gray tower with a white...crown.

Hadrian laughed to himself.

Royce turned to look.

"Crown Tower," he said, pointing. "I get it now."

Royce rolled his eyes.

⁂

The village of Iberton hugged the shore of a narrow lake that disappeared into foothills of yellowing grass. Dozens of boats bobbed at piers that jutted into the water like gapped teeth. Houses were small, quaint things of stacked stone with plastered uppers. Each one blew smoke from chimneys and sported a garden of ripe vegetables. Children ran across the docks while a pair of black dogs chased. After almost two days of Hadrian listening to the wind, their laughter was musical.

Beyond the lake, beyond the foothills to the north, the real mountains began. Snow-capped teeth rising jagged against the sky. Past them lay Trent, a whole different country. They had come to the ceiling of Avryn. The tower was just up the road and loomed over everything, except the mountains. It felt as if they had climbed a tall ladder and had reached the top rung. The view was impressive, but it was an uneasy perch.

Royce veered off the broad way to the narrow track leading to the village and dismounted before a small building with a signboard that was no more than a picture of a frothy tankard. Although it was growing late, it was much darker inside, and at first all Hadrian saw was the flicker of lanterns that hung from roof beams. He stopped at the entrance to grant his eyes a chance to adjust, but Royce continued forward, moving to a little table between a small stone hearth and the windows.

"How ya doing?" The man behind the bar greeted him with a big smile. He extended his hand and Hadrian had to take a couple quick steps to meet him. The proprietor had a firm grip and a wholesome way of looking him in the eye. "I'm Dougan. Who might you be?"

"Hadrian."

"Nice to meet you, Hadrian. What can I get you?"

"Um…" He looked over at Royce, who was lost in the recesses of his hood again. "Beer."

The bartender looked regretful. "Sorry, lad. We don't offer *beer*. Beer is what you get in any shoddy tavern on any dusty road where they have barrels delivered by wagon after weeks of travel in the hot sun. This is Iberton. You'll need to be more specific."

All three of the other patrons seated at the rail nodded and looked his way with pitiable expressions. Each was an older gentleman, the sort he'd expect to find drinking while the sun was still shining. "I'm sorry. I'm not following. What do you offer?"

"Ale, and lots of it—the finest in Ghent."

"The finest *anywhere*," said the oldest of the rail's crew. He wore a lengthy gray beard that nestled on the bar and a tattered traveling cloak that was torn and mended with various colored threads. "And I should know—I've been there." He raised his mug. The rest imitated him, each taking a swallow, and the mugs all hit the wood again with a singular thud.

"I'll have an ale, then," Hadrian said with a smile.

Again the doleful looks.

"What kind?" Dougan asked, this time leaning over and resting his elbows on the counter. He jerked his head toward the walls where panel-painted advertisements hung. Each had some rendering of a mug, glass, or tankard spilling over and phrases such as *A Taste of Summer's Morn, Barley's Banquet, Bittersweet to the Last.*

The walls were covered and Hadrian just stared.

"Where you from?" Dougan asked, still looking up at him with that warm, cheerful smile.

"Rhenydd," he said. Hintindar was too small for anyone to know.

"Ah...down south. First time up this way, then?"

Hadrian nodded. He was still looking at what he realized was the tavern's menu scattered over the walls. Some were beautiful, lovely paintings of the lake or masterfully carved in bas-relief. Others were crudely chiseled or written on bark with charcoal.

"Okay, this here's a barley town," Dougan explained. "That's what everyone does. They grow barley."

"And fish." This time it was the fat gent nearest the door. He wore a priest's frock and spoke with his hands. He made a casting motion and added, "Lots of good fishing here, if that's what you're after."

"I thought Ghent was big on sheep and wool?" Hadrian said.

"Oh, there's plenty of that too," Dougan said. "And if it's a fine woolen tunic or cloak you want, I know the perfect place.

But if it's ale you're after, you need walk no farther. Now, *many* people grow barley, and most of them who do make their own ale. This here is the perfect place for that. Barley farms and that lake out there provide the best ingredients in Elan. Just walk out and scoop up a bucket of water, and you'll see that it's crystal clear. We don't even have a well. There's no need. So all the big farms hereabouts have their own brands like *Bittersweet* and *Summer's Morn*. Those are from farms up on the north shore, whereas *Barley's Banquet* and *Old Marbury* are from the south." Dougan pointed up at the shelf that ran near the ceiling that was lined in oversized, metal mugs. Writing was etched on each but was too far and too small for Hadrian to read. "Them's the trophies handed out each year, and there's a grand competition for the first place. So you can see Iberton takes its ale seriously."

Everyone at the bar—everyone in the tavern except Royce— watched Hadrian. Sensing pressure, he decided to play it safe. "What would *you* suggest?"

This caused the priest to shift uneasily on his stool and the bartender to sigh. "That would be putting me in a precarious pinch. Being the dispenser, I must remain neutral."

"You'll choke on anything other than *Old Marbury*," said the man farthest away, the only one besides himself who wore a sword.

"Before you decide," the priest said, "you should know this is *Lord* Marbury."

"Oh?" Hadrian straightened up and offered a bow. "Your Lordship."

Everyone smiled in an embarrassed manner, except Lord Marbury, who scowled. "Do that again and I'll stab you in the foot."

Hadrian looked to Dougan, who, by virtue of his winning smile, had become his helmet in a hailstorm.

"It's more of an honorary title now," the bartender said.

"The church doesn't recognize ranks of nobility within Ghent," the priest explained.

Marbury grumbled, "The church wouldn't recognize a—"

"Another drink, *Your Lordship?*" Dougan said loudly, snatching up the mug before the man.

"I wasn't done with that one."

"Oh, I'd say you were. And let's not forget we still haven't found out where this young lad's loyalties lie, have we? Or his friend's for that matter." Dougan stared at Hadrian expectantly. "Have you decided?"

Hadrian was confused and uncertain where the topic of conversation had wandered. Then Dougan gestured at the advertisements again.

"Oh...right. Um..." He glanced at Lord Marbury, who sat hunched over the rail glaring at Dougan. "I'll try Old Marbury, I think."

This brought smiles from both His Lordship and Dougan, and Hadrian felt as if he'd finally said something right and had made more than a drink order.

"I'm partial to Bittersweet," the bearded traveler who had offered the toast admitted. Hadrian noticed the man jingled when he moved, but instead of a weapon, he was ornamented with numerous metal trinkets that dangled from a wide belt.

"You're a tinker?" Hadrian asked.

"Tinker Bremey," he introduced himself. His handshake was weak and began unpleasantly before their thumbs met. "I have good hooks if you're here for the fishing."

"And what might your friend be interested in?" Dougan asked, pointing toward Royce.

"Good question. We haven't known each other long."

"Join up on the road, did ya?"

"No, we—"

"I'm not thirsty," Royce called.

Marbury glanced over. "Then why in Maribor's name did you come in here?"

"*He* was thirsty." Royce pointed at Hadrian. "I just wanted to get out of the wind. Is that all right?"

"Sure." Marbury nodded and turned to Hadrian. "Considerate fellow you're riding with."

"Oh yeah." Hadrian nodded and smiled. "That's exactly how I describe him to everyone—considerate to a fault."

Royce smirked and folded his arms across his chest.

"I sell a tight weave tent that blocks even the highest winds," the tinker informed him. "Comes with nautical-quality rope and pegs to hold it in place. You stretch this lady out and she'll keep you warm all night."

Dougan slapped Lord Marbury's and Hadrian's mugs on the bar, where both foamed over just like in the pictures. The bar went silent as Hadrian raised the drink to his lips. He was used to small, or table, beer in Calis, where they used an overabundance of hops. This was stronger, richer and fresh. He was grinning before he drew the mug from his face.

"Hah!" Marbury slapped the counter. "I told ya. I should win this year. Just look at him—there's a happy man, if ever I saw one."

Hadrian nodded. "It's good."

"He's just being polite," the priest said. "You can tell that's the sort he is. Raised well. Mother was likely a devout member of the Nyphron Church."

"Actually, my mother passed when I was young," Hadrian said. "My father...well, the only time he mentioned the gods was when he ruined a bit of metal or burned himself on the forge."

"A smith's son you are," the tinker said. "I should have known by all the steel you carry. I sell a fine set of tongs and hammers. I even have one I bought from a dwarven smith—finest you'll ever see."

"Why did the dwarf part with it?" the priest asked.

"Desperate to feed his family, I think. Sad story."

Hadrian took the opportunity to move over and join Royce, who sat with his back to the hearth and his sight on the windows. "I'd say you're being awfully quiet, but then I might as well follow with 'Oh look, you're breathing.' "

Royce leaned forward and whispered, "Why don't you just tell them we're thieves while you're at it?"

"What are you talking about?" Hadrian matched his tone, feeling uncomfortable whispering like conspirators in front—or in this case behind the backs—of strangers. "I was just being friendly."

"You told them your name, your place of birth, what your father did for a living, suggested which direction you were traveling in, and the fact you've never been here before. You would have told them who I was, and exactly where we came from if I hadn't stopped you."

"And exactly what would be so wrong with that?"

"First, when you're on a job, you don't want people to notice you. You want to be nothing more than a vague shadow on a person's memory. Leave nothing that anyone can use to track you. After we break into the tower, people will be looking for us and they'll remember a talkative stranger wearing three swords who likely went back south."

"If you wanted to avoid being noticed, why'd we come in here in the first place?"

"That's the second thing. I'm expecting some guests."

"Guests?" Hadrian raised his mug to drink.

"The five men who were on the road behind us."

Hadrian put the mug back down. "What are you talking about? I didn't see anyone."

"No surprise there."

"What? You think they're after us?"

"I don't know. That's why we're here."

"Wait...then they could be just other people traveling the same road?"

"I think everyone is after me until proven otherwise."

"That's ridiculous."

"They were also wearing swords and chain and have been riding hard."

"So?"

"So five is too many for a courier, too few for reinforcements, and no one else rides that hard unless they're hunting someone. Five would be just about the right size to send after two men accused of stabbing the son of a baron who were last seen riding north out of Sheridan."

Hadrian turned to look out the window. All he saw was the stone wall, the road, and the lake beyond. The setting sun gleamed gold across the water's surface.

"There's a door off the side here." Royce tilted his head toward a hallway that extended past the bar. "It opens to the trench where they dump chamber pots. When our guests arrive, we'll step out that door and wait. If they follow, we can be certain they didn't just happen to get thirsty at the same time we did. Arcadius says you're supposed to know how to fight. I hope so, because if they come out, we're going to kill them. All of them. And then we'll come back in here and kill these four."

"What? These four? Why?"

"Because you decided to get all friendly and chatty. We can't leave five bodies in the sewer and four witnesses to spread the word. The first one you take out is Lord Marbury—he's the only real threat. I'll kill the priest and the tinker. Then whoever gets done first can deal with Dougan. Try not to splatter too much blood around. After they're dead, we'll put all the bodies out back—with luck the sewage pit will be deep enough to cover them. If we don't make a big mess with the blood, it might be hours before anyone notices. By then we'll be lost in the streets of Ervanon."

"I'm not going to kill these people," Hadrian said. "They're nice people."

"How do you know?"

"I talked to them."

"You talked to me too."

"You're not nice people."

"I know, I know, I have those wolf eyes that good old Sebastian warned you about. Remember him? The nice man who, along with his nice lady friend, was planning to slit your throat?"

"He was right about you at least."

"That's my point. Pick anyone and the odds are pretty good that they're not *nice*. Everyone *looks* nice. Everyone dresses up in fine clothes and wears wide smiles like Dougan behind the bar, but I guarantee if you scrub the surface of that coin you'll find tin. People always pretend to be pleasant, kind, and friendly, *especially* cutthroats and thieves."

"*You* don't."

"That's because I'm surprisingly honest."

"I'm not killing them."

"Then why are you here? Arcadius said we were to be a team. I was to show you the business. He said you were this excellent fighter, a hardened soldier. Okay. I didn't like it, but I can see the benefit of having a skilled sword along, for just such occasions as this. So what's your problem?"

"I don't like killing."

"I'm not an idiot. I gathered that much. The question is why? Did Arcadius lie to me? Are you really some sword merchant and that's why you carry all that steel? Did he send you with me to get your first taste of blood?"

"I've drank more than my share—believe me."

"Then what's the problem?"

"I discovered it was wrong."

"Excuse me? Did you say *wrong*?"

"Yeah, you know, wrong, the opposite of right."

"How young are you? Do you also believe in fairy god-mothers, true love, and wishing on falling stars?"

"You don't believe in right and wrong? Good and bad?"

"Sure, *right* is what's *good* for me, and *bad* is what I don't like, and those things are very, very *wrong*."

"You really were raised by wolves, weren't you?"

"Yes, I was."

"So you boys are from Rhenydd, eh?" Lord Marbury came over, pulled up a chair, and sat down.

Hadrian hoped the lord hadn't overheard anything. Not that he was afraid of him. Even with his sword, the man wasn't a threat. As with most high-ranked nobles, he had no idea how to fight. To them swords were like fur and the color purple—emblems of nobility and power—but Hadrian would be embarrassed if the lord had listened to their debate about committing murder. He liked the man, and Marbury seemed the honorable sort.

"Any news from the south?" His Lordship asked. "Things are as boring here as a dead goat that can't attract a single fly." He let out a solid belch. "All I have to get me by is ale, and I wouldn't be surprised if the church took that away next. So what's the word from the palaces of kings?"

Royce stared directly at Hadrian with an angry look.

"Didn't really visit any palaces. Wouldn't let me in dressed like this," Hadrian said.

Marbury hit his fist on the table and chuckled. "Wouldn't

let me in either, I suspect. I'm like a mir—half human, half elf—only in my case I'm a cross between a noble and a peasant. A lord in a land where nobility is outlawed. Did you know my family fief goes back to Glenmorgan?"

"How the blazes would you know that?" the priest asked from his seat at the bar.

Marbury twisted around, nearly spilling his drink with his elbow. "Did I invite you to this discussion?"

"No, but they didn't invite you to theirs either."

"Harding, go *bless* yourself."

"*Bless* you too."

Lord Marbury turned back to Hadrian and Royce. "As I was saying, my family got our fief from Glenmorgan."

Hadrian nodded. "I just learned about him. He almost rebuilt the empire, except he never was able to conquer Calis. Too many fractured kingdoms, too many warlords, and of course the goblins."

"That's him. Wouldn't call him emperor. The church dubbed Glenmorgan the *Steward of Novron* because they refused to give up on their dream of finding the lost heir." He leaned back in his chair and waved his hands about like he was trying to clear the air of smoke. "Glenmorgan ruled all this, everything. Rhenydd too. He built the Crown Tower where the Patriarch and the archbishop live. You must have seen it on your way in. That was only *part* of his castle. You're right— he never took Calis, but his grandson Glenmorgan III, saved Avryn. My great-great-great—and so on—father fought beside him in the Battle of Vilan Hills, where we stopped the goblins from overrunning Avryn. That was Glen III's downfall really. His nobles and the church, who'd gotten fat under the pitiful rule of Glen II, didn't like that Glen III was as strong as his grandfather. All those comfortable gentlemen of fur and the bell-ringing bishops betrayed him. They locked Glenmorgan

III in Blythin Castle, down there in Alburn. They charged him with heresy. And when the people rioted, the church, being the virtuous sort, blamed the nobles and then frocks took over everything."

"Frocks?" Hadrian asked.

"People like me," the priest spoke up again. "He means the church."

"I do indeed."

"You realize that's both treason and heresy."

"I don't give a pimple off Novron's ass if it is. You gonna send for the seret to drag me off to some tribunal? Invite a sentinel to scourge Iberton?"

Hadrian had no idea what a seret or a sentinel was, but the prospect didn't sound pleasant.

"No."

"I didn't think so." Marbury lowered his voice, addressing the table again. "Some days I wish he would, but there's no need. I'm a castrated bull. Good for nothing but wandering the fields and making barley ale."

"Never saw a bull make ale this good before," Hadrian said.

Marbury laughed. "I like you, kid." He looked at Royce. "I like him too. A bit on the quiet side, but that makes him the smart one, right? Quiet ones always are. They know better than to babble like old, castrated, noble, ale-making bulls."

Hadrian looked across at Royce, who had dipped his head down, hiding his eyes. "He likes to think he is, but he doesn't know everything."

"I never claimed to know *everything*," Royce said. "Just what matters."

"To whom?" Hadrian asked.

"To me."

"Yeah, you're right. That's a long way from everything."

"It's enough to make intelligent decisions. You let emotions get in the way of sense."

"I have just the opposite problem," Lord Marbury said. "I let sense get in the way of emotion. For example, I should have put my sword through the belly of Harding over three years ago, and would have if I had trusted my emotions."

"I can still hear you," the priest declared.

"I know that, you miserable frock."

"He seems like a nice enough man," Hadrian said.

"He is. He's a damn fine fellow. I got the fever two years ago and he stayed with me when everyone else left for fear it was the plague again. Why, he even washed my backside for me. That's not something you forget. Harding is a pillar of this community."

"I heard that too," Harding said.

"Shut up." Marbury took a swallow from his mug. "The point is he's still one of *them*—the snakes that slither and poison everything. The ones that crashed Glenmorgan's empire and put families like mine out to pasture. The ones that turned me from a knight serving an emperor into a farmer serving ale, and if I was half the man my great-grandfather was, I'd have lopped his head off years ago."

"It's not too late," Royce said.

Marbury laughed and slapped the table. "Hear that, Harding? The one in the hood here agrees with me."

Outside, the sun had slipped behind the hills, leaving the world in a ghostly light of diminishing sky. The children had disappeared, the dogs curled up on the side of the trail, and lights spoke of life in the settling darkness.

Royce's head tilted up abruptly. He leaned forward and said, "Prove me wrong." Then Royce stood and moved for the rear door. A moment later Hadrian heard the sound of footfalls approaching.

⚥

Hadrian watched as five men entered. Each wrapped themselves in dark cloaks, but the sound of chain mail was unmistakable and in Hadrian's mind conjured the smell of blood, the
squish of mud, and feet that were never dry. Their faces were
flushed from the wind, hair tangled and thrown back. They
scanned the room, eyes intent.

"Welcome, lads, name's Dougan." He held out his hand but
none moved to shake it. "What can I do you for?"

One of the men threw his cloak back over one shoulder,
revealing the red underside and a broken crown crest on his
chest. He also uncovered a sword—a Tiliner rapier with a
knuckle guard and sharpened pommel. Hadrian had seen
hundreds. They were the blade of choice among professionals.
Made in Tiliner Delgos, it was a solid working weapon, an
effective and practical instrument of murder.

"Looking for two men out of Sheridan who knifed a boy,"
the man said.

Dougan's eyebrows rode up. "Are you now?"

"We are." The men spread out, scraping their heavy boots
on the worn wood. They eyed the tinker and the priest; then
three made a small circle around the table where Hadrian sat
with Lord Marbury. "And who might you two be?"

"That there is Lord Marbury," Dougan said in gentle warning tone. "He owns most of the land south of the lake."

Harding turned around. "And he's had a few to drink, so I
wouldn't say he's in the best of moods today."

"I'm not," Marbury growled at the priest, "and you're not
making it any better."

"We were told one of the pair carried three swords," a different man said. Thick eyebrows, a trimmed beard interrupted

by a half-moon scar across his chin, he stood hovering over Hadrian. "Some sort of soldier, a mercenary maybe."

"This here is a friend of mine up from Rhenydd," Marbury declared. "And he's a smith. Made those swords himself, am I right?"

Hadrian nodded.

"So you're saying these are samples of your work, then?" The man hovered over him, his head cocked to the side, one finger pushing and pulling the pommel of the great sword.

"They are," Hadrian confirmed.

"Let me have a look." He held out his hand.

Hadrian couldn't see behind him now without appearing suspicious, but he was certain at least two of the three had moved up. Royce was outside near the sewer waiting in ambush to slit the throat of anyone who followed him out. He was likely listening to every word. Hadrian glanced toward the rear door. If he ran for it, at least two would grab him while the others drew steel. If that happened, he could yell and Royce would hear. It would be a bloody fight then, and afterward…

Prove me wrong.

He was testing him. *Arcadius says you're supposed to know how to fight.* Maybe he wanted to know for certain before the job. Maybe he wanted to know he could stomach shoving a foot of steel through a man, and if he could kill innocent bystanders if it came to that.

Prove me wrong.

Hadrian looked across at Lord Marbury and decided he would do just that.

Hadrian drew his short sword from its scabbard and, careful to take it by the blade, extended the pommel to the man hovering over him. He watched how he placed his fingers around the grip. He knew how to handle a sword, but he was shaking hands with the weapon, not planning on shoving it into his chest—not yet.

"Why are seret involved in a petty knife fight?" Marbury asked.

So this is a seret.

"The boy who was stabbed is the son of Baron Lerwick." He lifted the short sword, flicking it from side to side; then he spun it, rolling the hilt over the back of his hand, catching the grip again.

"Lerwick, eh?" Marbury nodded. "How long ago this happen?"

"Few days."

"Kid dead?"

"No." The man turned the blade back and forth in his palm.

"Close to it?"

"No."

"Seems like a lot of trouble for nothing, then."

"The baron doesn't agree and neither does the archbishop."

Marbury smirked at him. "Oh? My congratulations on owning such fine horses," Marbury addressed the bar in a loud voice. "These men must have the fastest mounts in Avryn to be able to learn about this knifing, ride to Monreel, speak to the baron, then to Ervanon to speak to the archbishop and get back here, all in one day."

The man ignored him. "This sword is awfully worn."

"It gets a lot of use," Hadrian said.

"I thought you were a sword smith and this was only a sample."

"Of course it is," the tinker spoke up. "That's why it's so worn. I should know. I've been a tinker longer than anyone in this room has been breathing. When you sell tools, you know that people do all kinds of stupid things with them. Hit rocks, chop wood, stab them in the ground...just while trying to decide. You can't afford to have your stock ruined by such abuse. Instead, you pick one and use it as the sample that everyone beats on."

The man looked at the weapon again and licked his lips. "Not very pretty work."

"I'm not a very good smith."

"How long has this man been here?" The seret holding Hadrian's sword looked to Dougan.

The bartender shrugged. "Hard to say."

"Three days," Marbury said. "Been staying with me at my house on the north shore. I have him working on a new copper tub for boiling the wort for my ale."

"That right?" the man asked the bartender.

Dougan shrugged. "How would I know what goes on at His Lordship's house?"

"What about you, Reverend? Can you confirm this man's story?"

Harding glanced at Marbury. "I would never dispute the word of His Lordship. He's a fine upstanding member of this community."

"He is?"

"Absolutely."

"Anyone else stop by?"

"My nephew's here too," Marbury explained. "He's out back with a chamber pot. Got hold of a bad chicken this afternoon and is still paying for it. You want me to drag the lad in so you can harass him too?"

The man scowled and dropped Hadrian's sword on the table with a *clang*. He led the others back to the door, then paused. "We'll be back this way. The pair we're looking for is actually a big man and a little guy—dressed in black. If you do notice anyone, I would appreciate you let us know."

"Will do, and come back again when you can stay and drink." Dougan smiled and waved as they walked out.

Hadrian looked at Lord Marbury as he returned his sword to its scabbard. "I've been building you a copper tub?"

"You're obviously incredibly lazy, as I don't think you've even started." He lifted his mug. "Your friend abandon you?"

"No. He's waiting out back. He was planning an ambush in case they got physical."

"He's the one who stabbed that kid, then?"

"Yeah, but he was—"

Marbury held up his free hand. "No need to explain. It's just a shame he didn't stick the knife into the baron himself."

"Don't care for Lerwick?"

"Not at all. The man is a liar, a cheat, and a disreputable scoundrel."

"He's also good friends with his holiness the archbishop," Harding said.

"Which is how he has a troop of Seret Knights at his disposal."

"What are seret?"

"Soldiers of the church," the priest explained.

"*Enforcers* of the church," Marbury said. "Bullies and brutes. Started out centuries ago as the Knights of the Order of Lord Darius Seret—another ruddy sod if ever there was one. That whole family was touched. Lerwick is related to that clan somehow, which explains a lot. Mean bastards."

Hadrian watched the hallway to the back door.

"Maybe you should go look?"

Hadrian shoved back his chair, which made a hollow screech, and then crossed to the hallway. Just as Royce said, there was a door and a piss pot next to it. He lifted the latch and gave a shove. The wooden door swung back, revealing a dirt alleyway that ran behind the buildings.

"Royce?" He was greeted only by the cold air and the darkness.

Hadrian walked around the tavern to the front where Dancer remained tied to the post, but Royce's horse was gone. The long coils of rope she once carried were also missing.

Hadrian stepped back inside to the stares of Bremey, Harding, Dougan, and Lord Marbury, who had moved back to the bar.

"Probably two miles down the road by now," Marbury guessed. "Like I said, he's the smart one."

CHAPTER 14

BACK TO SCHOOL

The next morning Royce was still missing. Lord Marbury had made good his fiction by inviting Hadrian to spend the night at his house on the south shore of what he learned was Morgan Lake, known for its premium bass fishing and crystal-clear water. He declined, feeling it was best to stay at the tavern in case Royce returned. He had spent the evening talking and drinking, pressured to try each label until he had at least two too many. Besides discovering the name of the lake and its fame for white, striped, and bigmouth bass, he also learned that Agnes, Willy the shepherd's second wife, was expecting their third child—Willy's fourth. And that the village would once again be holding their annual ice-fishing contest during the week leading up to Wintertide. As always, first prize was a full keg of that year's blue ribbon ale. The award had been given out as part of the Wintertide celebrations held on the frozen lake that would be decorated with hundreds of lanterns and for a few weeks acted as the town's common. Between stories and news from visiting riders, Hadrian had watched the window and listened for the sound of a horse, but Royce never returned. When Dougan blew out the lanterns and went to bed, he had let Hadrian sleep in the storeroom.

With no means to proceed with the mission, not even having the rope, Hadrian saddled Dancer in the morning. With a dry-mouthed hangover, he thanked Dougan for the room and asked him to give his regards to Lord Marbury. Then he began riding back toward Sheridan. He rejoined the broad road that he had learned was actually known as the Steward's Way. He plodded along with an aching head, an irritable stomach, and a growing anger. By the time he made camp, he was talking to himself.

"I can understand why you might not trust me. You don't know me. I don't know you," he said to an imagined Royce. The conversation had begun as thoughts, but by the time he was lying down to sleep, the thoughts took voice. "And sure, you're as skittish as a bloodsucking mosquito, but if you planned on running, why not tell me?"

He imagined some sort of smirk or laugh.

"I tried." His voice went up in tone. Royce never spoke in such a singsong sarcastic rhythm, and his voice didn't have the timbre of a girl, but that's how Hadrian said his lines because that's how he would have heard them. "I said they were coming. I told you we had to kill everyone and you argued. Then Lord Marbury butted in. What was I supposed to do?"

"You could have interrupted. You could have excused yourself and said, 'Listen, if five guys with swords come to the door, we should run out the back.'" He liked how reasonable and confident that sounded.

Royce rolled his eyes in Hadrian's imagination. He had been rolling his eyes ever since Hadrian left Iberton's tavern that morning, and it really irritated him. "What's the point? I didn't want you along in the first place."

"What if they had grabbed me? What if they had hauled me off to whatever prison they have up here for the crime *you* committed? What if they planned to skip the trip and settle things right in the tavern with a quick beheading?" Hadrian nearly shouted this, slapping his palm against the blanket-covered grass. His eyes fixed on the stars while a few feet away Dancer shifted her weight and tilted her head with a questioning look.

"Not my problem," replied the imaginary Royce. The way he said it, the way he looked saying it with that smug little smile and those wolf eyes, made Hadrian wish he were there so he could smash the grin from his face.

The bastard.

Hadrian returned to Sheridan Valley the next night. He purposely took it slow to arrive after dark and waited until the common was clear before riding directly to the stable. He found an open stall, but he left Dancer saddled. He didn't expect to stay long. He would explain what had happened to Arcadius, stop in to check on Pickles, then...he really didn't know. He'd ride south again, maybe aim for that city the guy on the road to Sheridan had mentioned. The one on the north bank of the Galewyr where his friend sold pottery. He could get a hot meal and spend the night in a bed. If it was good enough for the potter, it would be fine for him. He'd resupply, then maybe go back down to Colnora.

Then what?

Hadrian had already seen half the world, made and spent fortunes, served queens and warlords. So why was it that he had so few prospects? He considered returning to Calis. It was a weakness, the sort he saw in drunks, and he hated himself for even thinking it. The tiger and the letter had woken him from a nightmare that he had only imagined to be a dream. He couldn't go back to that. He didn't want to be a soldier again either. He likened it to growing up. At some point he discovered girls were pretty; after that he could never return to calling them names. As a child, it had been necessary to watch, follow, and listen, but every man needed to graduate from servitude or accept a life of slavery. He'd seen the men who stayed, the career soldiers, and knew why—they wanted power. Rank granted privilege, authority, respect. Hadrian had no use for any of it. He'd achieved the zenith in each and found himself miserable. He could no longer draw swords at the demands of another any more than he could call women names. This was perhaps the only thing he was certain of—that and the fact he never wanted to see Royce Melborn again.

But what does that leave?

At least Pickles had a better future. He'd accomplished that much. Hadrian smiled thinking of the poor boy from Vernes in a school gown. His own life had taken the wrong turns, but Pickles was on a good road now. If nothing else, Hadrian could take solace in knowing he had played a major role in changing the direction of Pickles's life.

Hadrian climbed the stairs to Arcadius's office, managing to avoid students. The door was closed, leaving him to knock on the professor's door.

"Come in," called the now-familiar voice.

Opening the door, he found the office was the same old mess. The professor was back at his desk this time with a book open before him and a steaming cup of something in his hand. Hadrian was three steps into the room before he noticed Royce Melborn. The thief was on the far side of the clutter, just as he had been the day they were introduced, only this time he reclined on a chest, eating an apple. His cloak was off, draped over the shoulders of the nearby skeleton that dangled from the spear like a macabre marionette.

"You!" was all that Hadrian could think to say.

Royce looked at him equally surprised, then shaking his head in disbelief dug into his purse and pulled out a coin. He got up and set it on the professor's desk before returning to his seat on the chest. "I honestly didn't expect to see you again."

"I *hoped* I would never have to see you," Hadrian said. "You abandoned me."

"To be more precise, I left you for dead. How'd you survive?"

"I didn't fight them."

"You ran? You must be fast."

"I didn't run. I spent the night at that tavern thinking you might be back to get me."

Royce chuckled. "Not much chance of that."

"Obviously."

"So how'd you survive?"

"Lord Marbury, and the others at the tavern—the people you wanted to kill—they protected me, lied for me. He even lied for you, but that wasn't necessary because, being a coward, you were already gone."

"I wouldn't call it cowardice."

"What would you call it?"

"Necessary. I needed to get rid of you. Normally that's not a problem, but"—he tilted his head at Arcadius, who was still reading—"my first choice wasn't an option."

"Is that it?" Hadrian pointed at the small battered notebook the professor was reading.

"Yes, yes," Arcadius said. "Edmund Hall's Journal."

"My freedom was riding on the success of this job," Royce said. "I couldn't take the chance of you messing up."

"And yet you managed to do that all by yourself," Arcadius said.

Royce's head turned sharply. "What? You said it was the right book."

"The deal wasn't just to retrieve the book. It was for *both* of you to get it."

"What possible difference does that make? The book was the prize. You have it. We're done. He was only along in case of trouble, which there wasn't any."

"I was very explicit... Once again you failed to follow my instructions. You needed to take Hadrian up the tower."

"That wasn't going to happen." Royce took another loud bite of his apple and talked with his mouth full. "We didn't practice with the harness, and doing it that way was…" He waved the apple in the air, looking at the ceiling for the answer, then gave up. "It was just stupid to begin with. As you can see, I do very well on my own."

Arcadius closed the book and, taking the spectacles from his nose, looked at Royce. "I'm pleased you got the book. It is fascinating, by the way. But I was very clear on the conditions. The fact that you ignored them doesn't change that you cheated. The debt remains."

Royce stood up with a wicked look on his face and took a step toward the professor.

Hadrian put his hands to his swords and advanced a step of his own.

"It's easily fixed," Arcadius spoke quickly. "You can still free yourself of the obligation. You merely need to put the book back."

"What?"

"You need to put it back—but this time you *have* to do as instructed and take Hadrian with you."

"You can't be serious." Royce glared at him. "Now you're just—Wait. You only wanted to *borrow* the book, you said. You planned to have me put it back all along."

"It was possible you might have surprised me and actually taken Hadrian with you the first time."

Surprise stole over Royce's face and Hadrian watched as a reluctant smile slowly appeared.

"Yes, dear boy," Arcadius said. "I'm not as foolish as I look, and you're not that hard to predict. Now, in order to meet the terms of our agreement, you must replace the book—after I've finished reading it, of course. This time, however, you must take Hadrian to the top with you. I will insist *he* carry the notebook and be the one to deposit it."

"Why?" The thief stared, bewildered.

"Royce, you of all people should understand the problems associated with failing to follow clearly presented directions." Arcadius turned to Hadrian. "Just minutes ago he was lamenting on how problematic it was when you refused to slaughter the other patrons in a tavern in Iberton." He looked back at Royce. "*Can't even follow the simplest of directions*, you said. Fact is, Hadrian isn't your servant."

"No, he's baggage."

"No, he's your *partner*. His opinion is equal to your own. The two of you need to work together."

"But he's not needed. The proof is on your desk. And I managed it in less time than it took him to just ride back here."

"It's up to you, Royce, but if you want to be rid of me, this is the price. Help Hadrian put the book back where you found it, and no cheating this time."

Royce threw his apple across the room, where it bounced off the wall and was swallowed in a pile of parchments. Then with that same eerie speed, he got up and advanced on Hadrian, who instinctively drew his swords.

Royce ignored the weapons. "You better not screw this up. Be at the base of the Glen Hall's wall in five minutes. If we're really going to do this, we practice at night." He looked at the blades that Hadrian held crossed before him and sneered. "When I kill you, I won't let you see me coming."

⤧

Hadrian pulled himself up and stood on the roof of Glen Hall. A cold wind clawed at his cloak and whipped his hair. Below him, trees swayed and the statue in the common appeared but a toy.

"Well?" he asked, looking at Royce as the two stood there, wearing the leather harnesses, still joined by coils of rope.

"Better than I expected."

The disappointment in his words made Hadrian grin.

"Don't assume too much. You have no idea what I expected."

It didn't matter. Hadrian knew he had done well. There wasn't much to it really. Royce did all the work of scaling and punching in anchors. Hadrian merely pulled himself up, drawing the rope between two metal rings at his waist, which when they were taut held him in place with little effort. The trick, he quickly learned, was to keep the rope from getting tangled. The hard part was removing the anchors, which he had to do to continue pulling the rope through the rings. Royce needed them for the actual climb, so Hadrian had to slip each one into a pouch at his side. If he had three hands, this would have been easy. As it was, he had to hold both the weight-bearing line and the tail with one hand while he dangled a life-threatening distance above the ground, fumbling to stuff an iron wedge into a bag. Holding his life in one fist was enough to keep his stomach in his throat most of the way up. After he broke a sweat, he discovered at some unknown point he stopped thinking about where he was, his mind focused only on the task. Reaching the top came as an exhilarating surprise. He had done it and his reward was to stand on the windswept roof of Glen Hall next to the ledge where a hawk had built a nest, taking in a view he suspected few, except the builders and the hawk, had ever seen.

"Still got the book?" Royce asked.

Royce required Hadrian to carry a book he had chosen at random off the floor of Arcadius's office that was roughly the same size as Edmund Hall's Journal. Hadrian had *Fieldstone Economics: Rise of the Cottage Industry* stuffed in his shirt, trapped in place by his belt and the harness. He tapped his chest. "Still there."

Royce walked around him with an unhappy expression. "There's no need to carry those swords. They're just added weight and might tangle the lines. Besides, you're going to make noise."

"The scabbards are leather. There's no metal to ring. Trust me, I've fought against the Ba Ran Ghazel in the Gur Em. I know how to be quiet."

"I doubt that. I haven't been in a jungle, but I suspect it's louder there than a closed room in the middle of the night."

"Well, if you are worried about noise, these harnesses jingle like sleigh bells."

"Sound isn't a problem on the climb, and we'll take them off at the top before we go anywhere. I designed them to slip on and off easily. I just don't see why you can't get by with only that little sword. At least leave the big one on your horse."

"I might need it."

"You might need a piss pot, but you're not bringing one of those up. And why three swords, anyway? You got a third arm I can't see? 'Cause I'll admit that would be impressive." As he spoke, Royce began adjusting Hadrian's harness, tugging on the buckles, pulling it tighter.

"I use it for a different style of fighting."

"What's the difference?"

"You don't want to be the one fighting me when I pull that blade off my back."

"Really?" He didn't seem convinced. "Why don't you always use that one, then? Prefer to give your enemy a sporting chance of killing you?"

"It's a matter of choosing the right tool for the job. Most times, delicacy is what's called for. You wouldn't use a sledge-hammer to pound a nail. You use a little dagger, right? Why would you do that? It puts you at a tremendous disadvantage if the other fella has a sword."

"You'd think that, wouldn't you?"

"Just as you think I really don't need all these swords." He held up his pinky fingers. "I don't really need these either, but I'm bringing them too."

"Suit yourself. You're the one who has to haul them up and down." Royce walked back to the edge and stared down.

He stood on the lip so casually that Hadrian felt his own stomach rise, and he felt a sudden urge to grab him. Why, he didn't know. An hour ago he would have greeted news of Royce's death with a sense of satisfaction, perhaps even relief.

"The world always looks better like this," Royce said so softly Hadrian almost didn't hear. The wind pressed the thief's cloak against his back, the edges flapping to either side like dark wings—a hawk watching for mice.

"How's that?" Hadrian asked.

"Silent, still, dark, and distant. Far more manageable, less troublesome. People are small; they can be ignored." He raised his head toward the invisible horizon. "The whole world is small at a height like this. Almost makes sense the way it lays out, like watching an ant hive. You never look at one of those and consider the politics, the petty prejudices, and all the vanities that drive them, but it's the same everywhere. The queen has her favorites, her courtiers. The bigger ants lord over the smaller, the more productive over the weak, and the fortunate over the unlucky. We just can't hear their squabbles. We're too far above. Instead, they seem so pure of purpose, so simple, so happy. Maybe that's how we all look to Maribor and the rest of the godly pantheon." He peered up at the stars. "Perhaps that's why they never think to help."

He took a breath and glanced over his shoulder as if surprised Hadrian was still there. He checked his own harness, then smiled. "Now comes the fun part. Just try not to burn your hands on the rope by going too fast."

With a wicked grin, Royce stepped over the side and dropped. Hadrian could hear the whiz of the rope passing through the rings on Royce's harness as he flew down the side of the wall, pushing out with his feet, bounding his way until he was standing on the ground after only seconds.

"Your turn," he shouted, his voice echoing between the buildings.

Hadrian shuffled to the edge, unwilling to even lift his feet. His muscles shaking with tension, he lay on his stomach and inched over the side. He hung from the lip, afraid to let go even though he felt the harness supporting most of his weight.

"Sometime tonight, perhaps?" Royce called.

Hadrian double-checked the tail rope to make sure it was clear of tangles and not twisted. He wasn't certain if he was shaking because of fear, the cold, or the tension in his muscles.

"Let me make this easier," Royce said. "Imagine twenty tower guards with sharp swords running at you, and twenty more with crossbows shooting, their bolts pinging off the stone. The thing is, you don't just have to get down before they stab, hack, or shoot you. You have to get down before they realize all they have to do is cut the rope."

Hadrian let go, catching his weight on the line and thinking how crazy it was to trust his life to a twisted bit of plant fiber. Dangling, he inched the line through the rings, creeping down the wall. He let a bit more of the line slip through, and he felt himself fall. Terror tore through him. He pulled the tail rope up at an angle against the ring and he slowed quickly to a stop. He paused for a moment, letting his heart slip back down his throat, but he also smiled. He saw how it worked. Royce had told him, but nothing could replace experience. With a push of his feet, he swung away from the wall and let the rope slide.

The feeling was a rush of excitement and a sense of grace as he neatly let his toes touch the wall again, pushing off once more. He timed the rope release better and felt like a spider whirling from his web. He planned on really letting himself fly the next time he pushed off, only to discover his feet touching grass.

He looked at Royce. "We should do that again."

↭

Royce and Hadrian were confined to their room for the majority of the next day and told to keep the door locked. After the knifing of Angdon Lerwick, Arcadius preferred no one know they had returned. Hadrian was disappointed because he wouldn't be able to see Pickles, who had been reassigned to the freshman dorm since being accepted as a student, but he also knew it was probably for the best. After four days on the road and staying up all night climbing the side of Glen Hall, Hadrian was tired. The two slept most of the next day, waking only when a boy delivered what he thought might be breakfast, or perhaps lunch, but turned out to be the evening meal. The steaming bowls of vegetable stew and round loaf of brown rye arrived along with a note from Arcadius asking them to visit his office after eating and to do so while being seen by as few students as possible. There was a postscript for Royce explaining it was all right if *some* students saw them. This was underlined twice.

They ate in silence with Royce tearing the loaf in half and handing Hadrian the larger piece. This act kept Hadrian's mind occupied throughout the meal. *Is he being kind? Is this some subtle peace offering? Or is it some sort of logic on his part that because I'm bigger I should have the larger piece?* The half he handed Hadrian wasn't that much larger and he finally settled on the conclusion that Royce never noticed the difference in size.

They made their journey downstairs without incident, and
Hadrian was certain no one had seen them. By the time they
reached the professor's office, the sun had set and Arcadius's
room was illuminated only by candlelight. He had dozens
melting about the chamber with the same haphazard pattern
as everything else.

"All rested and fed I trust?" the professor asked.

They both nodded.

This appeared to amuse Arcadius somehow as he started
to smile, then wished it away. "I've finished with the book.
Fascinating tale, although most was in very poor penman-
ship. Quite choppy and disconnected near the end. Be that as
it may, it is ready for you to take back. Which I strongly suggest you do immediately, as your presence here is precarious."
The professor walked around his desk, stuck his finger into a
cage, and petted the head of a sleeping chipmunk. "You picked
a bad time to cause trouble. Councilor Sextant of the Ervanon Delegation visited the morning after you left. He makes a
habit of dropping by in the hopes of catching us doing something unseemly. I suspect the entire delegation believes all we
ever do here is corrupt the nation's youth, indoctrinating them
into heresy with the allure of witchcraft, which most believe is
what I teach."

"What do you teach?" Hadrian asked.

Arcadius looked surprised and glanced at Royce.

"He doesn't tell me anything," Hadrian said.

"Apparently not, but I am just as guilty, aren't I? I am the
headmaster of lore at this university."

"Lore?"

"History, fable, myth, and mysteries. All things that came
before their order and secrets."

"And Hall's notebook was a book of lore?"

"Absolutely—but as I was saying, Sextant and his men

arrived the morning after you left. With him came his usual entourage of a dozen knights and footmen and, unfortunately, Baron Lerwick, Angdon's father. He was obviously distressed to discover his son was attacked in—as Angdon framed it—an attempted assassination."

This brought a smirk and puff of air from Royce.

"Angdon identified the two of you as the culprits. His friends confirmed his story. They asked me, of course, and I explained I knew nothing of the incident and that you both left the night before without a word. Lerwick was incensed that his son had been mistreated by two common ruffians and demanded Sextant send the knights to deal with you."

"How did they know which way we went?"

The professor shrugged. "I think he sent a party in both directions."

"So those were the knights who came to the tavern in Iberton?" Hadrian asked.

"Yes, and they will likely be back soon."

"And if they see us here—" Royce said.

"Exactly. So I think it'd be best if you were gone before first light. You also might want to delay returning, as I suspect this will take some time to work out."

"How long?"

"Until Angdon is no longer present to identify you. Perhaps a year."

"I don't see a reason to return at all," Royce said. "He puts this book back, and we're done, right? My debt to you is cleared?"

"Yes."

"Then there's no reason for me to ever return, correct?"

Arcadius nodded. "True, but you might still wish to. How many places in the world can you go right now where you will be welcome? It might be nice just to visit on occasion. And

I would appreciate eventually learning how the two of you fared on this adventure. Perhaps you will shock me by returning together. As I said before, I think you would make a fine team."

"He and I, a team?" Royce smirked.

"Yes, a team, partners, as in two people working together, pooling their talents for a common goal. In elvish they have a word for it. They call it—"

"*Riyria*," Royce finished for him.

"You know elvish?" Hadrian asked.

Royce glanced as if annoyed that Hadrian was still there.

"The point is," the professor went on, "if over the course of this job you discover a mutual benefit in each other's skills, you might consider continuing together."

"Is that what this is all about, then?" Royce asked. "Because that's not going to happen."

"Yeah," Hadrian agreed. "I don't see either of us willingly sticking around the other. I'm not sure we could live in the same country. We're opposites."

"That's the point, really," Arcadius said. "What good is it to have duplicates? Opposites extend your range, your knowledge, your capabilities. If the two of you could learn to get along, you could be quite formidable, because you are so different. You are both at crossroads, unsure where to go next. Learn to trust each other, and you might find your way."

"Uh-huh." Royce stood up. "May I go start packing now, Teacher?"

Arcadius frowned.

Royce took this as a yes and walked out.

"Well, Hadrian, I hope you at least take me seriously."

"I don't have any plans for the future, but..." He sighed. There was just no way. He couldn't think of any possible means to salvage the situation. He realized he liked the old man and wanted to leave him with hope. The old professor had gone to great lengths, but what he wanted was impossible. "It's like you're asking me to trust a poisonous snake. He's a wild animal. One minute he seems fine and then I discover he's just setting me up. I can't trust him. Once he pays back whatever he owes you, I think it would be dangerous to keep him around. Once that restraint is gone...well, I know I'd never get any sleep."

"That would be exhausting, wouldn't it? Living in fear, unable to trust that the person next to you isn't about to cut your throat."

"Absolutely."

Arcadius took off his glasses and set them on the desk before stepping around it to face Hadrian squarely. His eyes softened, the white brows dropping. He laid his hands on Hadrian's shoulders. "And that's how Royce spends every day of his life. I believe there's a human inside that cloak, Hadrian. You just have to find a way to break through to it."

"I suppose I'd need a reason first," Hadrian said. "Honestly, if it wasn't for Pickles, I'm not sure I'd even be doing this tower thing."

A troubled looked washed over the professor. "I was afraid you'd say that."

"Why? They're still letting him in the school, right? You got him enrolled?"

"I did arrange for his enrollment, but, Hadrian, I'm afraid I have some bad news."

"Did he do something wrong?"

Arcadius ran a hand over his mouth, letting his fingers drag into his beard. "Pickles...is dead."

Hadrian didn't understand. *What does he mean dead? As in not breathing, dead?*

"Did you say *dead*?"

The professor nodded.

"I'm talking about *Pickles*. You know. The boy from Vernes—the one with the big smile. That's who I'm talking about."

"Yes, that Pickles. He's dead."

Hadrian just stared, still incapable of making sense of it.

"Angdon accused Pickles of trying to kill him."

"But—"

"Angdon's friends supported the claim. I did what I could, but the evidence was on Angdon's side. Five established and trustworthy students—the sons of nobles—against the story of an orphan boy no one knew and who had a strange way of speaking."

"What happened?"

"Pickles was executed for conspiracy to murder a nobleman."

"Why didn't you stop it? How could you let that happen? Pickles didn't have anything to do with it. It was Royce who stabbed that kid!"

"I'm sorry. I did what I could."

"What do you mean? You're the master of lore. People call you a wizard! You're telling me a wizard couldn't stop them from killing a little innocent kid?!"

Hadrian's hands were on his swords. He wanted to draw them on instinct. Usually when he felt this way his face was splattered with blood and he could swing at something. The only thing in front of him was an old man who looked near tears himself.

"I'm not a wizard," Arcadius said. "There were wizards once. People who could perform real magic, but they all vanished with the fall of the empire. I'm just a teacher. My influence extends to students, not to the theocratic rule of Ghent. The church holds absolute authority here, and they brook no interference. They already see me as a borderline heretic. Twice

I've been brought up on charges and barely escaped punishment. All I could do was tell them the truth, which believe me I did. But as I said, they don't put much value on what I have to say."

The professor lowered his head and turned away, walking slowly back to his desk.

Hadrian felt as if he'd been punched in the stomach—a wretched, empty sensation that made it hard to breathe. It wasn't Arcadius's fault. It wasn't even Royce's fault. Sometimes awful things just happened for no sensible reason. That didn't stop him from being angry. He'd just have to keep being angry until he wasn't anymore.

"What did they do with him?"

"I don't know. He was taken out of the school. Surprisingly, he wasn't made a spectacle. None of the students were even aware of it, I don't think. He was executed on one of the nearby hills. I asked after his body. They refused to tell me even that much, maybe because they were taking it to show Angdon's father."

Arcadius sat down, bending over his desk and lowering his head into his arms. "I'm so very sorry, Hadrian."

"Why didn't you tell me when I first arrived?"

"I had planned to, but you were in such a state about Royce leaving you. I thought it best to let you have a decent night's sleep."

"Thanks for that," Hadrian said. "And I'm sorry. I know it wasn't your fault."

The professor nodded. "I suppose this means you aren't going to finish the job with Royce. Now that I'm no longer of any use to you."

"Of course I'll do it." Hadrian let his palms glide over the sword pommels. "You held up your end of the bargain. You got Pickles enrolled. It wouldn't be fair for me to back out now just because..."

Hadrian's throat closed up unexpectedly. He swallowed several times, trying to clear it as tears welled up. He struggled to keep his breathing even, clenching his teeth.

"Thank you, Hadrian," Arcadius said. "And for what it's worth, I honestly believe that everything happens for a reason."

"What possible reason could there be in Pickles's death?"

"Perhaps that remains to be seen."

CHAPTER 15

ASSESSING THE FUTURE

The old pile of decay was gone from the end of Wayward Street. In its place was a beautiful new building with windows, dormers, and a fresh coat of paint—mostly white with accents of powder blue along the trim. White came cheap; blue was expensive, but Gwen remembered the house in Gentry Square and wanted at least a splash of that spirit, and that made all the difference between being just another building and something special.

The porch was just framed out, visitors still had to climb up crates and walk across planks to enter, and the interior had a long way to go. Gwen focused all the early effort on the outside, confident that a good exterior would get customers in the door. After that, she figured the girls would keep them there. She was right. People came from as far away as the Merchant Quarter to see the oddity going up at the end of Wayward Street. Gwen hadn't the money for a sign, and just about everyone simply called it the House.

Gwen was proud of what they had accomplished and stood smiling as she took Inspector Reginald from the Lower Quarter's merchants' guild on a tour. She tried to keep him to the finished rooms, but he insisted on exploring *off the path*, into the sections that were filled with excess lumber, sawdust, and tools. Normally the house was filled with the sounds of hammering, but Gwen had shooed the carpenters away for the duration of the inspection. However, she couldn't do anything about Clarence the Roofer and Mae, who were conducting *business* in the "grand suite." Mae knew to keep quiet, but she had no control over her client, and Clarence was a grunter.

"Two weeks..." the inspector repeated as they strolled through the parlor.

He had been saying that a lot, and to Gwen's dismay, it was just about the only thing he had said. The man was hard to read. His expression remained flat, the tone of his voice so consistently dull as to make silence jealous.

"How did you pay for all this?"

As if on cue, overhead Clarence went into a staccato series of pig imitations. Gwen merely smiled and looked up.

"Yes, yes, I understand the nature of your business," Reginald said. "But this is a lot of expense"—he peered at a doorframe—"and very good craftsmanship. And it has been only two weeks."

"We attract customers from the Artisan and Merchant Quarters, so we can charge more."

"This isn't the only brothel in the city."

"But the services we offer are of better quality."

"I've seen your stock, and while I would exempt you personally, I'm afraid your girls are no better looking and, in most cases, not as attractive as those found at other establishments."

Stock. The word shouldn't have surprised her, but it did. To him this was an enterprise like pig farming, and Clarence wasn't doing anything to dispel that idea. Overhead the bed had shifted and the headboard was starting to bang against the wall. She made a mental note to have the frames secured to the floor and the joints oiled.

"Appearances matter to a point," she told him. "A pretty

girl turns heads and attracts visitors. I imagine those other businesses get a lot of first-time traffic, but we benefit from repeat business and word of mouth."

"So what's your secret?"

"We aren't slaves, and we get to keep all that is made. For many of us, this is the first time we've ever been in control of our lives, in control of ourselves. You'd be surprised how motivating that can be. I guess you could say that these women try harder to please than at other brothels. Customers must like that, because they keep coming back."

She led him back out to the parlor.

"As soon as I can afford a stove, we'll offer food and perhaps drinks. I hope this is just a stepping stone. We're all working here for a chance to improve. Maybe one day this won't be a brothel anymore. It'll be a lavish inn like it once was." She sighed, knowing that sounded naïve.

Gwen followed the inspector out and down to the street, where he turned and looked back at the place. "You've done an amazing job here," he said, standing with his thumbs in his belt and nodding.

"So you'll approve the certificate?"

"Absolutely not."

"What!" Gwen was certain she hadn't heard him correctly. "Why?"

"Because you're smart and I believe you could make a success of this place. What kind of message does that send? What if women started demanding apprenticeships in guilds? You are a foreigner, and that's not the way things are done here. It's my job to protect this city from dangerous ideas like yours."

He turned to walk away.

"No, wait!" She couldn't let him go, not after everything they had accomplished. She grabbed the inspector by the hand.

"Please, no. You have to change your mind. You can't just shut us down."

"It's not my decision. I only give my recommendation to the assessor. Of course, in twenty years he's never overridden any of my recommendations, but maybe this will be the first."

She refused to let go of his hand. She turned it, opening his palm, pulling it into the light. He twisted and pulled free, but not before she had seen what she was looking for. He glared at her and wiped his hand as if she carried disease, then mounted his horse. "I have three other surveys to make, one all the way out in Cold Hollow, so I expect you have until tomorrow before the assessor orders you out."

"Grue put you up to this."

She saw a reaction on his face that looked like shock. "As I said, you're smart—too smart."

He wheeled his horse and trotted up Wayward Street, leaving her alone between The Hideous Head and the House.

⌘

Gwen watched a carriage roll by the office of the city assessor. White with gold trim, the coach was spotless, as if the owner's servants polished it daily. Along the streets of the Gentry Quarter, men in capes and doublets escorted ladies dressed in stunning gowns whose ground-sweeping hems remained pristine. The colors were shocking: reds, golds, yellows, greens. The spectrum was not limited to the clothing. Banners, flags, streamers, even the awnings of street vendors whipped in the breeze, adding brilliance and spectacle. And of course there were the buildings. As she and Rose waited once more for their chance to enter the little administrative office, the two faced the beautiful house across the street. Powder blue. What had been a beautiful building to her the last time was now a marvel.

With her newfound experience, she understood the price of each balustrade and windowpane. Medford House was but a shadow, and yet it was theirs—their home, their dream. She couldn't let Grue take it away.

"What are you going to do?" Rose asked. She had been asking that since before they left.

Gwen hadn't replied, because she didn't have an answer— not a complete one at least, but saying she was clueless wouldn't help. While sometimes evasive, she refused to lie. The girls had been lied to enough. If she failed, they would have no choice but to return to Grue and he would punish them each for disloyalty, especially her. Waiting for the door to open, Gwen's hands were shaking.

She had one hope, one desperate gamble—that the city assessor was just as greedy as any other man. "You'll see."

"Next!" called the footman, wearing a long coat and carrying a staff.

Once more, Gwen grabbed Rose's hand and pulled her inside.

The same old man in a different doublet sat behind the same table. Looking up, he squinted. "You're familiar."

"My name is Gwen DeLancy. I opened a brothel in the Lower Quarter."

"Oh yes." The assessor leaned back and called out, "Lot four-sixty-eight."

"How are things going?"

"Good and bad. You see—"

A clerk delivered the parchments and the assessor studied them for only a moment. "The inspector for the Lower Quarter has not yet delivered a report on your business."

"I know that. I also know that when he does, the report will say that you shouldn't grant us a certificate."

The man offered a sad look. "I'm sorry. I must rely on the

firsthand reports of the quarter guilds and ward administrators. If you've been declined, then there is nothing I can do for you."

"Perhaps there is something I can do for *you*."

This brought a curious look from the old man and he squinted at her. "I think you'll find one of the reasons I have this position is that I am not so easily persuaded by a pretty face or the promise of nighttime adventures."

"That's not what I'm offering."

"No?"

"In just two weeks I have turned an eyesore into the most attractive building on Wayward Street. In another two, it will be the nicest place in all of the Lower Quarter. Already I am drawing business from both the Artisan and Merchant Quarters—customers with heavy purses. Each of these men are looking for what they can't find anywhere else in the city— a clean, respectable place where, for a few hours, they can feel like kings.

"I've done all this with nothing more than a few coins and six girls. Together we've created what could be the most successful business in the Lower Quarter. This is our chance to escape men like Raynor Grue, and we can only do it if you help us. You see, Inspector Reginald Lampwick is going to reject me not because I won't be profitable, but because he has made a deal with Raynor Grue, who doesn't want to see the women he once controlled succeed. As soon as you reject my bid, Raynor will put in one of his own. Lampwick will approve it, and Grue will inherit all the work I've done."

"And why would Lampwick do such a thing?"

"Grue has agreed to make him a partner, providing him with a quarter of the profits." Gwen had seen some of this in Lampwick's palm. She had seen many things: that he had eaten a slice of lamb and squash for his midday meal; that he kept the key to his strongbox around his neck on a chain given to

him by his mother, who had hung herself in his bedchambers;
and that he would one day die by being run down by a wagon
in the Merchant Quarter. She had no genuine clue as to how
much Grue planned to give the inspector as his share, only
that they had made—or would make—such an agreement. She
merely guessed at the stated figure.

The assessor frowned. "There are guild inspectors who
accept gifts from business owners. It's not against the law. Perhaps if you had made such an arrangement with Mr. Lampwick,
you could have secured your business interest."

"That's exactly what I am doing. Only I am offering to give
you the deal that Lampwick wants with Grue. Lampwick told
me that the decision isn't up to him, that it's up to you, and I
will pay a quarter of all the profits of the brothel in return for
securing the certificate." She lifted up the purse and placed it
on the desk. "We have only just started. We haven't even officially opened yet, and most of the profits so far have all gone
into the building with just a little spent on food, but this is
what you can expect right away, and I promise you, there will
be more...much more."

The assessor looked into the purse and raised an eyebrow.

"You needn't take my word for it. Reginald Lampwick has
already seen the value in the property. What he doesn't understand is that Grue will never make a success of the place the
way I can. If he could, he would have by now. I'm the one who
made this happen, and I'm the one who will make it grow.
Why should Lampwick benefit from your decisions? Give me
the certificate and I'll be able to provide a good income for you
and your family for years to come."

He glared at her.

That was it. Her cards were out, and she had nothing left.
She didn't like his look. On their last visit, he had appeared
so friendly, so kind. He was one of the few people in the city

who didn't treat her like a disease. She had felt such affection for him that she didn't begrudge his sharing in their success, but now she knew she had underestimated the man. Looking at him, Gwen realized her mistake. His clothes were not like those of Dixon or Grue. He had money, perhaps more than he could spend. What would be the point in offering a few more coins each month?

Gwen felt the weight of defeat pressing down. She had failed, and now all of them would be—

"How often would I receive such a gift and be certain"—he raised a careful finger between them—"this would be a *gift* that you would bestow upon me and not a partnership?"

"Of course…ah, monthly would be best, but weekly if necessary."

"Monthly," he confirmed.

She nodded.

The old man took a quill and began to write. "See that such gifts are delivered each new moon."

Gwen couldn't help smiling. "I'll do my best to make certain you won't have the strength to lift it."

He smiled back. "I'm afraid Mr. Lampwick will be very disappointed by my decision." He looked to one of the clerks. "Bring the royal seal."

༄

The evening was milder than most as Gwen stepped out onto the planking of what would soon be Medford House's front porch. Behind her in the parlor, the girls talked and laughed. Rose was repeating the story again for the benefit of Dixon and Mae, who missed the first three renditions. With each retelling, the number of times Rose used words like *brilliant* and *marvelous* increased.

Gwen moved to the edge of the would-be porch, a framed

platform three feet above the dirt, and leaned against a rough beam that would one day support the porch's roof. Across the street, The Hideous Head was quiet. Lamps were lit, but the door was closed and she saw no one moving about. She wondered if Grue had learned the news yet. Hard to imagine anyone in the Lower Quarter not having heard. The way Rose told the tale, Gwen had vanquished a fire-breathing dragon merely by spitting in its eye. She had done the impossible. She'd saved them all. Gwen was a hero.

She leaned against the beam feeling strangely melancholy.

I've won the battle, but have I lost the war?

A pair of dogs zigzagged the length of Wayward Street, sniffing for food. Besides them and a corner of canvas that flapped in the wind, nothing else moved. She had spent the gold coins. She had traded them for this. She had saved herself, and yes possibly a few others, but perhaps none of that was meant to happen. Her weakness had likely ruined everything. Those coins were entrusted to her for a reason. Since the death of her mother, she had awakened each day with a purpose greater than herself. Standing on the porch, Gwen understood she had cast away the only physical proof that the man with the gold coins had ever existed. She had sold her faith for security, and it felt as if she had lost the best part of herself.

Was it too soon? Or too late?

It hardly mattered; the coins were gone. She could replace them. She hadn't lied to the assessor about the kind of money the House was making, but she didn't think it worked that way. That was the problem. She had no idea how it worked. All she ever knew were bits and pieces, like her skirt sewn from random bits of cloth. Both formed a pattern of no discernible sense. *This is how people feel when they have their fortunes told*, she realized. Her mother had left everything behind and died trying to get Gwen to Medford, but she had never said why. Maybe she didn't know. Only the man with the coins had *really* known. For the first time in her life, she had succeeded at something great, and yet never before had she felt like such a failure.

She stared down the length of the street. The man she was supposed to help would come this way. *Dressed in his own blood.* She knew it—felt it in her bones like an approaching storm. Who might he be to attract the attention of the man who had given her the coins? Someone great certainly, a king perhaps, or a priest. Maybe even—

"What are you doing out here?" Dixon asked. Rose had finished her bardic tale and the big man hovered in the doorway, blocking the light. "Isn't it cold?"

"Not too bad."

"That Rose tells a great story."

"It gets longer each time."

Dixon stepped out beside her, reaching up to steady himself with the rafters. "Wind is picking up. Storm is coming."

She nodded. "Good thing we got the roof finished."

"It will be nice to just *watch* the rain for a change." He placed a big hand gently on her shoulder. "You did a good thing here."

She smiled and nodded, again wondering at the sympathetic tone of his voice. *Do I look that sad?*

"I never did thank you for taking me in."

"I didn't *take you in.* I desperately needed your help. I still do." She placed her hand on his.

He moved closer and his arm reached across her back. She felt his body drift up alongside like a boat moving to meet a dock. His warmth circled her. It was a good, safe feeling. Dixon never availed himself of the obvious benefits of being the protector of a brothel. This was the first time he'd ever touched her. His arms and fingers rested lightly. She could sense the hesitancy, the self-conscious fear, and she loved him for it.

She put her arm around his waist as best she could and squeezed. "You're a good man."

"You're a good woman. You know this business looks like it might be a real success. You most likely won't need to do any of the day-to-day activities the way the other girls do. You'd be better off handling other affairs and such."

"I'm already too busy."

"See, that's what I'm saying. And that being the case, well... someone might consider making a proper woman of you."

"Someone like you?"

"Unless Roy the Sewer has made his intentions known. And if he has, there'll be a fight." He grinned and then let it fade before saying, "What do you think?"

"I don't know," she replied. This took the wind out of him, and it made her feel terrible. She felt him diminish, his arm drooping along her shoulders, his sight shifting to the street. "I think the world of you. I'm just not sure—"

"How'd you do it?" he said.

She didn't understand.

"How did you discover what the inspector was planning?" His arm was off her shoulders and he had moved a breath farther away, his eyes continuing to look down the street.

"Oh, that."

"Yeah, how did you know—about Grue and Lampwick?"

"I...ah..." She hesitated. "It's kind of a secret."

Dixon looked at her, surprised. "Really? You can't tell me?"

She could see the hurt look on his face deepen. "It's just that...I'm afraid you'll...Most people would be disturbed. I don't want you to dislike me."

The hurt turned to concern. "It's not possible for me to dislike you." He offered her a little smile. "So how'd you do it?"

"I read his palm."

Dixon looked at her. "You did what?"

"It's very common back in Calis. Lots of people do readings and none of them are witches. They have shops like cobblers and are respected members of the community."

Dixon held up his hands. "I wasn't going to call you a witch."

"No?"

"No."

"What were you going to say?"

"I was going to ask how you learned to do it."

"Oh." Gwen felt embarrassed. "My mother taught me the practice years ago. Like I said, a lot of people in Calis tell fortunes. Some are better than others and there are a few my mother used to call swindlers. But my mother was *very* good at it."

"How does it work?"

"I see patterns in the lines, like scholars do when they read books. I get impressions, images of the future or the past. Some are vague. Most don't make any sense at all—until later. Everything always makes sense afterward. But some can be very clear, very precise, like his. I got lucky. I really don't exactly know how it works myself. How do your eyes work? You don't know—you just see, right? It's like that. Just something I can do. I also have dreams sometimes that show the future, and sometimes I can see things just by looking in a person's eyes but that's rare."

Frightening, too, but she didn't say that, not wanting him asking too many questions that she didn't want to answer.

"So you really can see the future? It isn't a trick?"

"No trick."

Dixon held out his hands to her.

She looked at them and smiled gently. "What I see isn't

always nice. Most often I see bad things, which is why I don't do it often."

"I'd like to know. But you have to agree to tell me the truth."

She knew what he wanted to know. She smiled and nodded. Then, taking his hands, she led him over to the lantern and looked at his palms. The dominant hand was usually the best to read, and while she was deciding which that was, she noticed something strange.

She looked up, puzzled.

"What do you see?" he asked.

"That's never happened before."

"What?"

"The story on your right hand is shorter than the story on your left. This is so odd."

"Are you messing with me?"

"Huh? No, of course not."

"What's the difference?"

"I don't know yet. I have to read."

His hand was so large, the lines so clear it was an easy read even in the dim light.

A small boy in a little farmhouse between two pretty maple trees. His father is a strong man who works a plow like it's part of his body. She can't see his mother and guesses she died giving birth. So much of the skill was in the guessing, working from the clues available to complete the picture.

The farm burns; there is cracked earth where crops should have been; there are floods and storms. Gwen had no idea of the order; scenes were often out of sequence. *There is Dixon as a young man, standing in the rain outside of a pleasant house. It isn't his; it belongs to a girl with red hair. He's in love, but her father is giving her to another, a richer, older man. Dixon stands in the downpour watching the wedding from the far side of the stone wall. No one can tell he's crying.*

Heavy rain always reminds him of that day. Gwen is sitting next to Dixon, next to the cart in the downpour on Wayward Street—the day she hires him. He's thinking of the redheaded girl.

Dixon's horse goes lame, and he has to kill her. He cries that day too. He pulls the cart himself then. He trudges along country roads. Then the cart gets away from him on a hill, smashes against a rock, and the axle breaks. He doesn't have the money to repair it. In another rainstorm, he stands on the edge of the Gateway Bridge above the Galewyr, staring into the current. He comes very close to jumping. She couldn't tell if it was because of the cart, the redheaded girl, or something else. She couldn't even be sure if it was in his past or future.

A great battle, a war. Dixon is dressed in makeshift armor fighting in the Gentry Quarter near the front gates of the city. He charges a man and—

This was where the stories in the hands diverged.

"Your right hand stops in a battle here in Medford. Your left says you'll die in a different fight, at a fortress years later."

"But either way I die fighting?"

"Looks that way, but not for many years."

"That's good...I guess. Anything in there about you?" he asked hopefully.

She nodded. "We'll remain good friends our whole lives."

"Friends?"

"Friends."

He sighed.

"Not what you were hoping for?"

"It's still a good fortune. A damn good one, actually. Better than..."

She was still looking at his palm and stopped hearing him as she saw something new.

Dixon and his cart, a horse pulling it this time, but a different

horse. They aren't in the city—someplace else, maybe a farm.
Sheep are bleating and it's raining, a storm, a terrible storm.
Men lying on the ground, facedown in large puddles. "More
will be coming. Leave us or they'll know you helped."

The voice. It reached out of Dixon's future. It spoke to her.

"Over here!" An old man waving. "Help them—please.
You have to get them out of here. Just dump the wood and
hide them in the cart. Take them away."

Lightning flashes. No longer raining, but dark. The cart is
on Wayward Street. One of the men climbs out. Small, weak,
he staggers and beats on the door of the livery, calling for help.
He is covered in blood.

Dressed in his own blood.

"What's going on? Gwen, what are you seeing?"

She was shaking. "Have you bought a new horse?"

"No, I...ah..."

"What?"

"I was thinking about it. The money you paid me went
to fixing the axle on my wagon, and I was saving up for...
There's this horse this guy up in the Art-Q is selling cheap. A
bit on the old side, but—"

"Is it black with one white ear?" she asked, and Dixon
looked stunned. "What are you going to do if you get the
horse?"

"Well, I was thinking of talking to you about this later, but
with this place being near finished, I thought I'd resume my
hauling business. I'd still be here most of the time—in case
you needed me, you know. But I already got an offer. One of
the woodies, he needs a load of lumber taken north, and the
guy says the farmer who ordered it has a load of wool for the
weaver back here in Medford. In one trip I'd make more than I
have since before my other horse died."

"When are you leaving?" She grabbed him by the shoulders, her voice rising.

"I don't know that I am." Dixon looked flustered. "I don't actually have the money for the horse yet. I was thinking about taking a loan against the money I'd make by delivering the lumber, but that's dangerous, and I wasn't sure—"

"Do it." She almost screamed the words but forced herself to keep in control.

"You think it's a good idea? What if something goes wrong? I'd be—"

"I'll cover the loan. I'll buy the horse outright if necessary."

"Really?"

"It's *very* important that you deliver that lumber."

"It is?"

"Absolutely."

"Why?"

"It just is. Get the horse, get the lumber, and leave as soon as you can. Promise me."

"I will."

"Thank you." She took his face in her hands and pushed up on her toes to kiss him. "And, Dixon, when you get there, if it's raining and you find two men who are hurt, bring them back here, okay?"

"Sure."

"Thank you so very much."

She looked back out at the street where the rising wind of a coming storm was whipping the canvas.

He's coming!

CHAPTER 16

THE CROWN TOWER

The Crown Tower loomed before them, casting a shadow across the land like a behemoth sundial with Iberton village marking bedtime. Hadrian had watched the dark arm sweep the plains and hillsides, the tower growing larger with each mile. They were closer than before, having passed the turnoff to Iberton, which was already no more than a small cluster of buildings behind and far below. Each step brought them higher on the mounded plain and closer to the giant they were to challenge, but all Hadrian could think about was Pickles.

He could still see the boy's face, his giant smile, and the happy tone in his voice. *You are a great knight, yes?* The swords were all he had seen. Pickles had watched everyone exit the ship in Vernes and figured anyone with three swords had to be a wealthy knight, but Hadrian had let him down.

He was going to take me out of here. We were going to go north. We were going to go to a university.

Hadrian would have been kinder to have left him in Vernes. He'd still be chasing bags in the streets along the docks, still dodging the press-gangs, and maybe one day he would have found a real knight—someone who wouldn't leave him to die.

Hadrian was making a habit of leaving.

He had wanted to see the boy's body, to say goodbye. He couldn't even do that. Hadrian also imagined they had disposed of Pickles in a ditch or unmarked common grave. No ceremony would have been wasted on the likes of a poor child from a faraway city.

Hadrian squeezed the reins and glared up at the tower as if it were the source of everything evil. If he hadn't been here... if he had been back at Sheridan, Pickles would still be alive. The thought was made all the more bitter, considering Hadrian hadn't done anything on the last trip.

This time the two had traveled mostly by night, keeping their sleep patterns aligned with the job, as well as avoiding the expected return of the Seret Knights, who they imagined would ride by day. Royce turned off the road and cut through brambles and brush to a low, wet area concealed by a briar patch. The center had been cleared, and the remains of a campfire identified it as Royce's base. The tower was only a few hundred yards away, up a steep slope within a maze of narrow stone streets. At this range it no longer looked like a tower. The base was too wide. Without tilting his head up, Hadrian might have thought it a slightly curved wall.

Royce was the first to break the silence. "Can you cook?" he asked without looking up as he gathered leftover wood and began stacking it for a fire. "This is our last chance to eat. We'll enter the city as soon as the sun is below the horizon and will begin the climb once the stars appear. After the job, we'll move fast. No stopping. No eating." He glanced up. "Well, I won't be. You can do as you like. In fact, I'd prefer if you went a different way than I do. I'll likely head east toward Dunmore, so you can pick any other direction." He returned to his pack for tinder. "It will be a long exhausting climb, even with the harnesses, so a solid meal is important. I wouldn't chance a fire otherwise. I'm no cook, so if there's any truth to what

Arcadius said about us being opposites, I'm hoping you're a chef."

"Pickles is dead," Hadrian said.

Royce stared at him a second. "What?"

"You heard me—you hear every stupid thing anyone ever says. That's the most annoying thing about you. Well, not the *most*—it's actually really hard to order them. The list is so ridiculously long."

"Are you talking about that kid at the school?"

"Of course I am. What do you think I'm talking about?"

Royce shrugged. "Since I was asking if you could cook, I thought you were actually talking about, well, pickles."

"I'm talking about Pickles! He was executed for the crime you committed."

"Uh-huh." Royce nodded. "How does that answer my question about your ability to cook?"

"*Uh-huh?*" Hadrian repeated, astonished. "That's your response? They execute a kid because of what you did and your reply is *uh-huh?*"

Royce dragged a dead log over to sit on as he worked at starting the fire. "I didn't kill him."

"So you did know he was dead?"

"Like you said, I hear every stupid thing anyone ever says."

"And you don't feel any remorse?"

"Nope. He was hung by the sort of people who live in this tower, at the request of Angdon and his daddy. I wasn't even there."

"You committed the crime that Pickles was executed for."

Royce peered at him, puzzled. "I stopped them from battering you senseless, and you consider that a crime?"

"I didn't need your help."

"*Really?*" The tone dripped with sarcasm.

"Yes, *really.*"

Royce made a sound somewhere between a breath and a chuckle. "Five against one, each of them armed with clubs and you with just your hands? Forgive me if I don't believe you."

"Why didn't you just join me? Two against five would have given them a lot to consider, especially if you had brandished your dagger."

Again Royce looked at him confused, almost as if Hadrian were speaking in a different language. "What world do you live in?"

"One in which you don't stab boys and allow other boys to die for it."

"Boys? What does their age have to do with it? If someone comes at you with a stick, does it really matter how old they are?"

"Yes. They're just kids. They aren't old enough to understand what they're doing."

"And neither are you."

"Me? You're not much older."

Royce, who had just coaxed a flame to life and was carefully feeding it twigs, paused. "It doesn't matter. I imagine if you were Arcadius's age you'd still be just as ignorant. Here's something you really should have already learned: If someone intends you harm, and you have the opportunity, you kill them. Anything else leads to complications that you don't need."

"But you didn't kill him."

"Exactly. If I had, we wouldn't be having this conversation."

"So why didn't you?"

"I made a promise, so I'm on a leash, and Arcadius has rules—one is not to kill the students."

"I wouldn't think you're the type to care about promises. Why haven't you just killed Arcadius? That's how you solve everything, isn't it?"

"That was very much my plan, only the pledge I made wasn't to the old professor, and the promise I made was not to kill Arcadius—at least not until I had repaid my debt to him."

"Who did you promise?" Hadrian wondered what sort of person could instill such conviction in a man without morals.

"None of your business. Now, can you cook or not?" Royce left the fire and went to dig around in his pack. He pulled out a pot and a spoon and held them up. "Well?"

"You don't care at all that Pickles died?"

Royce scowled and stuffed the pot and spoon back into his satchel. "Not in the slightest. I also don't see how this conversation benefits us."

"It benefits me because I want to know how you can be so goddamn cruel."

"It's a gift."

"You're a bastard, you know that?"

"Being an orphan, I have no idea, but you might be right. Now, can we eat?"

"I'm not going to eat with you. And I'm sure not going to cook for you."

"Fine." Royce stomped out the fire. "Your loss. Truth is I was just being nice. Thought you'd like a *last* meal. You realize you're going to die in a few hours, right? Look up there." He pointed at the tower. "Does that look like Glen Hall to you? Do you think we've got a rope that long?"

This hadn't occurred to Hadrian, but he was right. They had long ropes, but nothing that would reach the top.

"Because you can't climb, we'll have to carry extra coils up and do the height in sections. That means you'll need to disengage from one rope, support yourself on these tiny anchors, and attach yourself to the next." Royce raised his hand above his head. "Feel that breeze? Down here, it's a nice gentle breath. Up there, you'll swear Maribor himself was trying to blow you off the stone. Your arms will get tired. Your muscles will cramp. You'll be dying of thirst but be too scared to drink. And it will be cold—real cold. That wind and the autumn night will numb your fingers until you won't be sure how tight you're holding the rope. You won't be able to get enough air either—taking a deep breath will push your body out into the wind, and your muscles will be too tight, too tense to allow it. Then, I'm guessing about the three-quarter mark, that's when you'll slip. Stupid mistake. Fingers too numb to know better, muscles too tired to care. You'll hit the street, bursting like a leather water-skin.

"Since you have the book and they'll find it on you, and because Arcadius already said that if you fall on your own it's not my fault, my obligations will be fulfilled. I'll drop down a second or two later, careful to avoid the mess. There's no guardhouse or patrol that works the base of the tower, so even if an alarm is raised, I could take my time and walk back here before anyone could catch me. Of course I'd run, and since we're leaving the horses saddled and packed, I'll ride in that direction." He pointed into the dark. "In just minutes I'll be far enough away that no one will ever find me, and in all likelihood they will guess you were the only thief. Assuming you are recognizable as human."

He reached into his food sack and pulled out a piece of salt pork. "Then I'll be able to find a nice comfy spot and celebrate with a veritable feast. I just thought you'd like to have yours now."

Hadrian glared at him. "I'm going to climb that tower. I'm going to put the book back, and then I'm going to show you what this big sword on my back can do. And we'll see who hits the cobblestones first."

～

The city of Ervanon was a study of opposites. While not much larger than a quaint country hamlet, it contained more buildings per foot than Colnora. The streets were cobbled, narrow, and numerous. Instead of thatched cottages, every building was made of stone—not haphazard fieldstone as in Windham, but large cut limestone, mini-cathedrals each. And while each of the homes and shops were never more than three stories, each gathered at the base of the Crown Tower that sprouted like some mythical beanstalk out of a central plaza of colorful mosaic tiles.

The city also did not have a wall.

Dressed in heavy coils of rope looped around their shoulders, Royce and Hadrian crossed the gully out of the scrub, through a narrow gap between two buildings, and into the constricted alleys that forced Hadrian sideways. The sun was down. Only a trace of light remained in the sky and few torches or lanterns had been lit. Pressed between the blocks of stone and anchored by the rope, he waited while Royce peered out at the streets.

Hadrian could hear wheels and hooves that echoed off the stone. A distant voice called out followed by a whistle. A brief bit of laughter and the clap of a wooden door. Beneath it all, Hadrian heard music, a low vocal chorus chanting words he didn't know. There was no telling its source. When it came to sounds, Ervanon was a house of mirrors.

After pausing for several minutes, Royce sprinted into the street, and Hadrian chased after. Royce wasn't likely to abandon him again, but having been fooled once, Hadrian wasn't taking chances. The job was personal now, and he would see it through.

The streets were not much wider than the alley. A single apple cart could block an entire thoroughfare, and wall-mounted cisterns, which acted as public basins, had to be recessed into niches. Otherwise anything with wheels and sides higher than two feet would become stuck. Royce led them into one such niche where the two stood to either side of an empty sink, allowing a carriage to pass. Built for Ervanon's streets, the black coach was noticeably oblong, as if squished and stretched by the crush of stone. This city was a world of its own, and Hadrian began to wonder if the inhabitants might all be unusually tall and slender or flat like sliced bread.

They squeezed through another alley. The walls were not precise and the space between the two adjacent buildings tapered narrower as they went. Royce wriggled through fine, but Hadrian needed to press his back flat and suck in his breath to squeeze through.

Was that another attempt to lose me?

Hadrian felt he might be looking for problems, but he also knew he had good reason.

Coming out of the alley, they stepped on mosaic tiles across from which was solid darkness. The base of the Crown Tower blotted out everything. No lamps illuminated the circle, the light in the sky was gone, and the moon—what little they would see of it that night—had yet to rise. Hadrian paused to look up and nearly fell over. The thing was monstrous. Up close he could see the blocks of stone were the size of houses.

This is insane.

Royce led them around the tower. He was looking for something. How he expected to find it in the shadow with no light was a mystery but one he had no interest in asking about. His days of questioning Royce were over. All that remained was the climb. And after that...

Royce finally stopped, slipped on his hand-claws, and without a word, began to scale the tower.

Hadrian waited. There was nothing else to do. This is how they had performed the climb back in Sheridan, yet somehow it felt different, as if Royce was intentionally subjecting him to inactivity, treating him as a servant waiting on his master's fancy.

Hadrian leaned against the tower, turning his head left and right, trying to penetrate the gloom, listening for the approach of footsteps. There was nothing except the growing howl of a rising wind. Looking up, he saw that Royce had already faded into oblivion, which added to his growing anger. He made it look so easy. He had found whatever mark he searched for in the night and scuttled up the tower like he was chasing a girl up a grassy hillside. Royce had even waltzed through the route there, passing between the alley walls as if he were a rabbit and the city his personal burrow.

Feeling the cold of the rock against his back, Hadrian looked out at the vague shape of buildings across from him and wondered...if he was the only one to return to this spot, would he be able to find his way out? What were his chances of finding that singular crack that formed the mouth of the alley they had entered through, and after that what street would lead to the other alley that led to the gully, the scrub, and their horses?

Not having paid closer attention, Hadrian realized he'd already made his first mistake. This only served to ignite his frustration. A moment later the tail of rope dropped, slapping the tile beside him.

Hadrian climbed, fueled by sheer anger. Hand over hand, he pulled himself up the rope, his eyes fixed on the dark form of Royce above. Being out of the shadow of the city, there was light—nothing more than timid starlight—but enough to see the black of Royce's cloak. Just watching the way he practically scampered up the stone was infuriating. Everything about the thief enraged him now. The feeling was mutual, he was certain, as neither had spoken a word since they had left the horses.

The first three coils passed with hardly a notice. The climb wasn't a hardship for Hadrian; he welcomed it. His temper was up and his muscles begged for use. The first half of the climb was consumed by fury. No thought was given even to the transfers. He took a grip and disengaged from the safety, hooking to the other line, oblivious to where he was. He took satisfaction from the surprised expression on Royce's face each time he looked down to find Hadrian keeping up. Royce hadn't lied about the climb, nor the cold and the wind. Currents of icy air blasted him. One shoved him so hard that Hadrian spun to his back, where for a moment he dangled like a turtle on a string. Right about then he realized his hatred was not an unlimited source of energy. As his fury abated, all that remained were his muscles—muscles that were becoming exhausted.

While hard to gauge from his position, he guessed he was above the three-quarters point when he conceded to rest. He tightened the rope, pulling the line, twisting it in the rings so he could hold himself securely with one hand and let himself just dangle. For the first time he looked down, and it didn't seem real. Everything was too small. The buildings and streets were lost to darkness; only the pinholes of light that appeared as a cluster of stationary fireflies told the story of a city below. Another set of lights indicated Iberton. Hadrian spotted a silver wiggle, a river that caught the starlight and drew a meandering line from almost directly below them out to Lake Morgan. Other than these landmarks, he was surrounded by nothing but stars.

A gust of wind pushed him out and away from the stone. He felt his stomach rise as he imagined himself falling. He hovered for a moment, spinning. A toy for the wind, his heart pounding. Then the gust coughed and gave up the game. He slapped back against the wall, hitting his shoulder. He was slick with sweat, something he hadn't noticed before but something the wind revealed with its cold breath. Overhead Royce had paused.

Is he stopping for me, or is he tired as well?

He dangled as Hadrian did, but he didn't look nearly as concerned. The thief appeared to have no fear of death, and in a moment of clarity Hadrian wondered why he did.

What am I afraid of losing? My life?

Looking out at the starry universe, he didn't feel small—he didn't even exist. A copper coin had more worth.

Does it really matter? Is wishing to live another day enough?

Most people had reasons: loved ones, goals—making something, going somewhere, seeing something. Hadrian had left home to see the world and make a name for himself. He set out to be a hero, to right wrongs, save maidens, slay dragons. Instead, he became a butcher, a killer. That was the name he gained, the one he had earned. At first he thought Luck had been his friend. That's all there was to it—a bad day for them, a good day for him. He was younger and they were older, or they were younger and he had more experience. Then they came at him in groups. Not even a cut. Awe hardly described the looks of those in the stands. It was so easy to think he was special, chosen, picked by the gods. Everyone said so. Some even worshiped him as a god. Those were his days of insanity, the months of blood and wine, the days that ended when he fought the tiger and watched it die. He wasn't a hero. Heroes didn't slaughter the innocent or let poor boys die.

Heroes also don't climb insanely tall towers and steal books from priests.

The road he searched for, he couldn't find.

Maybe it doesn't exist.

He felt the rope twang and Royce was on the move again. That's when he realized he did have a reason to live. If nothing else, he refused to give that bastard the satisfaction of being right.

He caught the rope with both hands again and, setting his feet, resumed the climb. Step, pull, wrap, hold; step, pull, wrap, hold; up he moved. The last leg was climbed on the long rope. They had one length twice that of the others. Royce wanted it at the top so they could drop out of sight if necessary. Hadrian had carried the coil up. Removing it from his shoulders made him feel buoyant.

"From now on, no talking," Royce told him, having to shout to be heard over the wind as he hoisted the coil over his head.

Is that supposed to be a joke?

They were just beneath the alabaster stone of the "crown," and here Royce scaled up freehand; then like a spider he worked his way to the outer ring while inverted before setting the rope and dropping the length. The line hung out away from the wall two feet beyond Hadrian's grasp. They hadn't practiced this. He looked up, but Royce was climbing once more.

From now on, no talking.

He had done it on purpose. To follow, Hadrian would need to disengage from his safety and lunge out in midair to catch the other rope. Only two feet, but any distance separated by death felt too far.

Does it really matter?

He hadn't come all that way to fail. And who would really care if he died? He focused on the dangling line and half imagined Royce above him, poised, ready to shift it the moment he jumped.

See, Arcadius, I told you he couldn't make it.

The bastard.

That was all it took and he jumped. Catching the rope was easy, but the swing and the sudden drop was unexpected, and he struggled to stop himself from sliding down the length. His skin began to burn as his weight dragged him down. He felt the heat between his thighs and wrapped his feet tightly, catching the cord. Together, his legs, feet, and hands left him alive and swinging out and back where he slammed hard against the stone, slapping his knuckles and cheek.

Above him, Royce was already on the parapet.

CHAPTER 17

ROYCE

D*ifferent.*
Nothing was ever the same the second time around. Not that Royce made a habit of doing anything twice, but on those rare occasions he found it impossible to repeat the sequence exactly. This held true with the Crown Tower. None of it was the same. Of course it wouldn't be, given the oaf he had in tow, but that wasn't the issue. That aspect was behind him, and what he was feeling was out front.

Different.

The trip to Ervanon illustrated his point. The first time, he had moved invisibly except for the bumbling seret, who had no idea the real threat he posed. Once he dumped them on Hadrian, he had become a ghost, inconspicuous and unseen. This second time, the road had been alive with riders. Not that Hadrian had noticed. The man noticed nothing, not even his own stupidity, which followed him as loyally as a dog. Stealing that book had set all of Ghent on edge, and he was still being hunted. Soldiers, even those who worked for the church, were animals of habit. They hunted by day and slept at night. Avoiding them had been a simple task, but still indicative of a problem Royce hadn't faced previously. Never before had he returned to the site of a crime within days of committing it.

Such an act certainly benefited from being unexpected, but it also threw all the elements into a kind of tornado.

He had planned the job carefully. He knew the routine of the servants and patrols, the merchant caravans, and even the drunk they called Mosley, who wandered home past the tower each night. As a result, he had a high level of confidence even though he had little idea what lay at the top. Precious little information had been available on that. The alabaster portion of the tower was rumored to be the personal living quarters of the Patriarch, the head of the Nyphron Church. As much myth as man, only the archbishop, and perhaps the sentinels, ever actually saw him. If he had servants, he kept them with him and none ever saw the light of day except through tower windows.

While from the ground the top looked small, Royce had determined the "crown" was not just one floor. Arcadius had helped with that part. He sent Royce to take visual measurements using sticks and string; then he calculated with numbers and determined the alabaster portion was as many as four stories, or two if it had high ceilings. The sheer girth of the tower suggested a living space bigger than most castle keeps and could house a large staff of servants. Guessing that a patriarch was much like a king, Royce anticipated a personal chapel, a library, an impressive reception hall, an opulent bedroom, and a study. The top of the Crown Tower was famed to house the horded wealth of Glenmorgan and the church, so he could also expect a treasure room of some sort. A simple strongbox was unlikely, unless the tales were only rumor, but he suspected they were true. If anywhere was perfect to keep a treasure, it was up there. All he needed was to find the room with the biggest lock.

Royce was wrong—about the lock. He had found the book in an unguarded, open room littered with a cornucopia of oddities, weapons, armor, books, chalices, and plenty of jewelry, each treated with no more respect than junk in an attic. To Royce's relief, there had been just a few books to search through and only one battered journal. He was in and out in minutes, never needing to explore the upper floors, despite his curiosity. This time, knowing exactly where to go, he expected to be faster. The only variable was Hadrian.

Looking down, he saw the dolt was still dangling, swinging like a clown near the end of the rope. Arcadius had chained him to a mindless cow.

Unlike Hadrian, Arcadius wasn't an idiot, and the old man's motives vexed him—but then everything the professor did was puzzling. After paying to get Royce out of prison—something he never gave a reason for—he provided Royce with a room at the school, where he had fed and educated him. Initially, Royce hadn't seen anything strange in his actions. He was confident Arcadius had old scores to settle, and being in need of a good assassin had simply bought one.

Genius really—save a killer from certain death and such a beast might just be tamable. Having a pet assassin could be handy to anyone. Yet for all his education, Arcadius knew nothing about the ethics of killers—or maybe it was just Royce he had read wrong. Royce had no intentions of being domesticated.

Royce had already known letters and numbers, which had surprised the old man and allowed them to move on to history and philosophy. Why the professor wanted to educate him in such matters was another of the many mysteries that he refused to answer—no, not refused. Arcadius never flatly refused anything. He always gave an answer, just never the one Royce expected. This was one of the early indicators that the old man was clever. *I feel very strongly that everyone should have an education. Ignorance is the bane of the world.*

Knowledge brings understanding, and if men understand the difference between right and wrong, they will, of course, do what is right. It was this sort of absurdity that the professor would spout, leaving Royce to puzzle about his real motives. In the two years they had spent together, he had never found it.

Months went by.

Royce had expected Arcadius to provide him with a list of people to eliminate, but he had never received one. The old professor had even accepted Royce's prolonged leave of absence, "to close out some unfinished business." Arcadius hadn't asked a single question before or after, and the topic was never brought up since, not even in jest. This, more than anything, convinced him that Arcadius had known exactly how he'd spent those months away, confirming Royce's belief that the professor was dangerously intelligent and absolutely puzzling. Over a year had passed, and until this job, escorting Hadrian to Sheridan, he had never requested a thing. Now Arcadius was tossing Royce the key to his freedom, but why? If it had been anyone else, Royce would have assumed the job had been designed to fail. He had been on enough setups to recognize the smell. But why? Why buy him out of prison just to send him back or see him killed?

Different.

Everything was out of place with this job, the reasoning, the purpose, the stupid conditions. Nothing made sense. He was being manipulated; he just couldn't tell how or why. *I want the two of you to pair up,* Arcadius had told him. *You can be a good influence on the young man. Hadrian is a great swordsman—any weapon really. In a fair fight, no man can beat him, but I am concerned that not all his battles will be fair. He lives in a make-believe world, trusting that people are good and honorable. Such an attitude will make him easy prey for those wishing to harness his considerable talents. You can*

help put his feet on the ground, anchor him in reality, intro-
duce him to the real world—a world you know all too well.
And he will be a great asset. You could use a good sword at
your side.

All this must have been a lie. Hadrian hadn't drawn any of
his three swords, despite nearly being killed twice. Not to mention he had been stupid enough to get caught unarmed during an ambush. But the biggest indication was that he didn't
have the killer instinct. The man was soft. Royce concluded
the weapons were a ruse, a costume to give the impression of
a threat that didn't really exist. The question then remained:
Why had Arcadius gone through all this effort? What was the
old man really after?

Different.

Royce slid the remaining *escape* coil of rope to the side and
looked over the edge. He had expected the idiot to be dead by
now. His insistence on living was more than a little annoying,
but his persistence in climbing had solved the problem well
enough.

Royce reached inside the folds of his cloak and drew his
knife.

I told you, he pictured telling Arcadius, *he fell to his death
just as I said he would.* At least that wouldn't be a lie.

The rope supporting Hadrian was tied to the merlon,
twisting and sliding with Hadrian's pendulum weight. Royce
reached out with his knife and Alverstone's blade caught the
moonlight. The dagger shined its pale white light, nearly
blinding him. It was a good dagger—a great dagger—but at
that moment he wished for any other.

Royce shook his head, annoyed with himself. *I only promised not to kill the old man.* But that thought didn't change
the brilliance of the blade in his hand. He'd made a bargain
with the only person who had ever mattered. It was stupid.

The man was dead. It made no sense to keep a promise to a
ghost. Royce had managed to block out most of his memories
of Manzant prison, but the dagger was in his hand—a parting gift from a man who had saved more than just his life and
asked but one small favor. Royce had cut dozens of necks with
that white blade and never thought twice, but he couldn't cut
this one lousy rope.

It's my payment, Royce, he remembered Arcadius saying.

And that's it? After that I'm through with both of you?

*Yes. But I will hold you to an honest attempt—a fair treat-
ment. You can't set him up to fail.*

Royce sighed, sheathed the dagger, and got to his feet.

After the book has been delivered, I'm free of all vows.

A smile replaced the scowl. On the way out he would send
Hadrian down first—and then he would *untie* the bloody rope
if he had to. With any luck, someone below would hear him
scream and draw attention to his body. Royce would descend
the other side of the tower—the side nearest the exit, and disappear as planned. It would have worked better if they could
find the journal on him. Royce berated himself again for being
a fool.

When mentally scolding himself grew tiresome, and
Hadrian still hadn't reached the top, Royce had nothing else
to do but sit back and look at the view. Of all places, he loved
a good roof. The higher the better, and none had ever been
higher than this. The air smelled fresher, the moon felt closer,
and humanity was farther away. He leaned against the merlon,
listening to Hadrian's grunts while overhead the stars sparkled
even though clouds were quickly moving in. A storm was on
the way. That was good. Clouds meant a darker night. A storm
would hamper any search. Royce wasn't used to luck going his
way, but it appeared as if Novron was smiling on him.

Given his love of altitude, Royce found it ironic that most

of his life had been spent in the gutter. All that could change now. He was done with cities. Nothing to go back to—he had made certain of that. He hadn't just burned bridges; he had obliterated them in apocalyptic fashion. Only one more tie to cut, and he was severing it tonight. In an odd way he felt as much regret as pleasure. He would be on his own again, but he would also be alone.

I work best alone.

Royce wanted to believe that, but even after all that had happened, he still missed Merrick.

Back in his early days, when he was new to the city of Colnora, he had met Merrick. They were both new inductees to the Black Diamond thieves' guild. Merrick had started life better off than Royce—most people had. He had parents of means, not that they were still speaking to him by then, but they had raised their son, educating the boy with the hope he might follow his father's example and become a magistrate. Merrick chose a different path.

The guild paired Royce with Merrick to learn the city, but Merrick was always an overachiever. Royce was his pet project, and his new partner proceeded to instruct him on everything. He taught Royce letters, numbers, and the most reliable escape routes and safe houses. He also introduced him to his first bottle of stolen Montemorcey, shared one night on a rooftop. Doing so ruined Royce for any other drink and made high places his altar.

Royce had known nothing of the world and Merrick became his guide. Little wonder they turned out to be so much alike, kindred spirits in motives and attitudes. Royce had never known his family, and Merrick soon became the brother he never had. The two would still be terrorizing the streets, alleys, and rooftops of Colnora if only Merrick hadn't betrayed Royce and sent him to prison. The betrayal proved that no one could be trusted. People looked out for themselves. Not even the slightest act was ever without some form of perceived benefit to the person making it. Even kindness was the result of a desire for respect or admiration in the eyes of those helped. This was another lesson Merrick had taught Royce, and Merrick knew everything. When the noose pulled tight, when the wind blew cold, anyone—no matter who—looked out for themselves.

As he thought this, Royce felt a tremor on the wooden walk circling the crown. It wasn't Hadrian; he was still climbing.

The rising wind?

Possible, but he didn't like it. He had been lucky, but Royce was cynical by nature, and gods he knew to be fickle. He struggled to listen, but the same wind was howling and at that moment Hadrian finally pulled himself over the lip of the crenel, where he collapsed, panting on the walkway. Royce removed his harness and gestured for Hadrian to do the same. Once done, he pointed to the right, indicating their direction. The window he had entered last time was halfway around the tower. All he needed Hadrian to do now was follow him. Concerned about the vibration on the walkway, he wasted no time getting started.

He didn't trot although he wanted to. If the vibration was the result of footfalls, he didn't want to send a return message. Still, he moved with urgency, peering ahead and watching the bend for signs of anyone.

Different.

Previously there had been no patrol on the parapet, but he had rattled the beehive with his last visit. Had they found the horses? Had someone in the city spotted Hadrian blundering through the streets? Had they seen all the rope he was carrying and made an educated guess? They could have determined Royce's previous method of entry. Steps may have been taken.

Still, he needed only minutes. Royce reached the window—still unlocked. *Is that good or bad?* He pushed the panes in and entered. Dark, but not entirely silent, he could hear breathing. Creeping inside he found no one. The room was as empty as before. The breathing came from an outer chamber. Moving forward, he found a priest seated on a bench breathing heavily. The stairs were nearby and the priest's waistline indicated he might be unaccustomed to climbing.

The priest was a minor annoyance. He had his back to the window and panted so loudly, he invited a throat slitting. Royce pulled out his dagger and inched forward.

A heartbeat later Hadrian blundered in behind both. A moment after that, the priest turned—and screamed.

〜

The priest's scream was cut short by Royce, but while it lasted, the piercing wail had been loud.

"Drop the book and run for the rope!" Royce told Hadrian. "We're done. You're on your own."

Royce passed him and was out the window before Hadrian could respond, not that he had much to say, beyond, "Okay."

Hadrian did as instructed. He withdrew Hall's Journal and set it on the bench beside where the priest had fallen into a pool of blood. Then he climbed back out the window. Royce was nowhere to be seen. He might have run left or right, he had no idea, nor did it seem important at that moment. Hadrian ran to the right, back the way he had come.

Royce was leaving him behind. Hadrian could never hope to catch up; the man was too fast, too agile. He would already be over the side, rappelling down the tower long before Hadrian reached the rope. With the wind roaring in his face, and while still struggling to catch his breath after the climb, Hadrian reduced his run to a trot.

The wind wasn't the only thing shouting. Men were yelling, angry voices buffeted by the gale. Ahead or behind Hadrian couldn't tell for sure. All he knew was that Royce was gone and he was left alone on the tower to face the aftermath of the thief's handiwork. He thought of Pickles and gritted his teeth.

Silence, wind, silence, wind. Stone merlons interrupted the gale. Gaps of stars flashed on his left, solid stone to his right. Ahead he spotted the rope and the two harnesses.

Imagine twenty tower guards with sharp swords running at you, and twenty more with crossbows shooting, their bolts pinging off the stone around you. The thing is, you don't just have to get down before they stab, hack, or shoot you. You have to get down before they realize all they have to do is cut the rope.

Hadrian slid to a stop at the edge and picked up his harness.

How long do I have? Seconds?

"Why did I even take the thing off?" he muttered, glancing over his shoulder as he pulled the harness over his legs. Then he stopped. "Why two harnesses?"

Hadrian bent over the edge. The rope dangled, drifting lazily, abandoned in the breeze. No sign of the thief. As fast as Royce was, without a harness he couldn't possibly be at the bottom unless he had fallen. Hadrian looked at the other harness, even as he pulled the leather straps over his own shoulders. In the distance the sound of shouts continued. He felt vibrations through the wooden walkway. Men were on the parapet.

The walkway was a big circle. The window they had entered was halfway around the tower from where they had climbed up. Running in either direction after climbing out the window would eventually lead back to the rope. Hadrian had gone to the right, returning the way he had come. Royce, he realized, had gone left.

◈

Royce determined survival was still a possibility when there were just two. Three meant certain death, and now there were five. They were all tower guards at least, homegrown footmen—no seret. Still, their swords were just as long, which gave them a three-foot advantage. Trapped on the narrow parapet, he had little room to maneuver and nowhere to hide.

Royce glanced over his shoulder. No sign of Hadrian, but then there wouldn't be. He went the other way. They each had an even chance, and Hadrian had proved luckier. He'd gone around the tower on the side without guards and was back at the rope whizzing down the lines. In less than five minutes, his ex-partner would be back on the street heading for the horses. In fifteen, he'd be trotting away. Hadrian had done to him essentially what he had planned to do to Hadrian. Only in the fighter's case, it was accidental.

The guards advanced and Royce backed up.

There were other doors and windows along the parapet—none he would dare enter as he imagined the inside of the crown to be a hive of men eager to kill him. Royce had one chance. He could run back, circle the tower the way Hadrian had, and reach the rope. If he was fast enough, he could get over the lip and down a few feet before they cut the line. If he could get his hand-claws on and catch hold of the stone, he might be able to climb down. Still, they would probably have him. Men would be waiting at the bottom by the time he got down, but that was still his best option.

He lingered, curious as to why the footmen were hesitating. They inched forward a short step at a time with swords out, jabbing. No serious attempt was made to wound. They resembled a pack of old wives with brooms chasing Royce as if he were a squirrel on their roof. Men of this sort weren't usually this timid—unless they already knew him. He was missing something.

Time was not on his side. He turned to make good his gamble, but before he took a step he saw two more guards exit the tower to the parapet. They had him front and back then, and more were struggling to join the party.

So that's what you were waiting for.

None of the men jabbing their blades had said a word. No demands to drop his dagger, to give up, to surrender. It appeared the church had strict penalties for defiling the home of their holy leader. Royce's options were limited to just two: death by sword or death by falling. He put his back to the wall to see which side would lunge first. The guy to his right with the short beard gave him a sneer.

Royce crouched, ready to move. His best bet would be to dodge under whatever stroke came. Make a rabbit-stab to the heart or lung, then just push forward. They were clustered. He might be able to knock a couple down, stab another one or two before—

Someone screamed.

The cry was behind him.

Royce didn't have time to look as Mr. Beard took that opportunity to lunge. The attack was a jab. Royce avoided it, then rushed in tight. Leading with his shoulder, he ran into the man as hard as he could, thrusting Alverstone up and under his armpit. The initial resistance faded the moment the blade went in, and the man fell backward with a groan. The footman directly behind went down as well, knocked over by the collision. The third was quicker than Royce had hoped. He stabbed down. Royce rolled against the inside wall and the soldier's blade pierced the second man's thigh, wrenching out a high-pitched squeal. Royce scrambled up the piggish guard and got his dagger into the foot of the third man, still distracted by the shock of having wounded his comrade. The pain brought the man to his senses, and he swung at Royce, who again managed to roll clear. Limping, the tower guard retreated a step as his two remaining associates pulled him out of the way.

At any moment Royce expected a blade in his back. He hadn't had time to look and couldn't fight in both directions. The tiny army behind him had an open target and he wondered what was taking them so long to end this. Their tardiness almost annoyed him.

Then Royce heard the clank of steel and another cry. Finally taking the chance to look behind, he saw the bodies of at least four guards, blood-soaked and clogging the walkway. Amidst the slain, a stained sword in each hand, stood Hadrian.

Like everyone else still alive on the parapet, Royce stared in shock. Too many impossibilities bartered for his thoughts. The thief was paralyzed, unable to think because the world had just flipped. At first he refused to believe it was Hadrian. It had to be someone else. Perhaps it was Novron himself, who had overheard Royce's thought about fickle gods and had arrived to exact punishment. The guards had just been in the way. Somehow this seemed more believable to Royce than what his eyes revealed.

Is it possible the idiot couldn't find the rope?

Hadrian leapt the corpses and moved to his side. "Get behind me."

Royce did better than that. For some reason the gods saw fit to give him a second chance, and he was taking it. Slipping past Hadrian, he bolted for the rope.

It wasn't far, and just as he was nearing the anchor point, Royce stopped. Two more guards were on the walkway, blocking his passage. Only these were nothing like the footmen nor did they resemble seret. They didn't appear like anything Royce had ever seen before. They wore gold breastplates over shirts of vertical red, purple, and yellow stripes with long cuffs and billowing sleeves. Matching pants plumed out, gathering just below the knee into long striped stockings. On their heads, messenger wings decorated gold helms, which hid their faces behind cages of mesh. Each held unusual weapons, long halberds with ornately curved blades at both ends, which they held tight to their sides with one arm straight down and the other high across their chests.

Royce didn't know whether to laugh or run. They looked ridiculous. They were also big, and his inability to see their eyes worried him. They didn't hesitate. They didn't jab at him like old wives. They advanced with such determination that Royce settled on running away.

"By Mar!" Hadrian shouted as he ran across him again. "What have you found this time?!"

"I don't know, but I don't like them."

Hadrian stepped between Royce and the two golden guards as they marched single file. They showed no hurry but also no hesitation.

"Where are those others?" Royce asked.

"I persuaded them to leave."

"Good for you."

Hadrian used his sleeve to wipe the sweat and blood from his eyes as the walkway bounced with the coming of the colorful guards. "Once I start fighting, run back around the tower. Get to the rope and head down."

Hadrian was only lending voice to Royce's own thoughts. He took a step back and was about to run again when he noticed something that didn't make sense. "Hey, you're wearing your harness."

"I almost went down. You're lucky I realized you were in trouble."

The golden guard closed in.

Hadrian crouched, raising his swords. "Get going."

Hadrian lunged forward to meet the first of the pair. Royce watched in awe as Hadrian moved like a dancer, catching the pole-arm of the guard with one sword and stabbing with the other. It looked as if he got the sword up under the breast-plate, but the tip glanced away. The guard slammed Hadrian back with enough force to drive him into Royce.

"I told you to leave!"

"I'm going!"

Royce retreated as Hadrian attacked once more. This time the guard swung, spinning the top blade down. Hadrian blocked with his off-hand sword, and Royce watched in amazement as Hadrian's blade was cut in half.

"Whoa!" Hadrian retreated.

The guard pressed the attack. Hadrian ducked, letting the spinning blade spark against the tower's stone. Without pause, the guard brought up the bottom blade, which Hadrian deflected with the broken hilt, but that just gave the golden boy another downward slice. Hadrian should have been dead. Royce had seen enough fights to know that most were short affairs. One or two parries were all that could be hoped for, and that was only if both sides were playing by proper fencing rules. The golden gods before Hadrian weren't even using swords. The downward blow had speed and strength.

Clank!

Royce wasn't sure how he did it, but Hadrian had gotten his remaining sword up high enough to save himself from being cut in half. The same could not be said about his second sword, which snapped, the end of the blade flying out over the edge of the parapet. Hadrian only avoided being cleaved in half by falling to his knees.

"RUN!" he shouted.

Royce had seen enough and sprinted back around the tower.

He came to the dead bodies and vaulted them, skidding so far on the blood-slick walkway he nearly went out one of the open crenels.

There were eight bodies. Hadrian had killed seven.

Royce was nearing the rope's anchor point when again he faced a golden guard. Just one this time, but after watching Hadrian, that was one too many. *How many of these are coming up the steps after us?* No, he realized, this was the second of the two Hadrian had faced. Hadrian was probably dead. The other guard would be going around the opposite way, coming up behind him.

Fighting was stupid. He just needed to get by. If he could avoid one attack and push past, there was a chance to dive for the rope. Without waiting, without pausing, Royce ran at the guard and dodged left then right. The faceless golden helmet followed him and swung with incredible speed, just missing Royce's left leg. Pivoting and using his forward momentum, Royce punched his body through the gap between the tower wall and the golden armor. He remembered the second blade of the guard's weapon too late.

Royce felt the metal cut into his side, and where he intended to land on his right foot to keep running, his leg refused to obey. He collapsed under his own weight. Royce fell, skidding across the wooden walk, sliding on his own blood. Rolling to his back, he watched the faceless guard bring down the killing blow, the spinning scythe-like blade aimed for his chest.

Clank!

The pole was hammered to the wall, sparking and chipping out a fist-sized chunk of stone. Hadrian was there again, standing above him. He had his big sword out, and spinning in a full circle he caught the gap between the guard's collar and the flange of his helm. Or so Royce thought. His head should have flown a mile, but instead the guard was merely slammed into the wall where his helmet carved out another bit of stone.

Hadrian continued to ram forward, pummeling the guard with blow after blow, forcing him back. Royce struggled to get up. He pushed to his elbows and saw the cut in his side was deep, his tunic awash in blood. He struggled to slide himself toward the rope. The pain nearly caused him to pass out.

Almost getting inside Hadrian's defense, the guard halted his advance and reversed the momentum.

On his back, propped up on his elbows, Royce saw it coming but didn't have time to warn him. As Hadrian stepped into the blood, his foot slipped.

He managed to block the blow using both hands on his great sword as if it were a staff, but the impact bounced him against the stone wall of the tower. Unlike the guard, Hadrian didn't have a helmet. Still, he managed to anticipate the second blade. He tried to block, but not well enough, and he cried out as he fell alongside Royce.

The guard raised his weapon above both and it was a coin toss to determine which would die first.

Only Hadrian wasn't done.

The guard was now standing in Royce's blood too. With a scream that Royce thought was as much out of pain as determination, Hadrian drove the point of his long sword directly at the center of the guard's breastplate. Royce saw it as a feeble act of desperation, until he realized Hadrian wasn't trying to penetrate the armor. He shoved the golden soldier backward toward the edge of the parapet, aiming for an open crenel. When the back of the guard's knees hit the stone, he staggered. Blood-soaked feet offered no traction and without a sound the giant, gold-clad warrior vanished over the edge.

A moment later Hadrian collapsed beside Royce and the

two lay staring up at the black sky. The clouds had completed their process of covering the stars.

"Can you climb?" Royce asked.

"I think so," Hadrian replied.

"Then get going."

"Aren't you coming?"

"I'll be staying." Maybe it wasn't the clouds. Everything was blacker than usual. The edges of his vision were lost in an inky mist that was growing. "I'm either dying or about to pass out. One of us ought to survive this."

His heart hammered, thumping way too fast for a man lying on his back. Beside him, over the ringing in his ears, he heard Hadrian get to his feet.

"Why'd you do it?" Royce asked.

"What?"

"Come back. You were safe. You were at the rope. Why'd you come back?"

"Same reason I'm not leaving you here."

Royce heard the scrape of metal on stone as Hadrian gathered up his sword. A moment later he felt himself being moved. A sharp pain ripped through his center; then the black flooded in.

ॐ

When Royce opened his eyes, nothing made sense. He was upright, his face pressed against Hadrian's back, and the two were flying in the air. They slowed, and Royce felt the dig of the harness. Letting his head drop, Royce saw they were still halfway up the tower. The street below was a gray line no wider than a bit of string.

"What are you doing?" Royce asked.

"Welcome back."

"You're an idiot."

"I liked you better when you were unconscious." Hadrian let out another length and the two plummeted.

When they slowed again, Royce felt the pain rip through him, once more making his head fuzzy. There was a tight pressure around his waist squeezing him and making it hard to breathe. "I just want to make sure you understand how utterly stupid you are. You'll never get away dragging me with you."

"You know, I never really appreciated your silence before, but it really is one of your virtues."

They hung still as Hadrian prepared to jump a pin. "Don't move."

Royce would have laughed if he wasn't so concerned his insides would fall out. He couldn't see anything, but he could make guesses based on the sounds.

Hadrian grunted, shifted his body, grunted again. He made a fast jerk that bounced Royce's head; his cheek slapped the leather of the big sword's scabbard.

"You were right about the swords," Royce said. "You really do need three."

"You sound drunk."

"I feel drunk—and I hate being drunk. Nothing works the way it's supposed to. And it makes me act stupid...like you."

"You're aware I'm in the process of trying to save your life, right?"

"What part of *stupid* don't you understand?"

Hadrian moved again and Royce felt the harness tighten, and once more they dropped, swung out, slowed, pushed off, and dropped again.

"Those other two swords snapped like chicken bones," Royce said.

"Yeah, I don't know how that happened."

"This big one didn't."

"No."

"So why not make all the swords like that?"

"I didn't make that one."

"So in addition to being stupid, you're also a crappy smith?"

"I could drop you."

"But you are a damn fine swordsman. Arcadius was right about that—the bastard. I really hate that old man."

Another changeup, another couple drops, and they touched down. They could hear shouts, but they were on the far side of the tower. Royce looked but didn't see any sign of the golden guard's body. Hadrian must have pushed him off farther away than he remembered.

"Dear Maribor, you're heavy," Hadrian growled as he untied the rope.

"No, I'm not. You're wounded." Royce moved his hand and felt the blood-soaked clothes. "God, we're bleeding like a slit throat."

"You're bleeding more than me," Hadrian said.

"Oh, does that make you feel better?"

"Actually it does."

Free of the line but with Royce still strapped to his back, Hadrian began staggering up the street. They could hear the slamming of doors and more shouts but had yet to see anyone.

"Now what?" Royce asked.

"Why ask me? I'm the idiot, remember? You're the genius. What should we do? Go back to the horses, right?"

"We'll never make it."

"But you said it was an easy walk."

"That was when I could walk and when we weren't leaving a trail of blood. We really don't stand a chance."

"So far I'm not impressed with your genius."

"I'll admit, I think better when I'm not bleeding to death."

Hadrian ducked into a narrow gap between two stone

houses. Somewhere a horn sounded, impossible to tell where as the alarm bounced between the buildings.

"What about the river? I saw it from the tower. It's just over here, isn't it?" Hadrian moved deeper into the densely packed section of shops and homes. Staying to the alley, they reached the low wall that ran along a curving cobblestone street. Twenty feet below was the river. "We could jump."

"Are you crazy?" Royce said.

"We can float, right? No blood trail, and it will carry us out of town."

"I'll drown."

"Can't you swim?"

"Normally yes, but normally I can walk too. I'm just not confident I can do it *and* hold my guts in at the same time. And it's a drop. When I hit the water, I'll pass out."

"You're staying strapped on my back. I'll keep your head above the surface."

"Then we'll both drown."

"Maybe."

Hadrian peered over the edge as more horns sounded and then a bell began ringing.

"Okay," Royce said.

"Okay what?"

"Okay let's jump in the river."

"You sure?"

"Yeah. As long as we go in together—that way I'll know that if I die, you will too."

He heard Hadrian laugh. "Deal."

Hadrian took a step. As he did, Royce gained a clear view of the alley and saw the remains of a broken crate. "Wait."

"What?"

"Grab that wooden box in the alley."

Hadrian turned. "How did you see that?"

More bells chimed, and the horns continued to blare until it sounded like midnight on Wintertide. Then at last with box in hand, Hadrian climbed up on the wall. Royce felt the unsteady lurch as Hadrian pushed himself up and almost stumbled.

"Hold your nose," Hadrian told him, "and try not to scream. This is going to hurt."

"Probably only for a second." Royce chuckled. He'd given up caring and discovered all that was left was the absurd.

"Always the optimist, aren't you?"

"Jump already!"

"Okay, set?"

"Yes."

"One...two..."

"Before I die, please."

Hadrian grunted. Royce felt the lunge and the fall. Rushing air blew back his hair, then...nothing.

CHAPTER 18

ROSE

Rose stood behind Gwen, watching as she blocked the front door and shook her head, denying the customer entrance to Medford House. She did this while glaring at him, which required her to tilt her head back, as the man before her was huge. He was so tall he would have had to duck his head to enter, if she had let him.

"But I've got good coin!" the man bellowed at her, bending over so that their noses almost touched. Rose had never seen a bear, but that's how she saw him—a giant monstrous bear who was trying to barge his way into their home. She imagined this was how one would act, roaring into the face of a fox that for some inexplicable reason stubbornly stood its ground.

"I don't care if you've got the Crown Tower jewels in your purse," Gwen replied. "There are rules."

"I don't give a rabid rat's ass for your rules! I came here for a whore. I have money for one. I'm having one."

"Not unless I say so, and I won't allow it until you abide by the rules."

"I won't take no bath!" The bear puffed the words into her face so hard the air moved Gwen's hair.

Gwen's arms came up and folded in front of her. "Then you *won't take no lady.*"

"I don't want a *lady.* I want a whore, and you don't need to bathe to get a whore."

The bear's real name was Hopper, and he was indeed filthy, dressed as Rose had always seen him, in a wool shirt with dark yellow stains under the arms. He had two visible leaves caught in the combined overgrown hedge that was his hair and beard. It was possible he had no idea his head was gathering material fit for a squirrel's nest; it was also possible he knew and thought it made him more attractive in a rustic, manly sense.

"In this house you'll refer to the women as *ladies,* and you will present yourself clean and polite, or you can take your money across the street."

This confused Hopper the bear. Rose saw it on his face, but he soon worked it out and scowled. "Grue ain't got no whores. They're all here now."

"I meant go to Grue's place and drink."

"I don't wanna drink. I need a woman."

"Then go to another place."

"Other ones ain't worth paying for."

"What's wrong with them?"

"They don't smell so good." The bear wasn't one to talk. He had a scent that made Rose think he had firsthand experience with the sewers.

Rose didn't know Hopper personally. He'd visited The Hideous Head enough times that she knew his face, but they never spent any private time together. He was a regular of Jollin's, who had often remarked about his smell. To her, Hopper wasn't a bear so much as a skunk. A lot of the men they entertained fit that description, which was why Gwen had made a new rule.

"And you'd prefer a clean, sweet-smelling girl, is that right?"

"Yeah, that's right."

"Because licking dirt and week-old sweat is disgusting, right?"

"Exactly."

"The ladies here all agree with you, and that's why you'll wash before you visit us."

"It don't matter what they like. I'm the one paying. I call the tune."

"Not anymore. Now you can either go across the street and drink that coin away, or head to the barber and get cleaned up and come back. And if you do, I'll warn you to be polite and respectful."

"Respectful of a whore?"

"Respectful of a *lady of the house*, or you can go roll around in the muck with a whore."

He stood there breathing heavily, his lower lip pushed out. He let out puffs of air and looked down at the floor. "I won't have enough money if I pay to get cleaned up."

Gwen unfolded her arms. She reached out and touched the bear's hand. "Get clean. Get shaved. Rinse out those clothes and come back. We'll work out something. I don't just insist our customers are clean. I also require them to be happy too."

Hopper faced her and his stony mouth softened. "Really?"

"Absolutely."

He pulled his tunic at the shoulder and sniffed. "Maybe it could use a dunk or two." He nodded and left. As soon as he was gone, Gwen walked to one of the new soft chairs and collapsed into it.

"You're turning them away now." Rose crept up and sat on the bench beside her. It was one of the last bits of the old furniture, a simple plank that Dixon had built into a seat from the wreckage of the inn. Rose wasn't sure why it was still there among all the beautiful pieces that Gwen had handpicked from the craftsmen in Artisan Row, but it was one of the few relics, one of the few reminders of how it started, and Rose felt most comfortable on it.

"We can afford to," Gwen replied. "But he'll be back. You know…we should invest in a few more washtubs. We can bathe them right here—even charge them for the privilege."

"That's a great idea. You never cease to amaze me."

Rose smiled at her, and Gwen smiled back. They were all grins lately. At first Gwen had encouraged the practice, saying it was good for business; she didn't need to remind them any longer. And they all looked so pretty in their new dresses. Gwen snagged the material from the same place she got the curtains, getting a deal on both. They all looked so fine and respectable that Gwen took to calling them ladies—the Ladies of the House. She liked the sound so much she insisted everyone do so. "You won't get respect unless you act like you deserve it," Gwen had told them. She knew what she was talking about. Gwen had gained the respect of every craftsman on Artisan Row. Putting food on the tables of the carpenters, tar men, glass blowers, and masons, Gwen also treated them as kings when they visited. Men who had scoffed when she entered their shops were coming to her for advice. No one was inviting her over for supper or suggesting she run for ward administrator, but they smiled when she passed by and often opened doors for her. No longer a foreigner, she had become one of Medford's own. At last, she belonged.

Gwen had a million ideas. She held dances twice a week. Fiddle, Pipe, and Drum Nights they were called. It was free to dance, and no business was conducted until afterward. For a few hours they were gentlewomen at a ball, and besides it drew a nice crowd. Of course, they weren't really ladies. Ladies were nobles, and ladies didn't wear their old rags as slips under their dresses.

As the weather turned colder, Gwen invited the destitute in for free turnip-and-onion soup, but it wasn't a case of charity. "Everyone has a talent for something," she told each one, and she was right. Most of the poor used to do something: tin smith, rug hooker, farmer, chimney sweep. She put everyone she could to work, and those who were too old or sick were put to teaching others what they knew. Gwen put the farmers to work tilling a patch of dirt behind the House. Come next year it would help supplement their pantry. One old man used to sell honey and promised he would provide them with a beehive.

She wasn't like the rest of them. To some degree or other, they had all given up at one time, casting away their dreams and giving in to the demands of the world. Rose saw the differences in the way Gwen acted, even in the way she walked, and most notably by the way she spoke to men. While she called all of them ladies, Rose knew the only real lady in Medford House was Gwen DeLancy.

They heard steps on the porch, and then the front door opened. A cold gust of chilling wind flickered the lamps, and into the parlor walked Stane. Splashed with mud and reeking of fish, his oily hair stuck to his forehead, his face bristling with whiskers.

Gwen was out of her chair in a blink. "What do *you* want?"

"What do you think? This is a whorehouse, ain't it?"

Gwen was shaking her head before he finished. "Not for you."

"What'd you mean, not for me?"

"You're not allowed here—*ever*."

"You can't do that," he said, taking a step onto the new carpet with his muddy boots. "You stole all the good whores and locked them up here. You can't deprive a man entirely."

"Watch me."

He took another step and a sick little smile came to his thin, uneven lips. "I know Dixon isn't here. He left town two days ago and ain't back yet. It's just you and me now. You don't even have Grue looking out for you." He took another step. "You know, Grue would probably pay good money for someone to put this place to the torch." He looked around. "Be a pity to see it all burn away. Surprised he hasn't done it yet."

"Grue isn't as stupid as you are. I obtained the Certificate of Royal Permit on this place by partnering with the city assessor. Just like you, he knows how much Grue would like to see us fail. Any suspicious fire or deaths and who do you think the city assessor will blame? And burning any building in Medford is a crime against the king, because he owns this building—we only lease it. And if you hurt any of us—"

"I ain't gonna hurt nobody, just here for a good time."

"Go someplace else."

His eyes lighted on Rose. "I'll take this one."

Rose let out a stifled squeal and retreated three steps toward the stairs.

"Get out, Stane," Gwen ordered.

"Or maybe I'll just have you." He took another step.

Gwen didn't move, didn't blink. She stood toe-to-toe, staring back into his eyes, and as she did, her face grimaced. "Oh, dear Maribor," she muttered, and brought a hand to her mouth. On her face was a look of revulsion. "Oh, blessed Lord."

The sudden change surprised Stane, who looked confused. "What?" He glanced at Rose, then back at Gwen. "What kind of game are you playing?"

"Oh, Stane, I'm so sorry," Gwen told him, her expression turning to sympathy.

Rose was stunned. At first she wondered if Gwen was pretending, playacting, trying to trick him, only Gwen wasn't acting. There was a look of horror on her face like nothing Rose had ever seen.

Stane's expression changed too. Menace surrendered to concern. "For what?"

"For what's going to happen."

"What the blazes you talking about?" Stane took a step back. He turned, looking around the parlor, searching for the threat.

"He's going to kill you." Gwen's voice was eerie, gentle and shaken. She wasn't making this up. Her hands were quivering as they started to reach out weakly toward him.

"Who is?"

"It will be slow...painfully slow. He's going...he's going to cut you apart and leave you to bleed. Hang you up in Merchant Square and decorate you in candles."

"Who is? What are you talking about? Dixon ain't got the—"

"Not Dixon." She said this with weight, with power, with a sense of foreboding. "You won't know him. You'll keep asking why—he won't answer. He'll never say a word. He'll just keep cutting, and cutting, and cutting...while you scream."

"Shut up!"

"It will be late at night," she went on, taking a step forward. Her hands still out before her, shaking.

"Shut up!" Stane moved back off the carpet as if she held vipers before her.

"No one helps you, and the blood...the blood is everywhere. The blood is horrible. Can there be that much blood in a person?" Gwen paused, looking at the floor and shaking her head in genuine dismay. Her hands came up to shelter her ears. "You keep screaming as he hoists you up and lights the candles."

"I said shut your mouth!"

"After he leaves, as you die, people come out. They look up, but no one helps. They know what you are—they've always known, even though they never knew all the things you did. One person knows about Avon, but none of them know about Ruth,

Irene, and Elsie. And no one ever found out about Callahan's wife."

"How do you know about them?" Stane looked terrified.

"And Oldham's daughters—both of them. You're an awful, awful man, Stane."

Rose had never seen anyone's face filled with as much fear as Stane's—his eyes wide and darting.

"They watch you die," Gwen continued, though even Rose wished she would stop. "One man actually puts a bucket beneath your feet to catch the blood. He's going to mix it with feed and give it to his pigs. Oh, Stane, what you did to Avon, what you did to all of them was so terrible, and you should die for that, but even I wouldn't wish this on you... but, I suppose... you do deserve it."

No matter what effect Gwen's words had on Stane, they sent a chill deeper into Rose's bones than any wind ever could, but it was the look on Gwen's face, the genuine sympathy and revulsion that stopped her heart. Somehow Gwen could actually see Stane's death. And through her, he and Rose saw it too.

"You're a crazy bitch—that's what you are!" Stane shouted at her. "And you can just leave me alone." He retreated out the door, slamming it behind him.

Gwen wavered and reached out to steady herself.

"Are you all right?" Rose asked, racing to Gwen's side.

She grabbed Rose, squeezed tight, and cried.

✥

"Here," Rose said, holding out the steaming cup of tea.

"A porcelain cup and saucer?" Gwen looked at her, stunned.

"We were planning on giving it to you for Wintertide, but you look like you could use it now, and by then we'll be able to get you something better."

"Better than a porcelain cup?"

"You'll just have to wait and see."

The two were on the porch, which smelled of fresh paint and sawdust. They sat curled up on the wooden bench, their feet tucked, wrapped in a blanket that Rose had pulled off her bed. It was one of the original blankets they had wrapped in that first night they had spent in the dark parlor, sharing a loaf of bread and a brick of cheese.

That night seemed very long ago. So much had changed that it felt like another lifetime. The era they spent in servitude to Grue happened to a different set of women. It couldn't have been them. It certainly could never have been Gwen. Resting against her on the porch of their house, after having seen her drive off Stane as if he were an opossum routing in their garbage, Rose couldn't imagine Gwen ever having obeyed Raynor.

The night was cold and soon it began to rain. She first noticed it pattering on the roofs along Wayward Street; then the drops grew bigger, falling faster, and finally the patter became a constant hum. The porch was covered and the run-off from the roof made Rose feel like she was on the inside of a waterfall.

"How are you feeling?"

Gwen tilted her head against Rose. "Much better thanks to you. This tea is wonderful."

"Gwen..." She faltered. "What just happened? What did you do to Stane? Was that..."

Gwen set the cup and saucer down on the arm of the bench and pulled the blanket tighter. She had a stern, almost angry look on her face. "I'm not a witch, Rose."

"Of course not. I wasn't thinking that." Rose turned to face her, careful not to disturb the fragile cup.

"What *are* you thinking?" Gwen refused to look, staring instead at the rain, and though Gwen was enveloped in the blanket, Rose could tell her arms were folded.

"I don't know—that's why I'm asking."

Gwen huffed. "I just looked in his eyes, okay? I looked and I saw...I saw his death. It's hard to explain."

"Is it magic?" Rose asked in a soft voice. She knew magic was supposed to be evil. Her mother had said so. But if Gwen could do magic, then it couldn't be evil because as far as Rose was concerned, Gwen was perfection, and Rose's mother had been dimmer than a starless night.

"No," Gwen said quickly, still staring at the rain. "It's a gift." She finally turned to face Rose again. "That's what my mother always said. She called it *the Sight*. Some women, mostly Tenkins from the deep forests who are blessed with the Sight, can look at a person and actually see their future. Palms are the safest, but the eyes...the eyes can be an open window to the soul. Peering too deeply, you just topple in and become lost. You see, hear, and feel everything." Gwen took a breath. "My mother had the Sight and so do I."

There was a moment of silence that hung in the air.

"What are you thinking now?" Gwen asked. "Are you scared of me?"

Rose reached out and took Gwen's hand. "No. I've just never seen anything like that before."

"What I did with Stane...I didn't mean for it to happen. It doesn't usually. Almost never really."

"It was good that it did," Rose pointed out. "I doubt Stane will be back. Thank you, and not just for scaring Stane. What you did for me, for all of us really, is...well, you've given us a chance that we could never have had without you. You saved us all. You're my hero."

"We saved each other," Gwen insisted.

"I don't think so."

"Sure we did. We're like a family, and families take care of each other, support one another and—"

"Like a family?" Rose almost laughed, but it really wasn't that funny—not funny at all when she thought about it. "That's not how families work—trust me."

"What do you mean?"

"I'm just saying that's not how families work."

"That's how it was with me and my mother," Gwen said.

Rose shifted, turning away. She didn't like disagreeing with Gwen.

"How was it with you?"

"It's not important," Rose replied. "It feels like centuries ago. I was... Well, that's too long ago to remember."

"I know the others' stories," Gwen said gently. "I know Jollin's and Mae's and Etta's. You never told me yours."

"There's nothing to tell."

"Was it awful?"

Rose thought a moment, then shook her head. That was the worst part; it wasn't terrible. She hadn't been beaten or locked in a closet. Her family hadn't sold her into slavery, and they weren't murdered by highwaymen. Nothing so vile as that had driven her into the gutter. "No," she said at last. "Just sad."

"Tell me."

Rose felt awkward now. Foolish that the conversation had taken the turn it had. She shrugged as if doing so would assure Gwen that what she was about to say meant little to her. "My parents worked a bit of land just outside Cold Hollow—that's a couple miles east, between the King's Road and Westfield. Lots of rocks and briers but little else. I guess my father tried, but maybe he didn't know what he was doing, or maybe the land was bad—it looked bad. Maybe the seeds were no good or the weather too cold. My mother made excuses for him. Never knew why, as the only thing I know he ever gave her was blame. Then one day he was gone. He just left and never came back. My mother said it was because we were all starving and he couldn't take seeing us die. I guess she saw it as his way of saying he loved us. I saw it as just one more excuse—the last one at least."

Rose felt Gwen's hand rubbing her arm under the blanket, those dark, almond-shaped eyes looking so soft and kind. Gwen was being so sympathetic. She expected a horrible tale, and Rose felt bad she had nothing awful to give—nothing but the harvest stupidity brings.

"We had nothing after that," she went on. "My father, who loved us so much, took the mule and the last of the copper. We survived on roots and nuts that winter. My mother liked to joke that we lived like squirrels, but by then I had forgotten how to laugh. She wouldn't beg and refused to ask for help. She would say things like, 'He'll be back. You'll see. Your father will find work and come back to us with bags of flour, pigs, chickens, and maybe even a goat for milk—you'd like that, wouldn't you?' I was chewing bark for my dinner when she said this.

Gwen squeezed her hand, and Rose felt even more embarrassed that she was showing her so much concern. Rose also didn't know why she had started to cry. She didn't like crying in front of Gwen. She wanted to be just as strong, and crying over something so small and foolish was just weakness, and she hated weakness.

"My mother loved me," Rose explained. "She was stupid, but she loved me. She gave me what food we found and lied about having eaten. The following winter when we couldn't find any more nuts or roots, we ate pine needles.

"My mother died from a fever. By then she was not much more than a skeleton." Speaking about it brought back her face, the sunken cheeks, lips drawn back showing her gums. "It wasn't the fever that killed her. It wasn't starvation either. My mother died of pride—stupid, foolish, asinine pride. She actually died of it. Too proud to ask anyone for help. Too proud to admit her husband was a lousy, miserable bastard. Too proud to eat her share of the…"

She lost her voice. It stalled in her throat, which had closed without warning, as if the taste of what was coming up was far too bitter to suffer on her tongue. She took a breath that shuddered its way in and wiped the stripes of tears flowing down her cheeks with the heels of her hands. "She was too proud to eat her share of what little food we had. She told me she had. She swore she did. But every time I complained about being so hungry it hurt, she always offered me a nut or a partially rotted turnip, claiming she had just found two and already ate hers."

Rose sniffled and wiped her eyes again.

"After she was gone, I left my pride in that little hut and begged my way to Medford. I'd do anything. Once you've spent an afternoon chasing a fly around your house for dinner, once you've eaten spiders whole and drooled over worms found while burying your mother with your bare hands, there's nothing beneath you. All I wanted was to live—I'd forgotten everything else. A clod of dirt doesn't have dreams. A bit of broken stone doesn't understand hope. Each morning, all I wanted was to see the next dawn. But you changed that."

Gwen struggled to sip her tea, as she, too, had wet streaks on her cheeks.

"You aren't like my mother," Rose told her. "And you aren't like me. You stand up for yourself and for others. You make the world be the way you need it to. I can't do that. Jollin can't. No one can—no one but you."

"I'm nothing special, Rose."

"You are. You're a hero and you can see the future." They sat for a time listening to the rain drum overhead. The shower had turned into a full-on pour and the runoff a curtain of water. Somewhere a metal pail was making a muffled set of pings, and the road was filling with water as puddles joined together to form rivers and ponds.

"Why don't we talk about Dixon instead?" Rose offered a sly smile.

Gwen peered at her over the beautiful new cup with a suspicious squint. "What about him?"

"Rumor has it he proposed."

Gwen looked shocked. "He did not."

"Etta says Dixon offered to make 'a proper woman out of you.'"

"Oh...that."

"So he did!"

Gwen shrugged.

"What did you say?"

"I told him we would be good friends, always. He's a very good man, but..."

"But what?"

"He's not...*him*."

"Him? Who's him?"

Gwen looked embarrassed and shuffled her feet under the blanket. "I don't know."

"You don't?"

She shook her head, then covered her face with the blanket. "Maybe he doesn't even exist. Maybe he's something I've invented, pieced together over the years. Maybe I'm just trying to convince myself he's real and isn't just my hope of what is possible."

"You're turning away a good-living, hardworking, breathing man for the *idea* of an imaginary one?"

She peeked out from the folds. "Foolish, huh? Some hero."

"Well...it's very romantic, I guess, but..."

"You can say it—*stupid*. That's what I'm being."

"What if this white knight doesn't ever show up?"

"He's not a knight. I'm not sure what or who he is, but he's *definitely* not a knight. And if he's not just a figment of my imagination, then he's coming."

"How do you know?"

"Because I sent Dixon to bring him."

"What? How did you—"

"I read Dixon's palm and saw that he would be the one to bring him here."

"Wait. I thought this man, this not-a-knight, was just a dream, a fantasy of yours."

"He might still be." Gwen paused and looked as if she might stop there, but Rose was not about to let her quit now, not after being forced to vomit up her whole life story.

"Explain, please."

Gwen frowned. "On her deathbed, my mother made me promise to come here...to Medford. And I received those gold coins from someone telling me the same thing. That's why I was given the money. To help...*him*."

"To help who?"

"*Him.*"

Rose shook her head, frustrated. "Make sense, will you?"

"I can't, because it doesn't. I don't know why I was supposed to come to Medford. I don't know who this man is—or anything about him. I just know that I have to be here when he arrives. I have to help him and..."

"And what?"

Gwen tilted her head down, hiding her eyes.

"What?"

"I don't know. I've just been waiting so long, thinking about him, you know? Wondering what he might be like. Who he really is, what he looks like. Why I have to be the one."

"Are you saying you've fallen for a man you've never met?"

"Maybe."

"But that's okay because you're supposed to, right? The two of you are meant for each other, yes?"

She shrugged. "No one said anything about that. It's just what I want to believe. He could be married for all I know."

"Did they at least give you a name?"

She shook her head with an awkward smile. "I'm ruining my reputation with you, aren't I?"

"Are you kidding? You can do magic and have a mysterious destiny. I want to be you."

Gwen smiled self-consciously. "Everyone has a destiny."

Rose looked at her hand, then thrust it out. "What's mine?"

Gwen stared a moment. "You're not afraid? Even after seeing what happened with Stane?"

"I said I wasn't afraid of you, didn't I? And this proves it. Go ahead, look into my future. Maybe I have a mysterious stranger coming my way too. Only don't tell me about my death. I think I'd rather not know, okay?"

Gwen sighed. "All right, let's take a look."

Rose watched as Gwen opened her fingers and spread out the skin of her palm.

"This is interesting. You are going to fall in love. He's handsome, too, a kind face. You're going to fall in love and—" The tight grip she held on Rose's hand relaxed and while she continued to stare at her palm, Rose could tell she wasn't focusing on it. Her sight shifted to the decking of the porch.

"With who? Who will I fall in love with? Do you know his name?"

Gwen let go of her hand and reached for her tea. She lost control of the saucer and the beautiful porcelain cup slipped, fell, and shattered.

Gwen gasped as she stared at the broken shards of pure

white scattered on the porch. "I'm so sorry." When she looked up at Rose, there were tears in her eyes. "I'm so very sorry."

"It's okay," Rose offered. "We can get another one."

Gwen hugged her. Not like before, not like when Stane left. This time she squeezed as if Rose was all that kept her from being sucked away in the storm. She continued to cry, repeating, "I'm so sorry."

Chapter 19

Flight

Dawn rose gray over Lake Morgan. Only the lap of water and the honk of geese broke the stillness that, with the rising sun, had replaced the roar of rain. Drifting in the river, the showers made it hard for Royce to see. The splashing surface threw water, making him blink. Most of the time he left his eyes closed. At least he didn't need to worry about being soaked. They couldn't get any wetter. He and Hadrian had drifted the remainder of the night, clinging to the box like rats as behind them the peal of bells faded. Both had fallen asleep or passed out—it was hard to tell which. The river had ushered them along at a fine pace, but with the morning light they and their box bobbed in still water amidst a silent world of mist.

"You alive?" Hadrian asked.

"If I were dead, I don't think there'd be geese." Royce tilted his head up to catch the arrow of birds heading south. "But maybe they're evil geese."

"Evil geese?"

"We have no idea what goes on in the water fowl world. They might have been a gang that stole eggs or something."

"I'm guessing you have a fever." Hadrian looked around, and when he spoke he sounded both surprised and happy.

"This is Lake Morgan. That tavern we were in is along this bank somewhere."

"It's right there." Royce pointed to the cluster of buildings to their left. The slight movement jolted him with pain.

"All I see is a hazy clump," Hadrian said, squinting.

"Remind me when we get back and I'll see if Arcadius will lend you his spectacles. And we can't go to the tavern, if that's what you're thinking."

"Dougan will help us."

"Did you hear the bells last night? The roads will be filled with soldiers, and they'll be swarming that tavern."

"We could go to Lord Marbury's home. He invited me last time. He'd help us. He hates the church."

"Where's Marbury's home?"

"I don't know... but Dougan would."

"We can't go to the tavern."

"Only for a minute. We just need to ask. Besides, no one will be there at this hour."

"You're being stupid again."

"Like I was when I came back for you? Like when I hauled you down the rope, and when I insisted we jump in the river?"

"Yeah, like that."

"We need to get dry. I need to wrap your wounds better."

"Is that your belt squeezing the life out of me?"

"You wouldn't have lived the night without it."

"I can barely breathe."

"Better than bleeding to death."

Hadrian's shoulders were covered only by his wool shirt.

"Your cloak?"

"Part of it," Hadrian replied. "Hey, if we're going to survive, we need food, dry clothes, and proper bandaging. So we're going to the tavern, unless you know someplace else we can get those things?"

"Normally I'd steal them, but normally I can walk."

"You keep saying that."

"I like being able to walk."

"Okay, just hang on." Hadrian began to swim, jerking the box, dragging Royce. Each pull sent bolts of pain through Royce's stomach. He was thankful for the buoyancy. He let himself hang limp and felt his legs drag and sway as Hadrian splashed and panted.

The village looked dead. The only sounds came from a barnyard where sheep bleated and a goat's bell clanked with a lonely sound. Hadrian crawled out of the lake along a rocky beach across the street from the tavern. It was daylight, they were in the open, across the way from the village common, and they were conspicuous. Anyone looking from a window, alley, or distant hill would notice them.

"I don't think I can carry you," Hadrian said. "So I hope you can walk with some help." He unhooked the harness that had tied them together and slowly lifted Royce to his feet. The water had been cold, but as soon as he was out of it, the air hit him with a gut-wrenching blast that cut like ice. He shivered, sending dizzying stabs of pain through his body. His head grew hazy again. The darkness crept in, but he managed to hang on to both Hadrian and consciousness. He had little strength in his legs. They refused to work properly so that his toes often dragged. Almost all his weight was on Hadrian, who favored his own left leg as together they scraped across the gravel road toward the door of the pub.

Hadrian pushed on it. "Damn it. Locked."

"Push me up against the door, and I'll fix that."

"No, we're not breaking in. We're looking for help." Hadrian pounded on the wood, his fist making a soft muffled sound. They waited with Hadrian propping Royce against the doorframe. He pounded again. Behind them came the lonesome call of a loon. Hadrian turned to look out at the lake. "I hear they have good fishing."

Royce lifted his head to look at him. "You're a very odd man."

"You were the one talking about *evil geese*."

The door opened to reveal a sleepy-looking Dougan, who peered out with squinting eyes.

"Dougan," Hadrian said, "we need help."

The bartender took a quick look over their shoulders, then waved them in and closed the door.

"We just need some bandages, a needle and thread, some food, and maybe some dry clothes," Hadrian said. "I'll pay for everything."

Hadrian pulled Royce over to the biggest table in the main room, a nice long maple with four sturdy legs, and laid him on it. While much warmer in the tavern than on the beach, Royce couldn't stop shivering, and his head was clouding up.

Dougan, who was dressed only in a long wool shirt, wiped his eyes and yawned. "What did you two do this time?"

"Robbed the treasure from the Crown Tower," Royce said, and caught a stunned look from Hadrian. "But it's okay—we put everything back."

Dougan smiled. "Ha! I don't remember you being so funny."

"Oh yeah," Hadrian said, "he's a hoot once you get to know him."

Royce felt his cloak being pulled free of his arms. Then he was alone. He could hear Hadrian speaking to Dougan in another room. They were looking for cloth and a sewing needle. Water was dripping nearby as if the roof had a leak; then Royce realized he was the source. He lay like a sponge soaking the table with water...or was that blood?

The room was beginning to spin as Hadrian returned. "Okay, ah...we're going to take a look now. This might hurt."

Royce felt Hadrian jerk on the belt wrapped hard around his waist. It was like being stabbed again and for a moment Royce forgot where he was. He thought he might still be in the lake. It felt like he was drowning; then everything grew dark.

⌇

Pain.

He'd been out again. He didn't know how long. He didn't care. Royce knew he was awake because of the harsh ache that whirled around his body. He was certain that if he moved, the ache would change to something far worse. Lying still, his eyes closed, he heard nothing, smelled nothing. He could be anywhere, at any time. Back in Manzant, the loft in Colnora, the room in Glen Hall, somewhere on the road, in prison, in a coffin—so long as he didn't open his eyes, no single possibility was any more likely than any other. He lingered in a state of possibilities until he heard the creak of a nearby chair.

"How you feeling?" Hadrian asked.

Royce wondered how he knew, or had he been asking that same question for hours? His breathing pattern had likely changed. Royce didn't bother to open his eyes. "Like someone tried to kill me by slicing my stomach open, and then someone else tried to finish the job by drowning me in a river. How am I actually?"

"Not as bad as I expected. Not nearly as deep. Just cut through muscle and hit your lower rib, but I don't think it broke."

"Is that all?" he asked sarcastically.

"I'm sure it hurts."

"You think?"

"Loss of blood is the real danger—and shock to the body. I also put some salt on it. Dries things out and stops the wound from oozing and festering."

"You a doctor too?"

"In five years of warfare you treat a lot of wounds. Plenty of trial and error. You should be glad you aren't one of the first I tried to help. You'll feel a lot better now. Twenty-seven stitches."

"I'm so pleased you counted. Couldn't have lived without that."

Royce knew where he was the instant Hadrian spoke, but the whole picture was still forming. Tardy bits and pieces, slower than the rest, were ushered to their places. He remembered the call of the loon and Hadrian speaking about fishing before remembering that they had been in the lake. Recalling the swim, Royce was surprised to discover he was dry and dressed in a linen tunic. There was a blanket over him, several guessing by the weight.

"I have soup," Hadrian said. "You should eat."

Royce opened one eye and found Hadrian was sitting beside him with a steaming tin bowl he held with a towel. "Get that away from me."

"Nauseous?"

"Ready to vomit."

"Yeah, that happens. And you don't want to do that or you'll rip my stitches."

Royce opened both eyes to properly glare. "Oh yeah, that's exactly the reason I'm against it. I don't want to *ruin all your work*."

"Only trying to help."

And doing a lousy job of it! Royce opened his mouth to say it but stopped. It wasn't true. Truth was he'd be dead three times over if Hadrian hadn't risked his life to save him. In some dark corner of his mind he found he was as upset about that as he was about the hole in his side—maybe more so. It didn't make sense and was as disorienting as the pain. *Why'd he do it?* The question had been in his head ever since he saw Hadrian wearing the harness. *Stupid* didn't cut it anymore. No one was that dumb. And Hadrian had the brains to bandage him, get them down the tower, and all the way to Iberton. Hadrian wasn't stupid—crazy maybe, but not stupid. *Had Arcadius put him up to this? Was this planned? Can all this have been—*

No.

Even in his most diabolical, far-stretched, conspiracy-born theoretic imagination, Royce couldn't nail this calamity to the wall of premeditation. They both had almost died. They still might. No one ever gives a damn about plans or loyalties when their life is teetering on the brink, and Royce could still see Hadrian's swords snapping, the blade flying over the parapet. He remembered him slipping on blood and falling, getting a blade to his thigh. This hadn't been an act.

So why, then?

Royce didn't have an answer. They barely knew each other. They didn't like each other. Royce would go so far as to say they hated each other, and yet...it didn't make any sense. The one thing Royce did know, the one thing he was positive of was that he should be dead.

"Thanks."

Hadrian looked up. "What?"

Royce scowled. "You heard me."

"Maybe the struggle to get that word out is what was making you nauseous."

Royce sneered, but wondered if there wasn't some truth to it. He had only ever said *thank you* twice before. This made three. Far from being appreciative, he hated each time. The words were always bitter and came after weakness. "How's your leg?"

Hadrian looked down at the bands of linen peeking through his torn trouser leg. "Not too bad."

They weren't in the bar anymore. Royce was lying on a bed in a small room with simple furniture. "We at that Lord Marbury's place?"

Hadrian shook his head. "Dougan's bedroom. He's been very accommodating."

"We going to Marbury's?"

"Dougan says he was arrested."

"When?"

"Couple days ago."

"Where's Dougan?"

"Went to fetch water."

"Are you sure? How long does it take to walk across the street and back?"

"The well is in the village."

"Well?"

"That's what he said," Hadrian replied.

"We need to leave—now."

"Now?" Hadrian looked stunned. "Can you walk?"

"Push me up, and we'll find out."

Hadrian scowled and helped him to his feet.

The pain was sharp but tolerable—so much better than… was it the day before? Royce pushed off the bed as if he were a boat launching itself and stood hovering vertical. "See, I'm better," he said through gritted teeth. "Let's go."

"What's the hurry?"

"Dougan's betraying us. Probably sending word to the nearest patrol, or maybe he's standing on the highway trying to flag one down."

"How do you know?"

"Who do you think got Lord Marbury arrested?"

"Why Dougan?"

"See anyone else here you remember? They covered for you, and now all of them—except Dougan—are gone."

"That doesn't prove anything. Dougan lives here. The others were customers."

"Uh-huh, and the last time we were here, Dougan told you everyone drew their water from the lake. Just walk out with a bucket and scoop it up, crystal clear he said. This village doesn't even have a well, remember?"

"I'll get our things."

Hadrian left the bedroom, and Royce could hear him shuffling about the bar. Gingerly Royce followed, testing himself. He walked slowly using his hands, going from bedpost to doorframe to support post to corridor wall. Hadrian appeared with a bundle under his arm and his sword on his back. Giving an arm for support, they limped outside.

The sun was high, and in the distance Royce could hear villagers: the bang of doors, laughter, and the squeak of a wheel. Mostly he listened to the pounding of his heart in his head. His body wasn't pleased. It had liked the idea of lying down on a soft mattress under layers of blankets and didn't mind shouting that it wasn't up to any more.

Progress was incredibly slow. They shuffled instead of walked as Hadrian drew him along like an anchor. They moved up the road but swung around the south side of the lake before reaching the highway. Houses clustered around the water's edge. The only way to get free of people was to head southwest, uphill, into the heather.

They walked for what Royce guessed to be hours, a slow but steady pace into the hills of bristling grass and thorny bushes. Eventually Royce did vomit. He fell on his hands and knees and retched for several minutes, groaning in agony.

"What do you say we camp here?" Hadrian asked.

Royce was still on his hands and knees, staring at the grass and spitting. "Sounds good." He crawled a few feet away and then collapsed onto his back, staring up at the darkening sky.

Hadrian dropped to the grass beside him and the two lay shoulder to shoulder, panting for air, moaning in pain.

Royce wiped his mouth with his sleeve. "Where's that pitch-coated canvas you were going to make for me?"

"I forgot."

"Can't count on you for anything."

"Nope. I'll abandon you at the first sign of trouble."

Royce turned his head to face him and waited until Hadrian looked back. "You know I would have," he confessed. "I would have left you to die. Tried to, in fact."

"I know."

Royce stared dumbfounded. "And still you came back?"

"Yep."

"Why?"

"I'm stupid, remember?"

Royce rolled to his side, spit, and lay back down. "No, really—why?"

Hadrian looked up at the sky. "You're my partner."

Royce laughed and then cried out, "Don't do that—it hurts!" He carefully sucked in air, taking several minutes to get his wind back. "Are you . . . you're serious?"

Hadrian didn't reply, and the two lay beneath the night sky just breathing as the first stars appeared overhead.

Merrick had tried to teach the constellations to Royce long ago. He only remembered the Great King, a series of stars in the north that were supposed to resemble a man on a throne, wearing a crown. People also called it Novron after the first emperor, claiming that having been part god, he had ascended into the heavens. Royce spotted the first of the familiar crown stars winking out of the twilight.

Merrick had taught him almost everything he knew—reading, writing, numbers, the stars—but if he'd been on that tower with him, Merrick would have let him die.

"You realize the moment you dropped that book, we stopped being partners," Royce said.

"Oh yeah—you're right. Huh. I should have left you for dead after all."

"What's the real reason? Just before we started up, you said that you were going to kill me after the job. You were going to show me how you use that big sword."

"I did. Weren't you watching?"

"Yes, I was, but you were going to use it to kill me."

"Damn it—you're right. I forgot." Hadrian reached up weakly to touch the pommel of his sword. "Can we do that later? I'm pretty comfortable right now." He let his arm slap back on the grass.

"Why'd you come back? Why didn't you just leave?"

"This really bothers you, doesn't it?"

"Yes. Yes, it does."

Hadrian shifted his legs and grunted, then took a breath and let out a long sigh. "I came back because that's who I am." He paused, then added, "You probably can't understand that, can you?"

"It's not a reason."

"Okay, look, try this—I ran away from home, ran away from Avryn, ran away from Calis. And all I ever did was kill. I'm tired of it."

"Killing?"

"Everything—you name it—I'm tired of it. Right now I'm even tired of breathing. Call it frustration if you want. I just got tired of running away. Mostly I'm tired of leaving people to die."

"That kid? Pickles? The one I got killed?"

"You didn't get him killed. Maybe I didn't either, but it just seems whenever I run away, people I leave behind die. So if you're looking for a reason, maybe it's that simple. I was just too tired to run again."

They both lay for a moment, panting against the hillside; then Royce shifted and grunted with the pain. "You realize we can't go back to Sheridan."

"I know."

"Have to keep heading southwest now, and I don't know anything about the area. We'll probably get lost or walk into a road and a patrol."

"Well"—Hadrian looked down at Royce's side—"you're bleeding again, and I think I am, too, so the good news is we'll likely die before morning. Still, I suppose it could be worse."

"How?"

"They could have caught us at the tavern, or we could have drowned in that river."

"Either way we'd be dead. At this point I'm inclined to see that as better off."

"Anything can always be worse," Hadrian assured him.

They lay staring up at the sky and watching clouds blot out the stars. Royce heard it before he felt it. A distant patter on the blades of grass along the hillside. He turned once more to Hadrian. "I'm really starting to hate you."

ॐ

Burrowed into his cloak, Royce woke to the same roar and drumming of rain that he'd fallen asleep to, but the cold and wet had forced him to abandon any further efforts at sleep. With a shiver and grunt, he carefully inched himself up to his elbows and peered out of his hood. A thick curtain of rain muted everything, leaving the world as colorless as a corpse. Water flushed down the hillside, and because he was in a cleft, a rivulet had formed beneath him. His body acting like a dam left Royce sitting in a patch of water.

They were on the slope of a grassy hill scarred with rock and littered with bristling thistle and juniper bushes, everything prickly, a sea of burrs and nettles. Below, like rows of teeth, were stone walls bleached white and overgrown with moss and ivy. The mountains of Trent—if they were there—were lost to the rain. Royce had no idea where they were. He remembered little from their flight the night before and the opaque sky made it impossible to tell direction. He could see roads—nothing familiar, but the thin gray lines slicing through the hills below them were alive with riders. Men in pairs raced with cloaks flapping. There were larger groups, men on foot walking in formal lines. He also heard bells. At first he thought it might be a trick of the rain or his own tortured mind, but the sound came from every direction. It wasn't until he managed to separate out different rates and pitches that he understood. Every village and town for miles was ringing the alarm.

Hadrian had bent himself upright as well. Pale and gray as the day, they both appeared as risen cadavers bewildered and surprised to find themselves still tethered to the world.

"What do we have for food?" Now that his stomach had settled, Royce was famished.

Hadrian looked about the slope. "Some of these look like berry bushes."

"I meant, what did you get from the tavern?"

"I didn't get anything. I never had time to ask Dougan for any."

"Ask?" Royce was in the treacherous process of hoisting himself out of his tiny lake when he paused. "Why didn't you just grab something? I thought that's what you were doing behind the bar."

"I was grabbing our clothes. I had them drying there."

Royce looked down at himself. "Thank Maribor you dried the clothes."

"What did you want me to do, steal from Dougan?"

Royce nodded dramatically.

"I'm not a thief."

"Yes, you are, and you'd better get used to it."

"You have to steal something to be a thief. I put the book back."

"Tell them that when they catch us. I'm sure it will help."

Royce flinched and winced his way to higher ground. Muscles stiff and sore, his abdomen burned, and he suffered bolts of pain when moving. He felt worse than before, not surprising after spending the night soaked in a cold puddle. Shaking with the chill and his waterlogged skin, just lifting his arms was exhausting.

"Do you hear bells?" Hadrian asked.

"Yes."

"Those can't be the ones from Ervanon still."

"They aren't."

"You think it might be a religious holiday?"

"Nope."

"This is bad." Hadrian turned his head left and right, peering out through the rain.

His hair plastered to his head, his face pasty white, he looked beaten. Royce knew that stare; he knew those eyes. He'd seen them every day on the streets where he grew up. They were like the windows along Herald Street after the Sickness.

The fevers came every year to the city of Ratibor where Royce grew up, usually in winter, but once when Royce was young the Sickness invaded the city in midsummer. Unprecedented, they called it an ill omen. Everyone knew that was bad—it turned out to be worse than bad. Herald Street was one of the nice neighborhoods, one of the few in Ratibor. Royce liked to walk there when he was troubled, just to look at the pretty homes. It was how he dreamed, when he couldn't anymore. That summer the houses looked different. It was hot and dry. The windows should all have been open trying to catch any breeze, but they were all shut, the curtains drawn. Pale lace that behind the dirty glass took on a particular color of gray—the washed-out hue of hopelessness, a sort of pallid vacancy that came with having time to dwell on tragedy. Hadrian's eyes looked like the windows of Herald Street. They had the same color, the same closed-off emptiness, the same look of surrender.

"How's your side?" There was hesitancy in Hadrian's voice, a tinge of fear.

"A little better than yesterday," Royce lied. He wasn't sure why. What difference did it make? "So are those berries edible?"

Hadrian hesitated a moment, then turned to the bushes as if it had taken that long for the words to reach him. He stood up, slow like an old man, and Royce heard a sharp intake of breath when he put weight on his left leg. Walking over to the bushes, Hadrian stood there as if he'd forgotten what he was doing.

Royce watched. If it was going to happen, it would happen now.

Having lived through worse, Royce knew it could be done. He had never felt the gods had singled him out for punishment. That would presume he was important enough to be noticed. He was just one more overlooked life that should have ended early. He was just too stubborn to lie still and over the years had grown too mean to give in. But he knew nothing about Hadrian. He was a soldier, but what did that mean? Had he spent his few adult years riding on a fine horse with plenty of food, slaughtering unarmored footmen while he remained safe in a steel suit? Had he ever been alone, abandoned, and facing death?

If he was going to break, this would be the time. Few ever

lost it in the heat of the moment. It was always afterward, once they had time to think. Then the windows were shut and the lace curtains drawn. Royce watched silently. The day before he might have taunted him, tried to push Hadrian over the edge. Instead, he just waited. He felt no sympathy—no one ever had for him. The moment stretched as Hadrian stood in the rain, looking out across the valley, not seeing, just staring.

Then he bent over and plucked a berry.

In a few minutes he returned with a cupped hand. "Blueberries," he said, sitting down beside him. Royce tried one. Tart. He realized that while his stomach was better it wasn't perfect.

"So what's your story?" Hadrian asked.

"My what?"

"Your story—your history."

"I don't have one."

"Do you know who your parents were?"

"No. My earliest memory"—Royce paused to recall—"was fighting a dog for food."

"How old?"

He shrugged. "I don't even know how old I am now. I was at a workhouse—a place for orphans. I escaped. I was five or maybe six by then. Stole my food after that, ate a lot better as a result. Got in trouble pretty quick."

"City watch?"

"Wolves."

Hadrian stared at him, confused. "What is this about wolves?"

Royce tried a second berry. Sweeter. "A kids' gang. Finest group of pickpockets under the age of twelve. There are a lot of orphans in Ratibor. Competition is fierce. Must have been fifteen rival groups fighting for hunting rights. And there I was going it alone—oblivious. I didn't stand a chance. Still, I was better at stealing. The Wolves saw me. I was in their area and they didn't like it, so they offered me a deal. I could be drowned in the cistern, leave the city entirely—which was a death sentence at my age—or join them."

"How were they?"

"Like anyone—only more so. Nice until you have something they want. They kept me alive." He plucked another berry from Hadrian's palm. "How about you? How'd you learn to fight like that?"

"My father. He started training me almost from the day I was born. Day and night, no days off, not even Wintertide. Not that there was much else to do in Hintindar, but he was fanatical. Combat was like a religion to him. I figured there was a purpose, a reason behind it. I expected he was grooming me for military service, thought he would send me to the manor to start as a guardsman, thinking I would work my way up to sergeant at arms maybe. If I was lucky, Lord Baldwin would be called to service and I'd go along. If I was really lucky, I'd do something heroic on the field and King Urith would knight me. That's what I thought my father was thinking anyway."

"What *was* he thinking?"

Hadrian shook his head slowly as he looked out at the lake far below. "I don't know. But when I was fifteen, I asked when I would apply to the manor. Most boys started as pages much younger—fifteen was the age to sign up to be a squire if you were noble, or man-at-arms if you weren't. My father said I wasn't ever going to the manor. I wasn't going to Aquesta either. I wasn't going anywhere. He wanted me to replace him as the town blacksmith when he got too old to swing the hammer."

"Then why'd he train you like that?"

"He never told me." Hadrian popped the last of the berries into his mouth and chewed.

"So that's when you left."

"No. I was in love with a girl in the village—maybe not love, but as close as I've ever been, I suppose. I was going to marry her."

"What stopped you?"

"I got in a fight with my rival—nearly killed him."

"So?"

"He was also my best friend. We were both in love with her. Hintindar is a small place and didn't have a future for me. I figured everyone would be better off if I left—me included. So I hiked out and joined the army. Been fighting ever since."

Far below, two perhaps three miles away, Royce noticed a dozen men moving along the road. One was on horseback wearing black plate armor and a red cloak. The rest were footmen, some with pikes and some with bows. Out in front was a pack of hounds.

"What is it?" Hadrian asked.

"They've got dogs—I hate dogs."

"Who does?"

"That patrol." Royce gestured down toward the valley.

Hadrian peered out. "What patrol?"

"The huge patrol down there."

Hadrian squinted and shrugged.

"Trust me, there's a dozen or so footmen and a knight wearing black armor, so he might even be the seret you met at the tavern. You didn't leave anything at the tavern, did you?"

"What do you mean?"

"When you dressed my wound, what did you do with the part of your cloak that was around me? Did you leave it behind?"

"Didn't see any point in bringing a bloody rag."

"Damn."

"What? They have hounds?" Hadrian asked. "The dogs are hounds?"

"Yep."

"But dogs can't scent in the rain, right?"

"No...of course not." Royce didn't really know but he wanted it to be true.

"What are they doing?"

"Just walking."

"Where?"

"Right below us."

As Royce watched, the dogs veered off the road into the brush on their side. "Uh-oh."

"Uh-oh, what?"

Royce lost sight of them as they disappeared under the heather. A moment later he heard them bay.

"Did I hear something?" Hadrian asked.

"They have us." Royce pushed himself up, feeling dizzy the moment he did.

"I thought hounds couldn't scent in the rain."

"These can."

Royce staggered up the slope, feeling like someone was sticking a hot blade in his stomach.

"We can't outrun them, can we?" Hadrian asked, catching up.

"Not even if we were healthy."

Behind them, the baying of the hounds blended into the rain and the sound of ringing bells.

Hadrian reached the crest of the hill first. "A farm!"

"Horses?"

"Not even a mule."

Royce looked back and saw the patrol rushing up the hillside. The knight was out in front just behind the dogs. He didn't think they could see them yet, but they would soon.

"Maybe we can hide in the farm?"

"Farm? What's their crop? Rocks?" Royce asked.

"Better than getting caught in the open."

The land wasn't rocky so much as filled with rocks, which lay scattered on the grass like the remains of a stony hailstorm gathering mostly in gullies and at the bottoms of hills. They worked as effective obstacles, preventing anything close to sure footing as the two blundered down the slope.

Not surprisingly, the farmhouse, the barn, and even the silo were built of stacked stone. A rambling wall corralled a small flock of sheep, and there were a half-dozen chickens wandering the space between the house and the barn where numerous puddles formed in the mud to either side of a stony path.

Smoke rose from the chimney that poked out of the thatch roof, and both men made for the front door. Hadrian paused to knock. Royce walked in. An elderly man seated at a weathered table and a woman working near the hearth started at his appearance.

"Don't move or you'll die," Royce said, struggling to stand upright and gritting his teeth to manage it. That was fine, clenched teeth just made him more menacing.

Hadrian followed him in. "Sorry about the intrusion."

A boy around the age of ten trotted from one of the back rooms and halted, wide-eyed. The old man grabbed his wrist and jerked him to his side. White-haired and balding, the man moved quicker than Royce might have expected. He wasn't as old as he looked.

"Who are you? What do you want?" the man asked.

"Just do as you're told," Royce snapped.

"My name's Hadrian, he's Royce, and we just need a place to get out of the rain for a bit." Hadrian's tone was gentle, and he was smiling—not sinisterly, not malevolently, or crazy-dangerous-like, just cheerful. If he were a dog, he'd be wagging his tail.

"You're wounded," the old man said. "Both of you—you're the two thieves they're looking for."

Royce drew his dagger and let it catch the light from the hearth. That always had an effect. Alverstone's blade looked like no other. "We're also armed, dangerous, and as you might imagine, desperate." Royce stepped closer, causing the man to stand up and move his son behind him where the boy tilted his head to see. "In a little while a knight leading a patrol of soldiers will arrive here. They will ask if you've seen two strangers—wounded men. You're going to say you haven't. You're going to convince them we aren't here and make sure they leave without entering this house."

"Why would I do that?"

"Because we'll be in the back room with your wife and boy." Royce paused to glance at his son for effect. "And if they come in, or if I hear you whisper—if you try to be tricky or sly—I'll slit their throats."

"He will not!" Hadrian said.

"*Yes, I will.*" Royce glared back over his shoulder with a whose-side-are-you-on look.

"Listen, we haven't done anything wrong," Hadrian said. "There was a misunderstanding, and a fight, and we defended ourselves. Now they're after us, so we'd appreciate it if you could help."

All three just stared.

Royce shook his head and glared at Hadrian. "They don't care. All they know is we're in their home, and they want us out. You can't reason with these people. Those are *their* troops coming to protect them. They aren't going to side with us."

"Lord Marbury sided with us," Hadrian said.

"And they arrested him for it, remember?" The house

lacked windows, but he could see well enough through the gap between the door and the frame. Through the cracks he had a fine view of the barnyard and the chickens snapping up worms among the puddles. He could also see a bit of the main road. Nothing yet.

Hadrian took a seat, rubbing his leg above the point where he'd tied a strip of his cloak.

"You know Lord Marbury?" the old farmer asked.

Hadrian nodded. "Good guy. Had a drink with him recently."

"When?"

"Four, five days ago."

"Where?"

"Iberton, in a little tavern at the edge of the lake."

The man exchanged looks with his wife, who maintained a scowl.

"Keep quiet," Royce growled.

"We're in their house looking for help," Hadrian said. "The least we can provide is answers."

"I don't think you understand the meaning of the word *least*."

A pot began to bubble.

"See to the pot, woman," the man said. "No sense letting the meal burn."

The woman hesitated. "Why not? They'll just be taking it for themselves."

"A little food *would* be nice," Hadrian admitted. "We haven't eaten for..." He hesitated.

The man nodded. "Get them each a bowl."

"You're a fool," the woman said. She was plump with baggy cheeks, an extra chin, and pudgy fingers. Royce couldn't help wonder how she got that way farming rocks.

"We don't deny food to anyone under this roof."

"They're not guests," she hissed.

"They're under my roof." He turned to her. He didn't look like any farmer Royce had ever known. The body type was wrong, especially for his age. Decades behind a plow had a way of stunting a man, but he was tall, broad shouldered with powerful forearms and a straight back. "I won't be accused of lacking generosity to strangers." The voice was odd too—proud. Royce didn't know too many farmers and had never spoken to one of these northern rock growers, but pride in the face of invasion was unexpected.

"They're criminals—outlaws on the run with the justice of the church on their heels."

The old man leveled a harsh look. "Lord Marbury is no criminal, but that didn't stop him from being arrested. Now dish them each a bowl."

"These two aren't Lord Marbury. You shouldn't help them. It'll get you in trouble."

"I've been in trouble before."

"It will get *us* in trouble too. Think about me. What about your son?"

The man paused only a moment, then pulled the boy around so he could look the lad in the eye. "There's doing what's right, and there's doing what's safe. Most of the time you do what's safe because doing different will get you dead for no good reason, but there are times when doing what's safe will kill you too. Only it'll be a different kind of death. The dying will be slow, the sort that eats from the inside until breathing becomes a curse. Understand?"

The boy nodded, but Royce knew he hadn't a clue. Probably wasn't the point, though. The farmer expected that one day the boy would have cause to remember the time thieves had burst into their house. Maybe then everything he was saying would make sense, or more likely it wouldn't and he'd shake his head thinking what a fool his father had been.

The woman glared, then sighed. Grabbing a stack of wooden bowls, she moved to the hearth.

"What's your name?" Hadrian asked the farmer.

"Tom. Tom the Feather. This here is my son, Arthur."

"Good to meet you. And thanks for the hospitality."

Bowls were set out. Royce ate his near the door, sitting on a bench he managed to drag over. He wanted to keep an eye out but couldn't keep standing.

The rain pinged the puddles and ran off the thatch roof into a narrow gutter that circled the house as a drain. *How can dogs track in the rain?* It didn't seem fair. Dear Maribor, how he hated dogs. Still, the rain must make it harder for the dogs to follow a scent, and there was always a chance that a squirrel or rabbit would ruin the whole affair. If nothing else, the weather would take a toll on the men. A knight used to sitting out storms in warm castles must hate the idea of wandering rocky fields in the wet. When faced with the expansive countryside, might he trade the soggy search for a dry hearth and a hot meal?

The woman handed Royce some lamb stew—a thick gravy rich with generous chunks of meat, carrots, and potatoes. He could taste thyme and even salt. Everything was fresh. It was the best meal Royce had eaten in months, which left him puzzled. Royce imagined that the life of a farmer would be miserable, repetitive, filled with backbreaking labor easily destroyed by the fickle nature of weather. Yet, he supposed, when times were good, when the harvest arrived with a smile, they ate like kings.

Yip!

Royce heard the singular faint sound and paused, holding his breath.

Yip! Yip!

Dogs.

He pressed his forehead to the door where it met the jamb, staring out the crack. His sliver of the world revealed the road and movement.

"They're coming."

CHAPTER 20

TOM THE FEATHER

First the yelp and bay of dogs, then the shouts of men followed by the beat of hooves. Hiding in the back room with Hadrian and Tom the Feather's wife and son, Royce caught bits of conversations as they took their time getting to the door.

"Miserable sods."

"...sheep farm..."

"...any daughters would be..."

"...always clean them up..."

"Still, you'll never get the stink of sheep off."

"Not often."

"By Mar, why would you?"

Laughter.

The farmhouse and its three rooms were built around the chimney and the open-back hearth, allowing it to heat and light each of the rooms. The four of them clustered in one with little more than a great straw-mattress bed while Tom waited in the main room. Even though everyone had waited for it, they all jumped when the hammering began on the door.

Royce could tell when the door opened by how the voices lost their muffled sound.

"Who are you?" a voice demanded.

"Tom the Feather."

"The feather?" Someone farther away chuckled.

"He is a bit lean," another remarked.

"We're looking for two men. Thieves. Wounded. One my size, the other a bit smaller."

"You're the only strangers I've seen."

Royce heard the door bang against the wall.

"We're not strangers. We're your church. That's Sir Holvin of the Seret Knights outside."

Silence.

"Our dogs tell us the thieves came here."

"Then your dogs are mistaken."

"Uh-huh."

A shifting of feet and Royce heard the table move.

"This is my home. You can't—"

"You miserable little woolly, out of my way!"

"You have no right to—"

A grunt, a stumble, then the sound of a sword pulled from a scabbard.

Royce saw in Hadrian's eyes what he was going to do even before he moved. Royce was a fast learner, especially when it came to the study of people, and Hadrian wasn't much of a mystery. The man was suicidal as long as he was acting for the benefit of someone else. He didn't try to stop him, because this time it didn't matter. After the knights killed Tom, they would be coming in anyway. But guessing Hadrian's mind a second before he moved, Royce was able to follow right behind him.

Entering the main room, he saw Tom on the floor, a stool turned over. Two men in leather and helms waited near the door. One in chain mail stood over the farmer. The guy near Tom was drawing his sword, his eyes on the fallen man, lips in a sneer. He was angry at the impudent farmer who dared to do whatever it was he'd done. He also wasn't wearing his helm.

The soldier stood sideways to the bedroom, his head turned slightly, presenting the hollow of his neck.

Hadrian still had three steps to go when Royce threw Alverstone, which flipped half a turn before lodging in the man's throat. The man collapsed with a gurgle and metallic thud as if someone had dropped a pot filled with rags. What surprised Royce was how Hadrian reacted. Without missing a beat, without surprise or pause, he ignored the falling man and went for the ones at the door. Neither of them had time to draw steel, and with a free swing, Hadrian's massive sword cleaved the next closest man's head from his shoulders. What impressed Royce the most was that his initial swing was from left to right, leaving the point of his sword aimed at the last man at the end of his stroke. A quick thrust and Hadrian finished the fight. At least in battle Hadrian saw three moves ahead.

A heartbeat later Tom's wife saw the scene and screamed.

"The door!" Royce shouted.

Outside, the rest of the troop started for the house, but Hadrian was able to slam the door and slide the wooden brace into place, locking it. A moment later pounding began, making the door rattle.

"Now what?" Hadrian asked as everyone stared at the door.

"I'm pretty sure this is the point where I remind you I was right," Royce said. "You should have left me on that tower."

Royce retrieved his dagger from the guard's neck and wiped it off. As soon as Hadrian was sure the door would hold for a while, he returned his big spadone to its scabbard and picked up two of the soldiers' swords. The farmer's wife clutched the boy to her as she stood between the rooms, staring at the dead bodies. Getting up, Tom went to her. They embraced as a family, the wife whimpering into the chest of her husband.

"Hobart! Beecham!" someone shouted from outside, and they continued to throw themselves against the door.

"There's no other way out of here," Royce said.

"Wouldn't matter," Hadrian replied. "These guys are professionals. They have the place surrounded. Another door or window would just make one more point of entry we'd have to secure. We're actually lucky to have only two."

"Two?"

"The door and the roof."

Royce looked up at the rafters covered in widespread planking and thatch.

"Think they'll burn it?"

"If it wasn't pouring."

"Rain won't last forever."

"No . . . no, it won't."

The pounding on the door stopped.

"Nice door," Royce said.

"Thanks," Tom replied. "Oak."

"I'm guessing there's an axe in the barn or a woodshed out there?"

Tom looked to the boy, who said, "I brought them in the house on account of the rain. Pa don't like the heads to rust."

"They might have brought their own," Hadrian said. "Standard gear for a patrol is an axe, a pot, and a shovel."

"They'll be a long time cutting that door down. Wood is hard as stone. I dulled three saws."

Now that the soldiers had stopped beating on it, Royce peeked out the cracks again. Four men stood right outside, including the knight, who remained on horseback. A few more lingered to the rear. The rest he couldn't see. They spoke quietly.

"A shame we couldn't have gotten the knight," Hadrian said. "He's likely the only thing keeping the others here."

Royce took a seat at the table. He was feeling dizzy again, and the nausea was coming back. He had eaten too much too quickly. "So what else can they do? Find something to batter their way in? Figure out a means to tie on to it and have the horse rip the door off? They can climb on the roof and cut through it easily enough, or they could just wait for the rain to stop and set us on fire. Or they can do absolutely nothing. Time is on their side. They've likely sent a rider announcing their hounds have treed us."

"Right." Hadrian nodded. "The way those bells have been ringing, in a few hours we'll have an army out there. We'll have to make a move sooner rather than later."

"What kind of move?"

Hadrian looked back at the door as if he could see through it. "We need that horse. We can't hope to escape without it. If we can kill the knight and get on the horse, we'll have a chance of getting away."

"I think there's about nine men out there. Nine men—some with bows—and a plated knight on horseback. What do you want to do? Throw the front door open and rush them? You with your wounded leg and me with a hole in my stomach?"

"Do we have a choice?"

Royce didn't have an answer.

Hadrian said, "They're going to kill us whether we sit here and wait or go out there. That doesn't matter. But if we sit here, the rain will stop and they'll burn these people's home. Possibly kill them too. They didn't do anything wrong. They gave us food, remember? If we charge them—we'll die, sure, but this family will be safe."

"How is that a benefit?"

"Okay, let me rephrase. We can sit here and let them kill us with fire and smoke or we can try and take a few with us."

Royce smiled. "Better."

Hadrian bent down and rolled the chain mail–dressed corpse over. "Looks big enough," he said, and began pulling the mail over the dead man's head. "Nice throw by the way. I didn't know you could do that."

"I'm full of surprises."

"You in there!" They heard a shout from the far side of the door. "I'm Sir Holvin of Ervanon, Knight of the Order of Seret. Drop what weapons you have and come out. You are hereby under arrest in the name of our Lord Novron and the Nyphron Church."

Royce glanced at Hadrian, then at the family, still clustered and terrified. He shook his head and sighed, then stood up. "We have a family in here. A farmer, his wife, and a boy. I have a knife to the man's neck as I speak. If you try and come in again, we'll slit their throats. Do you hear me?"

"You can't win. You have nowhere to go. If you come out now, I promise you will live to stand trial."

"I mean it. I'll kill these people in here," Royce yelled.

Royce faced Hadrian, saying softly, "Happy?"

Hadrian smiled back and nodded.

Tom looked concerned, his wife terrified.

"Relax," Hadrian told them. "He just said that so they won't think you're helping us."

"Go ahead," the knight replied. "I don't care—but the longer you make me wait in the rain, the worse it will be for you."

Royce noticed the surprise on the face of the farmer's wife. "I would have said the same thing," he assured her, but the woman did not appear comforted.

"Give yourself up," the knight shouted. "Trust to Novron!"

"This guy is hilarious," Royce said, and sat back at the table. If they were going to make a suicidal charge, he wanted to rest first.

Hadrian pulled the chain mail over his head. He struggled for a bit before pulling it back off. "Too small. You want it?"

Royce shook his head. "I can barely hold up my own weight."

"Might deflect an arrow."

"I'll dodge them better without it."

"You can dodge arrows?"

"Sometimes."

"You *are* full of surprises."

"I don't make a living doing it."

Hadrian slipped his spadone onto his back and picked up the two swords again, feeling their weight. "I miss my own. These are awful. You about ready?"

"Wait," Tom said, and pried himself out of his family's grasp. He disappeared into the back rooms, then reemerged holding a huge shield and a bow as tall as he was. "I used to be an archer in the service of Lord Marbury. I fought beside him. He granted me this farm. His Lordship is a great man, but just yesterday the seret arrested him on the charge of treason— aiding fugitives from the church's justice. You two I imagine. If Lord Marbury felt you were worth standing up for, I won't dishonor his good name by doing any less. Besides, you just heard how concerned the church is for the safety of my family."

"My pa is the best shot in the county," the boy said.

"Tom the Feather." Hadrian nodded.

Tom held out the kite shield to Hadrian. "It's designed to stop arrows, covers the body fairly well." Over his shoulder, the farmer wore a full quiver.

"What are you going to do with those?" Royce asked.

"Zephyr and I are going to provide some assistance—going to fight for His Lordship one last time."

Royce closed his eyes and dropped his head into his hand. "I just convinced them you're not helping us. We're going out there so they don't burn your house and kill you. If you start shooting, they'll know different."

"If I shoot, you might survive."

"You're that good?" Hadrian asked Tom.

"With Zephyr, I can hit a rabbit at two hundred yards and release six arrows a minute. And she's made of fine northern yew—if I pull her deep, she can punch an arrow through plate armor."

"And if we don't kill all nine, you will be executed," Royce said. "This is the first and last generous thing I will ever do. Don't spoil it."

"He's right," Hadrian said. "We're just..." He looked at Royce. "We're just a pair of no-account thieves. Think of your son."

The old man looked down at the boy still gathered in his mother's arms. "I am."

"Let him do as he wants," Royce said. "I'm in pain, and if I'm going to die anyway, I don't see the point in suffering. Let's get this over with." He moved to the door and peered out. "Four right outside and the knight's still on his horse. No idea where the archers are. Frontal assaults aren't my specialty. Any ideas?"

Hadrian slipped the shield over his left arm. "Pull the brace and let me out first. Stay close behind. When we meet resistance, I'll push left, you move right. Don't fight the footmen unless you have to. Go for the horse. If you can, cut the stirrup and pull. The knight's own weight will drop him. Then grab the horse, stay low, and let me do the rest."

"That will leave you to kill five men, not including the archers."

"You're in no condition to fight. Besides, if you get that knight off his horse, you won't need to worry about the others. Once I clear the field, we'll hop on the horse and run for it. I just hope the archers can't hit a moving target. Ready?"

Royce stared at Hadrian, at his eyes. It was high summer on Herald Street, and the windows in that home were wide open.

"You realize we're about to die," Royce said, then sighed. "It's a real shame. I'm just starting to like you."

⌇

The door to the farmhouse flew open and they pushed out into the rain. The chickens were gone, but the puddles were still there, and so was the drumming roar of falling water. It was like jumping in the river again.

Hadrian rushed forward and got the first swing before any of them reacted, before the first arrow flew. They had caught the patrol by surprise. And even when the men in the barnyard reacted, they failed to see the threat. Soldiers spread out as if Royce and Hadrian were pigs bolting from a sty. One didn't even draw his sword but held his hands out as if to tackle them. This left an open path to the one destination none of them could have expected a small wounded man with only a dagger would take.

The moment Hadrian swung, Royce clenched his teeth and sprinted for the knight.

Stabs of pain jolted through his body and brought back a wave of nausea and dizziness, but fear kept him running. He splashed through the puddles that threw brown water up to defy the gray water coming down. Something whizzed by Royce's head, sounding like a bee with a purpose. He really could dodge arrows, if there was only one and he saw it coming, but in the rain he had only luck. Maybe the downpour caused just as much havoc with their aim as with his sight.

He didn't have far to travel. The whole barnyard was only a few yards across and the knight was in the middle sitting majestically on his white horse. He loomed above everything, all metal down to his shoes. Water rang off his plates and his horse puffed clouds, adding to the haze—a beast of the gray. He sat well above the muck, safe and aloof. Royce wondered if this was why he was the last to react.

Whatever Hadrian was doing caught his attention. The

knight's visor was up, shielding his eyes from the rain—eyes that were not focused on Royce until he was only a few steps away. When he moved to draw his sword and spur his horse, the knight was still not looking at Royce.

Royce had to time it right. He needed to shift his momentum, catch the knight's leg, while avoiding being chopped in half or slipping in the mud. As it turned out, falling was unavoidable.

The pain ripping through him was so intense he could have been hit by several arrows and not notice the difference. The dizziness was gaining strength. He could hear a ringing that was beginning to overtake the roar of the rain and that darkness was closing in again. He caught the knight's foot. The move was inelegant—less an action of assault as one of trying to keep from falling. With his other hand he sliced the stirrup's strap. He caught some of the horse in the effort and it jumped. Royce was amazed that a three-quarter-ton animal could jump so nimbly. That's when he slipped. Royce was holding on to Sir Holvin's foot as the horse jerked, and the mud was no help. He was still hanging on even as he fell, intent on pulling the knight to the ground, but he was too low. He didn't have the angle. Using Alverstone the way he used his hand-claws, Royce gouged his way up the knight's side, punching holes in the metal—by Mar, how he loved that dagger. Sir Holvin had no trouble noticing him then. Too close for the knight to swing, he hammered at Royce with the pommel of his sword. Holvin struck Royce in the head, and again in the face, but Royce refused to let go. He knew all he need do was hold on. The knight was right-handed and Royce was on his left. Sir Holvin was trusting to his stirrup for support—but it wasn't there. All that metal, that vast tower of iron defense, lost its foundation and toppled. They were all falling. Not just the knight, not just Royce, but the horse as well. It had jerked twice more after Royce thought he heard more bees, and soon he had fifteen hundred pounds of horse and a metal giant crashing down on him.

He pushed off, shoving away as best he could, and the forward momentum of the horse did help it move a step and a half forward before it landed. This left him clear of the knight, but the horse was big. The rear flank crushed Royce's left leg into the mud and wrenched his hips. Royce cried out as his leg broke. The pounding in his head and ringing in his ears reached a maddening pitch as if all the bells of the world were ringing alarms and his head was the clapper. The horse rolled and kicked, trying to right itself, driving Royce deeper into the mud.

"Royce!" He heard Hadrian and saw his figure moving toward him out of the gloom.

He still held the kite shield, only now it had five arrows decorating it. He planted the shield in the mud and struggled to pull Royce free.

"The knight!" Royce shouted.

"He's dead," Hadrian said, digging in the mud to gain enough clearance.

At the doorway he spotted Tom with his longbow, exchanging fire with bowmen near the barn.

"Why isn't the horse getting up?"

"It's dead too. The archers are lousy shots."

Royce let his head fall back into the muck where the rain pelted him in the face. "We needed that horse."

Hadrian slipped his arms under Royce and pulled. As his body slipped out from underneath the horse, as he felt the pressure subside, he heard another bee and Hadrian stiffened. Tom cursed and let another arrow fly and across the barnyard Royce heard a grunt.

Hadrian, who was already down on one knee, fell forward.

Royce caught him as best he could, his hands brushing the arrow shaft in his back.

"That's nine!" Tom shouted.

Hadrian lay with his head across Royce's chest, wheezing and coughing up blood. "Did you hear that...we won?"

৵

The rain poured.

What had been a shower became a flood. The skies opened and an ocean came down. Royce couldn't see. He couldn't stand up. His leg was broken and buried in the muck. He and Hadrian were wallowing in a pool of brown water that had mixed with their blood, making it the color of tea.

Hadrian collapsed on him like a wet rag. He'd stopped coughing, maybe breathing too. He had no way to tell.

"Hadrian?" Royce gasped for air and got mostly water. He struggled to prop his head above the water. It wobbled like a broken wrist.

Loud splashes and both Tom and Arthur were beside them.

"Leave us," Royce growled. He tried to stand on his own but couldn't even sit up. The stitches were ripped. He could feel the skin on his side open. "More will be coming. Leave us or they'll know you helped."

The world was swimming. Hadrian's head lay still on his chest. Except for the mud and the blood, he might have been sleeping.

"He's alive," Tom the Feather shouted over the crash of rain, maybe to his son, maybe to Royce. "Lucky the cheap bastards used bodkins instead of broadheads." He pulled the arrow out. Hadrian didn't even flinch.

Tom had a cloth he stuffed under Hadrian's shirt.

Amidst the violence of the downpour came another sound—the clopping of horse hooves. It wasn't the knight's.

His mount was still on its side in the mud. Sir Holvin looked to have drowned in a huge puddle after the horse crushed him. It was also possible he was dead before then. Royce had opened parts of his armor with Alverstone and his puddle was just as tea-like.

The horse he was hearing was a new arrival. *Reinforcements? That didn't take long.*

"Over here!" Tom shouted, a note of desperation in his voice.

Smart. Old Tom, you're not as dumb as I thought. You got your wish, Hadrian... They'll be fine, and it was a great fight. How did you manage to beat all of them while wounded? Arcadius was right about you. Too bad I didn't see it earlier. But you were a fool. You should have left me on the tower. You'd be kicking back in some tavern by now, not dying in a mud puddle.

Royce groaned as he felt himself lifted by strong hands. He was placed in a wagon.

They really are taking me to trial! Joke's on them. I'm going to die before then.

Hadrian was moved and laid beside him and a tarp thrown over both. The pelting rain disappeared and was replaced by the loud patter on canvas two feet above his face. It mingled with the ringing and the pounding, and finally darkness closed in and wouldn't take no for an answer. Not that Royce was fighting anymore—he was ready to die.

He felt around and found Hadrian's arm, patting it. "Old lunatic was right... We did make a good team."

CHAPTER 21

HIM

The halting of the cart woke Royce, and he wished it hadn't. He was in agony, feeling like a horse had fallen on him.

Oh, right.

Royce opened his eye—only one responded; the other was swollen shut. Everything was dark and silent. Hadrian was still beside him and the canvas still over their heads. He reached up and pulled, but the tarp was tied. He felt around and discovered Alverstone had made the trip with him. The handle was crusted with dry mud.

How long have we been traveling?

With little effort, Royce cut a long slice through the canvas. Cold fresh air spilled in and overhead he saw stars. The rain and clouds were gone. Royce inched up and peered over the sides.

Buildings. Dirty wooden shacks with mud splattered halfway up the sides. They were on a narrow dirt road, deep with ruts and still decorated in puddles. Royce turned his head, which made him woozy. More buildings. They were in a city. A crappy, miserable-looking town. A place he didn't recognize. The buildings to either side were dark, the street deserted. Looking forward, he saw the driver of the cart was gone. No soldiers either.

They were alone.

Maybe it wasn't soldiers at all. The wagon was small. It looked like a peasant's cart.

Royce heard him then. Hadrian was still breathing.

Weak and wheezing, his breath struggled like he had a garrote tied around his throat. If they had lived this long, they might yet have a chance.

Using the sides of the wagon, Royce drew himself upright. The pain in his midsection screamed again. He ignored it. His arms were all that held him up and they were shaking so badly they made the wagon quiver. He could think of no other way out of the wagon. He couldn't climb.

How long have we been in that wagon? How long does he have left?

Hadrian sounded like he was choking, or close to it.

For perhaps the first time in decades, Royce acted without a plan. Merrick had taught him never to make a move without a goal and a means of getting there. At that moment he had neither, just a vague sense that Hadrian was dying, and he needed to do something to stop that—and there was only one thing to do. He pulled himself up on the side guard and let himself fall over.

He couldn't help crying out as he hit the ground. The jolt was almost enough to send him back into unconsciousness, but this time he couldn't let that happen. He sucked in a breath and pushed up with his good leg. On palms and one knee, dragging one leg, he crawled to the closest door and hammered the foot of it with his fist. No sound, no light. He moved back out into the street. The agony was becoming too much. He couldn't think. His clothes had dried stiff, but there was a new wetness to his shirt. He was bleeding again.

In desperation he cried out, "Help!" It didn't sound like his voice. He couldn't recall having used that word since boyhood. He hated the sound, hated the taste it left. "Help us!"

He heard the slap of shutters against the upper-story windows.

Whatever doors may have been open were now bolted. No one wanted anything to do with them.

Royce lay in the street, his palms slapping the dirt, and he whispered, "At least save him...He didn't do anything wrong. He just tried to help." Tears formed in his eyes as he said it. "He doesn't deserve to die with me."

In one last effort, Royce threw his head back and cried, "Help us!"

He felt a hand on his arm, gentle and soft. "I've got you. You'll be all right now—you're safe."

Royce opened his eyes. The darkness was back again, closing in. The sea of pain was swallowing him once more, but in the haze at the center of the dark tunnel he saw a woman. Long dark hair, almond-shaped eyes, a kind face. She pulled him to her.

"Hadrian...in the wagon. You have to—"

"Dixon, hurry. Get the other one out of the cart."

Boots splashed through mud. Royce heard Hadrian cry out in pain.

"How is he? Is he okay?" she called.

"Alive—took an arrow," said a man's voice, deep and husky. "I think he'll live."

"Get them both inside, then fetch the doctor—Linderman, from the Merchant Quarter, not Basil."

"On it."

The rain continued to fall, though Royce hardly felt it anymore. He was passing out again.

"Save Hadrian," Royce begged. "He..."

"I know," the woman said. "I know everything, and I'm going to save both of you. You'll see. I've been waiting for you—I've been waiting for so very long."

CHAPTER 22

WHAT'S IN A NAME

R ehn watched as Professor Arcadius broke the wax seal on the dispatch and, pushing his glasses high up the bridge of his nose, began to read. The old man appeared visibly upset. Arcadius could never be described as neat and tidy, but the professor of lore had appeared more frazzled than ever before. His hair a wild storm of white, his robes even more wrinkled than normal—Rehn was certain that was the same jelly stain that had been on his chest before he left. As he watched, the professor's shoulders drooped, the muscles in his neck relaxed, and his breathing went from short gasps to longer, deeper draws.

Not knowing how long the document was, Rehn looked for a place to sit. As always, the lore master's office was a disaster, and Rehn found a seat wedged in tight between a caged pigeon and a barrel of vinegar. He shivered. He'd paused the moment he'd entered the school to shake off most of the snow, but enough had melted to leave his clothes damp. He rubbed his arms for warmth, tapped his feet together to knock off the remaining flakes, and listened to the chatter of the caged animals.

"Good news?" he asked, growing impatient. He had at least a little stake in this too.

The professor only held up a finger, his eyes never leaving the page.

Rehn slumped a bit and looked over at the pigeon. All white, with black eyes, maybe it wasn't a pigeon after all. Might be a dove or some more exotic bird the professor had obtained from parts unknown.

Where did all of this stuff come from?

Rehn looked out the window at the still-falling snow that gathered on the sill and muntins—the first real snow of the year. It had been a long time since he'd seen snow.

"They're safe," Arcadius said at last. Lowering the dispatch and pulling off his glasses, he leaned back with a great sigh. "At least there has been no report of them being killed or captured, so I have to assume they made it out alive."

"Where are they?"

"The city of Medford in Melengar, but as far as the church is concerned, they've disappeared. The search for the thieves of the Crown Tower has been called off. Officially they are saying the burglary never happened. Internally, Ervanon authorities are baffled. They have half a dozen dead tower guards, but also the returned book. They can't figure out what happened or why." The old professor displayed a self-satisfied grin. "The only clue they have is the testimony of a tavern keeper in Iberton saying Royce and Hadrian had been there and were badly wounded."

Rehn leaned forward, nearly knocking the pigeon cage over. "How badly?"

"Hard to say. The tavern keeper mentioned that Royce was barely conscious and that Hadrian stitched him up on one of the tables."

Rehn didn't care about Royce. "What about Hadrian?"

"He was wounded, too, but Royce was worse. It couldn't have been too serious, as it wasn't worth noting. One odd thing is that a patrol under the command of Sir Holvin—a Seret Knight—disappeared in the same area."

"Disappeared?"

Arcadius shrugged.

"How many in the patrol?"

"Ten, including Sir Holvin."

"Ten?" Rehn said, surprised. "You don't think..."

The professor smiled and nodded. "I suspect the metal has been tempered at last."

"But ten? And Hadrian and Royce were wounded."

The professor got up and, using a soup bowl, he scooped birdseed from a bin behind his desk and went to the cages, sifting the seeds through the cage bars. "We won't know what happened for certain until they return."

"Are you sure they will? It's been a long time."

"Royce knows better than to come back here right away. He'll play it safe. Wait a year, maybe two."

"But hang on," Rehn said over the flutters and squawking. "If the church lost track of them in Iberton, how do you know they reached Medford?"

Grinning, Arcadius looked over his glasses and winked. "Magic."

"Seriously?" he replied with a smirk.

"Oh, absolutely."

"Okay, don't tell me." Rehn sighed. It was just like the old man. Working with him was like teaming with a stone. Arcadius refused to give anything away, but Rehn guessed he had his reasons. They all did. "So then I can—"

"No." The professor shook his wild head of hair. "We can't take the chance of them coming back unexpectedly and finding you here. You're dead, remember?"

Rehn frowned. "Please don't tell me I have to go back to Vernes." He slipped into the voice. "I am not so much the believing this is a good idea, yes?"

"No, not Vernes."

"Why did you send both me and Royce there anyway?"

"Because when I send Royce to fetch someone, I never know if that someone will arrive on their feet or in a box, and I can't trust his account. You were my eyes and ears."

"So if not Vernes, then where?"

Arcadius set the bowl of seed down on the tall pointy hat that Rehn had never seen the professor wear. "Nowhere."

"You're cutting me loose?"

"For now."

Not like he didn't expect it, but still Rehn couldn't help feeling disappointed. The sudden depression surprised him. He'd never been all that interested in anything beyond his own survival before.

"That's the nature of this work. You know that. That's the way it has always been."

Rehn continued to frown, looking at the dirty puddle at his feet.

"You did a good job," the professor offered in a sympathetic tone.

"Ha!" Rehn mocked. "I couldn't even get on the stupid barge. Blasted disguise was a little too good. And then I let Hadrian catch me *reading* in the dormitories. I thought I'd ruined everything."

"And then there was the pie."

Rehn frowned. "You said you wanted me to get on his good side. I thought defending Hadrian was a good way to do that. That and Angdon is a royal ass. I'm surprised you didn't reprimand me earlier."

"I thought the beating was punishment enough, and it worked. One can't argue with results. You secured his trust, his sympathy. If it wasn't for Pickles, Hadrian never would have gone."

"Then why did you tell him Pickles was dead?"

Arcadius let go of the parchment and took off his glasses to begin cleaning them. "I couldn't risk Hadrian having divided loyalties. You were quickly becoming his adopted family."

Rehn smiled. "I like Hadrian."

"He liked Pickles too. I could see it in his eyes—that's why the little urchin had to die. Hadrian needed to be just as alone, just as isolated as Royce for this to work."

"Was a risky gamble."

Arcadius rolled his eyes and took a moment to stroke his beard. "If this could get any whiter, it would have."

"Why'd I have to be executed? Why not an accident?"

"Royce wouldn't have bought it. He'd be suspicious. In his world real accidents don't happen. On the other hand, vicious, irrational deaths are expected. It also increased the heat, got Hadrian on edge. It takes a lot to get under his skin."

Neither one said anything for a time. Rehn glanced out the window. "I should be going, then, before the snow gets too deep." He stood up and faced the professor with an honest face. Perhaps the most honesty he'd shown anyone in years. "By the way, did you get what you needed from the book Royce stole? What was so important about it?"

The professor smiled again. "Absolutely nothing at all."

"Huh? Then why?"

Arcadius bobbed his head in a whimsical manner, that childish twinkle in his eyes. "Just an impossible goal—the furnace to forge a bond."

Rehn nodded. "Say, I want you to know how grateful I am to you. I don't know what I would have done."

Arcadius put his glasses back on. Perhaps it was Rehn's imagination, but the old man looked moved, saddened. "Where will you go?"

"I don't know. Back home maybe."

"I hear Ratibor is lovely this time of year."

Rehn smirked. "Ratibor is never *lovely*. I'll let you know where I am when I find where I'm going. You'll contact me if needed, right?"

"Of course."

Rehn knew he wouldn't—too risky. His contribution to the cause was over. Rehn made his way across the room but hesitated at the door. He looked back at the professor. "There's a war coming, isn't there?"

"I'm afraid so."

"We still have a chance, right?"

"There's always hope," Arcadius said, but his tone lacked confidence. The old professor looked out the window as if he could see Royce and Hadrian out there hiding somewhere, buried beneath the snow, and added, "We've planted the seeds. All we can do now is wait and see what grows."

GLOSSARY OF TERMS AND NAMES

ABBY: Prostitute at The Hideous Head Tavern and Alehouse in the Lower Quarter of Medford

ALBERT WINSLOW: A landless viscount hired by Riyria to arrange jobs with the nobles

ALVERSTONE: Name of dagger used by Royce Melborn

AMBER FALLS: Huge waterfall south of Colnora

AMRATH ESSENDON: King of Melengar

ANDREW: Draft horse driver working for Billy Bennett's barge service

ANGDON LERWICK: Son of baron, who is studying at Sheridan University; bully

APELADORN: The four nations of man, consisting of Trent, Avryn, Delgos, and Calis

AQUESTA: Capital city of the kingdom of Warric

ARCADIUS VINTARUS LATIMER: Professor of lore at Sheridan University

ARTISAN QUARTER: The geographic region of Medford where most of the goods are produced

AVON: Former prostitute at The Hideous Head Tavern and Alehouse, killed by Stane

AVRYN: The central and most powerful of the four nations of Apeladorn, located between Trent and Delgos

BA RAN GHAZEL: The dwarven name for goblins, literally "Goblins of the Sea"

BARGE: A flat-bottomed boat pulled by draft animals and used to transport goods and passengers on a river

BARTHOLOMEW: Student at Sheridan University in Ghent

BEECHAM: Soldier in the command of Sir Holvin

BERNUM RIVER: Waterway that joins the cities of Colnora in the north and Vernes in the south

BILLY BENNETT: Proprietor of barge service running between Colnora and Vernes

BLACK CAT TAVERN: A disreputable establishment in Vernes

BLACK DIAMOND: International thieves' guild centered in Colnora

BLACKWATER: Last name of Hadrian and his father, Danbury

BODKIN: A simple type of arrowhead, essentially a squared metal spike

BREMEY: Tinker of Ghent

BROADHEAD: A deadly type of arrowhead, usually with two or four sharp blades designed to cause massive bleeding

CALIAN: Pertaining to the nation of Calis

CALIANS: Residents of the nation of Calis, with dark skin tone and almond-shaped eyes. An isolated people, not much is known about them in the northern and eastern kingdoms of Avryn, except that their women are among the most beautiful in existence, but the suggestion of their use of magic makes them reviled and outcast.

CALIS: Southern- and easternmost of the four nations of Apeladorn, considered exotic and strange as most in the north have little interaction with people from that part of Elan. The region is in constant conflict with the Ba Ran Ghazel.

CARTER: A person who makes their living by moving goods from place to place, usually employing a horse-drawn cart

CITADEL: A fortress that protects a town

COLNORA: Largest, wealthiest city in Avryn, merchant-based city, grew from a rest stop at a central crossroads of various major trade routes

CROWN TOWER: Home of the Patriarch and center of the Nyphron Church

DAGASTAN: Major and easternmost trade port of Calis

DANBURY BLACKWATER: Father of Hadrian Blackwater

DANCER: Name of Hadrian Blackwater's horse

DANIEL: Wealthy merchant of Vernes; husband of Vivian

DARIUS SERET: Founder of the Seret Knights

DELGOS: One of the four nations of Apeladorn. The only republic in a world of monarchies, Delgos revolted against the Steward's Empire after Glenmorgan III was murdered and after surviving a goblin attack with no aid from the empire.

DIXON TAFT: Carter operating out of Medford

DOUGAN: Proprietor of a tavern in Iberton along the banks of Lake Morgan

DRUMINDOR: Tall, dual-tower, dwarven-built fortress located in southern Delgos

DUNMORE: Youngest and least sophisticated kingdom

DUSTER: Person (or persons) responsible for a gruesome set of murders one summer in the city of Colnora

EASTERN STAR: Large sailing vessel transporting passengers and freight between Vernes and Dagastan

EDMUND HALL: Professor of geometry at Sheridan University, declared a heretic by the Nyphron Church, rumored to have found the lost city of Percepliquis

EDMUND HALL'S JOURNAL: Heretical document, one of the treasures kept in the Crown Tower

ELAN: The world

EREBUS: Father of the gods Ferrol (god of the elves), Drome (god of the dwarves), Maribor (god of men), Muriel (goddess of nature), and Uberlin (god of darkness)

ERVANON: City in northern Ghent, seat of the Nyphron Church, once the capital of the Steward's Empire as established by Glenmorgan

ESSENDON: Royal family of Melengar

ESSENDON CASTLE: Home of the ruling monarchs of Melengar

ETHAN: Sheriff in the Lower Quarter of Medford

ETTA: Least attractive prostitute at The Hideous Head Tavern and Alehouse in the Lower Quarter of Medford

EUGENE: Young jewelry merchant who is traveling to set up a new shop in Colnora, nephew of Sebastian

FALLON MIRE: City where Merton prevented the spread of a terrible disease

FARLAN: Steersman in the employ of Billy Bennett's barge service

FROCKS: Derogatory term used to refer to priests of the Nyphron Church

GALEWYR RIVER: Marks the southern border of Melengar and the northern border of Warric and reaches the sea near the fishing village of Roe

GENTRY QUARTER: The geographic region of Medford where the wealthiest (usually noble or rich merchants) reside

GHENT: Ecclesiastical holding of the Nyphron Church

GLENMORGAN: Historical figure and a native of Ghent who reunited the four nations of Apeladorn 326 years after the fall of the Novronian Empire. He initiated the new Steward's Empire, founded Sheridan University, created the great north–south road, and built the Ervanon palace (of which only the Crown Tower remains).

GRETCHEN: Hadrian's childhood pet chicken

GUR EM: Thickest part of the jungle in Calis, as it butts up against the eastern tip of Calis

GWEN DELANCY: Calian prostitute who leaves The Hideous Head Tavern and Alehouse to build her own brothel, Medford House

GWENDOLYN: Given name of Gwen DeLancy

HADRIAN BLACKWATER: Originally from Hintindar, he left home at fifteen, spent two years as a soldier (with multiple armies) and three years as an arena fighter in Calis

HARDING: Priest of the Nyphron Church, stationed in Iberton

HEAD, THE: Nickname for The Hideous Head Tavern and Alehouse

HIDEOUS HEAD TAVERN AND ALEHOUSE: Brothel and tavern run by Raynor Grue in the Lower Quarter of Medford

HILDA: Ex-prostitute of The Hideous Head Tavern and Alehouse in the Lower Quarter of Medford who was killed after leaving to make it on her own

HINTINDAR: Small manorial village in Rhenydd, home of Hadrian Blackwater

HOBART: Soldier in the command of Sir Holvin

HOLVIN, SIR: Seret Knight operating in Ghent

HOUSE, THE: Nickname used for Medford House

IBERTON: Small fishing village in Ghent near Ervanon

ILLIA DELANCY: Fortune-telling mother of Gwen DeLancy

JOLLIN: Prostitute of the Lower Quarter working at The Hideous Head Tavern and Alehouse

KEFFIYEH: A head covering made from wrapping a square piece of light material, usually worn in the east

LADY BANSHEE: Large fishing boat operating out of Medford

LAKE MORGAN: Lake in Ghent renowned for its fishing

LERWICK, BARON: Baron from Ghent who is on good terms with the Nyphron Church

LOWER QUARTER: The geographic region of Medford where most of the impoverished reside

LUCKY HAT: A moderately priced tavern in the city of Vernes

MAE: Prostitute of the Lower Quarter working at The Hideous Head Tavern and Alehouse

MALET: Sheriff in Colnora

MANDALIN: A city in Calis, once the capital of the Eastern Empire

MANZANT: Infamous prison and salt mine, located in Manzar, Maranon

MARANON: Kingdom in Avryn, rich in farmland and known for breeding the best horses

MARBURY, LORD: Honorific noble of Ghent who can trace his family history to Glenmorgan

MARES CATHEDRAL: Center of the Nyphron Church in Melengar

MARIBOR: God of men, third son of Erebus

MEDFORD: Capital city of Melengar. The town is divided into four distinct quarters: Artisan, Merchant, Gentry, and Lower.

MEDFORD HOUSE: Brothel in the Lower Quarter of Medford started by prostitutes who once worked at The Hideous Head Tavern and Alehouse

MELENGAR: Small but old and respected kingdom of Avryn ruled by King Amrath

MERCHANT QUARTER: The geographic region of Medford where most of the goods are sold

MERRICK MARIUS: Former best friend of Royce Melborn, known for his strategic thinking

MERTON: Pious priest of Nyphron Church reputed to have stopped a plague

MONTEMORCEY: Excellent wine imported through the Vandon Spice Company

MURIEL: Goddess of nature, only daughter of Erebus

NIDWALDEN RIVER: Marks the eastern border of Avryn and the start of the elven realm

NOVRON: Savior of mankind, demigod, son of Maribor, defeated the elven army in the Great Elven Wars, founder of the Novronian Empire

NYPHRON CHURCH: Predominant church of mankind. Worshipers of Novron and Maribor.

OWANDA: Ancestral Tenkin tribe in Calis of Illia and Gwen DeLancy

PACKER THE RED: Tinker of Avryn who was one of the few visitors to Hintindar

PATRIARCH: Head of the Nyphron Church, lives in the Crown Tower of Ervanon

PERCEPLIQUIS: Ancient city and capital of the Novronian Empire, destroyed and lost during the collapse of the Old Empire

PICKLES: Street urchin from Vernes

PRESS-GANG: Hired thugs in the employ of sea merchants who force men into naval service

RATIBOR: Impoverished capital of the kingdom of Rhenydd, home of Royce Melborn

RAYNOR GRUE: Proprietor of The Hideous Head Tavern and Alehouse in the Lower Quarter of Medford

REGINALD LAMPWICK: Assessor for the Lower Quarter of Medford

REHN: Employee of Arcadias

RHENYDD: Poorest of the kingdoms of Avryn

ROSE: Prostitute of the Lower Quarter working at The Hideous Head Tavern and Alehouse

ROYAL PERMIT: Legal paperwork allowing a proprietor to operate a business

ROYCE MELBORN: Thief, assassin, and former inmate at Manzant Prison

SAMUEL: Jewelry merchant from Vernes, cousin of Sebastian

SEBASTIAN: Successful jewelry merchant from Vernes

SENTINEL: Inquisitor generals of the Nyphron Church, charged with rooting out heresy and finding the lost Heir of Novron

SERET: The Knights of Nyphron. The military arm of the church, first formed by Lord Darius Seret, commanded by sentinels.

SHERIDAN UNIVERSITY: Prestigious institution of learning, located in Ghent

SIGHT, THE: Ability usually possessed by Calian women to see the future

SPADONE: Long two-handed sword with a tapering blade and an extended flange ahead of the hilt allowing for an extended variety of fighting maneuvers. Due to the length of the handgrip and the flange, which provides its own barbed hilt, the sword provides a number of additional hand placements, permitting the sword to be used similarly to a quarterstaff and as a powerful cleaving weapon. The spadone is the traditional weapon of a skilled knight.

SQUIRE: Errand runner or servant of a knight

STANE: Net hauler for the *Lady Banshee*

TENENT: Most common form of semi-standard international currency. Coins of gold, silver, and copper stamped with the likeness of the king of the realm where the coin was minted: 1 gold = 100 silver; 1 silver = 100 copper.

TENKIN: Most mysterious of the people of Calis, living in the deep jungles. It is rumored that they are a cross between man and goblin.

THAWB: A long garment, similar to a robe, worn in the east

TILINER: Superior side sword, used frequently by mercenaries in Avryn

TOM THE FEATHER: Farmer and former archer for Lord Marbury

TRENT: Northern mountainous kingdoms of Apeladorn, generally remote and isolated

TRIBIAN DEVOLE: Easterner hired by Arcadius to locate Hadrian Blackwater in Calis

VERNES: Port city at the mouth of the Bernum River

VIVIAN: Wife of wealthy merchant Daniel from Vernes

WARRIC: Most powerful of the kingdoms of Avryn, ruled by King Ethelred

WAYWARD INN: A defunct establishment that used to reside at the end of Wayward Street in the Lower Quarter of Medford

WAYWARD STREET: Road leading to the most impoverished section of the Lower Quarter in Medford

WILLARD: Bartender at The Hideous Head Tavern and Alehouse in the Lower Quarter of Medford

WILLY: Shepherd in Iberton

WINDHAM: Small village on the banks of the Galewyr River

WINTERTIDE: Chief holiday, held in midwinter, celebrated with feasts and games of skill

WOLVES: Ratibor street gang of children

ZEPHYR: Name of Tom the Feather's bow

ACKNOWLEDGMENTS

While this is my seventh published novel, this is the first time I've written an acknowledgment. It's not that I'm an ungrateful person. It's just that my other six were self-published, and in that world the author is an army of one, and we're used to doing everything ourselves. When Orbit signed The Riyria Revelations, we were on an accelerated schedule. The books had been fast-tracked into the next editorial calendar, and we had three volumes (and the contents of six books) to get produced and released in quick succession. There was only a little more than sixty days between the release of *Theft of Swords* and *Heir of Novron*. More than a few things fell along the wayside, including an afterword that I had written for the series.

One of the best things about being traditionally published is you are no longer constrained by the serial efforts of a single person. Instead you have an entire team working on your book's behalf, and while I'm going to recognize a number of them here, there are many more toiling behind the scenes whose names I don't even know. They are the proofreaders, layout people, administration assistants, and an entire sales staff that work so hard to get my books in as many places as possible. To each of you I give my thanks.

As with Revelations, Devi Pillai was my primary editor. For Revelations, Devi inherited a series of books that had already been widely read and had a devoted following. She made many wonderful suggestions, asking for more detail here, some clarification there, and was instrumental in the addition of the new beginning section, but mass changes for the series really weren't possible. The books were woven from multiple threads, and pulling one could unravel the whole tapestry. With *The Crown Tower*, no such restrictions existed, and Devi provided many great insights and suggestions that helped improve the story, all while orchestrating the entire publishing process and keeping everything on track.

There were several readers who also aided me in the editing process. I took advantage of the Internet's capability to provide a conduit for authors to communicate with readers and started a private and supersecret Goodreads group called the Dark Room. It is a place where lovers of the series can meet and where I can answer questions I could never reply to in the world at large for fear of spoiling the story for those yet to read it. (By the way, if you want an invitation to join, just e-mail me at michael.sullivan.dc@gmail.com.) Several members of the Dark Room volunteered to beta read the novel for me and provide feedback on a very short deadline. Their biggest contributions were in validating that I was accomplishing my goals, but they also gave me keen insights on areas for improvement. To call out the individual contributions would be extremely lengthy, but I do want to mention them by name: Sarah and Nathaniel Kidd, Heather McBride, Melissa Hayden, Robert Aldrich, Jeffrey Carr, Lewis Dix, Sebastian Hidalgo, Lucian Wilhelm, Jonathan Lin, and Jim MacLachlan. I just want to say I love the members of the Dark Room and want to thank you for all your support.

The cover of *The Crown Tower* was once again the combined talents of Larry Rostant, photographer and artist, and Lauren Panepinto, creative director. I've long preferred not having characters on covers (because I wish readers will develop their own impressions), but there is no arguing with success. I've received many positive compliments about the covers for the Revelations series and *The Crown Tower* follows in the tradition of those original works. Out of all the covers, I think I like *Crown*'s best. The tower is beautifully done, and the Royce character is the closest I've seen to how I imagine him. You both deserve a rousing round of applause. I thank you for your efforts to produce such a beautiful wrapper for my story.

Having never written an acknowledgment before, I'm not sure about proper etiquette, but I couldn't write one without extending my thanks to Alex Lencicki, the marketing and publicity director at Orbit. Outside of Devi, he is the person with whom my wife, Robin, and I have the most interaction, and he is hardworking, smart, and just a joy to work with. I can't even imagine all the demands he gets from the gaggle of authors all competing for his time and that of his team. While I appreciate what Alex has done for my own books, I want to also mention how impressed I am with the treatment of all Orbit's authors. I'm constantly seeing his invisible hand in all sorts of projects, and I smile secretly at each success, knowing firsthand how much work it takes to produce such results.

Jenni Hill is an editor for the UK branch of Orbit who I'd like to thank for her role as a commissioning editor for the UK market. She has picked up all five books across the two series, and Revelation's sales from "across the pond" (and elsewhere in the English-speaking world), have greatly exceeded my expectations. No doubt this is directly related to her work on the book's behalf, and one day I hope to get overseas and thank her face-to-face.

I'd also like to thank Tim Holman. If you look up his title online, it reads "Publisher" and I'm sure that has a great deal of significance in the industry, but to translate for those who aren't plugged in, what that really means is he's the big cheese. I know there is a lot of bashing on traditional publishing these days (much of it by people who have found success in self-publishing), but there is something to be said about "traditional publishing done right." Orbit exemplifies this and is a standard by which other publishers should be judged. Such things do not occur through accident or happenstance. It's generally the result of a leader with vision, and the ability to trust well-chosen people. So I just wanted to say thank you, Tim, and tell you to keep fighting the good fight.

My agent is Teri Tobias, for whom I want to publicly acknowledge my appreciation. In a profession that is often filled with "hard people" with "cutthroat ambition," I feel truly blessed to have Teri by my side. Like me, she's a maverick. Breaking away from larger agencies, she has free rein to do business the way she wants—a trait I both recognize and value. Teri's business savvy is what keeps my family fed. Not only has she negotiated some very lucrative deals in the United States, but she has also augmented my income with contracts in twelve countries, including Germany, France, Spain, Poland, and even markets in Brazil and Japan. I'm sure there will be many more doors opened in the future and can't thank her enough for being the conduit to me living my dream as a full-time writer.

Besides this being my first book with an acknowledgment, it is also the first one that is not dedicated to my wife. So I would feel remiss if I didn't mention her here. I don't think anyone but she and I know how great her contributions have been to both my career and the final outcome of the books. She is my first reader, collaborator on changes, and the only one who can go toe-to-toe with me when advocating for revisions. Our discussions have been so heated that my daughter has come downstairs to discover what the heck was going on. And the books wouldn't be half as good without her efforts. Beyond all that, they probably wouldn't exist at all, as it is the gratification I get from her reading enjoyment that spurs me to the keyboard each day.

Speaking of dedications, you'll notice that this book is dedicated to my readers. For those who don't know, I once quit writing for over a decade and in that time I never thought I would have anyone other than friends and family read my stories. That thought was more than a little depressing. Even when I couldn't stay away any longer and started writing again, I never intended to publish. It was a dream that I had considered out of my reach. I just mentioned how rewarding it is to see my wife enjoy my books; imagine getting similar reactions by people whom I have never met. I'm a storyteller, but telling stories in the echo chamber of your own room isn't much fun. Sharing the tales and discovering people like them is the greatest gift I could ever receive. People online often thank me for being so "interactive with my fans." I find this almost laughable. Don't you know that my actions are selfish? That I get just as much (and probably more) out of the exchanges as you do? I'm amazed to find that people have enjoyed my tales so much that they have been compelled to write me. I'm eternally grateful for those who love the books so much.

Recently, my wife and I were discussing why J. K. Rowling came out with another book. Robin asked, "She obviously has more money than she could spend in a hundred lifetimes, so why write anymore?" I had no trouble understanding it, but maybe it's hard to explain to someone who doesn't write. It's not work. It's not something I force myself to do when I'd rather be doing something else. I should have the bumper sticker "I'd rather be writing," because if I was independently wealthy, I would still write, and I would still want people to read my books. You see, I'm one of the rare people privileged enough to wake every day faced with the prospect of doing what I love the most. I've spent a lifetime writing and a decade of abstinence trying to break the addiction that I thought was a time-consuming dead end. I failed. Even if I never make another cent or find another reader, I'll still write. Can't help it really. But it's because of people like you who support my efforts that I don't have to go to a day job and count the minutes until I can race back to the keyboard. So most of all, I thank you for the one gift that no one else can give: time. More time to create worlds, more time to breathe life into characters, more time to do what I love the most. To you I extend my most humble thanks.

extras

meet the author

Michael J. Sullivan

MICHAEL J. SULLIVAN is one of the few authors who have successfully published through all three routes: small press, self, and big six. His Riyria Revelations series has been translated into fourteen foreign language markets, including German, Russian, French, and Japanese. He has been named to io9's Most Successful Self-Published Sci-Fi and Fantasy Authors list as well as making #6 on EMG's 25 Self-Published Authors to Watch list. As of January 2013, his books have appeared on more than sixty-five "best of" or "most anticipated" lists, including:

- Fantasy Faction's Top 10 Most Anticipated Books for 2013
- Goodreads Choice Awards Nominees for Best Fantasy in 2010 and 2012
- Audible's 2012 5-star The Best of Everything List
- *Library Journal's* 2011 Best Books for SF/Fantasy

extras

- Barnes & Noble Blog's Best Fantasy Releases of 2011
- Fantasy Book Critic's #1 Independent Novel of 2010

Like many authors, Michael's journey to publication was a long one. In his twenties he became a stay-at-home dad and wrote while his kids were napping or at school. He completed twelve novels over the course of a decade, and after finding no traction, he quit writing altogether. During the next decade, stories continued to form, but he never put any of them down on paper. He finally relented and started writing again, but only on the condition that he wouldn't seek publication. He decided to write the stories that he wanted to read and expected to share them only with his family and close friends. His wife, Robin, had other plans.

After reading the first three books of The Riyria Revelations, she became dedicated to getting them "out there." Since Michael refused to jump back on the query-go-round, she took it upon herself and after more than one hundred query rejections, she finally landed an agent. After a year of submissions, without any interest, she switched to querying small presses and *The Crown Conspiracy* was signed to Aspirations Media Inc. They later signed the second book, *Avempartha*, but when they lacked the funds for the print run, the rights reverted and Robin started releasing the books at six-month intervals through her own imprint. When foreign language deals started to come in, she hired Teri Tobias to pick the right publishers and negotiate the deals. By the publication of the fifth book, Robin asked Teri to try New York again and the series received a much different reception. Out of the seventeen publishers they approached, almost half expressed interest and in less than a month, a deal was signed with Orbit (fantasy imprint of big six publisher Hachette Book Group).

extras

After finishing The Riyria Revelations, and while waiting to evaluate the reaction to the series, Michael wrote two
stand-alone novels: *Hollow World* (a science-fiction novel) and
Antithesis (an urban fantasy). Work on these was temporarily
suspended because of the public's demand for more Royce and
Hadrian stories. In response, Michael wrote the two prequel
novels (The Riyria Chronicles), which have been sold to Orbit.
The Crown Tower will release in August 2013 and *The Rose and
the Thorn* in September 2013. Find out more about the author
at www.riyria.com.

interview

Will there be a sequel to *The Riyria Revelations?*

It's possible that there will be more stories going past the events that ended in Revelations, but probably not in the way that most would like to see. I get quite a bit of feedback from readers who would like to see the story pick up directly after (or just a few years later) from where Revelations ended. My propensity would be to go far into the future, when most of the people and events have evolved into myth and legend.

Revelations lives up to its name and as such has a lot of... well... mysteries revealed. It would be impossible to write any series using existing characters that starts after the Revelations timeline without introducing spoilers for the Revelations series. This would violate my first rule, which is to ensure each series exists without prerequisites and doesn't impact other books. Because the series was carefully designed to end where it did, I feel that "tacking on" to it would tarnish what I consider to be the perfect ending.

Will there be more Royce and Hadrian stories?

I would like there to be, but I'm also very protective of the series as a whole and I don't want to ruin it by overstaying the welcome. For me there are two factors to consider. First,

I must have a compelling story to tell. We've all seen series that kept putting out books (or television episodes) long after the magic is gone. I won't jump the shark and would rather leave money on the table than tarnish something that I'm very proud of. Fortunately, I don't see this as being an issue, as I already have several story lines that I find compelling. As I've said before, my own internal barometer is usually a pretty good gauge.

The second component is demand, and I have no control over this. I wrote The Riyria Chronicles because there were a lot of people who still wanted more even after 685,000 words. For years we lived off my wife's income, and now I'm glad to repay the favor. I'll never write a book "just for the money," but I also can't afford to write a book that no one will buy. So I'll be keeping an ear to the ground as Chronicles roll out, and if people want more, then I have plenty of material to draw from.

After finishing a project, do you have problems starting or coming up with the next one?

I'm always amazed when I hear authors say it's difficult to get them to put their butts in the chair and write. For me, it's like being asked to play my favorite game, and I wake up every morning excited to get to the keyboard. I have many more tales waiting in the wings than I'll ever be able to write in my remaining lifetime, so as soon as I'm done with one, I'm happy to jump right into the next. I don't feel a need to decompress after finishing a novel. In fact, the process being what it is means I've usually been doing a lot of editing, and I'm generally champing at the bit to write something new.

extras

How do you decide what to write next?

It really depends. Recently I finished the draft for a science-fiction novel titled *Hollow World*. The idea came from out of the blue. It wasn't on my long list of pending projects and ended up bumping some other titles. It started because of a short story I wrote for an anthology. Because of word count limitations, I could only lightly touch on the world and themes in that piece, but the story was so well received by my wife and fellow authors that telling the whole tale became overwhelmingly attractive. I find everything works best when I write books that I want to read, and I *really* wanted to read this story.

The other factor that comes into play is what the fans want to read. I hadn't really anticipated writing any more books in the Riyria universe, but I got so many e-mails and saw posts from people who were saddened that it was over that I decided to write some more Royce and Hadrian stories. It was fun to revisit with these old friends and it certainly made me a hero with my wife, who is the series' number one fan.

Riyria is fantasy; Hollow World is science fiction. Do you plan on writing in any other genres?

A lot of people think of me as a "fantasy author" but that's really just because it was my fantasy books that were published first. I've actually written in a wide range of styles, including literary fiction, suspense, horror, mystery, coming-of-age, and so on. Going back to my long list of projects, those titles on the waitlist are pretty diverse. I would love to continue to put out titles in different genres, since I'm motivated by challenging myself to break new ground. It's probably not the smart move (as it means building a fresh audience from scratch with each release), but I've certainly never been accused of doing things the easy way. Challenging myself keeps me excited about what I'm doing, forces the writing to get better, and ultimately results in a better experience for my readers.

Do you prefer to write series or stand-alone novels?

In many ways series are more interesting because of the opportunity to weave overarching plot threads across several volumes. It's fun to drop hints and plant some seeds that won't be fully realized until a future book. Also, it gives me more room for world building and character development, because I can sprinkle a bit of each across several books instead of crowding everything into a single volume.

The problem with a series is it represents a much higher risk. I've been fortunate so far in that I've been able to write both series in their entirety before submitting/publishing any of them. This allows me to adjust earlier books as new ideas come up later on. Writing three or more books all at once means an extended amount of time with nothing new released, and there is always the possibility that upon completion I could discover that the work is no good and should be scrapped. In *theory* I could write the way many other authors do, and release each book as written, but then . . . no, I really couldn't do that. So I prefer to write series because of the bigger canvas on which to create, but I will do that only if I can finish the story before publishing. If I have to write and publish in quick succession, then stand-alone books will be the only way for me to accomplish that.

extras

What book would you say was the most difficult book to write and why?
The most difficult book was probably my literary fiction novel, *A Burden to the Earth*. It's not that I found literary fiction harder to write than genre fiction. I just didn't find it particularly interesting except as an exercise in craft. Literary writing requires a scaled-back plot with emphasis placed on prose, complex characters, and multiple themes. And while I enjoyed the challenge and learned a lot, such books don't thrill me as much. In this particular work, my protagonist is a flawed and disagreeable character that, quite frankly, I wouldn't like to spend time with. His personality is absolutely necessary for the story being told, but it also means that I'm not as drawn to this book as I am to my other titles. *Burden* is a marked departure from my other work, and remains the best novel I've ever written, but because I could not in good conscience recommend it to anyone, it remains unpublished.

What book would you say was the easiest to write and why?
The last book of The Riyria Revelations, *Percepliquis*, was simply a joy to write. The entire series had been building during my decade hiatus, and when I finally sat down to write it, the story just spilled forth effortlessly. By the time I got to the final book, I had all my dominoes lined up and it was just a matter of toppling the first one, then watching everything fall into place. I did have a few "alternate endings" and it took me a while to reach the right conclusion—but once the idea came to me, I *knew* this was *the ending* I was waiting for... that it was the perfect fit. Pushing back after writing the last lines of that book was extremely satisfying. I actually said to

myself, "Damn, that was good." To be honest, I was a little concerned that I would never feel like that again, given the long buildup that went into that series. To my great surprise I felt similarly when finishing *Hollow World*, even though that was a stand-alone story.

How would you describe your writing style?

Which one? It can change depending on the project. I adopt the style that best fits the work. As previously mentioned, my literary piece has very well-crafted prose and vivid characters, but an almost nonexistent plot. I also can write in a strong voice, where the narrator becomes part of the story. Then there are the Riyria books. My goal with them was to keep the writing unadorned and have it fade from the page so that the story played like a movie in the reader's mind. I didn't want the reader to notice the words, and I had to kill great sentences to avoid the chance that a reader might pause to consider how good, and subsequently how out of place, a particular passage might be.

While the style of the prose varies from work to work, I've come to settle on a few consistencies. What I choose to write now are those things I enjoy reading. This generally means that the characters will be likable, the pacing brisk, and the story will move readers emotionally. My goal is to make readers laugh, cry, and possibly learn something new. If I can do all three, then I feel that I've done my job. I honestly can't think of anything else a novel can be expected to do.

What advice would you give to readers looking to find a new favorite author?

In the old days, the bookstore was *the source* for discovering authors. You could spend hours roaming the aisles and often find someone new catching your eye. Nowadays, not only are there fewer bookstores but shelf space is also in decline. Room has been made for cafés, nonbook merchandise such as toys or games, and the stores are often stocking only a single copy of many books, which means a title might be out of stock on your visit. They are even forgoing bookshelf presence for new authors or those who have not sold well in the past. Even those who are stocked often have a short amount of time on the shelf. If they don't find an audience, they are bumped by a newer release.

For me, I find Amazon a better place to shop for new talent. While I appreciate that some have issues with them, there is no reason not to use their tools for author discoverability. Amazon benefits from the artificial intelligence that is possible by analyzing millions of purchases. Often the easiest way to find a new title is to go to one of your favorite books (or authors) and look at the Also Bought lists. I've found this to be particularly good at finding books that are similar to one another.

But suppose you want something completely different? Some lament that there are too many choices and it is difficult to find the gems in a sea of mediocrity. But here again Amazon can be a huge help. They now have features such as Author Rank, which will show you the top 100 authors in a given category (the lists are compiled by examining sales and ratings across all books by an author). While this will show many of the big names, even new authors like me or top-selling self-published authors appear on the Top Fantasy Author list. For instance, as of this interview (January 2013), I was on the Top 100 Fantasy Book List for most of December 2012 and all of January 2013. Also, the Kindle store has a Top Rated list for categories such as epic fantasy, contemporary fantasy, or historical fantasy, just to name a few. This shows titles that other readers have given high marks to, and my experience has been that these are indeed the cream that has risen to the top.

What advice would you give to aspiring authors?

I think the most inspirational thing I can think of is that the only way to guarantee failure is to stop trying. This is a business that rewards persistence. Many people say you need "luck" to make it, but I think we make our own luck by stacking the odds in our favor. If your first book doesn't catch fire, write another. Don't rely on others to get the word out, even if you are published through a large traditional publisher. Take responsibility for building your own audience. Set your sights toward continuous improvement and don't expect overnight success. Both Stephen King (who considers your first million words as practice) and Malcolm Gladwell (who claims success in any field is achieved by practicing a task for at least ten thousand hours) recognize that it takes time to develop your skills. If you think your first finished novel is a train wreck, you're right on track. Recognize that it is an investment rather than a waste of time. Think of the time you spend writing as the payment of dues necessary to get your work to a salable level.

What have you learned about publishing that you didn't know going in?

That every time you reach a goal there is always another (or several others) that lie just beyond your reach. In many ways it's like hiking in the Blue Ridge Mountains—just as you reach the top of a ridge, you find a whole series of peaks that stretch out to the horizon. I've been able to tick off many of my initial goals: finish a book, complete a series, get published, find an audience, get good reviews, break the Amazon top 20, earn a living, sell more than a hundred thousand copies, and so on. But I still feel there is so much left to do. I still dream that someday I'll hit one of the major best-seller lists such as the *New York Times*, *Publishers Weekly*, or *USA Today*. I'd love to see a movie based on the books on the big (or small) screen. And my next sales goal is to cross the million mark. I have no complaints about where I am now, but I also think it's good to have something more to strive toward, and the nature of this business means I'm not likely to run out of brass rings to reach for anytime soon.

What is the biggest misconception that readers have about publishing?

I don't think they realize just how little most average writers make and how few can earn a full-time living from their novels. Most authors I know have day jobs (including those whose names many readers would recognize and even those with multiple titles released). Many debut authors receive advances of just $5,000 to $10,000 per book and those payments can be spread across several years (generally one-third when signed, one-third when the manuscript is accepted, and one-third when the book is published). Also, authors have the additional self-employed tax burden because they have to pay both halves of Social Security and Medicare.

What is the biggest misconception that writers have about publishing?

I often hear writers say that they are avoiding self-publishing because they don't want to market themselves. This seems to imply that if they are traditionally published that they are somehow absolved of this responsibility. I personally think that the authors who will be the most successful are those who don't abdicate their role in building an audience. Social networking has made it possible for authors and readers to interact in ways that have never been possible in the past, and this makes it possible for authors to take the reins with respect to getting noticed. I contend that unless you receive a seven-figure contract, then your marketing responsibilities should be the same regardless of whether you are self-published or traditionally published.

Do you prefer traditional publishing or self-publishing?

The publishing landscape has become very polarized in recent years, an incredible change considering it wasn't that long ago that self-publishing was considered the last resort for the desperate or hopeless. There are pundits on both sides who claim their preference is the only "right" choice, but I see advantages and disadvantages in both paths.

Traditional publishing takes care of production tasks and therefore provides me more time to write. I have a whole team who works on the editing, layout, cover design, and the like, but on the downside it pays a fraction of the amount earned per book when I self-publish. I actually enjoy being in control of aspects such as price, cover design, title, and categorization of the books, but not all authors do. So depending on your perspective, having to take responsibility for these tasks can be a positive or a negative.

Self-publishing offers a very attractive income proposition. Not only am I paid monthly (as opposed to twice a year), I can also sell a book for less and earn more. As I mentioned, it's really hard to earn a full-time living through traditional publishing, and I think in the future the most successful authors will be those who become "hybrids": who combine the income potential of self-publishing with the credibility and audience expansion that traditional provides. For me, utilizing both seems to make the most sense.

introducing

If you enjoyed
THE CROWN TOWER,
look out for

THE ROSE AND THE THORN

Book 2 of The Riyria Chronicles

by Michael J. Sullivan

Two thieves want answers. Riyria is born.

For more than a year, Royce Melborn has tried to forget Gwen DeLancy, the woman who had saved him and his partner, Hadrian Blackwater, from certain death. Unable to get her out of his mind, the two return to Medford and are met with an unexpected reception—she refuses to see them. The victim of abuse by a powerful noble, she suspects that Royce will ignore any danger in his desire for revenge. By turning the thieves away, Gwen hopes to protect them once more. What she doesn't realize is what the two are capable of—she's about to find out.

Reuben should have run the moment the squires came out of the castle keep. He could have easily reached the sanctuary of the stable, limiting their harassment to throwing apples and insults, but their smiles confused him. They looked friendly—almost reasonable.

"Reuben! Hey, Reuben!"

Reuben? Not Muckraker? Not Troll-Boy?

The squires all had nicknames for him. None were flattering, but then he had names for them too—at least in his head. "The Song of Man," one of Reuben's favorite poems, mentioned age, disease, and hunger as the Three Cruelties of Humanity. Fat Horace was clearly hunger. Pasty-faced, pockmarked Willard was disease, and age was given to Dills, who at seventeen was the oldest.

Spotting Reuben, the trio had whirled his way like a small flock of predatory geese. Dills had a dented knight's helmet in his hands, the visor slapping up and down as it swung with his arm. Willard carried combat padding. Horace was eating an apple—big surprise.

He could still make it to the stable ahead of them. Only Dills had any chance of winning in a footrace. Reuben shifted his weight but hesitated.

"This is my old trainer," Dills said pleasantly, as if the last three years had never happened, as if he were a fox who'd forgotten what to do with a rabbit. "My father sent a whole new set for my trials. We've been having fun with this."

They closed in—too late to run now. They circled around, but still the smiles remained.

Dills held out the helmet, which caught and reflected the autumn sun, leather straps dangling. "Ever worn one? Try it."

Reuben stared at the helm, baffled. *This is so odd. Why are they being nice?*

"I don't think he knows what to do with it," Horace said.

"Go ahead." Dills pushed the helmet at him. "You join the castle guards soon, right?"

They're talking to me? Since when?

Reuben didn't answer right away. "Ah...yeah."

Dills's smile widened. "Thought so. You don't get much combat practice, do you?"

"Who would spar with the stableboy?" Horace slurred while chewing.

"Exactly," Dills said, and glanced up at the clear sky. "Beautiful fall day. Stupid to be inside. Thought you'd like to learn a few maneuvers."

Each of them wore wooden practice swords and Horace had an extra.

Is this real? Reuben studied their faces for signs of deceit. Dills appeared hurt by his lack of faith, and Willard rolled his eyes. "We thought you'd like to try on a knight's helmet, seeing as how you never get to wear one. Thought you'd appreciate it."

Beyond them, Reuben saw Squire Prefect Ellison coming from the castle and taking a seat on the edge of the well to watch.

"It's fun. We've all taken turns." Dills shoved the helm against Reuben's chest again. "With the pads and helm you can't get hurt."

Willard scowled. "Look, we're trying to be nice here—don't be a git."

As bizarre as it all was, Reuben didn't see any malice in their eyes. They all smiled like he'd seen them look at one another—sloppy, unguarded grins. The whole thing made a kind of sense in Reuben's head. After three years the novelty of bullying him had finally worn off. Being the only one their age who wasn't noble had made him a natural target, but times had changed and everyone grew up. This was a peace offering, and given

405

that Reuben hadn't made a single friend since his arrival, he couldn't afford to be picky.

He lifted the helm, which was stuffed with rags, and slipped it on. Despite the wads of cloth, the helmet was too big, hung loose. He suspected something wasn't right but didn't know for sure. He had never worn armor of any kind. Since Reuben was destined to be a castle soldier, his father had been expected to train him but never had time. That deficiency was part of the allure of the squires' offer; the enticement outweighed his suspicions. This was his chance to learn about fighting and sword-play. His birthday was only a week away, and once he turned sixteen he would enter the ranks of the castle guard. With little combat training he'd be regulated to the worst posts. If the squires were serious, he might learn something—anything.

The trio trussed him up in the heavy layers of padding that restricted his movement; then Horace handed him the extra wooden sword.

That's when the beating began.

Without warning, all three squires' swords struck Reuben in the head. The metal and wadding of the helmet absorbed most, but not all, of the blows. The inside of the helmet had rough, exposed metal edges that jabbed, piercing his forehead, cheek, and ear. He raised his sword in a feeble attempt to defend but could see little through the narrow visor. His ears packed with linen, he could just barely make out muffled laughter. One blow knocked the sword from his hands and another struck his back, collapsing him to his knees. After that, the strikes came in earnest. They rained on his metal-caged head as he cowered in a ball.

Finally the blows slowed, then stopped. Reuben heard heavy breathing, panting, and more laughter.

"You were right, Dills," Willard said. "The Muckraker is a much better training dummy."

"For a while—but the dummy doesn't curl up in a ball like a girl." The old disdain was back in Dills's voice.

"But there *is* the added bonus of him squealing when hit."

"Anyone else thirsty?" Horace asked, still panting.

Hearing them move away, Reuben allowed himself to breathe and his muscles to relax. His jaw was stiff from clenching his teeth, and everything else ached from the pounding. He lay for a moment longer, waiting, listening. With the helmet on, the world was shut out, muted, but he feared taking it off. After several minutes, even the muffled laughter and insults faded. Peering up through the slit, all he could see was the canopy of orange and yellow leaves waving in the afternoon breeze. Reuben tilted his head and spotted the Three Cruelties in the center of the courtyard filling cups from the well as they took seats on the apple cart. One was rubbing his sword arm, swinging it in wide circles.

It must be exhausting beating me senseless.

Reuben pulled the helmet off and felt the cool air kiss the sweat on his brow. He realized now that it wasn't Dills's helm at all. They must have found it discarded somewhere. He should have known Dills would never let him wear anything of his. Reuben wiped his face and was not surprised when his hand came away with blood.

Hearing someone's approach, he raised his arms to protect his head.

"That was pathetic." Ellison stood over Reuben, eating an apple that he had stolen from the merchant's cart. No one would say a word against him—certainly not the merchant. Ellison was the prefect of squires, the senior boy with the most influential father. He should have been the one to prevent such a beating.

Reuben didn't reply.

"Wadding wasn't tight enough," Ellison went on. "Of course, the idea is not to get hit in the first place." He took another bite of apple, chewing with his mouth open. Bits of dribble fell to his chest, staining his squire's tunic. He and the Cruelties all wore the same uniform, blue with the burgundy and gold falcon of House Essendon. With the stain of apple juice, it looked like the falcon was crying.

"It's hard to see in that helm." Reuben noticed the wadded cloth that had fallen on the grass was bright with his blood.

"You think knights can see better?" Ellison asked around a mouthful of apple. "They ride horses while fighting. You just had a helm and a touch of padding. Knights wear fifty pounds of steel, so don't give me your excuses. That's the problem with your kind—you always have excuses. Bad enough we have to suffer the indignity of working alongside you as pages, but we also have to listen to you complain about everything too." Ellison raised the pitch of his voice to mimic a girl. "*I need shoes to haul water in the winter. I can't split all the wood by myself.*" Returning to his normal tone, he continued, "Why they still insist on forcing young men of breeding to endure the humiliation of cleaning stables before becoming proper squires is beyond me, but having the added insult of being forced to labor alongside someone like you, a peasant and a bastard, was just—"

"I'm no bastard," Reuben said. "I have a father. I have a last name."

Ellison laughed and some of the apple flew out. "You have *two*—his *and* hers. *Reuben Hilfred*, the son of Rose Reuben and Richard Hilfred. Your parents never married. That makes you a bastard. And who knows how many soldiers your mother entertained before she died. Chambermaids do a lot of that, you know. Whores every one. Your father was just dumb enough to believe her when she said you were his. That right there shows you the man's stupidity. So assuming she wasn't lying, you're the son of an idiot and a—"

Reuben slammed into Ellison with every ounce of his body, driving the older boy to his back. He sat up swinging, hitting Ellison in the chest and face. When Ellison got an arm free, Reuben felt pain burst across his cheek. Now he was on his back and the world spun. Ellison kicked him in the side hard enough to break a rib, but Reuben barely felt it. He still wore his padding.

Ellison's face was red, flushed with anger. Reuben had never fought any of them before, certainly not Ellison. His father was a baron of East March; even the others didn't touch him.

Ellison drew his sword. The metal left the sheath with a heavy ring. Reuben just barely grabbed the practice wood, which had been left lying in the grass. He brought it up in time to prevent losing his head, but Ellison's steel cut it in half.

Reuben ran.

That was the one advantage he had over them. He did more work and ran everywhere while they did little. Even weighed down by the padding, he was faster and had the stamina of a pack of hounds. He could run for days if needed. Even so, he wasn't fast enough, and Ellison got one last blow across Reuben's back. The slice only served to drive him forward, but when he was safely away, he discovered a deep cut through all four layers of padding, his tunic, and a bit of skin.

Ellison had tried to kill him.

꒰꒱

Reuben hid in the stables the rest of the day. Ellison and the others never went there. Horse Master Hubert had a tendency to put any castle boy to work, failing to notice the difference between the son of an earl, a baron, or a sergeant at arms. One day they might be lords, but right now they were pages and squires, and as far as Hubert was concerned, they were all just backs and hands to lift shovels. As expected, Reuben was put to mucking out the stalls, which was better than confronting Ellison's blade. His back hurt, as did his face and head, but the bleeding had stopped. Given that he could have died, he wasn't about to complain.

Ellison was just angry. Once he calmed down, the prefect would find another way to demonstrate his displeasure. He and the squires would trap and beat him—with the woods most likely, but without the padding or helmet.

Reuben paused after dumping a shovelful of manure into the wagon and sniffed the air. Wood smoke. Kitchens burned wood all year, but it smelled different in the fall—sweeter. Planting the shovel's head, he stretched, looking up at the castle. Decorations for the autumn gala were almost complete. Celebration flags and streamers flew from poles, and colored lanterns hung from trees. Though the gala was held every year, this time would be a double celebration in honor of the new chancellor. That meant it had to be bigger and better, so they adorned the castle inside and out with pumpkins, gourds, and tied stalks of corn. When the question of too few chairs arose, bundles of straw were hauled in to line every room. For the last week, farmers had been dropping off wagons full. The place did look festive, and even if Reuben wasn't invited, he knew it would be a wonderful party.

His sight drifted to the high tower, which had lately become his obsession. The royal family resided in the upper floors of the castle, where few were allowed without invitation. The tallest point of the castle held its title by only a few feet, but it soared in Reuben's imagination. He squinted, thinking he might see movement, someone passing by the window. He didn't, but then nothing ever happened in the daylight.

With a sigh, he returned to the dimness of the stable. Reuben actually enjoyed shoveling for the horses. In the cooler weather there were few flies and most of the manure was dry, mixed with straw to the consistency of stale bread or cake, and it barely smelled. The simple, mindless work granted him a sense of accomplishment. He also enjoyed being with the horses. They didn't care who he was, the color of his blood, or if his mother had married his father. They always greeted him with a nicker and rubbed their noses against his chest when he came near. He couldn't think of anyone he'd rather spend the autumn afternoon with, except one. Then, as if thoughts could grant wishes, he caught the flash of a burgundy gown.

Seeing the princess through the stable's door, Reuben found it hard to breathe. He froze up whenever he saw her, and when he could move, he was clumsy—his fingers turned stupid, unable to perform the simplest of tasks. Luckily he'd never been called on to speak in her presence. He could only imagine how his tongue would make his fingers appear deft. He'd watched her for years, catching a glimpse as she climbed into a carriage or greeted visitors. Reuben had liked her from first sight. There was something about the way she smiled, the laughter in her voice, and the often serious look on her face, as if she were older than her years. He imagined she wasn't human but some fairy— a spirit of natural grace and beauty. Spotting her was rare and that made it special, a moment of excitement, like seeing a fawn on a still morning. When she appeared, he couldn't take his eyes off her. Nearly thirteen, she was as tall as her mother. But there was something in the way she walked and how her hips shifted when she stood too long in one place that showed she was more lady than girl now. Still thin, still small, but different. Reuben fantasized of being at the well one day when she appeared in the courtyard alone and thirsty. He pictured himself drawing water to fill her cup. She would smile and perhaps thank him. As she brought the empty cup back, their fingers would meet briefly and for that one moment he would feel the warmth of her skin, and for the first time in his life know joy.

"Reuben!" Ian, the groom, struck him on the shoulder with a riding crop. It stung enough to leave a mark. "Quit your daydreaming—get to work."

Reuben resumed shoveling the manure, saying nothing. He had learned his lesson for the day and kept his head down while scooping the strata of dirt cakes. She could not see him in the stalls, but with each toss of manure he caught a glimpse of her through the door. The princess wore a burgundy dress, the new one of Calian silk that she had received for her birthday along with the horse. To Reuben, Calis was just a mythical place, somewhere far away to the south filled with jungles, goblins, and pirates. It had to be a magical land because the material of the dress shimmered as she walked, the color complementing her hair. Being the newest, it fit well. More than that, the other dresses were for a girl—this was a woman's gown.

"You'll be wanting Tamarisk, Your Highness?" Ian asked from somewhere in the stable's main entry.

"Of course. It's a beautiful day for a ride, isn't it? Tamarisk likes the cooler weather. He can run."

"Your mother has asked you not to run Tamarisk."

"Trotting is uncomfortable."

Ian gave her a dubious look. "Tamarisk is a Maranon palfrey, Your Highness. He doesn't trot—he ambles."

"I like the wind in my hair." There was a certain flair in her voice, a willfulness that made Reuben smile.

"Your mother would prefer—"

"Are you the royal groom or a nursemaid? Because I should tell Nora that her services are no longer needed."

"Forgive me, Your Highness, but your mother would—"

She pushed past the groom and entered the barn. "You there—boy!" the princess called.

Reuben paused in his scraping. She was looking right at him.

"Can you saddle a horse?"

He managed a nod.

"Saddle Tamarisk for me. Use the sidesaddle with the suede seat. You know the one?"

Reuben nodded again and jumped to the task. His hands shook as he lifted the saddle from the rack.

Tamarisk was a beautiful chestnut, imported from the kingdom of Maranon. These horses were famed for their breeding and exquisite training, which made for exceptionally smooth rides. Reuben imagined this was how the king explained the gift to his wife. Maranon mounts were also known for their speed, which was likely how the king explained the gift to his daughter.

"Where will you be going?" Ian asked.

"I thought I would ride to the Gateway Bridge."

"You can't ride so far alone."

"My father got me that horse to ride, and not just in the courtyard."

"Then I will escort you," the groom insisted.

"No! Your place is here. Besides, who will raise the alarm if I don't return?"

"If you won't have me, then Reuben will ride with you."

"Who?"

Reuben froze.

"Reuben. The boy saddling your horse."

"I don't want anyone with me."

"It's me or him or no horse is saddled, and I'll go to your mother right now."

"Fine. I'll take ... what did you say his name was?"

"Reuben."

"Really? Does he have a last name?"

"Hilfred."

She sighed. "I'll take Hilfred."

VISIT THE ORBIT BLOG AT

www.orbitbooks.net

FEATURING

BREAKING NEWS
FORTHCOMING RELEASES
LINKS TO AUTHOR SITES
EXCLUSIVE INTERVIEWS
EARLY EXTRACTS

AND COMMENTARY FROM OUR EDITORS

WITH REGULAR UPDATES FROM OUR TEAM,
ORBITBOOKS.NET IS YOUR SOURCE
FOR ALL THINGS ORBITAL.

WHILE YOU'RE THERE, JOIN OUR E-MAIL LIST
TO RECEIVE INFORMATION ON SPECIAL OFFERS,
GIVEAWAYS, AND MORE.

imagine. explore. engage.